A whisper
of scandal is only
the beginning…

*She was an innocent.
There was no way she could know
what she did to him.*

He closed his eyes as her fingers explored down his jaw, over his chin, and across to the other side.

"Olivia," he said in a near groan. "I want you so badly. I've wanted you for so long."

Licking her lips, she hesitated, her eyes meeting his. She whispered, "I want you, too." She threaded her hand through his hair until she cupped the back of his head, drawing him closer to her. And then sensation washed over him, warm and drugging, as her lips touched his.

Sweet and tentative, but not cowardly. She moved her lips in her own slow rhythm, testing and tasting, one hand behind his head and the other slipping around his side, fingers questing up and down his back.

He felt her shudder in his arms. "So strong," she whispered. "So powerful."

He felt neither strong nor powerful. He felt enslaved. Completely at this beautiful, tiny, strong woman's mercy.

"Gripping . . . engaging . . . The writing allows the reader to get deeply involved and the emotional struggles of Serena are palpable . . . I'm looking forward to reading about the other Donovan sisters . . . *Confessions of an Improper Bride* is a great start to this series, and I would recommend it to all romance novel fans."

—TheRomanceReader.com

A HINT OF WICKED

"Full of suspense, mystery, romance, and erotica . . . I am looking forward to more from this author."

—*Las Vegas Review-Journal*

"A clever, provoking, and steamy story from an upcoming author to keep your eye out for!"

—BookPleasures.com

"Haymore is a shining star, and if *A Hint of Wicked* is any indication of what's to come, bring me more."

—FallenAngelReviews.com

"Debut author Haymore crafts a unique plot filled with powerful emotions and complex issues."

—*RT Book Reviews*

"A unique, heart-tugging story with sympathetic, larger-than-life characters, intriguing plot twists, and sensual love scenes."

—Nicole Jordan, *New York Times* bestselling author

"Complex, stirring, and written with a skillful hand, *A Hint of Wicked* is an evocative love story that will make a special place for itself in your heart."

—RomRevToday.com

"A new take on a historical romance . . . complicated and original . . . the characters are well crafted...surprisingly satisfying."

—TheRomanceReadersConnection.com

"What an extraordinary book this is! . . . What a future this author has!" —RomanceReviewsMag.com

"Ms. Haymore's talent for storytelling shines throughout this book." —Eye on Romance

A TOUCH OF SCANDAL

"Jennifer Haymore's books are sophisticated, deeply sensual, and emotionally complex. With a dead sexy hero, a sweetly practical heroine, and a love story that draws together two people from vastly different backgrounds, *A Touch of Scandal* is positively captivating!"

—Elizabeth Hoyt, *New York Times* bestselling author

"Sweep-you-off-your-feet historical romance! Jennifer Haymore sparkles!"

—*New York Times* bestselling author Liz Carlyle

"Haymore discovers a second fascinating, powerful, and sensual novel that places her high on the must-read lists. She perfectly blends a strong plot that twists like a serpent and has unforgettable characters to create a book readers will remember and reread."

—*RT Book Reviews*

"*A Touch of Scandal* is a wonderfully written historical romance. Ms. Haymore brings intrigue and romance together with strong, complex characters to make this a keeper for any romance reader. Ms. Haymore is an author to watch and I'm looking forward to the next installment of this series."

—TheRomanceReadersConnection.com

"A deliciously emotional Cinderella tale of two people from backgrounds worlds apart, *A Touch of Scandal* addicts the reader from the first page and doesn't let go until the very last word. Hurdle after hurdle stand in the way of Kate and Garrett's love, inexorably pulling the reader along, supporting them each step of the way. *A Touch of Scandal* is a surefire win!"

—FallenAngelreviews.com

"A classic tale . . . Reading this story, I completely fell in love with the honorable servant girl and her esteemed duke. This is definitely a tale of excitement, hot, sizzling sex, and loads of mystery."   —FreshFiction.com

"These characters are just fantastic and endearing. I just couldn't wait to find out what happened on the next page."   —SingleTitles.com

"4 Stars! Kate and Garrett were wonderful characters who constantly tugged at my heartstrings. I found myself rooting for them the whole way through . . . If you like historical romances that engage your emotions and contain characters you cheer for, this is the book for you."   —TheRomanceDish.com

A SEASON OF SEDUCTION

Secrets
of an
Accidental
Duchess

Secrets
of an
Accidental
Duchess

JENNIFER HAYMORE

FOREVER

NEW YORK   BOSTON

Copyright © 2012 by Jennifer Haymore
Excerpt from *Confessions of an Improper Bride* copyright © 2011 by Jennifer Haymore
Excerpt from *Pleasures of a Tempted Lady* copyright © 2012 by Jennifer Haymore.

Forever
Hachette Book Group
237 Park Avenue
New York, NY 10017

www.HachetteBookGroup.com

Forever is an imprint of Grand Central Publishing.
The Forever name and logo are trademarks of Hachette Book Group, Inc.

The publisher is not responsible for websites (or their content) that are not owned by the publisher.

Printed in the United States of America

First Edition: February 2012

10 9 8 7 6 5 4 3 2 1

ATTENTION CORPORATIONS AND ORGANIZATIONS:
Most HACHETTE BOOK GROUP books are available at quantity discounts with bulk purchase for educational, business, or sales promotional use. For information, please call or write:

Special Markets Department, Hachette Book Group
237 Park Avenue, New York, NY 10017
Telephone: 1-800-222-6747 Fax: 1-800-477-5925

For L, who hasn't yet gotten his wish that I'd add more epic battles and characters with superhero powers into my books, but who apparently still loves me anyway.

Acknowledgments

Many thanks to my editor, Selina McLemore, who always helps me find the way through the cobwebs of plots in my head. And to my agent, Barbara Poelle, who's stuck by my side since Day One. Thanks also to my good friends and readers Kate McKinley and Anya Richards, who offer me endless support. I'm lucky to have all of you!

Secrets
of an
Accidental
Duchess

Prologue

She was an angel.

Maxwell Buchanan, the Marquis of Hasley, had observed many beautiful women in his thirty years. He'd conversed with them, danced with them, bedded them. But no woman had ever frozen him in place before tonight.

He stood entranced, ignoring people who brushed past him, and stared at her, unable to tear his gaze away. With her slender, slight figure, delicate features, and crown of thick blond hair, she was beautiful, but not uncommonly so, at least to the other men populating the ballroom. As far as Max knew, the only head that had turned when she'd entered the room was his own.

The difference, he supposed, the singular element that clearly set her apart from the rest of the women here, was in the reserved way she held herself. There was nothing brazen about her, but nothing diffident or nervous, either. It was as though she held a confidence within herself that she didn't feel any desire to share with the world. She didn't need to display her beauty like all the other unattached ladies present. She simply was who she was, and she made no apologies for it.

Her small, white-gloved fingers held her dance partner's, and Max's fingers twitched. He wanted to be the man clasping that hand in his own. He wanted to know her. He would learn her name as soon as possible. He would orchestrate an introduction to her and then he would ask her for a dance.

"Lovely, isn't she?"

Max whipped around to face the intruder. The man standing beside him was Leonard Reece, the Marquis of Fenwicke, and not one of his favorite people.

"Who is lovely?" he asked, feigning ignorance, curling the fingers of his right hand into a fist so as not to reach up to adjust his cravat over his suddenly warm neck.

Fenwicke gave a low chuckle. "The young lady you've been staring at for the last ten minutes."

Damn. He'd been caught. And now he felt foolish. Allowing his gaze to trail after a young woman, even one as compelling as he found this one, was an imprudent enterprise, especially at Lord Hertford's ball—the last ball of the London Season. If Max wasn't careful, he'd find himself betrothed by Michaelmas.

The dance ended, and the angel's dance partner led her off the floor toward another lady. The three stood talking for a moment before the man bowed and took his leave.

"Most people believe her sister is the great beauty of the family," Fenwicke continued conversationally. "But I would beg to differ with them. As would you, apparently."

"Her sister?"

"Indeed. The lady she's speaking to, the one in the pale yellow, is the youngest of the Donovan sisters."

Max looked more closely at the woman in yellow. Indeed, she was what most people would consider a great beauty—taller than her sister, and slender but rounded in all the proper places, with golden hair that glinted where the chandelier light caught it.

"The Donovan sisters?" he mused. "I don't know them."

"The lady in yellow is Jessica Donovan." Fenwicke murmured so as not to be heard by anyone in the crowd milling about the enormous punch bowl. "The lady in blue is her older sister, Olivia."

The angel's name was Olivia.

Due to his position as the heir of a duke, Max was acquainted with most of the English aristocracy perforce. Yet from the moment he'd caught his first glimpse of the angel tonight, he'd known he'd never been introduced to her, never seen her before. He'd never heard Olivia and Jessica Donovan's names, either, though their surname did sound vaguely familiar.

"They must be new to Town."

"They are. They arrived in London last month. This is only the third or fourth event they've attended." Fenwicke gave a significant pause. "However, I am quite certain you are acquainted with the eldest Donovan sister."

Max frowned. "I don't think so."

Fenwicke chuckled. "You are. You just haven't yet made the connection. The eldest sister is Margaret Dane, Countess of Stratford."

That name he did know—how could he not? "Ah. Of course."

A year ago, Lady Stratford had arrived from Antigua engaged to one well-connected gentleman, but she'd ended up marrying the earl instead. Like a great stone thrown into the semi-placid waters of London, the ripples caused by the splash she'd made had only just begun to subside. Even Max, who studiously avoided all forms of gossip, had heard all about it.

"So the countess's sisters have recently arrived from the West Indies?"

"That's right."

Max's gaze lingered on Olivia, the angel in blue. Fenwicke had said she was older than the lady standing beside her, but she appeared younger. It was in her bearing, in her expression. While Jessica didn't quite strut, she moved like a woman attuned to the power she wielded over all who beheld her. Olivia was directly the opposite. She wore her reserved nature like a cloak. She stood a few inches shorter and was slighter than her sister. Her cheeks were paler, and her hair held more of the copper and less of the gold, though certainly no one would complain that it was too red. It was just enough to lend an intriguing simmer rather than a full-blown fire.

Olivia's powder-blue dress was of an entirely fashionable style and fabric—though Max didn't concern himself with fashion enough to be able to distinguish either by name. The gown was conservatively cut but fit her perfectly, and her jewelry was simple. She wore only a pair of pearl-drop earrings and an austere strand of pearls around her neck.

Her posture was softer than her sister's, whose stance was sharp and alert. However, their familial connection was obvious in their faces—both perfect ovals with full but small mouths and large eyes. From this distance, Max couldn't discern the color of her eyes, but when Olivia had been dancing earlier, she'd glanced in his direction, and he'd thought they must be a light shade.

God. He nearly groaned. She captivated him. She had from the first moment he'd seen her. She was simply lovely.

"...leaving London soon."

Fenwicke stopped talking, and Max's attention snapped back to him.

Fenwicke sighed. "Did you hear me, Hasley?"

"Sorry," Max said, then gestured randomly about. "Noisy in here."

It was true, after all. The orchestra had begun the opening strands of the next dance, and laughing couples were brushing past them, hurrying to join in at the last possible moment.

Fenwicke gazed at him appraisingly for a long moment, then motioned toward the ballroom's exit. "Come, man. Let's go have a drink."

If it had been an ordinary evening, he would have declined. He and Fenwicke had a long acquaintance, and Max had always found the man oily and unlikable. They'd been rivals since their school days at Eton, but they'd never been friends.

He glanced quickly back to the lady. *Olivia.* At that moment, she looked up. Her gaze caught his and held.

Blue eyes. Surely they were blue.

Those eyes held him in her thrall, sweet and lovely, and sensual too, despite her obvious innocence. Max felt suspended in midair, like a water droplet caught in a spider's web.

She glanced at Fenwicke and then quickly to the floor, and Max plopped back to earth with a *splat*. But satisfaction rushed through him in a warm wave, because just before she'd broken their eye contact, he'd seen the first vestiges of color flooding her cheeks.

"Very well," he told Fenwicke. Tonight he didn't politely excuse himself from Fenwicke's company, because tonight Fenwicke appeared to have information Max suddenly craved—information about Olivia Donovan.

He turned away from her, but not before he saw another gentleman offering her his arm for the dance and a bolt of envy struck him in the gut. Thrusting away that irrational emotion, Max followed Fenwicke down the corridor to the parlor that had been set aside as the gentlemen's retiring room. A foursome played cards in the corner, and an elderly man sat in a large but elegant brown cloth armchair in the corner, blatantly antisocial, a newspaper raised to obscure half his face. Other men lounged by the sideboard, chatting and drinking from the never-ending supply of spirits.

Fenwicke collected two glasses of brandy and then gestured with his chin at a pair of empty leather chairs separated by a low, glass-topped table but close enough together for them to have a private conversation. Max sat in the nearest chair, taking the glass Fenwicke offered him as he passed. He took a drink of the brandy while Fenwicke lowered himself into the opposite chair.

Holding his glass in both hands, Fenwicke stared at him. "I gather you haven't had the pleasure of observing the Miss Donovans prior to tonight."

"No," Max admitted. "Do they plan to reside in London?"

"No." Fenwicke's lip twisted sardonically. "As I was saying in the ballroom, I believe they're leaving before the end of the month. They're off to Stratford's estate in Sussex."

"Too bad," Max murmured.

But then a memory jolted him. At White's last week, Lord Stratford had invited a few men, including Max, to Sussex this autumn to hunt fowl. He'd turned down the offer—he'd never been much interested in hunting—but now...

Fenwicke gazed at him. The man had always reminded Max of a reptilian predator with his cold, assessing silver-gray eyes. "You," he announced, "have a tendre for Miss Donovan."

It was impossible to determine whether that was a question or a statement. Either way, it didn't matter. "Don't be absurd. I don't even know Jessica Donovan."

"I'm speaking of Olivia," Fenwicke said icily. It sounded like Fenwicke was *jealous*, but that was ridiculous. As the man had said, the lady had been in Town for less than a month.

"I don't know either of them," Max responded, keeping his tone mild.

"Regardless, you want her," Fenwicke said in an annoyed voice. "I'm well acquainted with that look you were throwing in her direction."

Max shrugged.

"You are besotted with her."

Max leaned back in his chair, studying Fenwicke closely beyond the rim of his glass, wondering what gave Fenwicke the right to have proprietary feelings for Olivia Donovan.

"Are you a relation of hers?" he asked.

"I am not."

"Well, I was watching her," Max said slowly. "And, yes, I admit to wondering who she was and whether she was attached. I was considering asking her to dance later this evening."

The muscles in Fenwicke's jaw bulged as he ground his teeth. "She has no dances available."

"How do you know?"

"I asked her myself."

Max stared at the man opposite him, feeling the muscles across his shoulders tense as the fingers of his loose hand curled into a tight fist. He didn't like the thought of his angel touching Fenwicke. Of Fenwicke touching her. The thought rather made him want to throw Fenwicke through the glass window overlooking the terrace across from them.

He took a slow breath, willing himself to calmness. He wasn't even acquainted with the woman. Didn't even know the sound of her voice, the color of her eyes, her likes and dislikes. Yet he was already willing to protect her from scum like Fenwicke.

He wouldn't want Fenwicke touching any young innocent, he reasoned. He'd protect any woman from the marquis's slick, slithering paws.

"How is your wife?" he asked quite deliberately, aware of the challenge in his voice.

Fenwicke's expression went flat. He took a long drink of brandy before responding. "She's well," he said coldly. "She's back at home. In Sussex. Thank you for asking." His lips curled in a snarl that Max guessed was supposed to appear to be a smile.

Max remembered that Fenwicke's country home was in Sussex, just like the Earl of Stratford's. He wondered if the houses were situated close to each other.

"I'm glad to hear she's well."

"You can't have her," Fenwicke said quietly.

Max raised a brow. "Your wife?"

"Olivia Donovan."

Max took a long moment to allow that to sink in. To think about how he should respond.

"She's not married?" he finally asked. He knew the answer.

Fenwicke's tone was frosty. "She is not."

"Engaged?"

"No."

"Then why, pray, can't I have her?"

"She'd never accept you. You would never meet her standards. You, Hasley, are a well-known rake."

"So?" That had never stopped any woman from accepting his advances before.

"So, you're not good enough for her." Fenwicke's smile widened, but it was laced with bitterness. "No man in London is."

"How can you possibly know this?"

"She told me."

Max nearly choked on his brandy. "What?"

"I propositioned her," Fenwicke said simply. "In the correct way, of course, which was quite delicate, considering her innocence. I dug deeply—quite deeply indeed—into my cache of charm."

Max's stomach churned. He could never understand what women saw in Fenwicke—but obviously they saw something, because the man never needed to be too aggressive in his pursuit before capturing his prey, despite his marital status.

Yet it seemed Miss Olivia Donovan didn't see whatever it was in Fenwicke that all the other women saw. Intriguing. Without ever having met her, Max's respect for her grew.

The thought of how many times Fenwicke had abandoned his young wife in the country left Max feeling vaguely nauseous. How many times had he seen the man with a different woman on his arm?

Perhaps what left the sourest taste in Max's mouth was that everyone knew about Fenwicke's proclivities but continued to invite him to their social events. No one spurned him. He was a peer, after all, a member of White's, and an excellent dance partner or opponent at cards.

Long ago, Fenwicke had decided that Max was an adversary and had pushed Max into a constant competition. They'd competed over sports, women, their studies, and politics. It had all started in Max's third year at Eton, when his cousins had died of influenza and Max became the heir to a dukedom just like Fenwicke was— Fenwicke's father was the Duke of Southington and Max's uncle was the Duke of Wakefield.

Fenwicke even had the audacity to claim he'd be more of a duke, since he was an eldest son rather than a nephew. That statement had enraged Max—no one could vex him like Fenwicke could. Something about the man brought out the worst in Max, which was why he'd tried his damndest to stay away from the marquis. Avoidance hadn't worked, however. Both he and Fenwicke had gone to Cambridge and now they belonged to the same gentleman's club. Max couldn't get rid of the man. And once they were both dukes and sitting in Parliament, they'd be required to see more of each other. Max had to come to terms with the fact that Fenwicke was a permanent fixture in his life, but that didn't mean he had to like it.

Now, thinking of Fenwicke's lascivious thoughts toward Miss Donovan in spite of his married state, Max's dislike of the man threatened to grow into something stronger. Something more like hatred. He closed his eyes and images of his father passed behind his lids. His mother...alone. The tears she'd tried to hide from him. Even at a very young age, Max had known exactly what was happening. Exactly how his father had betrayed his mother, how he'd hurt her, ultimately destroyed her.

Max would never do that to a wife—he'd never marry so there would simply never be a concern—and he'd never abide anyone who did.

Fenwicke set his empty brandy glass on the table with a sigh. "I'm afraid Miss Olivia Donovan simply isn't interested."

Max narrowed his eyes. "So because you failed to charm the lady, you assume that I'll fail as well?"

"Of course. She's frigid, you see. The girl is composed of ice as solid as a glacier."

Another of the many reasons Max disliked Fenwicke: He never took responsibility. If a woman rejected him, he'd think it was due to some defect in her character as opposed to a natural—and wise—dislike or distrust of the man himself. If a woman professed no attraction to the marquis, naturally she wouldn't feel any attraction to any man, because all other men were lesser beings.

"I sincerely doubt she's frigid," Max responded before he thought better of it.

Fenwicke's eyes narrowed. "Do you?"

Max met the man's steely glare head-on. "Perhaps you simply don't appeal."

Fenwicke snorted. "Of course I appeal. I'm a marquis, to begin with, and the heir to—"

"Perhaps," Max interjected, keeping his voice low, "she possesses no interest in engaging in an adulterous liaison, marquis or no."

At his periphery, Max could see Fenwicke's fists clenching. He braced himself for the man's lunge, but it never came. Damn it. If Fenwicke had attacked first, it would have given Max a good reason to throttle him.

Fenwicke gave him a thin, humorless smile. "I would beg to differ."

Max shrugged. "Perhaps we should agree to disagree, then."

"If she did not succumb to my charms, Hasley, then rest assured, there's no way in hell she'll succumb to yours." Fenwicke's voice was mild, but the cords in his neck bulged above his cravat.

Max shook his head, unable to prevent a sneer from forming on his lips. "You're wrong, Fenwicke."

Fenwicke's brows rose, his eyes glinted, and a sly expression came over his face. He leaned forward, greedily licking his lips.

"Would you care to place a wager on that?"

Chapter One

Sussex,
Two Months Later

Sussex in autumn was beautiful. Having spent most of her life on a small island in the West Indies, Olivia Donovan had never experienced the seasons in such dramatic fashion. The bracken surrounding the estate that belonged to her brother-in-law had turned a deep russet color. The brush bordering the forest abounded with the bright red berries of rosehips and haw, and the trees displayed a wealth of browns, reds, and yellows—deep, homey colors that gave Olivia a sense of peace and security. Antigua had never shown varying colors in such brilliant display.

Olivia turned from the drawing room window to smile at her sisters. It was so good to be together again, and it never failed to send happiness surging through her when she saw the three of them huddled together.

Serena—who'd changed her name to Margaret, or Meg—had married, and so had Phoebe, who was, at twenty, a year younger than Olivia. Phoebe had arrived in England with Serena last year. Jessica and Olivia hadn't arrived until late July this year. They'd gone straight to London and had plunged into the frenzy that was the Season.

Jessica had met droves of potential suitors. Olivia hadn't met anyone, though if you asked her three sisters, they'd all say it was entirely her fault.

She was too picky, they said.

She was too quiet.

She was too shy.

What she'd tried to tell them, over and over, was that perhaps she *was* picky, quiet, and shy, but none of that really mattered. What was most important was one simple fact that her sisters seemed either unwilling or unable to comprehend: No gentleman would have her, not once he learned about her ailment. Gentlemen wanted sturdy women, women who were capable of bearing strong, strapping sons. They didn't want women who could fall ill from a relapse of malaria and die on a moment's notice. Not pale, thin women prone to fainting and fevers.

She'd been aware from a young age that she was destined to be alone. It didn't matter. Knowing that they weren't in the cards for her, she had given up pining for marriage and children long ago. She was truly happy— no, utterly fulfilled—as long as she was surrounded by her sisters.

"Oh, drat," Phoebe muttered, glancing up at the mantel clock. "I must go. Margie will be hungry soon, and I simply can't abide it when her nurse feeds her."

Margie was Phoebe's eight-month-old daughter, a lovely child with the strongest lungs Olivia had ever heard on an infant. She took after her mother in temperament, though she possessed her father's strikingly dark hair and eyes.

Olivia smiled. "Give my darling niece a big kiss from her Auntie Olivia, will you?"

"Of course."

"*Must* you go, Phoebe?" Jessica complained, waving her cards. "We haven't finished the game."

They'd been playing cribbage while Serena was embroidering a bonnet for Margie.

Phoebe crossed her arms tightly across her chest. "You can't understand, Jess. What it's like to be a mother. I can *tell* when she needs me. I can feel it."

"How perfectly ghastly." Jessica grimaced at Phoebe's bosom. "I hope I never have children and never, ever feel any such thing."

"You can't mean that!" exclaimed Olivia. "What about all your suitors, Jess?"

All three of her sisters swung their heads around to stare at Olivia and she took a step back, feeling the window ledge push into her spine. "What?" she asked. "Why are all of you looking at me like that?"

"Suitors don't necessarily translate into motherhood." Serena's lips twitched. She was obviously fighting a smile.

"Well, they translate into proposals of marriage, eventually. Then engagements and weddings. And those, in turn, translate to motherhood."

"*Pfft*," Jessica hissed. "Not true. Not at all true."

Serena raised a brow at Jessica. "Care to explain how *that* works, Jess?"

Jessica shrugged and turned up her nose in a particularly Jess-like expression. "Not really. I just happen to know that there are ways to prevent conception."

"Ways that are utterly deadly to both mother and child," Phoebe muttered, frowning.

"Not necessarily," Jessica said, looking superior.

"If that's so," Serena said, "we don't want to hear about them. In any case, you're scandalizing poor Saint Olivia."

Their gazes all turned to her, and Olivia felt the burn of a flush crawling over her cheeks. "You're not scandalizing me!"

"Oh, yes we are," Phoebe said in the tone of a wizened old man. "There are certain topics best not discussed in Saint Olivia's presence."

Jessica shook her head soberly. "You're red as a lobster, Liv. Obviously this conversation is distressing you."

"It is not." Olivia pressed her hand to her heated cheek. "Not at all."

Jessica turned to Serena and Phoebe. "I think we'd best let her continue to think that suitors mean eventual motherhood."

"But will that make her more likely to seek one?" Serena asked.

Jessica turned back to her. "Well, Liv? What do you think? No suitors and no motherhood, or shall we find you a suitor forthwith so you can start popping out litters of babies?"

Phoebe wrinkled her nose. "Jess! Is it possible for you to be any more indelicate?"

Jessica snapped back, "And who are you to speak of indelicacy, Mrs. Run-off-to-Gretna-Green-with-the-first-man-you-meet Harper?"

"Oh, stop it, both of you," Serena said. "Before this escalates into a silly argument, I have something to tell you. Something important." As the sisters turned to her,

Serena looked down at her embroidery, scarlet spreading across her cheeks. "Well, Jonathan and I haven't been trying to *prevent* anything."

As Olivia frowned at her, trying to understand what on earth she was talking about, Phoebe dropped her cards and jumped out of her chair. "You're pregnant!"

Pressing her lips together, still staring downward, Serena nodded.

"Oh, Serena," Olivia breathed. "Really?" Serena had been hoping to conceive ever since Olivia and Jessica had arrived from Antigua.

"Yes," Serena whispered. "I'm sure of it. But you forgot to call me Meg again." The smile on Serena's face told Olivia she didn't really care this time. Olivia found it so difficult to call her sister by her new name. She'd always be Serena, her oldest, wisest sister, no matter what everyone else thought.

"I'm so happy for you, *Meg*," she murmured, grinning.

"Another niece or a nephew for us! How perfectly lovely." Jessica seemed to have forgotten her annoyance at Margie's demands upon Phoebe.

Jessica, Phoebe, and Olivia gathered around Serena, embracing her as one, kissing her cheeks and pressing their hands over her still-flat stomach.

"Are you happy?" they asked her.

"Are you excited?"

"Are you afraid?" Jessica asked.

"Yes, I'm excited and happy, and no, of course I'm not afraid."

Phoebe kissed Serena's cheek and rose. "I really must go feed Margie," she said softly. With a special smile at Serena, she took her leave.

• • •

Olivia spent most afternoons walking the grounds of Jonathan's vast estate. Some might say that Jonathan's lands were overgrown and dilapidated, but the area was so full of delights and treasures, Olivia found her new home to be utterly marvelous.

Jonathan had only recently moved back to Sussex and begun taking care of the property again, and he and Serena had just begun the work of refurbishing the house and grounds. Serena always laughed when she said that after having lived in Sussex for less than a year, she was glad she could walk from the front door to the carriage door without getting pricked by thorns or tripping over a fallen branch.

Some afternoons Olivia walked with Jonathan's mother, the dowager countess, a lovely, cheerful woman, and others she walked with her sisters. But she was diligent about taking the time to walk daily, and most of the time she ended up on her own.

In Antigua, Mother had rarely allowed her to step foot outside, because Olivia's doctor had always said that taking outdoor exercise would be detrimental to her weak constitution. But Mother wasn't here. This wasn't Antigua, this was England, and the climate, flora, and fauna were very different. If anyone objected to her walks, Olivia would simply say she was certain she was safer here.

Today, wearing her usual plain brown wool walking dress and sunbonnet, she ventured into the woods deep within Jonathan's properties. The terrain was more uneven out here than it was nearer to the house, but paths wound through the trees, one of them leading to a natural spring wedged between two rock outcroppings.

Olivia breathed in the fresh autumn air and gloried in the crackle of dry leaves and brush beneath her boots. Before she'd left the house, she'd tucked a loaf of stale bread beneath her arm—she came in this direction every few days to feed a gaggle of gray geese that had made its home by the spring.

Humming under her breath, she descended the curve in the path that led to the spring. Glancing up from her feet, where she'd been looking to prevent herself from tripping over the rocks, she jerked to a stop, leaving a broken note hanging in the air.

A man—a man surrounded by eager geese—was crouched by the water.

He looked back over his shoulder at her. Obviously he'd heard her crackling and humming her way toward him. She hadn't been attempting stealth.

Her pulse throbbed in her chest at a sudden realization. She was alone in the forest with a stranger. A *man*.

She licked her lips nervously, watching him rise to his feet. Trying not to watch the way his black Wellingtons encased his strong calves and his leather breeches clung to his muscular thighs.

It wasn't polite to stare at a strange man's thighs, she reminded herself sternly. Forcibly, she yanked her gaze upward.

He wore black gloves, and he gripped a small round burlap bag, likely food for the geese, one of which was pecking hungrily at it, trying to open it to spill out its contents. The bag hung at the man's side, and he didn't seem to notice the goose at all.

Olivia dragged her gaze farther upward. A richly tailored coat—like something made by a fine London clothier rather than the shabby homespun most men wore in Antigua—clung to broad shoulders.

A firm, square jaw, dusted with the growth of afternoon whiskers. Lush but stern lips. A strong nose. Dark hair that swooped across his forehead in a soft curl.

And…oh, those eyes. Penetrating, startling green. Staring at her.

Olivia managed to stifle her gasp. She *recognized* this man. This *gentleman,* she corrected. She'd seen him before, at the last ball she'd attended in London before coming to Stratford House. How could she forget?

"I'm sorry." Her voice emerged in little more than a breathy whisper. "I didn't realize the spring was… occupied."

Those stern lips tilted upward. Was he smiling? Was he laughing at her?

Heat rushed over her cheeks, followed by annoyance. She turned to leave.

"Wait."

Goodness, that voice! It was a low baritone, smooth as honey. She stopped midstep. Leaves crackled as he moved closer to her.

"There's room for two."

When she didn't respond, he added, "I can't possibly satisfy these greedy fiends. Look, they're already after your bread."

It was true. One of the geese had seen her bread and was warily walking closer, a hungry glint in her eye. "That's Henrietta," Olivia said softly. "She's always the first to want her dinner."

"Henrietta," the man said, "already ate half my bag of grain. She needs to give her brothers and sisters a chance."

Obviously, the man didn't know these geese very well. "Here, now." She broke off a chunk of bread and waved it at Henrietta. "It's the end. Your favorite part."

When the goose made a lunge for the piece of bread, she threw it directly into a cluster of haw bushes. Henrietta, who wasn't the smartest goose, waddled after it and began rooting around in the brush.

Olivia smiled at the stranger. "That's how you get her to leave the others alone. Otherwise, she'll bite them and scare them off and take the entire loaf for herself."

"Or the entire bag of grain, no doubt."

"No doubt," Olivia agreed.

His eyes twinkling, he opened his bag, took out a handful of grain, and scattered it over the ground around him. The geese partook happily.

"Poor Henrietta," Olivia said. The silly goose hadn't found her chunk of bread yet, and was unaware of her siblings feasting not three yards away from her.

"You're Miss Olivia Donovan, aren't you?" the stranger said.

His use of her name made Olivia freeze again. Trying to infuse some moisture into her dry throat, she said, "I'm afraid you have the advantage of me, sir."

"I'm Max."

She stared at him dumbly. Max? Just…Max? Surely that wasn't right!

He must have recognized the confusion in her eyes, because he corrected himself hastily. "Maxwell Buchanan." He bowed slightly, took her hand, and squeezed. She could feel the strength of his fingers through the layers of the leather of their gloves as her own fingers slipped from his.

"It's very nice to meet you, Mr. Buchanan." She tilted her head at him. "I'm certain I've seen you before, haven't I?"

"You remember?" His emerald eyes held steady on her face.

"It was in London, at Lord Hertford's ball."

He smiled, showing deep dimples, a startling contrast to his rugged features. And so handsome.

Olivia mentally swatted herself. She'd been startled by the sight of him at the ball, and she'd thought of him a few times since, because it was quite possible that she had never in her life seen anyone quite as physically commanding as this man. Men like this were an uncommon sight in her sheltered world, but she couldn't forget that he was still just a man. A human being, just like her.

Honestly, her reactions were utterly foolish. Next, she'd probably slap the back of her hand to her forehead and swoon.

"I remember," he said softly, and his voice stroked down her spine, licked across her chest—for heaven's sake, it felt like his voice *caressed* her.

She took a deep breath. "It's . . . good to see you again," she said. "But why are you here? Are you a neighbor?"

He chuckled. "Oh, no. I'm a guest of Stratford's."

Her brows shot upward. "You are?"

"Indeed. I just arrived this afternoon. Thought I'd go for a walk before dinner."

"And you just happened to bring some food along for any geese you might encounter?"

"The stable boy gave me the bag. Said there were loads of geese and ducks out here this time of year. Turkeys, too. He said I might lure them and perhaps shoot one."

Only then did she notice the rifle lying across a flat stone that lay near the water. She looked back at Mr. Buchanan, eyes wide. "You planned to *shoot* my geese?"

He laughed easily. "*Your* geese?"

"I've been feeding them for a month." She narrowed her eyes at him. "Don't say I've fattened them up just for you."

He looked like he was fighting another laugh. "Very well. I won't say it, then."

The geese had finished the grain and were eyeing both Mr. Buchanan and Olivia, waiting for their next course. Even Henrietta had consumed her bread and was now shifting assessing looks between Olivia and Mr. Buchanan, apparently wondering which of them would be a better target to accost for more food.

Mr. Buchanan solved the dilemma, first by distracting Henrietta with a small handful tossed into the deep patch of grass nearest her, then scattering a larger handful nearby for the other geese.

"You do know," he said, "that the reason Stratford invited us here was to hunt with him?"

She blew out a breath through her lips. "I know," she said softly, and looked down at her bread. She tore it into small pieces, slowly and deliberately tossing them to the insatiable geese.

"You don't approve of hunting?"

"I just..." She shrugged. "I don't like killing God's creatures. That's all."

Mr. Buchanan's features softened. "Ah."

"But I understand that it's a necessity for human nourishment and survival. I can't say I approve of it as a sport, however."

"I'll tell you a secret." Mr. Buchanan leaned forward conspiratorially. "I am not an avid hunter. In fact, I've never shot at any living thing in my life."

She frowned at him. "Really?"

He nodded.

"Then why are you here?"

He shrugged. "I thought I'd give it a try. I might learn something. And..." He paused, then gave her a sheepish smile. "I'm in need of a new diversion."

"Are you lacking in pleasurable diversions?" she asked, throwing the last of the bread toward the geese and brushing the crumbs from her hands.

"I am." A shadow passed behind his eyes, but when she blinked, it was gone.

"I've heard that's a common problem in England amongst gentlemen of a certain class."

"Have you?"

When Olivia and Jessica had spent the month at their aunt Geraldine's London house this summer, their aunt had gone on and on about the canker on society that was young men of their class. "Yes. You see, my sisters and I were all raised on the island of Antigua. It's a very different place from England."

"I'd heard your family was from the West Indies. I imagine it's very different there, indeed." Mr. Buchanan turned over the burlap bag and scattered his remaining grain. Then he brushed off his own hands and collected the rifle, which he slung across his back. He raised his brows at her and held out his arm. "May I accompany you back to your brother-in-law's house, Miss Donovan?"

She nodded. She'd cut her walk shorter than usual, but she was intrigued by this gentleman. In any case, it was time to leave the spring and the geese, which were finishing up the bread crumbs and within moments would be pestering them for more.

Side by side, they turned and walked down the unkempt path from which Olivia had come. Mr. Buchanan held Olivia's arm firmly tucked within his own, his flesh solid—hard, even—against hers. It was...disconcerting.

Men had held her arm before in her life, of course. Her brother-in-law, for one, was very sweet with her, and even though no one ever brought up her frail constitution to her face, he always put great effort into ensuring she was taken care of.

But this was different. This wasn't a family relation, this was a man she'd only just met, and in rather odd circumstances. If this had happened in London and someone who didn't know her had seen them, it would have been enough to spark gossip—probably even talk of an engagement. Of course, her sisters wouldn't blink twice when they saw her coming out of the woods on the arm of a stranger—they *knew* her.

But anyone else in the world probably *would* blink. Several times over.

"So tell me about them," Mr. Buchanan said.

She gave him a blank stare.

"The differences between Antigua and England," he clarified.

"Oh, goodness. There are so many."

"Well, let's start with the obvious. The visual. How is Antigua different from England in the autumn?"

"There are no colors," Olivia said softly.

He raised his brows. "No colors?"

"Well, there are colors," she amended. "The blues of

the sky and of the ocean, for one. The sky is only subtly different from the English sky. A shade crisper, I'd say. But the ocean is very different. It's such a bright, shimmering blue. Utterly clear and fathomless."

"Hm." Mr. Buchanan slid her a glance, opened his mouth as if he was going to say something, and then seemed to think better of it.

She took a breath and continued. "All in all, quite different from the grayish color of the English waters I've seen so far."

"I imagine so," Mr. Buchanan said. "I've heard much about the seas of the West Indies. I've heard the waters are clear. Are they warm, too, like they say?"

"Oh yes, much, much warmer than English oceans."

They rounded a copse of trees and stepped onto the ragged lawn. Olivia tensed. Now was the time they would be seen.

Still, she couldn't bring herself to pull her arm out from his. The afternoon had turned chilly, but her arm was warm where his flesh pressed on hers, and that warmth seemed to radiate up to her shoulder and through her body.

Nevertheless, when she saw a figure walking toward them from the direction of the house, she did slip her arm from his. She smiled up at him—goodness, he was tall. Probably a foot taller than herself. "Thank you for walking home with me."

He smiled down at her, warmth filling those sparkling eyes of his. "It was my pleasure, Miss Donovan."

The grass was tall here, and Olivia lifted her skirts a little so she could walk through the most difficult clumps without soiling her dress. Beside her, Mr. Buchanan clasped his hands behind his back—no, she wouldn't notice the way that made his coat pull so tightly across his broad chest—and walked along at her side, studying the figure growing closer with every step they took.

"Do you know who it is?" he asked.

"It's one of my sisters." But which one? Phoebe and her husband, Sebastian, were living in the caretaker's cottage, so she probably wouldn't be coming from the house. That left either Jessica or Serena. Soon, the watery sunshine sparkled gold over the woman's hair as she carefully picked her way toward them, and Olivia smiled. "It's Seren—" She sucked in a breath. Very few people knew Serena's real name, and it was a well-protected secret. The world thought of her as Meg now. "It's my sister, Meg. Lady Stratford."

Mr. Buchanan nodded. "I've met her, but only twice, and both times it was in a formal setting. I've known the earl since we were boys, though."

"Really?" She was genuinely interested. She had a difficult time envisioning her brother-in-law's childhood. All she knew was that it had been a generally unhappy one.

"Yes. We went to Eton together. Afterward, we went our separate ways for several years..." He hesitated.

Olivia smiled. "Those were probably his 'Years of Debauchery.' That's what Meg calls them."

Mr. Buchanan raised a brow at her. "Is that so?"

"It is." She sighed, and said softly, "He's changed entirely, thanks to my sister."

"I've heard about her influence on him. In fact, I've seen it in him." Mr. Buchanan sounded thoughtful. "He's a much happier man now."

"I'm so thankful he and my sister found each other again."

"Again?"

Olivia blinked several times. This was the problem with Serena's new identity—it forced her to be slightly dishonest at times, and that made her terribly uncomfortable. She wasn't a dishonest person by nature.

"I'm sorry," she said in a low voice. "I'm afraid... well, that I've said too much. You'll forgive me if I don't say anything more, I hope."

Mr. Buchanan slowed in his step. She looked up at him again to see him frowning, but not at her—it seemed as though he was frowning at himself, at something he was thinking. He caught her eye, saw that she was watching him, and his features relaxed.

"Somehow, I think I could forgive you most anything, Miss Donovan," he murmured.

"Olivia, is that you?" Serena called.

She waved, and Serena hurried closer. When she was near enough, they all stopped, and Serena and Mr. Buchanan exchanged a bow.

"You must be Lord Hasley. Jonathan said you'd gone for a walk. Welcome to Stratford House, my lord."

He made his thanks as Olivia gawked at him. *Lord Hasley? My lord?* Obviously, he wasn't a simple mister, and he hadn't bothered to correct her when she'd called him Mr. Buchanan. Her cheeks heated. Should she have known his title based on his name alone?

Serena bade him come into the house, where she'd show him to his room and offer him refreshment before dinner. Serena was in her element. She was so satisfied by her new life with Jonathan and as lady of her own domain, and now she was with child. Her sister's happiness made Olivia feel warm and soft, like a gentle light glowed inside her.

Devilry glinted in Mr. Buchanan's—*Lord Hasley's*—eyes. "I heard you plan to serve goose for dinner tonight."

Olivia's mouth dropped open.

"Oh, dear." Serena frowned. "Yes, I did plan on it. Please tell me you haven't an aversion to roasted goose."

Lord Hasley smiled, his dimples flashing more at Olivia than at Serena. "Not at all. I'll enjoy every bite. It's your sister I'm concerned about."

Serena's confused gaze moved to Olivia.

"No need to be concerned, *Lord Hasley*," Olivia said primly. "As long as they're not personal acquaintances of mine, I'm sure I'll be quite satisfied with roasted goose for dinner this evening."

Shaking her head at his low chuckle, Olivia followed them into the entry hall, where Jonathan and another man waited for them with Jessica.

"Olivia, I'd like you to meet our good friend, Captain William Langley, who has come from his home in the north of England," Jonathan said.

She curtsied to the man. He was tall—as tall as Mr. Buchanan, but not as wide in the shoulders. And she saw instantly that he had a serious nature about him. She understood that; she knew a little of his past with Serena. "Captain Langley," she murmured. "I'm so pleased to finally meet you."

"And you, Miss Donovan." His voice was grave and sober, his eyes lacking the sparkle of Mr. Buchanan's, and something panged in her chest. He'd been in love, once, with Serena's twin, and had only found out recently that she had been lost at sea seven years ago.

Serena and Jonathan led the two men off to their rooms, talking animatedly about their plans for the renovation of the house as they began to mount the sweeping staircase. Jessica pulled Olivia down the corridor leading to the drawing room. "Oh, Olivia," she whispered, "isn't Lord Hasley the handsomest man you've ever seen? Serena told me he's a marquis and heir to the Duke of Wakefield."

"Is he?" Olivia looked speculatively in the direction Mr. Buchanan—*the marquis*—had left with Serena and the other gentlemen.

If what Jessica said was true, Lord Hasley wasn't just any lord. He was so far above a mister, it was almost laughable. He was a marquis, but that was only a courtesy title until he took his place as a duke, essentially just a step below a prince.

Imagine that. The heir to a duke had been squatting and surrounded by wild geese, and hadn't seemed at all offended when she'd incorrectly called him Mr. Buchanan. A lofty man with a lofty title...yet he didn't behave as though he were superior to anyone. Olivia knew from her experiences in London that that was a rare kind of lord indeed.

"Well?" Jessica asked. "Isn't he just *gorgeous*?"

"Yes," Olivia murmured. "Yes he is."

Jessica stopped cold, her mouth dropping open. "Liv? Are you all right? You're not ill again, are you?"

"What?" she asked distractedly. Then she turned to her sister. "No, of course I'm not ill."

Jessica pressed her palm to Olivia's forehead. "Are you feverish?"

"Not at all, silly! Why do you ask?"

"Because, dear sister, I've pointed out handsome men to you about a thousand times. But you've never—not once—actually *agreed* with me."

Chapter Two

The doors to the breakfast room were wide open, and even though the floor needed sanding, the walls and table required refurbishment, and coal smoke had stained the hearth and part of the ceiling with sweeping black marks, the room had quickly become one of Olivia's favorites. The reason for that was the wall of eastern-facing windows that allowed the bright morning sunlight to stream inside.

Today was no exception. Although it had rained overnight, the sun peeked out from behind gray clouds and sparkled over the rangy wild grasses of the eastern lawn. Jonathan had told them that once upon a time, the lawn had been spotlessly manicured with topiary bushes cut to perfection along a curving path that wended through the eastern acreage and around the back of the house skirting the woods. If Olivia squinted hard enough, she thought she could see the remnants of that path—a winding trail of weeds a shade darker than those that surrounded it.

Serena glanced up from her plate as Olivia and Jessica walked into the breakfast room. "Good morning."

"You're up early," Jessica commented grumpily. Jessica was never pleasant company in the mornings until she'd had her sugared coffee—a habit she'd grown into long ago back in Antigua.

"It's almost eleven," Serena said, exchanging a knowing glance with Olivia.

Olivia scanned the dishes on the sideboard. She chose a thick slice of toasted bread and proceeded to smear gooseberry jam over it. "I don't believe I've seen you up before noon since we arrived from London," she said to Serena.

"I was…" Serena pressed her lips together and glanced down at her brimming plate before continuing, a pink blush staining her cheeks. Serena had never really been one to blush unless under extreme conditions, and Olivia found this new propensity charming. She just wanted to hug her sister to bits. "Well, I was quite hungry," Serena finished.

That precipitated a grin from Olivia. "Ah," she murmured. "Eating for two souls rather than one?"

Olivia smiled at Serena's unintelligible muttered response.

Jessica glanced at the door. Confirming no one was close, she murmured, "Have you told Jonathan yet?"

"Not yet." Serena bit her bottom lip. "I'm waiting for the perfect time."

"I can understand that," Olivia murmured. If she were in her sister's place, she'd want to wait for the perfect moment to tell her husband the news as well.

Just then, Lord Hasley entered with a cheerful "Good morning, ladies," and strode to the coffeepot, effectively ending any further discussion of Serena's pregnancy.

Olivia studied her toast, but from the corner of her eye she saw that the marquis was dressed in riding clothes—clothes that clung to his muscular frame in a most appealing way—and the same tall black leather boots he'd worn yesterday.

"Good morning, my lord," Serena said. "I trust you slept well."

He grinned at her. "Excellently, thank you." He sucked in a deep breath. "Ah, I've missed the country air."

"Has it been long since you were last in the country?" Jessica asked.

Having no excuse to remain at the sideboard, Olivia went to the table and took her seat to the right of Serena's.

Lord Hasley hesitated, then smiled, although not quite as jovially as he had when he'd first entered the room. "Many years," he said, his voice containing a subtle softness that made Olivia glance sharply at him.

He set his coffee on the table, and at Serena's urging, returned to the sideboard to fill a plate with food.

"What do you gentlemen have planned for the day?" Serena asked. "I know Jonathan's already at the stables."

"Yes, and Langley's with him. They're discussing the earl's stock." With his plate piled high, Lord Hasley took the seat beside Olivia. "Since I'm not the horse connoisseur those two are, I told them I'd prefer to spend the morning with the ladies."

"Oh, *wonderful*," Jessica said saucily, "perhaps you might help me with my embroidery."

Lord Hasley didn't hesitate. "Alas, I forgot my own sampler, so I'll be happy to assist you with yours, Miss Jessica."

Olivia's chuckle burst out of her, and she slapped her

hand over her mouth when her sisters' gazes snapped to her. "Sorry." She shrugged. "That was funny."

Lord Hasley chuckled too, easing her embarrassment, and Serena said, "I've an idea. It's something I've been thinking about for the past several weeks, and I was intending to recruit Olivia and Jessica to help me. But your assistance would be welcome as well, my lord."

"I am all ears," Lord Hasley said, and attacked his poached egg with gusto.

Serena spoke between bites of black pudding. "Well, as you know, we've made Stratford House our home for several months now, and while I've met nearly all of Jonathan's tenants, I've yet to meet some of the neighbors. Particularly our closest neighbors, Lord and Lady Fenwicke of Brockton Hall."

Olivia fumbled with her piece of toast, nearly dropping it onto the floor, but Lord Hasley's hand on her arm steadied it. She gave him a sidelong look, her heart pulsing wildly in her chest. His reaction—well, it was as if he knew. Yet surely he couldn't. That was impossible.

But that night she'd seen him at Lord Hertford's ball. Oh, goodness, he'd been walking with Lord Fenwicke. They'd appeared friendly with each other. Had Lord Fenwicke spoken of her? Had he told Lord Hasley what had happened between them?

Serena continued blithely on. "Lord Fenwicke is still in London, I believe, but Lady Fenwicke is in residence. She's very young—I'm told she married Lord Fenwicke just over a year ago, and I hear she's lived there since the wedding, but I haven't seen her at all. It promises to be a fine day, so I thought we could all walk over to Brockton Hall and call upon the lady."

"Well, that sounds like an absolutely lovely idea." Jessica was all eagerness.

A sick feeling curdled in the pit of Olivia's stomach, but there was no way she'd reveal that to her sisters. They'd worry. They always worried when she didn't feel well.

She remembered Lord Fenwicke's ugly smile. When they'd waltzed together, he'd pulled her body so tightly against his, she'd felt him not-so-subtly rubbing his erection against her belly. After the dance, he'd tugged her into a dark alcove, and she'd been so stupid and naïve for not dashing away from him before he'd taken her there.

He'd leaned into her ear and whispered nasty, horrid things to her. About how he'd tear her clothes off and lay her down. About how he'd take her so hard that she'd feel him for a week.

Then he'd pulled her against him again and his wet mouth slathered over her neck and his hand snaked down her bodice. She had pushed him off her, managing to hold back the scream threatening to reveal herself and Lord Fenwicke in a compromising position to half the London *ton.*

She'd turned to run away, but he'd grabbed her arm and yanked her back. Later, she'd found a ring of bruises around her arm. He'd said, "I'm a marquis, if you recall." As if it was unthinkable that she would turn down a man of his status.

She'd responded that she didn't want any man, any marquis, any wretched London rake, and especially not him, and that she intended to die a spinster. Then she'd turned on her heel and marched away. She'd felt disgusted and dirty for a week.

How could she look in the eyes of Lord Fenwicke's wife? Goodness, even thinking the man's name made Olivia feel all clammy and cold.

Lord Hasley's fingers still curled around her arm, but his touch was gentle, nothing like Lord Fenwicke's painful grip. Neither of her sisters seemed to have noticed her agitation, thank goodness. Now, Lord Hasley squeezed gently and then removed his hand. "Miss Donovan? What do you think?"

She tried to smile at Serena, but she was certain it came out as more of a grimace. "It is a good idea. Neighborly relations are important."

"Very true," Lord Hasley said.

"Are you acquainted with Lord and Lady Fenwicke, my lord?" Serena asked.

Olivia turned to him, curious as to how he'd answer. In truth, a description of the extent of his relations with Lord Fenwicke would go far in helping Olivia firm her opinion about Lord Hasley.

"Lord Fenwicke is an acquaintance," Lord Hasley said, "but not a friend. Stratford and I have known him since our school days."

"And his wife?"

Lord Hasley nodded. "I met her in London two years ago." He smiled, but it was a tight smile that didn't make his dimples appear. "She was a very charming, very lovely young lady."

"But you haven't seen her since?" Jessica asked.

"No. It's been almost two years to the day."

"But that's all right, isn't it?" Jessica asked. "At least we won't be a group of complete strangers bombarding the poor lady's privacy."

Nerves jumped along Olivia's spine. The woman probably wouldn't instinctually hate her, and of course, chances were that she knew nothing of what her horrid husband had said and done to Olivia. That had happened in London, far from here.

"It's settled then." Serena rose from her seat as a footman whisked away her plate and coffee cup. "We'll leave in half an hour, and I'll take some of those lovely tarts Cook made last night for her." She smiled. "She's just a little older than you are, Jessica. You never know, she may turn into a wonderful friend."

"Oh, wouldn't that be lovely?" Jessica clapped her hands at her chest in anticipation. Out of all the sisters, Jessica was the most outgoing. She made friends wherever she went. "A friend for us all."

Max loitered in the library, scanning the rows of old books while he waited for the ladies to come downstairs for the walk to Brockton Hall. He liked this room. It was large for a library, and spacious. Rows of books covered three of the walls from floor to ceiling. The fourth held two deep-set tall and narrow windows on either side of a very comfortable-looking chaise longue. Four old chairs, all of different designs and colors but all large and soft, were scattered around the room, welcoming anyone who desired to lose themselves within the pages of a book.

Max ran his fingers along the spines of a row of books at his eye level. There was no orderliness to the shelving of these books: *Pamela* was beside *The Science of Horticulture,* which was shelved in turn beside *The Truth of the Christian Religion, Book Three.*

The door opened behind him, and Max turned to see

Lady Stratford smiling at him. She wore a light gray dress that complemented her eyes. "Jessica and Olivia should be down in a minute or two." He nodded and she tilted her head at the bookshelf. "What book were you looking at?"

"Oh, none in particular."

She laughed softly. "It's difficult to find books in here. I intend to organize them someday, but there are so many, it seems a daunting task."

"It's a wonderful library," Max said. He knew he'd be spending more time in here.

"Thank you." She came up beside him and pretended to look at the shelf Max had been scanning when she'd walked in. After a moment, she said, "I was surprised to see you with Olivia yesterday."

"It was pure chance that we happened upon each other in the wood."

That was a lie. He'd been waiting by the spring because the stable boy had told him she would probably go in that direction, and Max had had this inexplicable desire to be alone with her for their first meeting.

"The wood is quite vast," Lady Stratford said softly. "Sometimes I worry about Olivia going off by herself, because if she were to get lost, it would be like searching for a needle in a haystack. And yet..." She paused significantly. "You two found each other."

"It's odd how the world is sometimes far smaller than it appears," Max said, shrugging.

"Indeed. Well, we all worry about Olivia going off alone, but we allow it."

Max raised a brow. *Allow it?* Olivia was a grown woman. Why wouldn't her family allow her to go for a walk within the confines of her brother-in-law's estate?

When Lady Stratford met his gaze, alarm bells rang through him. Her expression was a clear warning. It said, *Don't trifle with my sister. We are all looking out for her.*

He shouldn't be offended that the countess thought he'd consider trifling with Olivia. The lady probably knew a little of his past, which, as with many men of his age and class, involved quite a bit of trifling.

He forced a friendly look onto his face. "You must care for your sister very much."

"All of us do," Lady Stratford said. "Olivia is special. She might be the most guileless, genuine person you or I will ever meet, Lord Hasley."

He raised his brows. "That's high praise indeed."

"Don't take it from me." Lady Stratford's stern look softened. "I'm sure you'll discover it for yourself during your stay here."

At that moment, Jessica and Olivia entered. Jessica was dressed like her personality, in a vibrant red. Olivia wore a more sedate striped ivory walking dress with lace trim. The urge to trace that delicate line at her neck made Max's fingers tingle. What he wouldn't give to touch that pale, perfect skin above her breasts...and lower.

Max took a deep breath. The countess was looking at him. Watching him. He'd have to be careful with that one. Even more, he'd have to be careful with himself.

One day at a time. He'd be here in Sussex for a month, at least. There was no need to turn his interest in Olivia Donovan into more than what it really was. He would enjoy the time he had here and then return to London and get on with his life.

The countess led them outside and down the front drive to the main road. Max kept quiet, listening to the ladies—

mostly Jessica and the countess—talk. Soon enough, they turned off the road and onto a wide rutted path that Lady Stratford said marked the edge of the earl's property. They passed a sheep farm, and the countess stopped to exchange a friendly word with her tenants, leaving them with a package of her cook's famous lemon tarts.

When they returned to the path, Max found himself beside Olivia, following Lady Stratford and Jessica, who were engaged in an animated discussion about the wool business.

He smiled down at Olivia. "Not interested in wool?"

She gazed at him, her blue eyes seeming impossibly clear and bright against the smooth, uniform background of her pale features.

"Oh no, I am," she said quickly, then looked down, hiding her expression behind the brim of her bonnet.

When he remained silent, she looked up again, smiling ruefully. "I just wanted to walk with you for a while. Do you mind terribly?"

Max's chest tightened. Good God. She was...Max couldn't even come up with a word to describe her. "Delightful" seemed an understatement of grand proportions.

Ever since he'd agreed to it, he'd regretted that idiotic bet he'd made with Fenwicke. It didn't matter what happened between him and Olivia Donovan this autumn. He had signed the wager Fenwicke had written in a moment of furious weakness, and he'd strike the moment out of existence if he could.

He wouldn't compromise any woman—especially not Olivia—for the sake of a bet, not even to beat Fenwicke. That was something his father would have done, and damn it, Max had spent his whole life attempting to become the antithesis of his father. Fenwicke always seemed to bring that part of him out, though. Curse the man.

It looked like he was going to owe Fenwicke a thousand guineas on the first of the year. No matter what happened between Max and Olivia in the upcoming days, it had already become something that Fenwicke's involvement would soil. Despite Max's hot-headed actions and words that night in London, now that he was calmer, now that he *knew* the lady, he knew he would do everything in his power to completely dissociate Fenwicke from Olivia Donovan.

It would be one of the few wagers between them that Max had lost. For the first time in his life, Max found that he didn't even care.

He glanced at Olivia to see her looking at him with a furrowed brow.

"I don't mind you joining me at all," he said gravely. "I'm glad you decided to walk with me. I was beginning to feel lonely."

Her face crumpled into an expression of agitation. "I'm so sorry. We didn't mean to make you—"

He raised his hand, cutting off her words. "I was jesting, Miss Donovan."

"Oh . . . oh, dear." Her lips twisted prettily. "Sometimes I can be far too literal."

"I'll remember that," he said. "Next time, I'll be sure to warn you in advance when I'm not being entirely literal."

"Thank you, my lord."

"Please. Call me Max."

She looked up at him again, frowning. "I would like to do that, but wouldn't it be considered quite improper?"

"Not if you reserve it for when we're alone."

Her gaze flicked to her sisters, who'd stretched the distance between them. "Like now?"

"Like now," he agreed softly. He wanted to touch her again. But he didn't want to make her uncomfortable—she was having a difficult enough time using his name, for God's sake. So he kept his hands at his sides, more rigidly than was natural.

She was too lovely. So soft and gentle. She reminded him of a white rose petal. She made him want to gather her up and hold her close to him, not allowing anyone else to touch her, to mar that delicate beauty.

He glanced down at her and saw a smile tipping the edges of her lips. So beautiful, her lips. Such a deep pink. He wanted to run his thumb over the plumpness of her lower lip, feel its suppleness against his skin.

He inhaled through his teeth. Best not to think too much about touching Olivia Donovan. That was likely to get him into an embarrassing state, particularly since the day was warm so he'd slung his coat over his forearm after they'd left the sheep farm, and his waistcoat didn't completely cover the front placket of his breeches.

They rounded a bend and Fenwicke's house came into view. It was smaller than Stratford's, but unlike Stratford's, it was in perfect repair, with freshly painted gables and fronted by a perfectly manicured sweeping lawn.

As they approached, a heavy feeling settled through Max, and he looked at Olivia. She'd gone even paler than usual, and her plump lips had pressed into a thin, straight line. He wanted to reassure her, to tell her that Fenwicke's wife was a very different person from the man himself. That she could befriend her neighbor without worrying about what Fenwicke had tried with her, because

Fenwicke was very rarely in Sussex, and when he was, it was usually for short periods of time—certainly not enough time to mingle with the neighbors.

Watching her from the corner of his eye, Max wondered exactly what had passed between Olivia and Fenwicke. The two were like oil and water. It seemed obvious that Fenwicke's greasy charm wouldn't have worked on her.

Ahead, Jessica and the countess had slowed to allow Olivia and Max to catch up. When they did, Jessica gestured at the house. "Quiet, isn't it?"

"I wonder if she's home," Olivia murmured.

"I'm sure she is," Lady Stratford said. "I've heard she rarely goes out."

They approached Brockton Hall, the sisters clustering closer together and casting wary glances toward the house. They reached the graveled drive and stepped up into the entryway. Lady Stratford lifted the immense bronze door knocker, and the four of them listened as the sound resonated within the house.

For a moment, Max thought that no one would come to the door, but then an aged servant answered it. When Lady Stratford explained to the frowning man who they were and the reason for their visit, all he said was "Just a minute, if you please," before shutting the massive door in their faces.

The sisters looked at one another and then at Max, who shrugged. "Let's wait and see what happens."

They waited several minutes. Max was losing patience, and Jessica was pacing back and forth across the front landing when the door opened again.

The old man didn't meet any of their eyes. "Lady

Fenwicke will see you now." Turning, he made room for them to enter. They walked into a spacious entry hall, and the man closed the door behind them, then shuffled into a dimly lit corridor. "This way, please."

He led them in to an elegantly decorated drawing room with elaborate, expensive Oriental furnishings and heavy, dark-colored velvet draperies. A young woman stood beside the richly carved and spotless white marble fireplace.

If he hadn't known this was Lady Fenwicke, Max wouldn't have recognized her. She'd gained a good two stone, her vivacious dark eyes had gone flat along with her complexion, and even her dark hair seemed to have lost all the richness it had held just two years ago.

She smiled at them, but the smile didn't bring any light to her eyes.

A heaviness settled over Max. He knew that some would say that this was the result of any marriage, but one only had to look at the Countess of Stratford's glow to disprove that. No, this was the result of being married to one Leonard Reece, the Marquis of Fenwicke.

Lady Stratford seemed to have taken on the role of their speaker, but Max didn't mind. He was content to stand behind the ladies and allow them to do the talking.

"Good afternoon, my lady. I'm your neighbor, Lady Stratford. These are my sisters, Miss Olivia Donovan and Miss Jessica Donovan. And this is our guest, Lord Hasley."

She didn't seem to remember him. No recognition flickered in her eyes as her gaze passed over him. He'd only met her a few times before, but people usually did remember him, due to his position in society if nothing else.

"Welcome," she said. "I'm so glad you came. I've been looking forward to meeting you. I am Beatrice Reece."

She invited them to sit and called for tea. Lady Stratford gave her the lemon tarts, which she appropriately gushed over. Everything was all politeness and propriety, but there was something about Lady Fenwicke that just seemed... absent. Max glanced at Olivia. Her gaze was forthright and friendly—not that he'd ever seen it any other way— but there was the slightest crease between her brows.

Tea was served, and Max sat back and enjoyed the scorching, bitter taste of his. The sisters all took generous lumps of sugar for their tea, and Lady Fenwicke took sugar and cream in hers, but Max noticed that after she'd prepared it to her liking, she placed it beside her and didn't touch it.

The ladies discussed their plans for autumn and winter, briefly skimmed the topic of their past in the West Indies, and told Lady Fenwicke about their absent sister, Phoebe, who Max had met last evening. For her part, Lady Fenwicke hardly spoke but asked the sisters questions and offered them more tea and cakes. A proper hostess. Still, something in Max panged for her. She just seemed so damned unhappy.

Jessica dabbed her napkin to her lips. "That almond cake was simply delicious, Lady Fenwicke! I'll have to tell my sister's cook to ask for the recipe from yours."

"Thank you, but I must confess that I made the cakes myself." Sucking in a breath at her blunder—a lady of her status should never admit to doing something as common as cooking!—she looked down at her lap.

There was a short silence, then Lady Stratford said in a kindly voice, "Oh how lovely. You are a talented cook. I do hope you'll give my cook the recipe."

Olivia took her first bite of the cake and added her

appreciation, and Max ate his cake in silence. He liked these three sisters. It was heartwarming how they attempted to make their hostess comfortable.

"Do you like to cook, then, my lady?" Jessica asked. "Is it a hobby of yours?"

He also liked how forthright they were.

"I do," Lady Fenwicke said quietly. "I like it very much. It is . . . it is a great solace to me."

"I understand completely," Olivia said. "Going for long walks is my solace."

"Reading is mine," Lady Stratford added.

"And mine is dancing. Oh, how I love to dance," said Jessica, beaming. "Our sister Phoebe does, too. We used to dance together for hours and hours in our parlor back in Antigua before she came to England last year." She turned to Max. "What's your solace, my lord?"

That took him aback. His solace? Solace hadn't been a concept he'd considered for years. Perhaps ever. "Well. I can't think of anything."

"It must be hunting," Jessica said. "Since you're here to hunt with my brother-in-law and Captain Langley."

"No, that can't be it." A mischievous grin lit Olivia's features. "Lord Hasley has confided to me that he's a poor hunter."

"Perhaps horses, then," the countess said. "Many men take solace from their animals. I know Jonathan does, at times."

"No," Olivia said, sliding a glance at him. "Not horses, either. Don't you remember? Lord Hasley told us this morning that he wasn't the horse connoisseur that Captain Langley and the earl are," Olivia said.

"Ah, that's right." Lady Stratford gave Olivia an

appraising look, then set her teacup down. "Thank you so much for the tea and the lovely cakes, my lady. I didn't mean to march in like this today, but I've very much wanted to meet you."

"Me too," Jessica said, "and I'm so glad we came."

"I'm very glad you came, too," Lady Fenwicke said. "It's so nice to meet new neighbors."

"We must go, though," the countess said. "My husband will be wondering what has happened to us."

"But he won't worry." Jessica shot Max a saucy grin. "He knows Lord Hasley is here to protect us."

Lady Stratford rolled her eyes heavenward. "In the event of a dragon attack as we walk through the fearsome Sussex countryside, I daresay."

Max bowed his head. "At your service, ladies."

They all laughed, even Lady Fenwicke. Her lovely, tinkling laughter seemed to shock everyone else into silence again.

"Really, Sussex is so quiet, I do believe we'd have to conjure a dragon in order to find the need to be protected," Lady Stratford said.

"There are dangers in Sussex," Lady Fenwicke said quietly. "Just not where one might expect."

Everyone stared at Lady Fenwicke until the countess broke the silence. "Oh, I do hope you're wrong. I've found it to be very safe indeed, though I admit to not having lived here for very long."

Max glanced again at Olivia. The line between her brows had deepened, and he suppressed the urge to smooth it out with his fingertip.

Lady Stratford rose. Max stood instantly, and the two other sisters and Lady Fenwicke rose as well. Jessica invited the lady over for tea in a few days' time, and she accepted with a smile.

They left, turning from the gravel drive onto the wagon path. Max had a sinking feeling that the unexpected dangers Lady Fenwicke spoke of had to do with her husband. He hoped to hell he was wrong.

It wasn't until they turned the bend that hid the elegant house from view that any of them spoke. It was Jessica.

"I'm going to be a good friend to her," the youngest sister said solemnly. "I think she needs one."

Max nodded. He couldn't agree more.

Chapter Three

It was an unseasonably warm day, and Olivia had sat through the afternoon on the gallery bench, tucked beneath her parasol to protect her complexion from the sun. She was watching the others play—or attempt to play—tennis on the ancient court that had originally been erected on the grounds almost three hundred years ago in honor of Henry VIII's visit to Stratford House.

The court was long and narrow with high walls but no roof. One wall had partially crumbled and the uneven floor was not conducive to balls bouncing properly, but Jonathan planned to eventually fix both. In the interim he still enjoyed playing, and he had purchased a new net as well as racquets and balls soon after he'd arrived in Sussex this spring.

Phoebe and Jessica were trying their best, but they'd never played tennis—it wasn't a sport they'd ever seen in Antigua, and their lack of skill combined with the cracked floor and the crumbling wall made the game more about laughing, running, and fetching balls than actually hitting them over the net.

Jonathan and Captain Langley were fairly good, their skills obvious compared to the entirely lacking ones in her sisters, especially Captain Langley's. And Max... well, he seemed far too large to make any sense of the court and the ball, though he said he'd played on occasion when he was at Cambridge.

Olivia would have liked to try it, but she knew her sisters and Jonathan would object, and if they did grudgingly allow her to play, they'd be overly solicitous and embarrass her. She didn't want that kind of attention—not in the presence of their guests.

She'd long ago come to terms with the fact that her family would always believe that she would fall ill whenever she exerted herself physically. But that didn't mean she had to agree with them. Once, when she was fourteen and in a particularly rebellious temperament, she had experimented in the middle of the night when everyone else was asleep. She'd gone outside and run and run around the plantation. She must have run for an hour without stopping. It had felt so good. By the time she finished, sweat had caked her chemise to her body. And, not surprisingly—to her, at least—she'd felt wonderful the following day, and she hadn't come down with a fever.

She'd experimented in later years, too, though less overtly. She was fully convinced that exertion wasn't what caused the fevers, yet despite her protestations, her family didn't believe her. They were all convinced that if Olivia exercised, it might kill her.

Jonathan served. The ball hit the service penthouse and dropped into the gallery. Max tried to return the serve, but he hit the ball straight into the net. He dropped the racquet at his side, shaking his head, a hopeless expression on his face.

"Game and set!" Jonathan said in triumph.

"Yes, yes. Thanks ever so much for the reminder," Max said dryly. They ambled to the table the servants had erected beside the gallery bench, and each of them took a glass of cool lemonade.

Olivia smiled up at the two men. "That was a wonderful game."

Max snorted. "Once upon a time, I was semiskilled at this game. Now I look like quite the idiot lumbering around out here."

"On the contrary," Olivia said. *You looked marvelous.* And he had. He was, simply, a pleasure to watch, losing at tennis or at any other time, for that matter. He smiled back at her... and her skin prickled all over.

In the past few days she'd often felt Max's eyes moving over her like a warm caress, and when she looked at him, he'd smile faintly but he wouldn't look away. He'd just keep gazing at her with such heat in his expression she could feel it from across a room.

Jonathan gestured toward the house. "Did everyone else go inside?"

"Yes," Olivia said. "They were bored of watching you pummel Lord Hasley."

Max groaned, and Jonathan laughed. "I'd best join them. How about you two? Shouldn't you get out of the sun, Olivia? Max, want to go in?"

"No thanks," Olivia said. "I'd like to enjoy the sun for a few more minutes, and then perhaps I will take a walk."

"I'll stay outside for a while, too," Max said. "I'll come in after I cool down."

Jonathan said good-bye, gave Max a hard look of warning that Olivia found endearing, and trudged off toward the house.

"You needn't stay out here with me, you know," she said.

He sat on the narrow bench beside her, stretching out his long legs in front of him. After a few seconds gazing at the way the fabric of his trousers clung to his muscled thighs, Olivia averted her eyes from the disturbingly appealing view.

"I want to stay with you," he said simply. "Besides, I thought you might like to have an opponent."

"An…opponent?"

He raised the racquet he still held. "Yes. A tennis opponent."

She felt a slow smile curve her lips.

He went to retrieve the racquet Jonathan had abandoned and then returned to her. "Come. I'll teach you."

She smiled up at him. "How did you know I wanted to play?"

His green eyes twinkled. "I saw the way you watched us—you looked positively envious."

She rose, folded her parasol and left it on the bench, then walked out onto the court.

"Here. Hold it like this." He sidled close to her, demonstrating how to grip the racquet. She tried to concentrate, but the warm masculinity of the entire length of his body against her side made her feel rather…wild. Swallowing hard, she focused on gripping the racquet exactly like he showed her.

He led her to the hazard side of the court. "Now ... all you've got to do is hit the ball after I've sent it to your side. You just return it to me, either by sending it over the net or by hitting it off one of the walls."

"Right."

It had looked simple enough, despite the fact that Jessica and Phoebe had missed nine out of ten balls sent their way. Especially Jessica, who'd been laughing so hard at herself that by the end, tears were rolling down her cheeks and she'd declared she was hopeless and she'd never play any sport in a less friendly crowd.

The only person who hadn't been laughing was Captain Langley, but Olivia hadn't seen him laugh in the four days since the gentlemen had arrived. That wasn't to say he wasn't kind—he was a lovely man. He just wasn't the sort of man disposed to laughter, she supposed.

Max took the entire bucket full of balls and moved to the service end of the court.

Olivia smirked. "I see you don't have much confidence that I'll be hitting any of the balls you send my way."

"None at all," he said genially. When she laughed, he gently hit the first ball.

Anticipating where the ball would bounce, Olivia positioned herself quickly and pulled her arm back as she'd seen Captain Langley and Jonathan do, and she whacked the racquet through the air.

And missed. She spun around and watched the ball bounce wildly off the wall behind her.

She turned back to Max. "Again, please."

He repeated his motion, and she missed again. "Swing earlier," he advised.

She nodded, pursing her lips together in concentration.

He hit the ball to her, she swung, and pop! The ball went sailing over the net. And over Max's head, over the crumbling wall, and somewhere into the bushes beyond the court.

"Excellent!" he cried. She returned his statement with a pained look.

They went through the remaining balls in similar fashion. She managed to return a few of them directly to him so that he was able to hit them back. By the end, they'd actually engaged in at least one short rally of five hits, and she felt flushed and happy.

He gave her an enthusiastic grin as she knelt down to retrieve the ball that had landed closest to her. "You're very good."

"You're too kind." She laughed. "I'm quite awful."

He walked around to her side of the court, retrieving balls along the way. "No, really. Considering the fact that you've never played, I think you're quite good. Some practice, and you'll be a worthy opponent for someone like Langley."

"Not you?" she asked.

"No, you'll be far better than me."

"Perhaps we should practice together then," she said. "Because heaven knows, my sisters will have a fit if they knew I was running about out here." She glanced in the direction of the house, glad that Jessica, Serena, or Phoebe hadn't come to fetch her. Jonathan must have told them she'd gone for a walk.

"Why wouldn't they approve of you running about?" Max asked.

For a brief moment she went still, considering telling him about her malaria. She knew from vast experience, however, how people tended to react to that information.

Most drew away from her, as if they feared she'd pass the disease to them. Or as if they feared she'd drop dead at their feet at any moment.

The truth was, while she'd never be cured, she had the disease under control. Quinine, though it was expensive and had sometimes been difficult for them to obtain, cured her whenever the fevers came. Even though Mother had often hardly been able to afford their next meal, she had always made certain quinine was available to Olivia. And despite all her difficulties with her mother, that had been enough to prove to Olivia that she did love her deeply.

Olivia wanted to enjoy this autumn, and she wanted to have this time to pretend that she was a normal woman, just for a little while. Most of all, she didn't want Max fearful that she'd collapse when they played tennis together—and she wanted very badly to play with him again. So she simply shrugged. "My sisters are protective of me."

Max followed her gaze toward the house, and his hand closed around hers. She glanced down in surprise at their enjoined hands. His fingers were so big that they encompassed hers entirely. The heat of his touch permeated through the material of their gloves. Soft and gentle, yet firm. Hard and masculine. Her breaths came quicker, but she didn't move. She kept her gaze on the house, though she no longer really saw it.

She didn't pull away from him, although a small voice somewhere inside her said she should—she *must*. She simply didn't want to. She wanted to stay here, just like this. Touching him innocently, even though something about it felt intimate. Even carnal.

She curled her fingers tighter about his and dragged

her gaze to his. He was looking at her. No, not just looking at her. That implied he was doing something ordinary. But there was nothing ordinary about the way he gazed at her. His green eyes seemed to stroke over her, caress her. She didn't know how it was possible, but she could feel his touch in faraway places she'd never felt before.

"Max," she whispered. It came out as a question, though she hadn't meant for it to.

He bent his head toward her, so close she felt the warm whisper of his breath over her lips...Oh, Lord, was he going to kiss her? She'd never been kissed before. She'd never expected to be kissed. It simply wasn't in her realm of experience or expectation.

Suddenly, more than anything, she wanted him to kiss her. Every inch of her body cried out for it, rattling her, surprising her so much that she gave a violent shudder, and he jerked back, blinking.

"God." He raked his free hand through his dark hair. "God, Olivia. I'm sorry."

He'd called her by her given name. Her name sounded positively sinful in that low baritone of his.

She blinked at him. "You're...sorry?"

His fingers slipped away from hers, and it took almost all her willpower not to reach for the comfort of his hand again.

"Yes. I—" He shook his head, and his expression turned rueful. "I shouldn't have done that. Will you forgive me?"

Staring at him, Olivia caught her breath and slowly drifted back to earth, and with her returning senses came the truth of what she'd nearly just done. What she'd wanted more than her next breath.

She'd nearly kissed a man. Not only a man. Lord Hasley, probably the most virile, handsomest man she'd seen in her life. Not to mention the most eligible bachelor in England.

This wasn't her. She wasn't a wanton. She didn't crave touches or kisses.

If she didn't implicitly trust the people surrounding her, she might think she'd been drugged.

"I forgive you, Lord Hasley."

"Max."

She closed her teeth down over her lower lip. "Max," she whispered. The way it came out reminded her of how she'd said it before. A needy, desperate question. She swallowed dryly, then jerked her gaze away from him. "Really, I am the one who's sorry. I don't know what came over me. This...well..." She hesitated, then looked imploringly up at him.

"This what?" he asked.

Blowing out a breath, she shook her head. "It isn't me. I don't do"—she waved her hand back and forth between the two of them—"this."

He nodded, then gave her a pained smile. "I know, Olivia." He hesitated. "Neither do I. Not...like this."

She tilted her head at him, not understanding exactly what he meant but not daring to ask. What he did—what he'd done with other women before coming to Stratford House—was none of her business. None whatsoever. He was a bachelor, nine years older than she, and she had no doubt that he was far, *far* more experienced at encounters like this than she was.

Still, he'd said he understood that she didn't do "this." And he said he didn't do "this" either, so...

Oh, Lord. Was he intending to court her? To make whatever it was between them permanent? Was he thinking of her as a possible *wife*?

A thrill rushed through her, leaving her senses tingling and her heart pounding hard. She dropped her gaze to her feet, feeling hot and awkward, and at a complete loss for words. In her periphery, she saw the gray flash of a tennis ball, and she forced her body to turn and head toward the wall to collect it. She heard the sound of him taking the bucket handle and his soft footsteps over the pavement as he followed her.

Silently, they searched for the rest of the balls and deposited them into the bucket one by one. When they'd finished, she glanced at the far wall. "I suppose I should look for the ball that went over."

"I'll help you. The brush is thick, though—I doubt we'll find it."

"Well, it's worth a try."

They went behind the tennis court and picked their way through the deepening weeds and bushes, keeping an eye out for the ball.

"Your sisters obviously adore you," he said quietly. "But I can't understand why they shelter you so thoroughly."

She'd been kneeling down to search under a bush, and she smiled up at him. "I adore them, too. The three of them are so different, and yet I love them all. We lost a sister a few years ago, too. She was Seren—I mean, Meg's twin. It was the most horrible thing that ever happened to us—especially Meg—but in a way, I think it brought us closer together."

And further away from their mother, but that wasn't

a story she was ready to tell Max, even if they were addressing each other by their Christian names now. Even if they'd almost kissed.

Deep in the bushes, she saw a flash of gray. "Oh, there it is," she exclaimed. But then she frowned. The ball had been caught in the brambles of a rosebush, and there was no way she could retrieve it without ruining her dress.

Before she had the chance to say so, Max dove under the bush. Seconds later, he emerged, smiling, holding the tennis ball up in victory. "Got it!"

"Oh, dear. Your coat is torn!"

He looked down at the small tear in his sleeve, then back up at her. He gave her a wry shrug. "Ah well. My valet will have my hide. Then, he'll likely burn it, along with the coat."

"What a waste of a perfectly good coat." At his raised eyebrow, she added with a laugh, "And hide."

Max shrugged. "Gardner is far too fastidious to allow me to keep either now that I have damaged one of his fine works of art."

"For goodness' sakes!" Olivia patted his arm over the tear. "I'll mend it for you. He'll never need to know."

He looked honestly shocked, which made her laugh.

"You'd do that for me?"

"To rescue such a fine coat? And"—*such a fine hide, but, oh, she couldn't say that!*—"your hide? I certainly would."

"That is very kind of you." He grinned. "I *am* rather fond of this coat..."

This time the words tumbled out before she could stop them. "And I'm rather fond of your hide."

She felt her eyes widen in surprise at her own words

as the heat of a flush washed over her cheeks. A part of her, a deep, wanton part that she'd never known existed before, prayed that he'd try to kiss her again. It longed for the touch of those soft-looking lips against hers.

Instead, his lips curled into a smile, and he took her hand and led her back to the house. She didn't speak; she was too overcome by all the new sensations—the new desires—coursing through her.

The next few days went by in a flurry of activity. The gentlemen went hunting. The ladies visited with one another and with Lady Fenwicke, and Jessica was making good on her promise to truly befriend the lady, even to the extent that she visited Stratford House's kitchen with her and managed not to shudder as Lady Fenwicke and the cook discussed the many uses of pig stomachs.

Max and Olivia had met to play tennis on four separate occasions when everyone else was otherwise occupied. Even after such a short time, Olivia had seen a marked improvement in her own skills and a more subtle improvement in Max's. He was simply too large—too wide—to be able to scramble to a ball and flick it across the court. Olivia, although she was slight and not tall at all, was fast and nimble, and she prided herself on how quickly she'd learned.

They weren't playing true sets; instead, they enjoyed their short tennis games and approached them as lessons, as Olivia was still learning the rules. Today, they'd been playing for almost an hour, and the score was forty-love with Olivia serving. Excitement fluttered through her— this was the closest she'd ever come to beating Max in a game—and if she won this point, it would be a sound defeat.

She tossed the ball into the air and served. The ball bounced on the penthouse and down into the corner of the court. Max lunged, but Olivia's serve had been perfectly placed, making it awkward to hit, and the tip of his racquet only grazed the edge of the ball and sent it flying over the wall.

Olivia threw her racquet up into the air in a burst of joy. "I won!" she squealed, catching her racquet neatly. She couldn't help herself—she beamed at him proudly.

Shaking his head but with his lips tilted in a smile, Max went to the table for a glass of lemonade, and drank heartily. She danced over to him. "Did you see that? I beat you for the first time ever!"

"You did indeed. One game out of sixteen today." He handed her a glass of lemonade. "And here's your reward."

"Oh, you think you can remind me of my losses, do you?" She narrowed her eyes at him playfully.

He merely cocked a brow at her.

"Well, I won't let you spoil this victory for me."

"Won't you? How many times did I win a game at love, might I ask?" he said, all smugness.

"Why, Lord Hasley, I do think you're embarrassed. You're upset that you were beaten by a woman half your size."

He looked at her for a long moment, his dark eyebrows lowering, the humor fading from his expression.

"No. That's not it."

She felt her own humor draining away. "What, then?" she asked, almost breathless.

"I'm surprisingly...delighted that you beat me." The low serious tone of his voice sent skitters of pleasure down her spine.

"Did you allow me to win?" she asked, suddenly suspicious.

He chuckled and shook his head. "No. You won that game entirely fairly."

"Good," she murmured, accepting the return of that sweet sense of satisfaction.

"You're a very quick learner," he said sincerely. "I believe you possess more physical coordination than most women."

"Do you think so?"

"I do. It's too bad..." His voice dwindled, and he looked away.

"It's too bad, what?" she asked, setting down her glass of lemonade.

"Never mind. I don't wish to offend you."

She stared at him, one eyebrow raised.

He sighed. "Very well. I was going to say, it's too bad your family limits you so much. I've been watching since we last spoke, and you're right—your sisters and Stratford are extremely protective when it comes to you. *Over*protective. I think they're attempting to squelch your innate sense of adventure." He frowned. "They handle you like a porcelain doll. And while it's true that you're slighter and more slender than your sisters, I don't see that you are any weaker than them, yet they treat you as if you are."

She blinked at him. She didn't know what to say. Her family was the most important thing in her life, and she wanted to defend them, but there was no denying their tendency to stifle her at times. Hence, her walks. Her desire to run at night. Her need to be alone at times.

"Am I right?" he asked quietly.

She nodded. Another woman—a wiser woman—

would be more offended. She might lie to him and say he was a virtual stranger, he couldn't know the first thing about how her family—herself, in particular—operated. But Olivia had always been a forthright kind of person. She never thought of dissembling... until it was too late, of course.

Yet, allowing this man to get too close to her—that would be unwise. Surely he must know that. Even without taking the malaria into account, she was the daughter of an obscure, impoverished Irishman, hardly fit to be paired with the heir to a powerful dukedom.

And yet... and yet here he was, behaving like a suitor might behave. Like a potential spouse might behave.

"Oh, Max," she murmured, swallowing hard.

He tilted his head, questioning her with those startling eyes of his.

"We have become friends, haven't we?" The word "friends" sounded silly on her lips. She'd never really had friends apart from her sisters, but she was fairly certain that a friend couldn't make her feel the way Max made her feel.

"I hope so," he said in a low voice.

"Can I tell you something, then? Something that will be very embarrassing for me to speak with you about, yet I feel we must speak of it."

Max hesitated. She watched his chest rise and fall as he took a breath and set down his empty glass. "Come. Let's walk." He held out his hand, and she took it, nearly sighing aloud at the firm press of his fingers as they closed around hers.

They strolled into the woods, taking the path that led to the spring where they'd met. They walked slowly and without speaking. Beside Max, with his hand enclosing hers, Olivia felt even more vibrant and alive than she did on her solitary walks. Her senses were alert, every one of them abuzz. The sun shone brightly, causing the autumn forest to glow in deep and varying shades of gold and bronze. There were few sounds, but Olivia could discern between each one: a call of a jay, the stirring of the branches in the breeze, the crunch of dried leaves beneath their feet.

When they reached the spring, Max shrugged out of his coat and spread it across the large flat rock. They sat side by side, removed their gloves, and tossed pebbles into the water until he asked, "What is it you wanted to talk about?"

She swallowed hard. There was nothing to do but to get straight to the point. She lowered her hands, still clutching a pebble she hadn't thrown yet, and looked straight into his eyes. "I am concerned...I fear...you might misunderstand our...association."

He just gazed at her, a deepening frown creasing his brows.

"Please understand, I have no intention of..." She took a breath and tried again. "My future has been laid out for me, you see. I intend to live out my life here, at Stratford House, close to Meg and Phoebe and their children. I will not marry."

Still, he didn't say anything.

"I... You see, I *want* to be the spinster aunt."

When he didn't immediately answer, she jerked her face away from him and looked down at her fist wrapped around the little pebble. She uncurled her fingers and let it drop to the ground.

Finally, he spoke. "Do you think I was considering marriage?"

She went instantly hot all over. "No, of course not." Biting her lip, she looked up and confessed, "Well, not *today*...but the way you've been...I...don't know. If that was the direction of your thoughts, though...I just wanted you to know that I don't foresee marriage—to anyone—in my future. So there is no point in courting me, or in me accepting the...er...*advances*...of any suitor." She hesitated and then added a belated and breathy, "I'm sorry."

His hand covered hers, his palm heavy and all-encompassing. It was the first time he'd touched her skin directly with his own, and the effect sucked the remaining air from her lungs.

"I had no intention of asking for your hand in marriage."

Olivia went instantly stiff, humiliation threatening to choke her.

Glancing at her, he raked his free hand through his hair. "God, I'm sorry if that's what I..." He hesitated, and his expression gentled as he leaned in closer to her. "Listen to me, Olivia. Thank you for being honest with me. You're so special, so unlike any woman I've ever known, and you deserve my honesty in return. The truth is, I don't intend to marry, either."

"You don't?" she murmured. Didn't all dukes require wives and heirs?

"No."

"Why?"

He flinched, a subtle withdrawal. "It's very complicated." His lips twisted. "I suppose it comes down to the fact that I've always known I'd make a very poor husband. I wouldn't want to cause any woman unhappiness, so I've known for a long time that marriage wasn't for me."

"Oh." She looked up at him, confused on many levels. "Then what—why are you—Why did it seem like you wanted to—?"

She stopped speaking abruptly as the truth slammed into her. She didn't think she could get any hotter from embarrassment, but now she was certain she must be scarlet. She tore her gaze away from him again.

Suddenly, the pressure of his palm on hers took on a completely different meaning, and she yanked her hand out from under his like it had scorched her. She turned wide eyes on him. "Oh. Oh, dear."

His brow furrowed, and he leaned closer to her, the concern deepening on his face. "What's wrong—?"

She raised her hand to stop his words, then closed her eyes and bent her head forward with a groan, slapping her palm over her forehead. "I am so stupid."

"Olivia—"

"I should have known *that's* what you wanted from me." She braced herself, removed her palm from her forehead, and looked up at him. "I'm sorry, Max. I won't... I thought you understood—I'm simply not the kind of woman who's free with her...favors."

The last word almost caught in her throat, and she coughed, even as her traitorous body rebelled against her words. She was flushed and needy. Whenever his skin touched hers, it relieved some of the ache while at the same time spreading the desire for *more*.

Max spoke softly. "I know that."

"Do you? Are you certain? Because—" She hesitated,

then gazed at him. "I'm so confused. I don't know what this is..." She waved her hand between the two of them. "But...I can say with almost complete certainty that it is becoming a rather unusual friendship."

"I'm very attracted to you, Olivia."

His words made her body jolt backward. "What?"

Her voice came out in a squeak. There it was again— she sounded, and certainly looked, like a complete ninny.

"I'm attracted to you," he repeated. "And I believe you're attracted to me, too."

Her mouth went dry. She couldn't say she wasn't attracted to him—that would be a lie. "Be that as it may," she managed, "it doesn't...I can't..." She sucked in a breath. "I told you—I want to be the spinster aunt. By that, I don't mean the *disgraced* spinster aunt."

His green gaze narrowed. "Do you think that's what I'd do? Disgrace you?"

No, he'd touch her all over with those big hands of his. He'd relieve her need, bring her pleasure...

Oh, Lord. The way she was beginning to think about Max was utterly scandalous and improper. She must *not* think of what he'd do to her. Goodness, her body was running hot one second then cold the next. She was completely out of her depth.

"I don't know," she said breathlessly. She shook her head. "This discussion is highly..." *embarrassing, awkward, distressing,* "...improper."

He lifted one shoulder in a shrug, but a smile teased at the corners of his lips. "You brought the subject up."

"Because I felt it must be brought up before things went too far. I was feeling..." She searched desperately for the right word.

"...an attraction," he finished for her.

She screwed her eyes shut. "Yes. An attraction."

After a long silence, he murmured, "It doesn't need to be like this."

"Like what?" Her voice was a wisp of sound on the air.

"Upsetting."

"What should it be like?"

Her hand was resting flat on the rock, and he lifted it in his own. When she didn't move away, he turned it over and placed a soft kiss in her palm, his lips and fingers warm against her skin.

Olivia found the gentle touch so wildly erotic that she had to focus on her breathing—it was speeding up so quickly, the world was blurring.

"It should feel good," he murmured against her palm. "Exciting."

"It does," she said on a near groan.

He lowered her hand and squeezed it between both of his own. "Don't be afraid of me, Olivia. I will do nothing to you that you don't want. And I would never, ever see you disgraced."

God help her, she was tempted. So tempted. Every cell in her body demanded that she submit, that she say, *Yes, Max. Take me. Do whatever it is with me that you please.*

But she couldn't. She had to protect herself, her family, her *future*.

"This can't...we can't. I want to be your friend, but I think we should try to stay apart for a while, until..." She stumbled over the words as her body screamed for one thing and her mind—a mind that had been trained for many years to believe it held a specific place in the world,

and that place would never involve a man's touch—
screamed that this wasn't right.

His fingers slipped away from hers, and his expression
grew somber. "I'm a patient man, Olivia. I'll give you the
time you need. But understand that I'm not going anywhere. When you're ready, I'll be right here. Waiting."

She couldn't breathe, couldn't speak. So she nodded,
then rose to her feet.

He retrieved his coat, and quietly, they walked back to
the house.

Chapter Four

Olivia gazed out the drawing room window as Jessica sat at the desk agonizing over the dinner plans she and Lady Fenwicke had made for them all this evening. Olivia had been working on her embroidery, keeping her sister company.

But she couldn't focus on sewing. She couldn't focus at all.

She didn't know what was wrong with her. For the past week, Max had left her alone, for the most part. They still played tennis. They still laughed together. They were friends.

It felt different, though. And if she were honest with herself, she missed his charged touches, those looks he'd given her that were infused with such meaning...such *heat*.

She missed *him*.

Her gaze wandered toward the window. Outside, the sun had descended over the treetops of the forest. The men had gone off to hunt late this morning, but they'd stayed out longer than usual.

She turned to Jessica. "I'm going for a walk."

Jessica looked up from the scattered papers. "Oh, all right." She scowled at the clock above the mantel. "Beatrice is already ten minutes late."

"She'll be here soon," Olivia soothed.

"I know...I just..." Jessica shook her head. "I should have asked her to come earlier. That way we wouldn't have had to rush to prepare for this evening."

"You'll do wonderfully, Jess. I'm sure of it."

Olivia finished tucking her embroidery into her basket. When she rose to leave and was brushing smooth the dark patterned length of her skirts, Jessica asked, "Will you join Phoebe and Meg, do you think?"

Their sisters had gone visiting tenants after luncheon. "Perhaps," Olivia said noncommittally as she turned to leave. "I'll see you at dinner. It'll be spectacular! Don't worry so much." With those words of encouragement, Olivia went to her bedchamber to collect her bonnet, pelisse, and gloves, and then she slipped out the front door and into the crisp autumn air.

She walked for a long while, realizing that it had been days since she'd just come out to the forest and walked by herself. She'd been too caught up in all the activities of Jonathan's house party.

It was pleasant to be alone again. To be far from society, from people. She took a deep breath and looked up at the sky. Clouds had gathered, darkening the sky more than usual for this time of day.

She was just about to turn around to head back to the house when she heard the whicker of a horse, followed by the sound of plodding hoof beats, and her heart sped. She'd only half paid attention to following the trail, but she looked down now, and, yes, she could see clear imprints of horses' hooves in the mud. The gentlemen had ridden in this direction earlier today, and now they were returning home.

She saw Jonathan's horse first—a fine black gelding he adored. When he saw her, he reined in.

"Olivia!"

"Good afternoon, Jonathan. How was your hunting?" She smiled up at them, then greeted Captain Langley and Max, who were riding behind him.

"Excellent," Jonathan said. "We were able to shoot a few grouse today. Even Max got one."

She turned her smile on Max, who'd drawn up behind Captain Langley. "Well done!"

"What are you doing out here?" Jonathan asked. "Looks like it might rain."

"Just walking. Don't worry—a little damp won't kill me."

Jonathan gave her a dour look. Behind him, Captain Langley frowned up at the sky.

"You will ride home with us." Jonathan began to dismount so that he could lift her into his saddle.

Olivia held her ground. "Oh, no, please, Jonathan. Do go on ahead. I've no wish to ride home with you—I've been enjoying my walk."

Jonathan's look darkened even more. Behind him, Max was dismounting. "You two go on ahead. I'll see Miss Donovan home."

Blowing out a frustrated breath through his lips, Jonathan nodded at Max, then turned a scowl back down on her. "Are you certain you will be all right?"

"I'm perfectly fine." She addressed all three men. "I

don't need to be coddled, gentlemen. Rest assured, I am perfectly able to walk home."

Jonathan and Captain Langley exchanged a knowing look and Olivia pursed her lips—so Captain Langley knew about her ailment. It shouldn't surprise her, she supposed—the captain knew most of their family's deepest secrets.

"I think I'd prefer to walk as well." Max gave her a friendly smile as he handed Captain Langley his reins. "Stretch my legs a bit."

Captain Langley took the reins, and then he and Jonathan continued on, both tipping their hats to her as they rode by.

When they were out of earshot, Max said, "I really would prefer to walk with you."

She glanced back over her shoulder at him. "You do know I am quite capable of walking myself."

"I know," he said.

They walked in silence for a while, then she asked, "Did you enjoy shooting the grouse?"

"Not really," he said, and chuckled.

She laughed, too. "I suppose hunting isn't for you."

"I suppose not."

"And tennis isn't either."

"Unfortunately not, though I do enjoy it." He paused, seeming to hesitate, then added, "When I'm playing with you."

"Thank you. But I'm sorry you haven't found the diversion you've been searching for."

"But I have found a diversion."

From the low timbre of his voice, from the way he said the words, she didn't need to ask him what he meant. *She* was his diversion.

She wasn't offended. It was fair for him to say it. After all, he'd been her diversion, too.

"So have I," she admitted quietly.

Side by side, they walked along in comfortable silence. The terrain was jagged here, with mossy rock outcroppings on both sides of the horse trail.

The warmth of Max's body beside her did strange things to Olivia's insides. Max's sleeve brushed against hers, and she shuddered. Instantly, he began to fumble with his buttons. "You're cold. Here, wear my coat."

She slid her gaze toward his coat. It was the one she'd mended after he'd rescued her tennis ball from beneath the rose bush. She'd done the best job she could, and apparently it had been enough. Max's valet hadn't discovered the tiny flaw in the stitches and sacrificed the poor garment, along with his master, to the fire.

"No, it's quite all right. I'm not cold at all."

"Then why—" He sidestepped a rock and brushed against her again . . . and she shuddered again.

He said nothing. At that moment, she could have kissed him for his silence. And for so many other reasons.

"Thank you," she said quietly.

He raised his dark brows. "For what?"

"For the respect you have shown me in the past week."

He frowned, a muscle working in his jaw. "I like you, Olivia. And I admire you. I am not going to push you toward anything that makes you uncomfortable."

"I know. And I feel so grateful for that. Many men wouldn't care about such a thing." She thought about Lord Fenwicke and how he'd pawed her, and a cold sweat broke out along her spine.

His frown deepened. "They should."

"I know. But they don't." She didn't meet his eyes.

"Damned Fenwicke," he muttered under his breath.

She jerked to a stop, looking up at him in utter despair. "What?"

"What did Fenwicke do to you?" There was an edge of violence in his voice that she'd never heard before.

She took a step backward. "How do you know...?"

"From Lord Hertford's ball. He told me he'd propositioned you, and that you rejected him soundly. He didn't tell me exactly what happened, though."

She jerked her gaze away from Max and crossed her arms over her chest. "He is a terrible man. And I dislike him. Strongly."

"I dislike him, too. But tell me, Olivia. Did he hurt you?"

She squeezed her arms tightly. "No, he didn't hurt me. But... he would have, I think."

The muscles in his jaw moved, and he shook his head. "Stay away from that man, Olivia. I don't trust him. If he hurt you, I'd—"

"I'll stay away," Olivia said quickly. "Trust me, I have no desire to see him ever again."

"Good." Max blew out a breath. "It's unfortunate he's your neighbor."

"Well, it's fortunate that he's rarely in Sussex, I suppose. And when I hear he's in the area, I'll simply stay at home until he's gone." Her voice sounded far stronger and more confident than she felt about the matter. Truthfully, the mere thought of Lord Fenwicke turned her insides into burning acid.

They walked in silence for a time. Then Max murmured, "I've never met anyone like you before, Olivia Donovan."

She gave him a faltering smile. "All of us Donovans are rather odd. We attribute it to our pasts. Our lives have been…" Her voice dwindled and she shook her head. "You see, it has been…challenging for us. My father died of malaria soon after we arrived in Antigua." She swallowed hard. She'd survived the disease, but Papa had succumbed to the very first fever.

"I'm sorry," Max murmured.

"He left us stranded on an island far away from home and quite poor: five sisters and a mother determined to fashion us into proper ladies so we could one day marry proper English gentlemen."

"But you have rebelled."

Olivia shook her head. "Not overtly. My mother has no knowledge of my decision not to marry. It would infuriate her."

Mother had insisted she lie about her health when she came to London, but it was unconscionable for Olivia to do that. Her sisters knew her well enough to understand. So did Mother, really, but Mother was Machiavellian. She would command Olivia, or her sisters, to change her very nature in order to acquire a suitable husband. That was one of the many reasons Serena had made certain Mother stayed in Antigua, at least for now.

"What prompted this decision to never marry?"

"London, among other things," she answered, not exactly lying but evading the real truth. "Experiencing the Season."

"Why? Most young ladies are all a-flutter about marriage during and after the Season."

She shrugged. "It just made me feel…Oh, I don't know. Like an item of finery for sale at an auction, I suppose. I felt as though I should be flaunting my wares to be snatched up by the highest bidder. The whole business made me terribly uncomfortable."

"I understand."

"It was just me, though. Jessica enjoyed every minute of it. I drew great satisfaction from watching how she glowed at the parties and balls." She laughed softly. "And she had so many suitors."

"Not everyone is satisfied by the same things."

"Even sisters," she agreed.

"Yes, even sisters."

"But I do think I am odd. Most ladies enjoy the Season, and they should—it's exciting and so romantic. I suppose I'm just made differently from most ladies, though, because it didn't appeal to me at all. And the gentlemen... Well, the thought of marriage..." She hesitated, struggling to explain her feelings adequately. "In the midst of it all, I spent some time thinking about what makes me happiest in life—what I find most fulfilling, and what my future should entail. And I came to the conclusion that marriage to an upstanding London gentleman won't suit me nearly as much as remaining with my family. I never have such a feeling of satisfaction as when I'm surrounded by my sisters, and they're all happy."

"But what about *your* happiness, Olivia?"

She smiled at him. "Their happiness makes me content."

"Is that enough, though?"

"Well...yes."

But the answer hadn't emerged as strongly as she would have liked. In truth, his question rocked her. *Is it enough?*

Surely it was. Of course it was.

So absorbed was she in her thoughts that she didn't notice the raindrops until one struck her on the cheek and jolted her out of her reverie.

She blinked. Fat, heavy drops were falling all around them, plunking down on the branches and crisp leaves. She looked at Max in rising alarm.

"It's going to rain cats and dogs," he said grimly. "I can hear it coming."

Glancing up at the sky, she agreed. In a matter of moments, both of them were going to be soaked to the bone. "I'm sure Captain Langley and Jonathan are home by now. I suppose you're regretting your decision to walk with me."

It was raining harder every second.

"Not at all," he said smoothly. Then he gripped her wrist. "Look." He gestured at a tall outcropping of rock just off the trail. "Let's wait underneath those rocks until it passes."

She looked up doubtfully, only to have her face instantly drenched by a shock of cold raindrops.

"Yes...all right. *If* it passes."

"I think it will. There's a break in the clouds." He hurried her underneath the outcropping. He didn't seem to be upset by the rain—he was smiling as he shrugged off his coat and laid it on the ground for her to sit upon. His dimples were deep in his cheeks and his green eyes twinkled as he collapsed beside her, removing his hat.

His shirt was open at the top, and he wore no cravat, so she could see a bit of his chest at the vee of his shirt. His black hair was wavy from the moisture in the air, sparkling water droplets dripping from the sleek curls.

She stared at him, acutely aware of the heat of her blood pumping through her veins. He was...riveting. And she wanted to touch him. She'd wanted so badly the kiss that had almost happened after she'd won that first game of tennis. She'd thought about it, she'd dreamed about it, she'd secretly craved it for days.

Slowly, hardly aware of what she was doing, she raised her hands and slid them around his neck, filtering the bottoms of his curls through her fingers. His hair was cool and silky smooth.

"Mm," she murmured. The feel of him, damp yet so vibrant against her fingers, warmed her, made her feel utterly alive. The expression on his face, his wide green eyes, those dimples frozen into his cheeks with his surprise, made her want to draw him closer to her.

And that was exactly what she did. She tugged him closer, and closer yet until she felt his soft breath against her skin. She touched her lips to his dimple and pressed a kiss to the indent.

She pulled back, intending to move to the other side, but as she passed his lips, they caught hers in a tender kiss.

"Oh," she murmured again. The feel of his lips against her mouth was like nothing she could have imagined. He tasted wild, like the forest. He tasted like freedom.

He kissed gently but insistently, his lips moving with a rhythm that had her heart thumping and her nerves buzzing. He kissed her with a kind of raw power that made her feel utterly safe. And...*desired*.

The rustle of the rain pummeling the leaves seemed far away. It seemed as though she and Max were the only two people in the world, the only connection that mattered.

Ever so gently, his lips coaxed her mouth open, and his tongue touched her lip, making her gasp. His arm pressed around her waist, holding her firmly against him. His other hand cupped the back of her head, preventing her from pulling away.   .

Heat. And sweetness. Wildness, and such exquisite pleasure. She felt like a flower bursting out of its pod, unfurling its petals, opening to the beauty and warmth of the sun.

Crack!

Olivia jumped back, gasping. Max leaped to his feet.

Was it a gunshot? Olivia pressed her hand to her chest, trying to catch her breath, when lightning flashed, brightening Max's features for a split second.

He sank beside her, releasing a breath. "Just thunder."

She nodded, but she was shaking. Not from fear. Not even from cold.

He saw, and in an instant his arms were around her, drawing her close against him. He leaned his back against the surface of the stone, drawing her with him so that she lay pressed to his shoulder.

Holding each other close, they relaxed in relative dryness as the storm raged around them.

It was nearly dark by the time Max and Olivia returned to Stratford House. The rain had softened into a not unpleasant mist, but Max could tell Olivia was chilled to the bone. He herded her inside, sat her on one of the chairs in the entry hall, and called for her maid. When they were left alone, he studied her carefully. She was pale and shaking, even wearing his coat.

"Are you all right?" he asked.

"Perfectly fine." She smiled up at him, and the smile

reached her eyes, making them sparkle like sapphire jewels. "Just a little chilled."

Burdened with an armful of towels, Olivia's maid entered and proceeded to usher her out of the entry hall. Max started to follow them upstairs but stopped when he heard the sound of a door opening behind him. It was Jessica, coming from the direction of the kitchen.

"Oh, I'm so glad you're back, Lord Hasley. We've all been worried about you and Olivia caught out in the rain, though we knew you'd take care of Olivia. But Beatrice..." She sighed.

He remembered that tonight was supposed to be the night of the dinner Lady Fenwicke had planned with Jessica. "Hasn't Lady Fenwicke arrived?"

Jessica sighed. "No. And she was due hours ago. I'm afraid the dinner is a disaster—only half prepared. I haven't the talent she does for these things, alas."

"Ah. I'm very sorry, Miss Jessica."

"It's not that." Jessica waved her hand dismissively. "I don't really care about dinner—I'm just so worried about Beatrice. It's so unlike her not to come."

"Didn't she send a note?"

Jessica shook her head.

"Perhaps she forgot the date."

"Oh, no, that's impossible. She was just here yesterday, remember? We were working out the finishing touches to the dessert."

"Perhaps she didn't want to come out in the storm."

"Perhaps." But Jessica wasn't convinced. She shrugged. "I rushed in here because I thought you might be Jonathan. I was going to beg him to walk with me to Brockton Hall."

Max raised a brow. "At this hour?"

Jessica sighed. "I know." She gave him a hopeful look. "Do you think he'd let me borrow one of the carriages?"

"To ensure your friend is all right? I don't see why not. Why don't you ask him?"

She clasped her hands together at her chest. "Will you come with me? Since he's not here, he must be in the library."

"Of course." He gestured toward the corridor that led to the library. "After you."

Stratford wasn't in the library, but they encountered him, as well as the countess, as they retraced their steps back to the entry hall. Stratford was already dressed to go out, and his wife was beside him, wringing her hands.

"Oh, there you are, Hasley. I was just about to head out into the rain to find you and Olivia."

"We're fine, if a little damp."

"Is Olivia well?" Lady Stratford asked, her forehead scrunched with worry.

"She's damp and chilled, but well. We found shelter under a rock outcropping for the worst of the rain."

The lady released a relieved breath and then excused herself to go upstairs to help her sister.

"Beatrice never showed tonight, and I'm so worried about her!" Jessica exclaimed as Lady Stratford walked away.

After questioning Jessica on Beatrice's absence like Max had done, Stratford suggested the three of them ride together to Brockton Hall to make sure all was well with the lady. It was then that he noticed Max's state.

"You're soaking wet, man."

"I am," Max agreed.

Stratford eyed him. "I cannot fathom why you haven't gone upstairs and dried off. You're dripping all over my new parquet."

"Oh, it's my fault!" Jessica exclaimed. "I'm so sorry, Lord Hasley. I was so caught up in my worry over Beatrice that I failed to see how very drenched you are. Please forgive me!"

He assured her it was nothing.

"Go up and change, Hasley," Stratford said. "By the time you return downstairs, the carriage will be waiting."

Max nodded and took his leave. He hurried upstairs to the bedchamber that had been assigned to him, a long-unused room in the wing of the house that was mostly closed for refurbishment, and quickly took off his clinging, wet clothes and replaced them with dry ones. As he was pulling on his coat, his valet, Gardner, entered and eyed the puddle of sodden clothing on the floor with disdain.

"Really, sir."

Max shrugged. "Couldn't be helped."

Gardner harrumphed, but Max ignored him. Overly fastidious valets were all the rage, but the man tended to be overdramatic about expensive pieces of sewn fabric. Max couldn't care less about clothing.

As he walked downstairs, he revised that thought. He cared about clothing when it was on Olivia. When its neckline drew his attention to her breasts. When it cinched tight at her narrow waist, and outlined the swell of her behind.

Olivia's clothing did wonders for his imagination. Today, she'd been wearing a simple walking dress, but it was tight across her chest and clung to her arms, revealing their slender length, unlike most of this autumn's fashionable sleeves, which made women's arms look like mutton legs. The pattern on her dark skirt had a line of blue as bright as the sky on a clear day, bringing out the expressive blueness of her eyes. The skirt became full just below her waist, which made him wonder about the flare of her hips....did they really curve out like that, or was it an illusion caused by the cut of her clothing? Under those layers of skirts and petticoats, were her ankles as tiny and delicate as he imagined they'd be? Were her breasts as soft and creamy and pale as the top line of her bodice hinted?

He jerked to a stop halfway down the stairs. Olivia stood at the bottom, looking up at him. Her hair had been combed and it was piled on her head in sunlit glory. She wore a dress with an intricate deep purple print—butterflies and flowers. As always, her bosom peeked over the top, a tantalizing hint, but not enough. He wanted to see more. To touch that skin...

But he wouldn't compromise her. He'd be damned if he'd be the one to make her feel as though she'd been disgraced. He'd be damned if he brought out that look of absolute revulsion that had been on her face when she'd talked about Fenwicke.

If he ever touched her, it would be under far different circumstances. She'd have to consider his caress as something honorable, something real, something special. Never something impure or dirty. Never a disgrace. Never something comparable to what that bastard had thought of doing to her.

"Jonathan and Jessica are already in the carriage," she said. "I asked to go along, too."

"Will you be warm enough?"

"It's not so bad outside, as long as we remain dry. The cloud cover has made it warmer than usual."

"Still..."

He'd reached the bottom of the stairs, and she slipped her arm into his. "Don't tell me you're going to become as overprotective as a brother," she murmured.

He swallowed down a choking noise. "Brotherly, Miss Donovan," he murmured for her ears alone, "has nothing to do with the way I feel about you."

She pressed her lips together and looked away, but he didn't miss the hint of a smile curving her lips.

Her maid entered holding a blood-red cape, and she pulled it over her shoulders. He watched her adjust it, smiling a little as the slightest tinge of pink traveled across her cheekbones. When the maid left, she whispered, "Why are you watching me like that?"

He considered his answer. Definitely not to embarrass her, even though he loved it when color lit her pale cheeks. "Because I like to watch you," he said simply. And that was the truth.

Outside, twilight was giving way to night. The mist had stopped falling and a sliver of moon peeked from behind a cloud, lending a dim silver glow to the wet lawns. Max helped Olivia into the carriage, then took the backward-facing seat beside the earl.

They remained quiet for most of the ride. Jessica stared out the window, on alert as if she thought she might find Lady Fenwicke collapsed somewhere along the side of the road.

"That's odd," Jessica murmured as they made the final turn onto the long driveway that led to Brockton Hall.

"What's that?" Stratford asked.

"The house. It's all lit up. Usually Beatrice doesn't bother with so many lights. She thinks it's a waste when it's only her in residence."

Max looked at Olivia, meeting her eyes, registering the alarm in them before she returned her gaze to her lap.

She knew what this meant as well as he did. Damn it. This was a bad idea. He hadn't been thinking when Jessica said her friend hadn't come. He should have known.

"Someone must have seen us coming," Jessica said. "The front door has opened."

Max snapped his mouth shut. He'd been about to suggest they turn around.

The carriage drew to a halt. Stratford stepped out and reached up to hand Jessica down. As she stepped out of the carriage, Max murmured to Olivia, "We can stay here, if you like."

Olivia's eyes widened at him, then she slid toward Stratford, who was already holding his hand out for her. She didn't speak, just gave a quick shake of her head and reached for Stratford's hand.

Max followed close behind her as they mounted the steps, where a tall, thin servant of middle age awaited them. Max hadn't seen this man the last time they'd come to Brockton Hall.

"Good evening," the man said, but by the way he elevated his nose, he made it clear that he didn't think it was good at all.

"We're here to see Lady Fenwicke," Jessica said.

In a very haughty voice, the servant said, "Lady Fenwicke is not at home, ma'am."

Jessica frowned. "Well, where is she?"

Max winced. Clearly, Jessica wasn't familiar with the true meaning of "She's not at home," which was, "She's here, but she won't be seeing *you*."

The servant gave her a baleful stare. Stratford took her arm. "Will you inform her that the Earl of Stratford, his two sisters-in-law, and the Marquis of Hasley called?"

"Of course, my lord." The man sounded like he was huffing with every word he said, as if it were painful for him to appear polite.

Frowning, Jessica looked between Stratford and the snobbish servant. "But where is she? I didn't see her along the road." She focused on the man at the door. "She was due at Stratford House earlier today, and I am so very worried she might've fallen and broken her leg, or got lost, or was kidnapped—"

"I assure you, ma'am, she is well," the servant said.

"Come, Jessica." Olivia said quietly. "Let's go home."

"But—"

They all turned toward the click-clack of shoe heels on the marble floor, approaching from the western wing. As the figure came into view, Max repositioned himself behind Olivia in time to see the slight ripple of her shoulders beneath the red cloak as her back stiffened.

Fenwicke.

His cold silver eyes surveyed the crowd gathered at his door. His gaze lingered on Max for a time, the challenge in them obvious. Then he took in Olivia. Max fought a snarl as his gaze swept over her from crown to foot.

If the bastard touched her...

Max had moved so close to her, her bottom nudged his thigh. Olivia hadn't told him everything that had transpired between her and Fenwicke, but she'd given him enough information to make it clear that Fenwicke had attempted to use her very poorly indeed. That infuriated Max beyond reason.

Fenwicke raised his brows and nodded at Stratford. "Good evening, Stratford. Please come inside and out of the cold."

After they'd clustered together inside the entry hall, he added, "To what do I owe this unexpected pleasure?"

"Good evening, Fenwicke. You know Hasley, but have you met my sisters-in-law, the Miss Donovans?"

He raised his silvery brows into peaks. "I have met the lovely Miss Olivia Donovan. And what a pleasure it is to see you again."

Max ground his teeth as he bowed to her. She returned his greeting with strict, cool politeness.

Fenwicke then made a great production of flattering Jessica, and the naïve girl gushed about how very much she'd been looking forward to meeting their neighbor, and how she hoped he'd come call on them often. Then she said, "I understand everything now. Beatrice wasn't expecting you to arrive today. That must be why she forgot about our dinner."

Fenwicke tilted his head. "Your...dinner?"

"Yes," Olivia cut in, still the vision of politeness, but now with an added crispness to her tone. "We'd planned to have her over to dine at Stratford House this evening."

"I see," Fenwicke said.

"Well, that's not—" Jessica began. But Max saw Olivia squeeze her sister's hand, hard, and she broke off.

"When she didn't arrive at the appointed time, we were concerned," Stratford said.

"Completely understandable," Fenwicke said. "But

you're correct. She must've forgotten all about it. She was so excited to see me and relay the events of the past several weeks that she retired early this evening."

"Oh, well, that's too bad." Jessica sighed. "I was so looking forward to our dinner. I hope she will come see us soon."

"Of course."

"Tomorrow, perhaps?" Jessica looked up at Fenwicke hopefully.

"Doubtful," Fenwicke said, the gracious smile still plastered on his face. But a hint of annoyance flattened the edges of his lips.

"We must take our leave, then. We're so sorry to intrude on your evening, Fenwicke. Ladies?" Stratford gestured for Olivia and Jessica to precede him outside, then followed after them. As Max turned to go, Fenwicke caught his arm.

"How are you faring with our little slut?" the marquis murmured into his ear.

Rage shot through Max so quickly and so intensely that he'd jerked his arm away and raised his fists before he could think of what he was doing.

Then, through the red in his vision, he saw Fenwicke leering at him, daring him to throw the first punch.

Don't become your father, damn it!

Shoving away his anger, Max dropped his fists and shook his head in disgust. He turned his back on the bastard and followed after Stratford, hoping that he'd be able to wash the soiled feeling from his arm.

Chapter Five

Something was wrong with Beatrice, and Jessica was going to find out what it was.

She hadn't heard from Beatrice at all during her husband's visit, and not seeing her friend gave her a nervous, itchy feeling in her gut. Finally, several days after Lord Fenwicke's arrival at Brockton Hall, Olivia's maid told her that he had returned to London. Jessica would wait overnight to allow Beatrice to recover from her husband's visit, but the following morning, she would call on her friend and find out how the visit had gone.

The weather held, a fact Jessica was grateful for, because it was awfully cold and wet here in England. As soon as she'd taken her breakfast, Jessica headed to her friend's house alone. There was no reason to bring a chaperone—neither she nor Beatrice had bothered with one in the past few weeks. Their houses were only a mile apart, and few people traveled between them besides the residents and servants.

Less than half an hour after she'd left Stratford House, she was knocking on the door of Brockton Hall. No one answered at first, but she was persistent, and finally a man opened the door.

It wasn't the snobbish servant who'd answered when Lord Fenwicke had been in residence. The marquis must've brought that man with him. Instead, it was the older servant who'd been there on her previous visits to Brockton Hall.

"Yes?" the old man said, and Jessica nearly smiled. Fenwicke's man had made her uncomfortable, but this one... well, he was manageable. "May I help you, miss?"

"I'm here to see Lady Fenwicke."

"I'm sorry, she's not at home."

She narrowed her eyes. That was the same thing the pompous servant had said. She took a deep breath and plunged into her lie. "I've an important message for her, and I've been told I can only tell it to her in person."

She held up the reticule slung over her wrist. In truth, all that was inside the small purse was a good number of recipes Jonathan's cook had written for Beatrice.

The old man eyed her warily. "A message?"

"Yes, indeed. A very important message."

"From whom?"

"From... Lord Fenwicke. He stopped by Stratford House yesterday on his way back to London"—Lord, she hoped Olivia's maid's information had been correct—"and he told me to deliver the message first thing this morning."

The man scowled at her openly for a long moment, then said, "One moment, please, miss." He turned around and shuffled out of sight.

It seemed like forever before he returned.

"My mistress will see you."

Thank goodness. Bestowing her biggest smile on the man, she went inside. He led her upstairs to a room she'd never been to before. It was dazzling—as were all the rooms at Brockton Hall, with a beautiful marble fireplace carved with cherubs, rich carpets and furnishings, and walls lined with portraits of important-looking men— probably the line of lordly gentlemen who had preceded Lord Fenwicke as owners of this lovely place.

The room was empty, though. The man gestured her inside and instructed her to wait.

Another several minutes passed before the door opened again. Jessica popped up from the chair she'd been fidgeting in. "Beatrice!"

Beatrice paused at the door. "Good morning, Jessica. I'm told you've a message for me from my husband?"

Jessica frowned. Beatrice wore a giant bonnet that shaded most of her face, and she was partially turned away from Jessica, obscuring her face even more. Her back was hunched, and she wore an old, plain woolen dress.

Beatrice closed the door, her shoulders shaking. Jessica hurried to her friend. "Oh, dear Beatrice. What is it? What's wrong?"

"Do you have the message?" Beatrice's voice was high and tinny.

"No," Jessica admitted quietly, taking one of her friend's cold hands and chafing it in her own. "I just wanted to see you. And that was the only thing I could think of...."

Beatrice stiffened. "You shouldn't have done that,

Jessica. You don't—" She took a breath. "Please. I'm not feeling well. I'll call on you next week."

"Beatrice. Look at me."

"No, I don't think—"

Jessica released her cold fingers, pressed one hand on each side of Beatrice's head, and gently turned her so they were face to face.

"Oh!" Jessica breathed. *Oh no.* Beatrice's brown eyes were swollen and ringed with horrible colors: black, red, orange. Both of them. "What on earth happened?"

"I...fell."

It was a lie. Jessica knew that as surely as she knew she took her next breath. Suddenly, a furious hatred surged through her, and tears sprang to her eyes. "He did that to you," she choked. "Lord Fenwicke did it, didn't he?"

"Please go home," Beatrice whispered, still refusing to meet her eyes.

"Oh, Beatrice, I'm so sorry..."

Beatrice squeezed her eyes shut.

"I'm so very sorry."

Beatrice sighed. "Never mind, Jessica. It's my fault. I shouldn't have planned that dinner with you. I was over-stepping my boundaries. I know he can arrive at any moment. I know I should be prepared. I should have known that that would be the night he'd choose to come home."

Jessica grimaced. That awful man had pretended to be surprised when they'd told him about the dinner. And though she'd been leery about accepting his excuse that Beatrice was already in bed, she'd found him pleasant enough. She'd believed him. Had he beaten his wife before or after Jessica's visit?

Fury at the marquis boiled through her, but compassion for his wife kept her in a state resembling sanity.

Tears streamed down her friend's face. Jessica reached out and took her into her arms in the gentlest hug she could manage. Although she didn't want to simply hug Beatrice. She wanted to grab onto her and fly. She'd take her far away from here, far away from that horrible, disgusting man.

"It's not your fault," she managed to grind out. "How could it be? No one deserves to be struck. No one."

"But...but..." Beatrice sobbed openly against Jessica's shoulder, her body shaking. "I can't do it properly, Jessica. I'm a very bad wife. He says I'm too fat, that I'm a disgrace and an embarrassment..."

Jessica pulled away. "No! That's not true. You're lovely and sweet, and one of the prettiest ladies I know. You can't be a bad wife. You aren't. It's simply impossible."

Jessica untied the ridiculous bonnet and tossed it into a chair. Then she drew her friend into her arms again and stroked her hair until she cried herself quiet.

Finally, Beatrice drew away from her. Taking the handkerchief Jessica pulled from her reticule to offer her, she mopped her face with it. "I'm sorry."

"I'm your friend. Don't you know that? Don't be sorry."

Beatrice sniffed. "We've known each other for only a few weeks."

Jessica smiled. "I knew from the moment I saw you that you and I were going to be great friends."

Beatrice gave her a wavering return smile. "Really?"

Jessica nodded. "Yes. Really." She reached down and took Beatrice's hand. "Come. Let's sit for a while."

Beatrice nodded and allowed Jessica to lead her to the elegant pale green velvet sofa. Jessica watched as Beatrice dabbed away fresh tears with the handkerchief. When she lowered the handkerchief to her lap, Jessica touched her eye gently. "How many times has he done this to you?"

Beatrice raised a shaky hand to her left eye, the one with the darker ring around it. "This?" She shrugged. "I don't know."

"Do you mean you don't wish to tell me, or you've truly lost count?"

Beatrice stared into her lap. "I . . . I've lost count."

Jessica groaned out loud.

"He has every right—"

Anger heated Jessica's cheeks. "I suppose he tells you that?"

"But he does," Beatrice whispered. "There is no law against disciplining one's wife."

"Just because there's no law against it doesn't make it right. No honorable husband would treat his wife in such a way."

A tear pooled and rolled down Beatrice's cheek. "I suppose I haven't married a good husband, then."

No, she hadn't. "Oh Beatrice, you deserve so much better than this. Tell me you know that."

"If I was prettier, if I wasn't so fat . . . he'd be proud of me. He'd take me with him to London."

Jessica took a breath. The awful man hadn't only abused his wife—he'd convinced her that it was her fault. Jessica had never thought herself capable of such hatred before this moment.

She slid off the sofa and knelt before Beatrice, placing her hands on her friend's knees. "Listen to me. It's not your fault. How can I convince you that you are pretty? Tell me, how many offers of marriage did you have before you chose Lord Fenwicke?"

"Six," Beatrice said. "But Papa said I must choose Lord Fenwicke because he will be a duke someday."

"See? If you were ugly, you wouldn't have received six offers, believe me!"

Beatrice smiled a little, but then her lips quivered. "But I wasn't fat then."

Jessica shook her head. "I've never known you at any other size, Beatrice. I've never thought you were fat, and I've always thought you utterly lovely."

"Really?"

"Yes."

"Promise?"

"Yes. I promise."

Beatrice's smile grew a little stronger. "Thank you," she whispered. "You're such a good friend."

Jessica took her hand and squeezed. "You're welcome. But I'm not saying that just to make you feel better. I'm saying it because it's true. Now...do you know when your husband will return to Brockton Hall?"

Beatrice shook her head. "He never informs me in advance before he arrives. I never know he's coming until he pulls up in the drive. And...now..." She took a shaky breath. "I fear I must be home the next time he comes. What if he were to arrive and look for me while I was at Stratford House? He'd be so angry with me."

"That's all right," Jessica said quickly. "You know we wouldn't abandon you, don't you? I'll come visit you here. So will my sisters."

Beatrice smiled.

"But... you could leave him, you know," Jessica said quietly.

Beatrice's eyes widened. "Jessica, are you mad? I couldn't leave him!"

"Why not?"

"He is my husband!"

"He is a bully and an abuser of ladies. He doesn't deserve you."

"But I couldn't. My family would be so ashamed..."

"It's not your fault!"

"But I would be dishonored. Embarrassed..."

"Nonsense. The only one who would be embarrassed is him."

Suddenly, Beatrice grabbed both of Jessica's hands with her own. "Oh, Jessica, you won't tell anyone, will you? Please promise me you won't tell anyone. If you do... oh God, please, Jessica..." She began to sob again.

Jessica blinked at her. She hadn't even considered keeping this information from her family. She usually told her sisters everything.

"You don't wish for me to tell my sisters? But, Beatrice, they'll help you."

Beatrice closed her eyes and moaned, twin tears trickling down her cheeks. "I don't think I could bear the shame. Please..."

"Very well," Jessica said soothingly. "I won't tell them until you give me leave to."

"Thank you." Raising Jessica's hand, Beatrice pressed it to her cheek.

"Well then..." Jessica took a deep breath. "Let's speak of a happier topic, shall we?" She reached for her reticule. "I brought you some recipes."

She laid out the pieces of paper and listened to Beatrice expound over ingredients and measurements, but the whole time, her mind was working hard.

Jessica Donovan wasn't going to allow any friend of hers to be beaten. She simply wasn't going to allow it.

Max could hardly believe November was half over. Time had flown since he'd kissed Olivia beneath the outcropping on that rainy afternoon. They'd spent many afternoons together since then: reading in the library, talking in the drawing room, playing tennis when the weather permitted, though that was rare these days. But he hadn't kissed her again. Not for lack of desire to feel her sweet lips against his. He just hadn't been alone with her since that day. If he had been alone with her, he doubted he would have been able to keep his hands off her.

He strode into the breakfast room. For the first time since his arrival at Stratford House, none of the ladies were sitting down and drinking their chocolate. Instead, Stratford was in the room. He was prowling along the sideboard as if unable to decide what to choose for his breakfast, and Langley was speaking to him in low, urgent tones.

"Is something the matter?" Max asked when they both fell silent and looked up at him.

Stratford sighed. "It's Olivia. She came down with a fever last night. The ladies are upstairs tending to her."

Stratford's features were pinched with worry. Max's heart surged, then his heartbeat sped. "A fever? Is she..."

He couldn't finish the sentence. *Is she in danger?* No, she couldn't be. It simply wasn't possible. She'd seemed perfectly healthy yesterday. Still, Stratford's demeanor was making his heart thump unsteadily against his breastbone.

Stratford seemed to understand his unfinished question. "She's not in immediate danger, no. But it is cause for concern whenever she has a fever. Meg feels each one leaves her weaker."

Stratford turned back to the sideboard. He spooned some eggs onto his plate and sat at the table across from Langley. He looked up at Max, who'd stood frozen to the spot since he'd opened the door, and gestured toward the food. "Have some breakfast, Hasley."

Max forced himself to nod. He forced his stiff legs to move toward the breakfast offerings, and he blinked hard against the blur in his eyes so he could distinguish between the elegantly laid out dishes. He shoveled something onto his plate and then went to sit beside Stratford.

Each fever weakened her? God, how many fevers had she had?

He wanted to ask if he could see her. But that would be too presumptuous. He wasn't a member of their family. He wasn't even Olivia's suitor—officially. Even if he were, it would be quite forward to ask permission to go to her when she was ill.

"May I see her?" he blurted. Hell. He just couldn't control it. Couldn't stop this raging need to see her, to make sure she was all right.

Both men's gazes snapped to him. Stratford froze with a slice of toast halfway to his mouth. "Er," he said, frowning, "well, I will certainly ask Meg."

"Thank you."

Langley had been silent since Max had entered, and now he gave Max a sympathetic look. "You and Miss Donovan have become quite friendly."

His tone was not accusatory or prying in any way, yet

Max suddenly felt like he was a piece of meat the other two men planned to chop up and devour, piece by piece.

"Yes," he said evenly. "We enjoy each other's company."

"You spend quite a bit of time with her," Langley said conversationally. "Both of you seem to like playing tennis."

"We do."

"It has been too cold for that." Stratford cradled his coffee cup in his hands. "Especially for someone with as delicate a constitution as Olivia. Tennis is a summer sport, even for the sturdiest of souls."

"It's true the weather hasn't cooperated very often. We haven't played more than once or twice in the past fortnight—" Something inside Max clenched. They'd played tennis yesterday. "You don't think...Well, you don't think the tennis caused the fever, do you?"

God, he sounded so anxious and needy. But what if he were responsible? Perhaps he should have insisted they not play, that it was too cold, too windy.

She would never have agreed.

"I don't know," Stratford said.

Langley shrugged. "Really, there's no way of knowing for certain."

Stratford sipped his coffee. "Meg assures me that she, Phoebe, and Jessica have been through this many times with Olivia. They know what to do. Meg said the fever's already come down a bit."

There it was again—talk of this being a recurring problem. Max jumped on it this time.

"Many times? Are you saying Miss Donovan is susceptible to fevers?"

Stratford raised his brows. "She hasn't told you?"

"Told me what?"

"When she was nine years old, Olivia contracted malaria. She nearly died from it."

Max tried not to show any response, but he felt like his insides had been crushed. Imagining Olivia as a child, deathly ill... He took a slow, deep breath. "Like her father."

"Yes," Stratford said. "She recovered from that first affliction, whereas he did not. However, she still suffers from occasional relapses of fever. Each fever weakens her, and every time she has one, her sisters' darkest fear is that she won't recover."

Their protectiveness of Olivia made so much more sense now. But why had she kept this important part of herself from him? He wasn't angry with her—she was under no obligation to tell him, after all, but a part of him felt like it had been rubbed raw enough to ache. This meant she didn't trust him. Not completely.

"Truthfully, none of us likes it when she goes on all those long walks, because we worry she'll come down with a fever and no one will be near to help her. But"— Stratford shrugged—"I quickly learned that that is Olivia. She's a very solitary person, and she needs her freedom. She needs to feel strong... and she *is* quite strong, really. If not physically, at least in other ways."

Max didn't know what to say. This information seemed like too much to assimilate all at once. Olivia— his Olivia—had a horrible, deadly disease. She was lying upstairs right at this moment, suffering from it. He didn't want to be down here discussing it with these men. He wanted to be at her side.

Stratford clapped a hand over Max's shoulder and squeezed lightly. "Let's go for a ride this morning. It'll be better than sitting in the house and worrying."

Max thought about that—God knew he didn't want to go farther away from her. What if she needed him? But then he gave a slow nod. She didn't need him—he didn't have the first idea how he could possibly help her. It was the doctor and her sisters who would help her most right now.

Stratford was right. Max wouldn't stop worrying, but he might go mad if he was confined to the house and unable to see her.

By the following afternoon, Olivia felt much better. The fever still raged, making her head ache and her eyes sting. She'd kick off the covers, and moments later she'd be shuddering from cold.

One of her sisters stayed with her at all times. Phoebe had given her a dose of the quinine she'd brought from Antigua and then had gone off to tend to Margie. Jessica had just come in and was fussing with the covers.

"Keep the blankets over you, Olivia," she admonished. "The doctors always say you must sweat the poisons out, you know that."

She mustered a smile, then closed her burning eyes. "Too hot."

"Humph." Jessica plumped into the chair someone had left beside the bed and took her hand. "This one has been an easy one, hasn't it?"

"Isn't over yet," Olivia murmured.

"But you're stronger already."

"True. I'll be out of bed tomorrow, certainly."

Jessica snorted. "I doubt that."

Keeping her eyes closed, Olivia smiled. After a short silence, Jessica said, "Someone's been asking to see you."

Olivia's eyes popped open. "Max?" she breathed.

She'd been thinking about him. Missing him. Wondering what he thought about her illness. Serena had told her that Jonathan had been surprised Max hadn't known about the malaria, but they understood why Olivia hadn't told him.

Would he avoid her now?

"Lord Hasley, yes. He's quite worried about you, the gentlemen say."

Olivia sighed, allowing her eyelids to sink shut again. *Max.* She'd dreamed about him during the height of the fever last night. A strange dream that kept repeating itself, about being in his arms while he carried her over water, running at top speed.

What was she supposed to think of that? Was her dream telling her that Max walked on water? She might have laughed, but it hurt too much to laugh right now.

"So I assume this means you want him to visit you."

"I'd like it very much," Olivia murmured. "But... will he come?"

"Oh, I think so."

"And would anyone think anything of it? If he comes to see me, I shouldn't want Jonathan and the others to think it means more than it does..."

Jessica's brows rose nearly to her hairline. "Goodness, Liv. What do *you* think it means?"

"He's a concerned friend?" Olivia asked hopefully.

Jessica rolled her eyes heavenward. "You're in your chemise. In *bed.*"

"Well, goodness, Jessica... There isn't much of a chance he'll compromise me in my condition. Not to mention that I'm sure I look a fright."

Jessica crossed her arms. "You can't fool me, Saint

Olivia. Though I think it's high time I stop calling you a saint."

"What do you mean?"

"You know, I believed it was impossible for you to attempt to pull the wool over anyone's eyes. You're honest to a fault. And yet you're trying to hide it from us."

"Trying to hide *what* from you?" The headache stabbed endlessly between her eyes.

"Your affection for Lord Hasley."

"Of course I feel affection for him. We've become good friends."

"Oh, indeed? Well, do you know what? I think your feelings for him surpass friendship, dear sister."

Do they?

"Yes, I think they do."

Olivia blinked at Jessica, then realized she'd spoken the words aloud.

"I've seen the way your gaze trails after him. I've seen the way you light up whenever he's near." Jessica smiled. "And do you know what? I approve. I like Lord Hasley."

Olivia wished she could think. She wished the fever would allow her to focus. But, as it usually did, it took her faculties in random snatches.

Max.

They'd been talking about Max.

She'd missed him. How long had she been sick this time? It seemed like forever.

"You're tired," her sister murmured. "Get some rest, Liv."

Olivia closed her eyes and allowed dreams of Maxwell Buchanan to take her away.

Chapter Six

Max leaned forward in his chair. "Your sisters say you're much better."

"I am, thank you." Sitting up in her bed, surrounded by pillows, Olivia took Max's hand. It was the fourth day after the sickness had assaulted her body, but last night her fever had broken, Olivia hoped, for the final time. She felt weak, but better than usual, and happy. She'd defeated it yet again, and soundly this time.

And the way Max was behaving toward her made her feel even better. There was a softness in his eyes and a gentleness in his touch that soothed her worries about how he'd react to her now that he knew about her illness.

"The countess told me your fevers usually last longer than this."

"It might be the change in weather. I think England might be a better climate for me than Antigua was."

"I hope that's true." Squeezing her hand, he smiled at her, but there was a hesitation, a hint of pain, in that smile. After a moment of silence, he asked, "Why did you keep this from me, Olivia?" When she didn't answer right away, he blew out a harsh breath. "Never mind. I know I shouldn't ask. I know I have no right to demand anything from you, including personal information. Yet..."

She saw his Adam's apple moving as he swallowed.

She squeezed his hand. "I did want to tell you about it. But... I was afraid."

"Afraid of what?"

His voice was rough, and his eyes were glassy, as if her fear of telling him caused him pain.

"Oh, Max." How to explain to him all the years of reactions ranging from pity to disgust? How to explain to him her fear of him becoming so afraid of her fevers that he stopped giving her all those freedoms with him that she enjoyed so much?

"I was so afraid you might change," she said softly. "And I liked the way you were—the way *we* were together. I didn't want you to think differently about me. I still don't."

Max blinked hard, and tenderness replaced the pain in his expression. "It would only have helped me to understand you, Olivia. You and your family."

"I wanted you to believe I was a normal woman. I didn't want you looking at me with pity or disgust. I just wanted to pretend for a while."

"If you thought your illness would change my opinion about you in any way, you were wrong."

"It changes everyone's opinion about me."

"Not mine," Max said firmly.

"Are you truly saying that once I leave this bed, nothing will change? We'll still be... friends? We'll still walk together and play tennis together?"

"Nothing will change," he said solemnly. He leaned forward, and without releasing her hand, smoothed his other thumb over her eyebrow. "I've missed you."

His rich, low voice washed over her, comforting yet raising awareness of his proximity all over her body.

"I missed you, too," she breathed. She'd dreamed about him constantly. Ever since Jessica had told her he'd been asking to visit her, she'd hoped to see him every time she opened her eyes. And this time, here he was. She was so happy he had come.

"Will you be able to leave bed soon?"

"Tomorrow, I hope." She frowned. "But I fear I won't be able to play tennis with you for a while."

He shrugged. "I doubt if we could, anyhow. Not sure if the ball would bounce properly. There was a frost last night, and it's growing colder. I'd wager the ground will be icy tomorrow."

"Drat," she muttered. "How long will the weather work against us?"

He smiled. "Spring will be here before we know it. And until then I think we shall find other happy pursuits together."

Her eyes widened but her body rejoiced at the wicked glint in his eyes. "Are you teasing me, Lord Hasley?"

"I'll let you determine that." He leaned closer to her, his expression sobering. "Any pursuit will be a happy one, as long as I pursue it with you."

She felt the same way, she realized with a jolt. She always felt so free when she was with him. She loved the way he tilted his head slightly when he was listening to her, as if he found every word that came out of her mouth to be meaningful and important. She loved how he asked questions about her life and her family and appeared to be genuinely interested in her answers. And she loved it when he touched her, which, if she were honest with herself, she'd admit he'd touched her far less in the past few weeks than she would have liked.

"I finally understand why your family is so overprotective," he said. "They just want to keep you safe. To prevent relapses of the fever."

She made a small dismissive noise. "They believe that every walk I go on will be my last one."

"And you disagree? You don't believe all your physical activity causes the fevers?"

"No, I'm quite sure it doesn't."

"What does cause them, then?"

"I'm not certain. They seem to be quite random."

"How often do they occur?"

"Once or twice a year. The last one was last winter."

"I've been thinking about it. It seems to me that if you were to get a fever from walking or being outside, you would have come down with one that day it rained on us. You were chilled and soaked to the bone."

Olivia nodded grimly. "Meg was furious with me, and she was furious with Jonathan for not throwing me over his saddle by force and galloping me home before the rain struck."

"And yet you didn't fall ill from that. You fell ill now. What could possibly have caused it to happen now? Do you think it was the tennis?"

"I'm sure it wasn't the tennis. How many times did we play tennis together, and in even colder weather, without it making me sick? I wish I knew what really causes the fevers, Max. But I've no idea, truly."

Still holding onto her hand, he drew closer, and her eyes drifted shut, anticipation buzzing on her skin.

"Are you tired?"

"No," she breathed.

And his lips brushed over hers, warm and soft, and then pressed, coaxing her to respond. She did respond, opening to him and moving her lips in a slow dance that made her heart thump wildly. Sensation curled through her body like a tendril of sweet smoke, caressing every part of her. She inhaled deeply, taking in his masculine presence—so different from the feminine essences that had surrounded her for so many years. There was a hardness, a toughness, to this man. But he had never been anything but gentle with her. He was the contradiction of strength and muscle with softness and compassion. She loved that about him.

Further, deeper, she sank into his kiss. His free hand moved up to her face. His hand was so large that when it cupped her cheek, he touched her from chin to crown. His fingers stroked at her hairline, swiping wisps of hair out of her face. And she realized that his hand was trembling.

The door glided open on its hinges. The only reason Olivia heard it was because she'd been so focused on Max, on the intensity of how her body responded to his touch, that the foreign noise snapped her into reality. Still, she didn't jerk back. Even if she could have, she truly didn't want to.

Slowly, seemingly with great effort, Max drew away. Olivia opened her eyes, tearing her gaze from Max to see Serena standing in the doorway.

Heat rushed to Olivia's cheek as Max's fingers slipped from it. Rising, Max bowed. "My lady."

"Lord Hasley." Serena's voice was a trifle more clipped than usual.

There was an uncomfortable silence, and then, sighing audibly, Serena came inside, closing the door behind her. "I believe I shall pretend I didn't see anything."

Still smiling politely, not looking the least bit embarrassed, Max nodded. He looked down at Olivia. "Tomorrow, then?"

Still mortified, she nodded.

He was still holding her hand. With a final squeeze to it, he took his leave.

Serena watched him until the door clicked shut behind him, then she took the seat he had vacated.

"You're feeling better," she said.

"Mmm." Her embarrassment fading rapidly, Olivia stared up at the bed canopy, looking at the curve of the rose stems in its pattern and the petals of the various roses it depicted. The roses bloomed in different stages, from tiny buds to voluminous blossoms, all pale pink offsetting the dark green of the fabric.

She slid her gaze toward Serena. "Do you intend to play big sister with me, Serena?" she asked softly. "Will you scold me now?"

Serena looked at her for a long moment, clearly considering that option. Finally, she said, "No."

"Good." Olivia returned her gaze to the ceiling.

"I know you and Lord Hasley have been developing an affinity for each other."

"Hm. Is that what you call it? An affinity?"

"I think so." Serena crossed her arms over her chest. "In truth," she murmured, "I never expected this of you, Olivia."

"I never expected it of me, either." But, oh, how she liked Maxwell Buchanan. And, oh, how she liked his kisses...She sighed. "I suppose I'm no saint, after all."

Serena smiled. "I suppose not. Still, after your experience of the London Season, you made it very clear to Jonathan and me that you wished to live with us. That you had no interest in gentlemen and no intention of marrying."

"That's all still true."

Completely unconvinced, Serena raised a brow. "Really?"

"Of course. Lord Hasley will be gone in a few weeks"—and he'd take his kisses with him—"and my life will continue as I planned it. This is only a temporary... diversion."

"Do you really think so?"

"I can't see how else it might go." She knew Max had a life outside Stratford House. She knew he'd be a duke someday and could never think of marrying someone like her, a woman of no fortune, flimsy connections, and questionable health.

The end of their relationship was inevitable, yet the thought of Max leaving still made her ache deep inside.

"Oh, Olivia." Serena looked almost sorry for her. "What, exactly, do you believe is happening between yourself and Lord Hasley?"

"Well," Olivia said slowly, "I like him very much. I enjoy his company."

"And plainly he enjoys yours as well," Serena said. "And from the way he's worried about you in the last few days, I'd say he cares for you."

"Yes, I think he does." Olivia thought of his kiss. No wonder so many women were utterly bespelled by men's caresses. The way he kissed her made her feel like he'd do anything for her, anything at all. He'd offer her the world on a silver platter.

Yet despite her inexperience, she possessed at least a modicum of wisdom. Even if he did care about her, she wasn't cut from the cloth of a duchess.

She'd never thought of herself as mistress material, either... until recently.

"Dearest," Serena murmured, "above all, I want you to be happy. I don't want him to hurt you."

Olivia took a moment to ponder this. "Do you really think Max is capable of hurting me?"

"Yes. I do. I don't think he intends to hurt you, but it appears he has taken a bit of your virtue and probably desires more. He is a man, after all. And when he leaves Stratford House, he'll take that part of you with him, and you'll never see it again. Can you face that loss without feeling hurt and betrayed?"

Olivia didn't answer right away. She thought about how she felt when he kissed her. Like she'd do anything to continue to experience the feeling his touch gave her. How her skin prickled with excitement, her heart pounded, her nerves hummed with anticipation. How she craved that sweetness that poured through her with each one of his caresses.

Could she savor those feelings he offered her for such a short time of her life, or would he leave her with a lifetime of regrets?

"I don't know," she admitted quietly. She looked up at her sister, for the first time really thinking of her future, of the life she'd lead with Serena and Phoebe and their husbands and children. It was still what she wanted...

Wasn't it?

She could never leave them...she knew that much. She'd already lost one sister, and she'd never survive the loss of the three she had left.

"I might want to..." She took a breath, steadied her voice, and continued. "I think I might want more from him."

"Marriage?" Serena asked gently.

"Oh no," Olivia whispered. "Not marriage. That would be impossible." She looked at her sister imploringly, hoping she wouldn't be forced to explain it.

Serena just looked at her, blank-faced. "What, then?"

"If I'm to live my life as a spinster...well, I might like to have the experience, just once, of...of a lover." Heat rushed over her cheeks, hotter than when Serena had first entered the room. But she forced herself to continue. "I am very inexperienced in these matters, as you know, Serena. But...but I think Max would be a very gentle lover to me."

She felt light. Breathless. So embarrassed she wanted to melt straight into the bed sheets. But if she couldn't share her true feelings with her older sister, then she couldn't be honest with anyone.

"Oh, Olivia. I want you to experience that singular piece of heaven," Serena said. "I truly do."

Olivia looked at her, waiting for the "but."

"But I'm so worried about you. I don't want to see you hurt."

Long ago, Serena had fallen in love with Jonathan one summer and had spent some of the most joyful, erotically charged days of her life with him. But then he'd spurned her and for seven years she'd struggled to overcome her shattered heart.

Serena and Jonathan's journey to happiness had been very long and fraught with difficulty. But Olivia knew her sister's story was one of the rare ones. It would be more common for a lady in Serena's position to spend her life mourning that lost love. Was that what Olivia would do after Max left her?

Olivia reached out from under the covers for her sister's hand. "Don't worry," she said, her voice firm. "It probably won't even happen."

"If it does, promise me you'll be careful."

"I will." She hesitated. "There is a difference between what is happening with me and Max and what happened with you and Jonathan so long ago, you know."

"What's that?"

"You expected him to marry you. It was an unspoken agreement between the two of you, or so you thought at the time. But I have no such misconceptions, Serena. I know Max cannot marry the likes of me. I know that whatever happens between us will only be temporary."

"Are you *sure*, Liv?"

"Yes. I'm sure."

"Don't allow him to . . ." Serena hesitated.

Olivia frowned. "Don't allow him to what?"

". . . get you with child," Serena finished.

"How can I prevent it?" Olivia chewed on her lower lip. "Do you know? Perhaps we should ask Jessica. She seemed to know of something—"

"Ask him not to finish when he's inside you."

"Oh." Taking a deep breath, Olivia nodded. "I will do that, then. If it . . . comes to that."

"Promise me you will."

"I promise."

"Good." Serena squeezed her hand, much like Max had done a few minutes earlier. "I just pray that when it's over and he returns to London, he won't take your heart with him."

"Don't worry, Serena. My heart is firmly encased right here." And she pressed her palm against her chest. "Trust me. It's not going anywhere."

A week after Olivia had resumed her daily routine, she sat in the drawing room surrounded by family and feeling very content, despite the fact that she and Max hadn't had a moment alone since she'd left her bed. The weather had been awful, and though it had stopped raining for a time in the middle of the day today, clouds now threatened the afternoon light. Olivia turned away from the window.

"Another day without my walk," she grumbled.

"Good," Phoebe said. "I don't like it when you walk. Maybe if you stopped walking altogether, you'll stop having those awful fevers."

Olivia sighed, but her mood was too light to argue with her sister. Instead she traded a silent look with Max before going to Phoebe and holding her arms out for Margie, who reached for her with her two chubby fists. Olivia gathered the baby into her arms and walked past the men, who'd set up the card table and were playing a game of whist.

Olivia took Margie to the sofa and sat beside Jessica. She bounced Margie gently on her knees while the baby gave her a big gummy grin and grasped on to her fingers. "You sweet thing. Such a big, big girl I think you weigh almost two stone now, don't you?"

"For goodness' sakes!" Phoebe exclaimed. "She's not *that* big!"

"She's a big, healthy, adorable baby, and you should be very proud," Serena murmured from her chair near the hearth, where she was working on embroidering a baby bonnet—for her own baby, Olivia knew. Although, as far as she knew, Jonathan still didn't know Serena's news. Why on earth had Serena kept such important, wonderful news from her husband for so long?

"*I* am proud." Sebastian, Phoebe's husband, looked up from his cards. "She's the most beautiful baby that was ever born, I guarantee it. And she's the perfect size, too."

Serena had often said how much it surprised her what a doting husband and father Sebastian had become. He'd once had a reputation of being difficult and temperamental, but it was widely agreed that Phoebe had soothed his fighter's spirit.

"I'm proud, too." Phoebe's expression softened as she gazed at the pretty dark-haired baby on Olivia's knee.

"Good," Jonathan's mother, the dowager countess said, looking up from her book and over her spectacles at Phoebe. "One should always be proud of one's children." She smiled fondly at Jonathan. "As I am."

Jonathan doggedly ignored her, but the tips of his ears turned pink, and Olivia smiled. Jonathan had hardly spoken to his mother for several years, but his marriage to Serena had mended everything that had once been sour between them.

"Speaking of familial love," the dowager continued, "I've just received a letter from my own mother."

"Oh, have you?" Serena asked. "How is she?"

The older woman chuckled. "She claims she is dying and summons me to London."

Jonathan didn't look up from the cards. "She says

that every year. She isn't dying. That woman is tough as leather—I'm sure she'll outlast us all."

"Nevertheless," the dowager said, "I think I shall go in the new year."

"Oh, we'll miss you," Serena said. "How long will you stay?"

"A month, possibly two."

Jonathan shook his head. "My grandmother is so odd. She always chooses to winter in London. Why not go in the spring, when it is more welcoming? And when all her friends are there?"

"She prefers it that way." The dowager sniffed. "She can do as she pleases without running into Lady X or Lord Y and being forced to make pleasant conversation."

"Well, I know firsthand how much she dislikes being pleasant."

Serena shot Jonathan an admonishing look. "I should like to meet her sometime."

"Oh, you will, my dear," the dowager said. "I intend to bring her home with me."

Jonathan snorted. "I wish you worlds of luck in that endeavor, madam. You'll need it."

The dowager gave Jonathan a serene smile. "I'll do my best."

Jessica leaned over and kissed Margie on the cheek, and then she rose. "Well, rain or shine, I'm off to Beatrice's."

"Are you sure?" Olivia looked toward the window at the ominous clouds gathering in the sky. "I really do think it's going to rain."

"Take a carriage," Jonathan offered, glancing up from his cards.

"Oh, thank you, Jonathan. I think I will, if you don't mind," Jessica said. "Honestly, I don't mind getting wet and I can carry an umbrella, but I'd rather not ruin my dress with mud." She swiped her hands down her light pink lawn.

Jonathan rose to summon a footman. "I know you'd walk through mud for your bosom friend, but I think it's best you take the carriage."

"But what I don't understand is why Lady Fenwicke hasn't visited us since Lord Fenwicke left Brockton Hall," Serena said.

"Oh . . ." Jessica hesitated. "Well, she prefers to stay at her house."

"But why?" Serena pressed.

Jessica chewed on her lower lip. "Well, I promised not to say."

Everyone stared at Jessica. Even the three seated gentlemen all looked up from their cards.

Olivia smiled. "You're a good friend, then, Jessica. An honest one. I'd like to have a friend like you."

Jessica turned to her. "Oh you do, Liv. I'm not only your sister, you know."

"I know."

"But why would she want you to keep a secret?" Phoebe asked. "Is she in trouble?"

Jessica looked at Phoebe, fidgeted, and then just shrugged. "I truly cannot say. Please don't force me to, Phoebe."

Jonathan closed the door behind the footman and returned to his chair at the card table. "The carriage will be out front in a few moments."

"Thank you, Jonathan. I'll run up to fetch my things,

and I'll wait at the front for it. I want to be home in time for dinner. I do want to taste the oxtail soup Cook and Beatrice have planned for us all this evening."

"Of course," Serena said. "Have a nice time, Jess."

Jessica left, and Phoebe frowned after her. "I'm worried about that girl."

"Jessica?" Olivia asked.

"No. Lady Fenwicke."

"Me, too." Olivia pulled Margie close, stroking her fine, dark hair. In return, Margie grabbed a fistful of Olivia's hair and shoved it into her mouth.

"Do you like the taste of my hair, Margie?" Olivia murmured.

"She finds it delicious, I'm sure." Phoebe groaned. "That girl will eat anything."

"She tried doing away with my toes last night." Sebastian cast a doting smile in Margie's direction. "Didn't you, love?"

Hearing her papa's voice, Margie turned her head. She pulled the hair out of her mouth and reached out a chubby fist for her father. "Pa-pa!"

Sebastian's dark eyes widened. He turned to the other men. "Did you hear that? She called me papa!"

As the other gentlemen slapped Sebastian on the back for the obviously superior intelligence of his progeny, Phoebe jumped up from her chair and came rushing over. "Oh, Margie, did you say papa? Say it again, darling!"

Margie had found Olivia's hair again, though, and was yanking on it.

"Ooh! That hurts." Olivia pried the chubby fingers from her hair.

A whimper sounded from the opposite side of the

room. It took Olivia a second to realize it hadn't come from Margie. She and Phoebe looked across at Serena, who'd risen from her chair.

"Oh." Serena's voice was half cry, half moan. "Oh dear."

The front of her skirt was covered with blood. She swayed, and there was a loud crash as Jonathan jumped up, overturning the card table, and rushed to her. He caught her in his arms just as she crumpled in a faint.

Jonathan carried Serena up to their bedchamber while Max and Captain Langley rushed to the village to fetch the doctor. Two hours later, the doctor had just left Serena's bedchamber, confirming that she was losing the baby. He was now downstairs telling Jonathan the bad news.

Serena lay in bed, her skin so pale it looked almost blue. She had lost a great deal of blood, and though the doctor said she was out of immediate danger, he advised her to stay in bed for a day or two. Phoebe and Jessica sat at the edge of the bed across from Olivia.

"Oh, Serena." Phoebe swiped away a tear with her handkerchief. "Does it hurt very much?"

"It hurts a little," Serena said.

"I'm so sorry," Olivia murmured. "I know how much you wanted this."

"There will be another." Serena had forced her voice to sound determined, but the pain was evident in her eyes. She gave Olivia a wavering smile. "I'm used to looking down at you in bed, Liv. Not up at you."

"I hope I never have to stand at your bedside again. Well, except to hold your hand at the birth of your healthy baby, that is."

Serena closed her eyes, squeezing tears out from the edges. "Me, too."

The door opened and Jonathan strode in. He had eyes only for his wife—he didn't even seem to notice her sisters' presence in the room.

He went straight to the bed, sat on its edge, and leaned down to Serena, gathering her in his arms. "Serena," he said, his choked voice muffled against her skin. "Why didn't you tell me?"

"I thought... I wanted to wait for the right time. But now I think that maybe, deep in my heart, I knew something was wrong and I didn't want to build your hopes prematurely."

Olivia and her sisters rose at the same time and headed for the door to give Serena some privacy with her husband.

"You should have told me. I need to know these things.... I need to know how you're feeling, what you're thinking..."

Olivia gently shut the door behind them. Standing alone in the darkened corridor, the three sisters exchanged a desolate look.

Chapter Seven

Olivia couldn't sleep. The rain had turned into sleet, and the wind had risen, whipping a branch against her windowpane. She lay there, staring up at her bed canopy but unable to discern the blooming roses in the darkness.

She was cold tonight. And lonely. And sadness swept in waves through her, cresting, peaking and crashing and then pulling away in a strong tide before the process began all over again.

She thought of Max in the opposite wing of the house. Except for his bedchamber, there were no rooms in use in that wing. She wondered if it was quiet there, or if the sleet beat like little pellets against his window. Was he awake and cold and lonely tonight, just like she was?

Well. There was only one way to find out.

She rose, swinging her feet over the side of the bed, then hesitated. Would he think her too forward?

The answer came quickly. No. She didn't think so. He was always happy to see her. She'd never awakened him before, but while she could imagine a host of reactions from him, ranging from curiosity to confusion to happiness, she couldn't imagine him being angry or thinking less of her.

She took her woolen robe from its hook and tugged it on, tying the belt around her waist. Opening the door to her bedchamber, she peeked into the darkened corridor. All was silent. Everyone was fast asleep, including the servants.

She walked down the corridor, hesitating only as she passed Serena and Jonathan's room. All was quiet inside. Closing her eyes, Olivia imagined Serena sleeping soundly, tucked into her husband's arms. Serena had told her once that that was how she slept, and Olivia hoped it was the case tonight.

After she passed their room, she continued on, now in the darkest wing of the house, unused for several years before Max had come and taken the refurbished bedroom at the very end of the passageway.

Olivia stopped at the door, hesitating yet again, suddenly terribly nervous.

Half the civilized world would think she was mad right now. Or unforgivably brazen.

Or, perhaps, both.

Wide awake, Max clasped his fingers behind his head and stared up at the ceiling.

It had been a hell of a day. It had started out fair enough despite the weather. He'd hoped he'd spend the afternoon walking with Olivia, but the weather had not cooperated.

Perhaps it was for the best. Olivia wouldn't have wanted to have been away when her sister collapsed.

Still, the look of terror on Stratford's face. The looks of fear on the sisters' faces. The countess was much-loved. And even though she was out of danger, she'd lost a child, and the tragedy of that had shaken the household. Even Langley, the most sober and even-tempered fellow Max had ever known, had been affected. At one point, Max had glanced over at him and seen tears glistening in his eyes.

Something creaked just outside his door, and Max frowned. It was usually dead quiet in this wing of the house. He didn't mind that. He had slept like a baby since coming to Sussex, and that was part of the reason. The other reasons had to do with how much he'd been enjoying himself here.

Creak. There it was again. Max slipped out of bed, pulled on the pair of loose trousers he'd slung over a nearby chair, and crept toward the door. When he reached it, he pressed his ear against it, listening intently.

Silence.

He grasped the handle and yanked the door open, his other hand curled into a fist, prepared to slam into the intruder's gut, if necessary.

She had just been turning away, but at the sound of the opening door, she froze. Slowly, she turned to face him.

Olivia. His hand opened at his side.

She didn't speak. Neither did he—he was too surprised.

Finally, she whispered, "You're naked."

He looked down at himself, confirming that he was indeed wearing trousers. He hadn't dreamed he'd pulled them on. He gestured at his legs. "No I'm not."

Her lips tilted in a wry smile. "Sorry to disturb you."

She gestured weakly down the corridor in the general direction of the opposite wing, where her bedchamber was located. "I'll—I should be going now. Good night."

"Wait." His voice sounded harsh, and she took a step back.

"I mean...I'm happy you came. Thanks for coming." He shrugged. "I couldn't sleep."

She seemed to relax a little. "Neither could I."

He opened the door wider. "Will you come in?"

Blanching, she gazed into the room as if she were looking into a cavern of danger and malice. He laughed softly. "My bedchamber won't bite. I promise."

She jerked her gaze to him.

"And neither will I."

"Are you...Are you sure?"

He nodded. "I'm quite certain."

"All right, then." Taking a deep breath, she threw her body into his room as if she were plunging into an ocean teeming with sharks.

Amused, he closed the door behind her and then leaned back on it, crossing his arms over his chest.

"I take it you've never been in a man's bedchamber before."

Pressing her lips together, she shook her head back and forth slowly.

"Ah." He raised his brows. "Well, it's been several seconds and I haven't ripped your clothes off and ravished you yet."

"Max!" she choked, her eyes widening.

He laughed and gestured to one of the chairs. The room was large, meant to be a full apartment rather than just a guest bedchamber. "Sit down. I'll stoke the fire."

Like an automaton, she walked toward the chair and bent her body into it. He lowered himself in front of the hearth. When the fire was going, he rose and turned toward her. Her face glowed with a pearly sheen in the firelight.

"You're so pretty," he murmured.

She was. Slender and elegant, so small that the richly upholstered chair dwarfed her. Her complexion was so smooth and pale, and her blue eyes...

He closed his own eyes. As much as he'd like to, he wouldn't tear those wispy clothes away and jump on top of her like some hairy barbarian. She deserved far more than that. She deserved respect; to be sheltered, cradled, and protected. Worshipped.

He took a deep breath and opened his eyes, turning his head to find her watching him.

"I'm sorry to disturb you. I was just—" She hesitated, and sadness washed over her expression. "I'm sorry," she repeated in a low voice. "I was... lonely."

He understood. All three sisters had felt the countess's tragedy deeply.

"I'm so sorry for your sister's loss."

She gave him a bleak look. "Me, too."

He sank into the chair beside hers, reached out and took her hand. They sat in silence, both of them gazing at the flickering flames of the fire. He held her delicate hand in his own, trying to somehow pass comfort into her.

"Tell me about you," she murmured after several minutes.

"Me?"

"Yes. I want to know more about you. We're always talking about me. I don't know enough about you."

Max hesitated, then rose abruptly. "I need a drink. Would you like one?"

Olivia glanced around. "I suppose so, but are you going downstairs?"

"No. I have a bottle of wine." He went to his bureau, opened the cabinet, and pulled out the bottle he'd stored there, holding it up for her approval.

"Oh," she murmured. "All right, then."

He withdrew a glass, uncorked the wine, and poured. Returning to his seat, he handed her the glass.

"Thank you."

"You're welcome."

"But what about you?"

He shrugged. "I only have one glass. We'll have to share."

She took a sip, staring at him over the rim with that clear, direct gaze of hers. "So are you avoiding my request deliberately?"

"Your request?"

She handed the glass back to him. "To tell me more about yourself."

"Ah. That." He took a hearty swallow of wine. "Perhaps I am."

She nodded but didn't take her gaze off him. "If it makes you uncomfortable, Max, you needn't speak of it."

All of a sudden, and quite surprisingly, he did want to tell her about those things he usually tried to shove out of his thoughts, out of his life. All those memories he never spoke of to anyone.

He took another deep swallow, draining the glass. He rose and went to refill it. She watched him in silence.

How was it that she knew how to get to him? How to insinuate herself under his skin so permanently that he felt her even when she wasn't in the same room as him? How did she know the right words to say, the right expressions to make, to affect him in this way?

When he returned to his chair, he smiled at her. "I will tell you anything you want to hear. But talking about myself is something I generally try to avoid."

"I understand."

"What do you want to know?"

"Do you have brothers and sisters?"

He would have... if—

"No," he said.

She hesitated before asking, "Will you tell me about your parents?"

"They're dead."

"I'm so sorry," she said softly. "What were they like? Do you remember them?"

Good God. This was harder than he'd thought it would be. He looked down at the dark liquid in the glass. "My mother was..." He swallowed hard. "She was very beautiful. She died when I was ten years old."

"Oh no. That must be so difficult for a young boy." Reaching over, she covered his hand with hers. "I lost my father when I was nine."

Max nodded.

"How did she die?"

"I don't know... exactly." But he did, didn't he? "It was my father." His voice was low and scratchy. "He... killed her."

The color drained from her cheeks, and her hand tightened over his

"I don't mean... Well, it was nothing overt. He didn't pull out a pistol and shoot her. But he was cruel to her in many other ways, sometimes subtle, sometimes not. I'd watched her since I was a very small boy. Saw how his actions affected her, how she carried his bruises inside and out. How those bruises grew and festered, and eventually killed her. Even though I didn't really understand it at the time, I do now."

"Oh, Max," she whispered.

He looked from the red liquid he was swirling in the glass to her face. Tears welled in her eyes. "Olivia." His voice was gruff. "Don't cry. Please."

She blinked hard, and for a moment, her hand left his while she swiped at her eyes. "I'm sorry. Ignore me."

It was that thing about her, her innate caring and empathy, that made something inside him swell to near bursting. Hell, she'd never even met his mother, and yet here she was, feeling so intensely for her.

She replaced her damp hand over his. He looked down at the slender, pale fingers and his too-big, blunt-tipped, darker fingers beneath them.

He reached up with his thumb and stroked the smooth, warm flesh of her hand.

"My father never loved my mother in the way she deserved to be loved," he said. "After I was born, she lost a few other babies, and he blamed her for it, even though each loss devastated her. He began to ignore her, to hardly spend any time at our home in the country. Whenever he was at home..." Max hesitated, remembering how he'd been hiding in his mother's room once and had watched, terrified, as his father beat her. "He behaved quite brutally toward her. And the women." With a soft groan, he thrust his free hand through his hair. "My father flaunted them. He was...cruel about it."

Max spied that the wine glass was empty. He reached for it. "More?"

Pressing her lips together, she nodded and handed it to him. "Yes, please."

He poured the wine and returned. She gave the glass a baleful look as he gave it to her. "Perhaps you should have just brought the entire bottle."

That made him smile. "Probably."

"What happened to your father?" she asked as he took his seat.

"He died a few years after she did. My father and his brother—my uncle—had a very close but very competitive relationship. Both of them were fascinated by new-fangled devices and the newest inventions, and they bought them all and showed them off to each other incessantly. They shared many of their new toys and trinkets—in fact they shared just about everything except the title. My uncle had the dukedom all to himself, and my father never forgave him for that. He was consumed by jealousy. In the end, I believe his own bitterness killed him."

He passed the glass of wine to her. "Thank you for telling me about your parents, Max. It explains..." She hesitated.

He frowned. "What does it explain?"

"Well...I think it accounts for how gallant and protective you are. You're a champion of ladies now, because you couldn't be one for your mother when you were a boy."

His frown deepened. "I don't know. I've never been a particularly successful champion of anyone." His gaze met hers. "In fact, in most circles, I'm known as a rake and a seducer of women."

She shook her head soberly. "You might have earned

that reputation at one time, but I've met at least one rake, and you're nothing like him. You've been nothing but a champion of me."

"Are you sure?"

He noticed she'd not responded to his reputation as a seducer of women. Could she predict his intentions? Because, damn it, she was in his bedchamber in the middle of the night. Why had she come, unless she wanted something more from him as well? No matter what her intentions were, he couldn't guarantee he wouldn't be doing any seducing tonight.

Her hand, which she'd replaced over his the moment he'd sat down, tightened, squeezing his fingers. "Every word you tell me has been either support or encouragement. I admit to not knowing many men"—she bent her head shyly—"but from what I witnessed during my brief time in London, very few were like you. They analyzed my looks and were either dismissive or flattering based on their assessment of my external attributes. They didn't seem to care what came out of my mouth, as long as whatever it was that I said didn't emerge as overly insightful."

Max chuckled, then sobered. "I've been known to be that way, too," he said. "Just . . . well, just not with you."

She gave him a soft smile. "And my illness . . . it didn't scare you away like it does others. You even . . ." That pink tinge he loved to see returned to her cheeks. "Well, you even kissed me when I was recovering when most everyone, save the closest members of my family, tends to stay as far away from me as possible."

"Why? I can't contract malaria from you."

"I don't know why. Sickness doesn't appeal to anyone, I suppose."

"Well, it certainly *doesn't* appeal to me," he said. "I don't like that it hurts you. But that isn't any fault of yours."

He was shocked that the malaria could lessen anyone's regard for Olivia. Yet, thinking of his peers, he could imagine how some of them might distance themselves from something like that.

He leaned closer to her. "When I look at you, Olivia, I don't see a sick person. . . . I didn't see that even when you were in bed after the fever. I see only a woman." A beautiful, honest, serene woman. "A woman different from any woman I've ever known. You say you're different because of how you grew up in Antigua, yet you're different from your sisters, too."

"Well, unlike my sisters and their friends, I kept indoors most of the time. I rarely went outside, rarely associated with anyone but my family. I suppose that fashioned me into a different sort of person than I might have been otherwise."

The thought of Olivia's free spirit trapped inside for so many years made him ache. "But I imagine you didn't want to stay indoors."

"No, but I had no choice. Long ago, the doctors convinced my mother that if I went out, the resulting fever might kill me."

"So you were her prisoner."

Olivia laughed softly. "That's one way of putting it." She rose and reached for the glass. "I'll fetch some more wine."

He shook his head, instead taking the glass from her and setting it on the small table beside his chair. He reached for her hand, and when she took it, he tugged her toward him.

"Sit with me," he murmured.

She stumbled a little, then sat in an awkward position on his lap. He reached around her and settled her more comfortably against him.

He bent his head into the crook of her neck and breathed her in. So sweet. All freshness and flowers. She was warm but light on his lap. She was so tiny, she made him feel like a giant. He wondered if it had come naturally that she was the tiniest of her sisters or whether the malaria had prevented her from growing as tall as they were. It didn't matter. Her size suited him perfectly.

She snuggled against him, sighing contentedly. The motion had all his senses flaring.

She was an innocent. There was no way she could know what she did to him. But damned if his cock wasn't growing harder by the second.

Turning to him, she reached up to cup his face. "So rough," she murmured.

He closed his eyes as her fingers explored down his jaw, over his chin, and across to the other side. Soft fingertips circled the shell of his ear, making him suck in a breath. And then she touched his lips gently, almost reverently. Opening his eyes, he pressed a kiss to her fingers.

"Olivia," he said on a near groan. "I want you so badly. I've wanted you for so long."

"I've been thinking..." Licking her lips, she hesitated, her eyes meeting his. She whispered, "Well, what it comes down to is...I want you, too."

"Are you sure?"

Slowly, she nodded. "I am. I want this."

She moved her hand away from his lips, pushing over

his cheekbone and threading her hand through his hair until she cupped the back of his head, drawing him closer to her. She was pulling him in for a kiss, he realized. And then sensation washed over him, warm and drugging, as her lips touched his.

Sweet and tentative, but not cowardly. She took the lead, questioning and probing, moving her lips in her own slow rhythm, testing and tasting, one hand behind his head and the other slipping around his side, fingers questing up and down the side of his back.

He felt her shudder in his arms. "So strong," she whispered. "So powerful." And she kissed him again, less tentatively this time.

He felt neither strong nor powerful. He felt enslaved. Completely at the mercy of this beautiful, tiny, strong woman.

His hand stroked over the material of her robe. The dip of her waist, the subtle flare of her hip, the smooth contours of her body inflamed him, made him ache for more. For all of her.

He found the hem of her nightdress at her thigh, and realized that the dress must've hiked up when she'd sat on his lap. Moving his hand lower, he touched her knee, then cupped the rounded back of her bare calf. His breath hitched—she was so utterly slender and smooth.

Then he noticed that she'd stopped breathing altogether. She'd stopped kissing him, too, though her lips were still pressed against his.

"Tell me to stop," he whispered against her lips.

"What?" Her voice was breathy and high. Was she panicking?

"I still want you. So much, it's nearly killing me. But I should stop. Tell me to stop."

She pulled back. "Why should you stop, Max? I already told you it's what I want."

His hand stilled on her calf but didn't leave it. "I shouldn't... I don't want to compromise you. I don't want you to regret..."

"Shh." She pressed a finger to his lips. "I'll have no regrets."

He squeezed his eyes shut. "It's the wine speaking." She'd had at least two glasses—maybe more. His own memory was fuzzy. Certainly she wasn't accustomed to drinking potent wine, and she was so slight, even a small amount would affect her.

She was drunk, she wasn't thinking, she'd regret this— He dragged his hand off her leg.

"It's not the wine." She brought her hands up and held his face between her palms. "Look at me."

He opened his eyes.

"The wine did not affect my decision."

"Are you sure?"

Gravely, she nodded.

"I want you, Olivia."

"I want you, too. So badly."

He shook his head, hopelessly confused but at the same time completely bewitched. His heart was hammering. His cock was like a steel pike. Just the thought of her flesh bared, of her mouth open in ecstasy...

"Olivia." It was a groan of agony, of prayer, of need.

In response, she shrugged the robe off her shoulders and reached down to untie the belt. It fell over his legs. Now all that separated his flesh from hers was the single flannel layer of her nightgown.

She reached up and pulled the string, letting the gown

gape open at the neck, revealing the creamy swell of her breasts. Slowly, Max bent down and pressed his lips to the curve of her breast.

Warm, soft, and sweet. The three adjectives that best described her.

Sighing, she arched back, giving him better access to her breasts. He cupped the swell through the material but nudged it aside with his lips, finding her nipple and taking it into his mouth. She made little panting noises, and her fingers tightened, her nails biting into the flesh of his back.

Her nipple responded to his ministrations, tightening and budding. He suckled, then circled it with his thumb while his lips explored the rest of her breast and higher, over her collarbones and up her jaw until he found her lips again.

He kissed her gently, then stood, lifting her. He walked toward his bed, and set her down at its foot. Kneeling, he grasped the hem of her nightgown and lifted slowly, dragging his fingertips over her shins, knees, and thighs. When the fabric snagged at her bottom, he hesitated and looked into her eyes.

"Tell me one more time," he said. "Tell me you want this."

She licked her lips. "Must I be naked?" she asked in a voice so thin it barely resembled a whisper.

"No."

She stared at him.

"You don't need to be naked, Olivia. But I'd very much like to see your body. To touch it."

Her eyes drifted shut. "Yes. I want that, too."

His lips twitched into a smile. "Good."

He raised the nightgown over her buttocks, hips, waist, and breasts. She reached around and grasped the hem, helping him pull the garment over her head. When it was off, she tugged it over her arms and tossed it away. Then, fists clenched, she lay back stiffly, straightened her arms at her sides, and gazed at him.

He could stand and stare at her all day. In the yellow-gold light of the fire, she was perfection. No harsh edges and rough corners like he had. She was all smooth roundness and curves, more so than he could have ever imagined with her clothes on. Her flesh was an even color—pale ivory—and flawless. He could see hints of her hipbones, collarbones, and ribs, but she wasn't so thin that any of them jutted out.

"God, you're perfect," he murmured.

She shuddered.

"And cold." He groaned softly. "I'm sorry." He gathered her into his arms, pushed back the blankets and laid her down, then went in beside her before pulling the covers up to their chins.

She turned to him, tucking her body against his. Her skin was cool against his heat. Her hands roamed over him, learning his body's contours, until she reached the waistband of his trousers. "Take them off."

It was a whispered command, but it surprised him nonetheless. Despite her smallness and her innocence, Olivia proved over and over that she was no coward.

Without a word, he complied, unbuttoning them, then kicking them off and tossing them onto the floor to join her nightgown.

When he turned back to her, she was staring up at him, wide-eyed. "I'm naked. In bed. With a gentleman."

"A gentleman who wants you. Who..."

Loves you?

Holy hell, was he falling in love with Olivia Donovan? Had he already fallen? Max had never been in love before—he'd actively avoided such irrational entanglements. But was that what this odd, fuzzy feeling was? Was that what made him feel like he wanted to take this woman into his arms and worship her body for the rest of his life?

Whatever this feeling was, he didn't want it to stop.

"I want you, too," she whispered.

He pushed a stray strand of bronzed blond hair away from her face so he could see it. Then he moved his hand down her side, past the dip of her waist and down the front of her thigh until he cupped the curls between her legs. All the while, he watched her eyes widen.

"What do you think is going to happen, Olivia?"

"You're going to...penetrate me," she breathed.

Gently, he pushed his fingers between her legs, stroking her damp, hot folds. "Here."

"Yes," she gasped.

He nudged her until she lay on her back, then he knelt over her, all the while smoothing his fingers over her. He touched her in that most womanly place, finding her hot and wet, feeling smug that he was the only man who'd ever touched her here. And if he had his way, he'd be the only man to ever do so.

The only man.

He couldn't contemplate the significance of that thought—not right now.

He slipped a finger inside her, and her body arched up to meet him. The action made him grind his teeth. She

was so tight. Her body squeezed the length of his finger.
And she was receptive as hell, shockingly so. Passion
glazed her eyes, and her channel clamped over his finger.

He stroked in and out of her, watching her face with
rapt attention. A sheen of perspiration covered her cheeks,
and her blue eyes were bright and needy, staring into his
with such trust.

God, did he deserve such a look? Did he deserve such
a woman?

His body had tightened all over. His cock was so tight
and hard. He was in a precarious position—one light
stroke would set him off.

"Max?"

"Yes, sweetheart?"

She wiggled against his hand. "I need...I should...
We must...Oh..." Her eyes fluttered shut as he pushed
his finger into her.

"Oh," she whispered. "I never knew...I couldn't
imagine...But..."

"Shh," he murmured. "Stop talking. Just enjoy it."

"But...But..." She opened her eyes, and even as she
pushed against his finger, and even though her voice croaked
with dismay, she said the words that nearly killed him.

"Max...you must stop."

Chapter Eight

Olivia watched Max draw away from her, not only physically, but his expression, too, turned still and then shuttered.

"No," she murmured as an ache for his touch swelled within her body. "No...I meant..."

"What did you mean?" His voice was gentle enough, but it held a flatness that hadn't been there before.

"I meant...Well..." She swallowed hard. How did men and women discuss such things? It was one thing to be so intimate with a man, although even when she didn't seem to know what to do, her body did. But to find the words to speak about such intimacy seemed a thousand times more difficult.

He lay on his side, supporting his upper body on his forearm as he watched her patiently. Yet a muscle worked in his jaw.

"You're angry with me," she whispered.

Releasing a harsh breath, he rolled onto his back. "No, Olivia."

"I'm so sorry," she said, choking back a moan. "I've ruined it, haven't I?"

He remained silent.

"I didn't want to stop," she said. "I just...Well... well, we're not married, Max. And I'm...I'm afraid. I do want you—desperately—but I don't want this to result in a child out of wedlock." She hesitated. He didn't move, didn't speak. His chest—his beautifully golden and muscular chest—rose and fell as he breathed.

Finally, he turned his head toward her. "If we ever engage in carnal relations, Olivia, I'll do whatever I can to prevent conception. Unfortunately, nothing is guaranteed."

Olivia pressed her lips together and then nodded. "And what if I do conceive?"

Max rolled back onto his side to face her. "I'd marry you, of course. I'd take care of you, and of our child."

"Would you?" she asked. "Many men wouldn't. And...you're going to be a duke someday..."

"Ah, but remember—you yourself said that I am not like most men. Not with you."

She already knew that he wasn't like other men, and she believed him. "I trust you," she whispered, and burrowed into his arms, thinking of the way he'd said "our child." Not "*your* child" but "*our* child."

He took her into his arms willingly, and she felt the press of his lips on her head.

"Did you doubt me?" he murmured.

"I didn't know whether men ever thought about such things," she said, her voice muffled against his muscled chest. "It's chiefly considered to be the woman's responsibility, is it not?"

"No. It's my responsibility. And it's one I will uphold."

She smiled against his skin. "It's mine too, though. It would change my life, after all."

He said nothing, but his arms tightened around her.

"My sister said you must withdraw—"

"Your sister?"

"Yes."

He pulled back to look down at her, aghast. "You told her about us? You told her that you intended...?"

"I told her I was considering engaging in carnal relations with you."

He groaned. "You make it sound as though you two were discussing what you should have for dinner."

"Well...it wasn't quite like that."

"Which of your sisters was it?"

"Meg."

He bowed his head, releasing a slow breath against her scalp. "I suppose this means I can expect a challenge from Stratford tomorrow morning."

"Of course not!" she exclaimed. "My sisters and I are very close. I must talk to them about such things. How else could I learn about the things in the world that are most important to know?"

"Most young ladies wouldn't ask at all."

"But these are things everyone should consider, don't you think?"

"Yes, I do."

Olivia sighed with contentment. They held each other in comfortable silence. Olivia drank him in—the hard maleness of him, the clean smell of him, the warmth emanating from his skin.

"Max?"

"Hm?"

"I was scared for a moment when I wanted to talk to you about this. But you listened to me. You stopped what we were doing, and you didn't judge or become angry. And it seemed like you'd...well, you'd progressed quite far. I wasn't sure if you *could* stop, even though I'd asked you to."

"I didn't want to stop, Olivia. It was difficult, because you're right about me having progressed far." He frowned. "When a man reaches a certain point, it's painful to stop."

"Oh, dear. Did I cause you pain?"

He shrugged. "It wouldn't matter even if you did. I'd never press if it was something you didn't want."

"I did want it, though...I just...well, I wanted to thank you." She gave him a shy smile. "I feel like I can talk to you about anything."

"Like you can talk to your sisters about anything?"

"No, not exactly." Revealing herself to Max was different from revealing herself to her sisters. She'd spoken of carnal relations to Serena, but being with Max, sharing herself with him, was so different. With Max she felt a level of intimacy that didn't remotely reach her relationships with her sisters. "With you...I can be...well... *naked*."

He laughed, and she laughed with him. It was a freeing sensation, confirming her hope that while she might have jolted his body, she really hadn't upset him with her request for him to stop touching her. Although now she wished he'd start touching her again.

"I don't only mean naked on the outside, you know," she admonished with laughter still in her voice.

His lips pressed against her head again. "I know."

His body was flush against hers, his manhood nudging against her hip as it grew larger once again.

She looked up into his eyes. "Do you still want me, Max?"

"I want you every minute of the day, sweetheart. I've wanted you ever since the day I arrived here."

She smiled at the endearment. He was the one with the sweet heart, she thought. In every way.

"I still want you, too," she whispered.

"I suppose we'll have to do something about that, won't we?"

In response, she leaned forward and pressed her lips to his chest. His hands trailed up her spine. When they reached her shoulders, he pushed her gently onto her back once more. He looked down at her through those startling green eyes and smiled.

"Can I kiss you, Olivia? I want to kiss you everywhere. I want my lips to move over every inch of your body. I want to taste you. To know you."

As he spoke, he began, moving from her cheeks and nose, and lower, his lips a tickling caress down her neck and across her collarbones.

Olivia's muscles stiffened with anticipation as he drew closer to her breasts. And then his lips traveled up the curve of one and settled on the tip. It felt as though his lips connected her to a stream of warm light that traveled from her breast and wended its way through her, leaving heat and something else. Something that made her want to squirm out of her skin.

Need. That was it.

If he sank to his knees and worshipped her breasts, it wouldn't have been any more compelling. He cupped them in his big palms and moved from one to the other, kissing, licking, sucking. The band of warm light grew stronger, more powerful, until her toes curled and she trembled from head to foot.

"Max," she breathed. "I ... I need ..."

"What, sweetheart?" he murmured against her nipple. The vibrations of his voice against her made her arch her back up until he'd captured the hardened nub between his lips. "What do you need?"

"I ... don't know. I need ..."

She gasped as he tugged lightly on her nipple. "I need something, but I haven't the faintest idea what it is."

He left her breast and in the next moment he'd pressed himself between her legs. His mouth rested at the top of her most private part. She gasped, her legs stiffening, her hands automatically reaching down to hide the area from his gaze. From his lips.

He kissed her fingers, gently nuzzling them away. "I want to taste you, Olivia. Let me."

"You mean ... ?" Raising herself on her elbows, she stared at him in complete shock. Was this part of carnal relations? How could it be that no one had told her? How could it be that she'd never even imagined such a thing?

"Will ... you like doing that?" she breathed.

He looked up at her, his green gaze sparkling and positively sinful. "I'll enjoy every moment. I promise."

"But ... will I enjoy it?"

He nodded soberly. "I think you'll enjoy it very much. If it doesn't give you pleasure, all you need to do is tell me to stop. All right?"

"All right." Her voice sounded very small. She lay back, closed her eyes, and forced her hand to slide away.

Her body still hummed with the effects of his ministrations on her breasts. She was tense and warm and nervous and excited—she felt like a compact bundle of tightly contained energy on the verge of exploding into a million pieces.

He pressed kisses down until he was fully settled between her legs. But she hardly knew—or cared—where he'd settled. She grabbed handfuls of the covers and ground her teeth so she wouldn't cry out from the pleasure of his lips and his tongue moving over the most wickedly sensitive part of her body.

"Oh," she murmured. "Oh. My. Goodness."

Then she couldn't even speak. For many minutes, the heat filtering through her sped up and flushed through her until her every nerve buzzed. And suddenly, sensation poured through her, so intense and so overwhelming, she couldn't move, couldn't vocalize a cry. Her body undulated under Max's hands and mouth as the fiercest pleasure Olivia had ever known swept through her.

She came back to awareness for moments at a time, each one stretching longer until she could take a breath. Then she shuddered, suddenly cold. Max was instantly over her, his warm body covering hers.

"You came," he murmured.

"Did I? Was that what that was? An...orgasm?"

"You tell me." His body was sliding against hers, the long length of him rigid against her thigh.

"Yes," she breathed weakly. "I think it was." Serena had told her about orgasms once, back in Antigua what seemed like eons ago.

He smiled down at her.

"You look quite self-satisfied," she murmured.

"I am."

His smile faltered, and she saw that he was gritting his teeth. "Is something wrong?"

"Very," he said quietly, shifting ever so subtly so she could feel the hard ridge moving against her skin. "I need you now, Olivia."

She released the bedcovers she'd been clutching and slipped her arms around him. "Then let me give you what you need."

He reached down and adjusted himself between her legs. She looked into his face, into his eyes. Feelings flooded through her: trust, admiration, respect...love. She wanted him. Wanted *this*.

He gazed back at her, his crystalline green gaze boring into her with intensity that sent bright little tingles beneath her skin.

He held himself there at her opening. On the verge of something monumental. Life-changing. She could feel his need for her—his body vibrated with it. Yet he hesitated.

"This will hurt you," he whispered.

She arched her body, welcoming him inside. "I don't care."

Slowly, he pushed into her. At first, it didn't hurt at all. She felt utterly, wickedly stretched, but it didn't pain her. And then pressure built until it seemed impossible he could continue on, but his progress, though slow and steady, didn't falter.

Then the pain came on the heels of the pressure. Olivia gritted her teeth. He wasn't breaking her, wasn't tearing her apart. This was a natural thing, to lose one's virginity. It would change her permanently, but it surely wouldn't do permanent damage.

And then he sank deep, breaching her fully, and she

tried to stifle a whimper. There was more than just the pain—far more. There was pleasure, too. The feeling of being filled, of her sensitive tissues being stroked in a way they'd never been touched before. The feeling of Max, all around her, gentle and yet so masculine. She wanted him to move again. She wanted to feel the press of him inside her. She wanted...more.

He groaned softly. "I've hurt you."

She didn't want to lie to him. She didn't want to describe the pain, either. Although her orgasm had taken away the sharp edge of her longing, it was still there, lush and warm, and so she said the only thing she could: "Don't stop, Max. Please, don't stop."

He released a relieved breath and moved tentatively inside her, tilting his head as if to ask her permission to continue.

"It's better now," she murmured, and it was the truth. The pain was still there, but the other sensations were beginning to dwarf it—the sensations of a man inside her. Max inside her, stroking her in her most intimate place, and all through her. He seemed to touch every part of her from the top of her head to her toes, including her heart. And her soul.

His eyes glittered as he looked down at her, as pleasure washed through his expression.

"So sweet," he murmured. "So tight."

His thrusts quickened until the velvet slide of his body through hers made her gasp—not with pain but with pleasure.

His movements became stronger, more forceful. His tension became a palpable thing, his body all taut muscle beneath her hands. Strength. Power.

His arm muscles flexed and tightened on either side of her, and he seemed to grow inside her. She was surrounded, encompassed by his masculinity, by his virility.

He rocked harder over her, faster, and then every one of his muscles tightened impossibly, and he jerked out of her, gathered her in his arms, and rolled to his side, holding her tight against him.

He groaned low in his throat, and she felt the warm damp of his release against her thigh. Wave after wave rocked his body until he shuddered and relaxed deep into the bed, keeping her locked against him.

"Beautiful Olivia," he murmured. "So sweet. So damn beautiful."

He sounded half asleep, but he also sounded happy. She knew she'd just pleased him greatly. And that simple fact made her happy.

With pleasure and contentment rippling through her, she drifted off to sleep.

Max awoke with a jolt. The pale gray light of early dawn had just begun to filter through the curtains. The heaviness against him shifted, and he looked down at Olivia.

His chest clenched. She was pressed up so tightly against him, he couldn't see much beyond her delicate profile and the red-gold hair that fanned out over the sheet.

So beautiful.

She'd given him the precious gift of her virginity last night. He didn't know why she'd chosen him to be the recipient of that gift, but he was damned thankful for it. And he wouldn't forget it.

He moved a strand of hair away from her face, and with great reluctance, he murmured, "Olivia?"

"Mmm."

She snuggled more tightly against him, and within a moment she sighed deeply, asleep again.

"Olivia, sweetheart. It's almost morning."

After a long pause, he heard a murmured, "Noooo..."

"I know."

She slipped her arm around him and looked up at him, blinking sleepy blue eyes at him. "I like sleeping with you so much. It's so warm and comfortable."

"I like sleeping with you, too."

She rolled her shoulders, stretching, then glanced in the direction of the window. "I should be rushing out of here, terrified that someone might catch us. But do you know what? I feel like one minute longer with you would be worth it."

"Mmm. Me too." He bent toward her, inhaling the fresh smell of her hair.

She sighed, long and low. "But that's selfish, isn't it?"

"I wouldn't have thought so."

"My family would be mortified. And furious with you."

He chuckled. "I thought you'd told them your intentions." That thought was deuced uncomfortable. He'd never had a brother or sister, so he could only imagine the potential intimacy between siblings. He'd never thought a sibling relationship could be *that* close, though.

"Only Meg. And even she wouldn't approve of me flagrantly revealing the fact that I've spent the night in your bed in her house."

He shrugged. "I have no hope of ever understanding her point of view." If Olivia was his sister, and she'd spent the night with a man—

Well, that thought was far, *far* too disturbing. He flung it away.

Olivia rose, clutching the sheet to her chest. She caught his gaze lingering there, probably caught the wicked glint in his eye, because she laughed softly.

He raised his hand and stroked a finger down her cheek. "Are you sore from last night?"

She looked at him through her lashes with a shy expression that squeezed his heart. "A little."

He sat up, hooked his hand around the back of her neck, and drew her face toward his for a soft kiss before he pulled away, allowing her to decide whether to stay or go.

She looked straight at him, her blue eyes clear. Then she glanced down to his lap and back into his eyes again. She bit her lip, then let it roll under her teeth before she spoke. "Do you think...Can we do it again before I go?"

Max hadn't expected that—at all. He sucked in a harsh breath, because her words had an instantaneous effect on his body. His cock, which was already hard, pulsed. His skin prickled, his body recalling his release last night.

He'd been so enthralled by the experience of bedding Olivia Donovan that he'd almost forgotten his promise to do whatever he could to prevent conception. He'd managed to tear himself away from her at the last possible moment, but doing so had nearly killed him.

"I'd like that," he said solemnly. "More than anything in this world." Yes, he needed one more taste of her. One more time.

She lay back and raised her arms to him, welcoming. Gently, he moved one of her hands downward, until her fingers skimmed his cock.

"Oh," she murmured.

"Wrap your hand around it," he said gruffly.

The touch of her cool fingers, so hesitant as they curled around him, was excruciating pleasure while at the same time an excruciating tease.

Gritting his teeth, Max guided her hand through the motion that mimicked the glide that his cock had made last night when stroking through her body. She concentrated hard, staring at her work, though she could only see the shape of him in her hand beneath the covers.

She glanced up at his face and tightened her fingers over him as she slid her hand downward. "Oh," she murmured, "you liked that."

"I did," he agreed without opening his clenched teeth.

Squeezing him tightly, she pulled back upward, this time swiping her thumb over the crown as she reached the top, watching his expression intently as she did so.

He lay on his side and allowed her to torture him with pleasure for a few more moments. She stroked him up and down, learning from the expressions on his face and the small noises he made what he liked most.

Hell...she was a fast learner. He was going to burst if she kept this up.

"I want to see," she said softly.

He opened his eyes and met her blue gaze. "You could command me to jump..." He sucked in a breath as she slid her hand downward once more, her fingertips skimming over his ballocks. "...jump off a cliff right now... and I'd gladly go."

She grinned. "Is this how to control a man?"

"Not... 'a man,' " he corrected. "Me. And hell, Olivia. All you really needed to do was...ahhh—" He let out a strangled groan as she pulled back upward, squeezing. He felt the tightness in his lower back—the sign that always told him when his release was imminent.

"What?" she whispered. "What did I need to do?"

"Just smile at me. That's...ah...all you had to do. One smile and I was...lost."

She tugged on his cock one more time, seeming to pull the release straight from him. "No," he ground out. "Not yet."

He removed her hand from him, then murmured, "Go onto your hands and knees, sweetheart."

Her eyes widened, but she nodded. He took a moment to gaze at the curtains of hair falling down the sides of her face, the smoothness of her spine and back, and the tight roundness of her behind. He trailed his fingers along her pale, even skin from her neck down to her bottom, cupping one smooth cheek in his palm.

"You're perfect," he murmured. He lowered his fingers between her legs, feeling the subtle tremble of her skin beneath him. "Don't be afraid," he murmured. "This will feel good." His worries were allayed when he found her wet and ready for him.

He stroked her until she was panting and thrusting her body back against his fingers, then he aligned himself with her entrance and slowly pushed himself in.

God, it was heaven. She was so warm, so tight, clasping him like a hot, wet glove. "I'm not going to last, Olivia."

Her only response was a push against him, seating him all the way inside her. He held there for a moment, his eyes closed in pleasure at the feel of her velvet clasp over him.

He held her hips and pulled out and then in, a rhythm as slow and old as time. But after only a few strokes, that feeling welled from the base of his spine, and he knew he couldn't control it this time. His thrusts became harder, frantic. Release pooled low in his cock, and then—

Still gripping her hips tightly, he pulled out of her and pressed himself against her behind as his orgasm tore out of him. She pushed back, exerting just the right amount of pressure to make him groan. It seemed to go on forever. He thought he'd given everything last night, but this morning he came and came until he was spent. When it stopped, he collapsed to the side of her, pulling her against him, feeling the slickness of his release between them.

He bent down to kiss her head. "Thank you."

"Mmm," was all she said in response.

He lay for a few minutes, gathering his strength. Then he rose, yanked on his trousers, and stumbled to the basin. He wet a towel and, warming it between his hands, he returned to her.

She jumped a little when he pressed it against her back. "Shh," he said. "Just lie there, sweetheart. Let me take care of you."

Carefully, he swiped the cloth over her skin and between her legs, cleaning her gently and thoroughly. When he finished, he fetched her nightgown and helped her put it on, tying it at the neck in a bow like she'd had it last night.

She glanced down then back up at him. "Thank you for last night," she said quietly. "Thank you for this morning."

He nodded, suddenly not able to find words to answer her. And then, as he watched her leave him, something strange lurched in his chest.

He didn't like watching her walk away.

Chapter Nine

Olivia went to Max's bed every night for a week, but then her courses arrived, and for the next few nights, when she went to his room they only held each other. And talked. They talked for hours on end—about their pasts, their hopes, their beliefs, and their dreams for the future.

Autumn had given way to the short, cold days of winter. Olivia ignored the cold as much as she could, and she continued to take her walks whenever the weather came close to permitting it, and Max often joined her.

On their walk the day before yesterday, Max finally told her exactly why he never intended to marry. He explained how he'd always been terrified that if he married, he'd become just like his father.

"But why?" she had asked. "Do you think you won't be faithful?"

He shrugged. "I've never felt any compulsion to be faithful to a woman, until now."

The offhand admission had surprised him, and he'd

stared at her for a long moment, the expression in his eyes undecipherable. It hadn't surprised her. Even though they hadn't really been with other women besides her sisters and Beatrice, his focus had been entirely on her. And she could say with some measure of confidence that he hadn't thought of anyone else since he'd arrived in Sussex.

"And you would never abuse a woman like your father did," she added.

"Never," he said through gritted teeth.

"So what have you to worry about, then?" she asked, although a part of her wondered why she was pursuing this line of questioning—why would she encourage him to marry when it was obvious he could never marry her?

He looked away from her, his gaze seeming to search through the trees. "There's a violence in me, Olivia. A rage I sometimes cannot control. I could never expose an innocent woman to that. I couldn't live with myself if I did."

She glanced at him, surprised. She'd never seen him angry. Dismayed and frustrated, perhaps, but never in a rage. "I don't understand," she said softly. "That's not you, Max."

"But it is me. A part of me I pray you'll never see."

Something in her chest had tightened into a knot.

Today was blustery and cold, but sunny enough. Olivia had spent most of the night with Max, and she'd slept in this morning. Her maid, Smithson, told her that Serena, Phoebe, and Jessica had all gone to Lady Fenwicke's house for a visit, and the men were off hunting. But when she came down to breakfast, Max was reading the newspaper at the breakfast table, a cup of steaming coffee in front of him.

He rose when she entered the room. "Miss Donovan." He smiled at her, his green eyes twinkling.

"Good morning, my lord."

She sat, feeling suddenly shy. It felt so awkward to speak to him outside of the privacy of his room or their walks. She must pretend he was simply a friend, and it made her uncomfortable. A silly, wanton part of her wanted to sit in his lap and smack a kiss on his cheek. But a servant or someone else could walk in at any time, and she just couldn't allow herself that level of unseemliness. Not in her brother-in-law's house.

Max's low, silky voice washed over her. "So you slept late this morning, too?"

Turning from the sidebar, she raised her brows at him. "I did. I was told the men had already gone off hunting."

"They did. I woke too late and discovered they'd gone without me."

She gathered her plate and sat across from him, nodding at the footman who came to offer her chocolate. "And my sisters went to Lady Fenwicke's house."

Max folded his paper and looked at her. The corners of his mouth lifted upward in a smile. "It's just you and me, then."

Oh, there was so much sin buried within that seemingly innocuous statement that a delicious shiver rushed through her.

She cocked her head. "Perhaps I can interest you in a walk after breakfast, my lord?"

He chuckled low and nodded, as if to say, *I'd had other plans—wicked plans—but I suppose a walk will do.*

She returned his smile, and they simply sat for a long moment, grinning at each other. Anyone who walked into the room at this moment could see very well what besotted loons they'd become.

She broke the look first, conscious of the servant who'd just walked into the room to bring her chocolate and to refresh the dishes at the sideboard. She gazed down at her cup, circling its rim with her fingertip. Finally, she looked up at him.

"Tell me, my lord, where in England did you grow up?"

"Not too far from here. In Hampshire. My uncle's seat, Forest Corner, is located there."

"So you spent your childhood there?"

"After my mother died, my father spent most of his time at my uncle's house. My cousins lived there, too. During my years at Eton, it was where I returned during school holidays."

"A place to go," she murmured, "but not home."

"Not home," he agreed softly. He took a contemplative sip of his coffee. "Forest Corner is a vast, cold place. It's scrubbed until it shines daily. It was entirely different from the house my mother kept. Entirely different from this house, for that matter. Every carefully rendered detail is for aesthetics rather than comfort."

"I understand. It does sound cold. And yet it will belong to you someday, won't it?"

"I suppose it will."

"But you said you had cousins. Are they all girls?"

"No. My uncle fathered one daughter and two sons, and all three died of influenza one year. The eldest of them was twelve, the youngest was six. Their mother caught it too. I'd been gone at Eton that autumn, and when I arrived at Forest Corner for the winter holiday, they were all...gone."

"Oh," Olivia murmured, "how horrible."

"Yes." There was a hint of desolation in Max's expression as he gazed down at his coffee cup. He grasped it between both palms. "It was a long time ago...but my cousins were my closest companions during my childhood. I miss them."

"I'm so sorry, Max. I can't imagine." A part of her felt hollow inside, thinking about how much loss this man had suffered. At least he still had one family member remaining. "What about your uncle? Did he take you under his wing after that happened?"

Max pressed his lips together and shook his head grimly. "Not at all. He never believed I could be as good a Duke of Wakefield as Charles or Henry." He took a slow breath, then looked up at her. "He told me once that he wished it was me who'd died rather than his sons."

She flinched, but he shrugged. "I cannot blame him, really. He lost two sons, a daughter, a wife...I never wanted a dukedom, and I wasn't raised to be a duke. But Charles and Henry were his heir and spare—both born and raised to perform the job."

Olivia nodded.

"My uncle was in London when they became ill. He was in Town with my father and their mistress."

"Their mistress?" Olivia repeated, her eyes widening.

He nodded, then swallowed the rest of his coffee. "Yes." His voice lowered. "I told you they shared almost everything, didn't I?"

Olivia couldn't do anything but stare at him, completely aghast.

"When I was nineteen," Max said softly, "I called my uncle to task for that and for his many other crimes against his family while they were alive. We haven't spoken since then."

"Oh Max. I'm so sorry. That is a horribly tragic story...." With a horribly tragic ending.

"It was a long time ago. Most of it happened almost twenty years ago. The years since haven't been all bad."

"Well, I think the years have treated you quite well," she said before she could think to recall the words. Her face went instantly hot, and she realized that she'd called him by his first name, too. And in the presence of a footman standing near the door.

"Care to explain what you mean by that?" Max drawled.

She sent a quick glance to the footman, who stared straight ahead. Then she narrowed her eyes, ever so subtly, at Max and said, "Well, you've told me you spent many happy years in London doing..." Doing what? She gave an offhand flick of her wrist. "Whatever it is that men do."

"Mmm, yes, very true, Miss Donovan."

She looked down at her empty plate. The toast she'd buttered at the sideboard was long since gone. She placed her napkin on the table and rose. Max's chair scraped against the floor as he rose along with her.

"Please excuse me, my lord. I'll go upstairs and prepare for our walk." She'd asked Smithson to ready her bath while she was having breakfast. She'd be quick about that, then change into her walking clothes so she didn't keep him waiting too long.

"Please," he said with utter straight-faced politeness, "allow me to escort you upstairs."

The mere idea that he'd "escort her upstairs" to her bedchamber made her blush deepen. He walked around the table and held out his arm for her. When she took it, he pulled her against his body—a touch more tightly than was strictly polite—and she felt him shaking with laughter. As they exited from the breakfast room, she sent a glare up to him that promised retribution.

When they were out in the corridor, he lost the battle with his twitching lips and broke into a broad grin. He bent his head down and whispered into her ear, "You're adorable, Olivia."

"And you're wicked," she said primly. But she was fighting a smile herself.

"Hm...and what, pray, did you really mean when you said the years have treated me well?"

"You know very well what I meant," she hissed as they turned the corner to mount the curving staircase. "I meant you're enormously, impossibly handsome, of course."

"I'm glad you think so." His expression was smug, and she couldn't help it. She had to physically restrain herself from pressing her lips to those deep, delectable dimples of his and kissing that expression off his face. Turn it into one of desire. Of need.

She shuddered. She'd thought she'd hidden it, but he tensed against her. "What is it, sweetheart?"

"Max," she groaned softly as they reached the top of the stairs. "Please. We can't talk this way. Not anywhere but in your—" She broke off.

He raised a brow. "In my bedchamber?"

"Yes."

And they were approaching *her* bedchamber. She slowed her step, drawing her arm from his. "Thank you for walking me up here."

Max looked pointedly at the door, and she leaned on

her tiptoes and whispered, "You *cannot* come inside. My maid is in there!"

Max sighed. "Unfortunate," he murmured. Then he bowed. "I'll see you downstairs, then?"

"Yes. In an hour?"

"Of course."

He bowed, and when she opened the door he gave her a nod and turned away. As she walked inside, clicking the door shut, she saw a final glimpse of his tall, broad form retreating down the corridor.

Smithson helped her remove her clothing and take down her hair, and Olivia stepped into the tub. She sank deep into the piping hot water on a sigh.

"Would you like me to wash your hair for you, miss?" The young maid's freckled face swam in front of her half-lidded gaze.

"No, no, that's all right. You may go. I'll call when I'm ready for you."

"Yes, miss."

She heard the click of the door as the maid left, and sank deeper into the water. It was tempting to relax until the water was lukewarm, but she couldn't dally today. She took the soap and washcloth from the small bronze tray left on the table beside the bath. When the cloth was fully lathered, she started at her feet and had begun to work her way upward when she heard the click of the door again.

"What is it, Smithson?"

"Who's Smithson?" asked a very low, decidedly male, voice.

She whipped her head around, holding the washcloth to her chest. It did little good covering her, considering that it was nothing more than a tiny square of cloth.

"Max," she breathed out. "What on earth...?"

He was standing in the center of her room, calmly removing his coat. "I thought there ought to be more locations where we can speak freely with each other." He looked up from his task for a moment to give her a lopsided grin. "This seems like a good place to start. And when you opened the door to come here, I saw the bathwater steaming up behind you." He shrugged out of the coat. "Did you think I'd be able to resist?"

Before she could say a word, he'd untied the string at his neck and had pulled his shirt off, leaving his torso deliciously bare.

"Max!" she squeaked. Good heavens. It was broad daylight. There was no lock on her door. Her sisters and the gentlemen could return anytime, although she didn't expect them until later this afternoon. But servants could—and would—walk in at any moment. "You can't...someone might...oh..."

She still held the cloth against her chest. It was growing cold, and she looked down at it hopelessly. In two strides, he'd approached the tub and knelt at its side.

"Allow me." He gently pried the cloth from her resisting fingers and turned to resoap it.

"A servant could—"

"Don't worry," he said softly. He dipped his fingers in the water, stretched her leg long, and began to wash it.

Oh, Lord. There was something far, *far* more erotic about being cleaned by a handsome, shirtless man than cleaning oneself....

"No one will come in. The chambermaids work on your room in the afternoon, and none of the other servants have any reason to come here, do they?"

"Smithson."

"Ah, the mysterious Smithson." Max's green eyes focused on her, and his hands stopped their gentle ministrations. "My unknown competition. Tell, me, Olivia, does he touch you like I do?"

His tone was jesting, but something in his expression was not.

"Max," she breathed. "Surely you're not jealous. Smithson is the maid!"

His lips twitched. "Ah. The lady's maid. Did you tell her to return?"

"Yes, when I call her."

"Well, then." He raised his brows. "Since I doubt you'll be calling her while I'm here, it seems we're safe. But if you're concerned, I'll block the door with your desk chair."

She glanced at the door, imagining servants hovering outside, gripping the door handle, preparing to open the door. If he slid the chair in front of the door, it would take a few seconds for them to get in. A few seconds in which she could...Do what?

She blew out a breath. "No, that's all right. You're right. No one's coming in here. Not until later."

"Much later," he corrected.

"Yes," she agreed, "much later." She stretched out her other leg in a not-so-subtle hint for him to wash it.

"Good." He went to work, rubbing soapy circles all over her skin. She crossed her arms over her chest and lay back, closing her eyes and sinking into the soft comfort of his strokes. She felt him tugging at her arms, trying to uncross them, and she released them, knowing she was exposing her breasts to him and not caring. In fact, she was curious whether he'd clean them, and if he did, how it would feel.

The cloth moved up her stomach, gentle but not light enough to tickle her. She sighed in bliss. "Mmm, it feels so good when you touch me like this."

"Does it?" he murmured. "I'll do it more often, then."

And then the cloth brushed over her breast. She gasped lightly. He didn't clean the area in smooth, swift strokes. He paid special attention to her breasts, cupping each in his palm, swiping the cloth over it, softly squeezing her nipple between his fingers in that way that made her womb clench with longing.

And then he moved up to her shoulders and neck, exerting a little more pressure with the cloth in this area.

"Sit up and I'll wash your hair."

She hadn't planned to wash her hair, but she didn't resist. She scooted her bottom forward and sat upright. Using the large ladle on the table, he wet her hair and then soaped it. His fingers pressed firmly into her scalp as he rubbed and washed, taking his time to clean each strand.

Closing her eyes, Olivia sighed in pleasure. He left her hair for a moment to wash her back using the same firm strokes that seemed to permeate through her tight muscles and soften them.

"Ooooh," she murmured. "You're going to put me to sleep."

He chuckled softly. "Not precisely my intention."

"No?"

"No." He resumed rubbing her head and then asked her to tilt back so he could rinse. When all the soap was washed away, he rinsed her back, then poured water over her front. As the stream flowed over the sensitized tips of her breasts, she instinctively arched her body for more.

Max didn't hesitate. He refilled the ladle and poured it over her again, sending sensation so deeply through her body that her toes curled.

"Stand up, sweetheart."

"Mmm. All right."

She rose, her legs feeling rubbery, but Max caught her as she wavered, wrapped a towel about her, and lifted her from the tub. She pressed a kiss against his neck as he walked her toward the bed.

"Thank you for that."

"I should thank you."

"You're the one who did all the work."

"I was also the one who was able to see your beautiful body dripping wet." He laid her on the bed. "I don't think I've ever seen anything more arousing."

"I don't think I've felt anything more arousing," she murmured. And she wanted more. She reached both arms up, welcoming him to lie beside her. "There are so many things we've done in the past days that I never dreamed I'd ever have the opportunity to do."

Lying beside her, he pushed a damp strand of hair off her face. "Are you glad to have had the opportunity?"

"So very glad," she said. And she was. Now, she couldn't imagine living her life without the brand of Max's touch on her skin. And it *was* a brand. Invisible to others, but she knew she'd feel it for the rest of her life.

He smiled down at her, but there was a dark edge to his appearance that she noticed for the first time. She hadn't really been studying him in the bath—her eyes had been half-lidded and she'd been so focused on her own pleasure that she hadn't seen what was now so obvious in his expression.

"Max...is something wrong?"

He nodded, and her heart clenched hard.

"What is it?" she breathed.

"I have to leave. I'm needed in London."

She went cold. "No."

"I'm sorry, sweetheart." He took a shuddering breath. "But it's something I can't avoid."

"What is it? Has something terrible happened?"

Leaving the bed for a moment, he retrieved his coat and withdrew a folded sheet of stationery. "A letter from London. It arrived just before I returned to your bedchamber."

Returning to bed beside her, he handed her the letter. She rolled over onto her side and propped herself up on an elbow as she unfolded it.

There wasn't much to it:

Hasley,

I am dying. I'm told, much to my dismay, that it is an event that is likely to occur sooner rather than later. Since you are the wastrel who is to take my title as your own upon my demise, I demand your presence at my London house immediately. I have a great deal of instruction I must impart to you prior to my passing.

Wakefield.

"Oh, Max," she whispered, looking up at him through damp lashes.

Max stared down at the note. "My uncle never speaks to me."

She nodded.

"He never sends me letters." Max's Adam's apple moved up and down as he swallowed. He stared at the letter for a long while, unmoving, unspeaking, and then he said, "Odd that the first time I speak of him in months is the first time I receive any correspondence from him in years."

Finally, Olivia asked, "Is this unexpected?"

"By all accounts, he has been very healthy," Max said. "I assumed he'd live forever—or at least a very long time. I wouldn't have been surprised if he'd outlived me."

"I'm sorry," she murmured.

He still gazed down at the letter, his distress evident from the grooves creasing his forehead and the flat line of his lips. "I must leave immediately. Today."

"Of course you must." A flush of misery washed over Olivia. She didn't want him to leave. But that was utterly selfish. Max's uncle was dying. Max would be a duke soon. This letter meant that his very existence was about to change.

He looked at her, his eyes shining. "I must leave you."

She nodded, for she suddenly couldn't speak. A lump welled in her throat.

It was over. She knew this would happen eventually, and she thought she'd been prepared for it. Yet now that he was really leaving Stratford House, her heart felt cracked and hollow, like it was on the verge of shattering into a million pieces.

Max had been very clear about his intention to never marry. Even if he eventually changed his mind, he'd never consider someone like her. Everyone believed Serena had married far above her station when she'd married an earl. Max would be a *duke*. With new, likely overwhelming responsibilities, not to mention that everyone would have new expectations of him.

She was a nobody, but she would not be his public mistress, so she was destined to remain a simple, short-lived romantic affair. A splash of fun in his otherwise lofty and busy world. A mere memory. As he would be to her.

She burrowed against him. "I don't want you to go."

He drew her into his arms and held her tight.

"But you must. I know you must," she said against the warmth of his chest.

"Yes, I must."

His lips grazed hers, pressing gently at first, then more demanding. Her body, so attuned now to his kisses, flushed. As he worked the front placket of his trousers, tightness gathered in her center. A deep ache—an undeniable need for him she'd grown accustomed to.

His fingers slid down her side to her thigh, then swiped down it. He lifted her leg, and before she could recognize his intention, he pushed inside her, forcing the air from her lungs in a sharp gasp.

But he didn't hesitate. He took her hard, thrusting so deeply within her it felt like he touched her very soul.

She looked up to find him looking down at her, his green eyes narrow and glittering as he thrust again until his pelvis pressed against hers. Sliding her arms around his rock-hard shoulders, she held on. He didn't stop, didn't pause. His body was a long length of steely muscle. He maintained a hard, almost brutal pace, holding her gaze trapped in his. Each thrust sent sensation shocking through her, anything but gentle, anything but delicate.

She reveled in it. Arching into him, she whispered, "Yes, Max. More. Please."

He pistoned in and out of her, his iron length touching every part of her, sending sparks boiling through her from her fingertips to her toes.

Within a few moments, the shudders began. Starting from her womb and spreading outward in a flood of heat—sharp, almost painful ecstasy. Dimly, she felt his arm wrap around her like a steel band. Keeping her pressed against him, safe and secure.

Olivia lost control. She fell headfirst, her body arching with the jolt of the orgasm as it overtook her as thoroughly as if a bolt of lightning had slammed into her body. Infinitely hot, decadently sweet pleasure overwhelmed her. She didn't breathe, didn't make a sound. She couldn't. All she could do was allow it to run its course, infuse every part of her with electric joy. Spots exploded before her closed eyes. She wasn't afraid of falling or of fainting. She wasn't afraid of anything, for she knew Max held her close. Protected her. *Loved* her.

Sensation returned slowly, and she drew in a gulping breath. Only then did she realize that Max had withdrawn.

She looked up at him, realizing her eyes were damp. He brushed a tear away with his thumb and looked down at her, his expression tender.

She blinked. "Did you . . . ?"

"Yes."

"I didn't . . . I was . . . That was . . ."

"I know," he murmured. "For me too. I almost didn't withdraw in time." Sudden concern etched itself across his face, and he frowned. "You would let me know . . . if anything should happen. Wouldn't you?"

She squeezed her arms tighter around him. "Of course."

They lay in silence for a while, their limbs entwined. The heaviness of sleep drifted over her. She knew from experience that falling asleep in Max's arms was a dangerous thing. It was the most relaxed state of sleep she'd ever been in. So many times he'd ended up carrying her back to her bedchamber.

But it was afternoon. Anyone could walk in. Smithson was expecting her to call. Someone would come in to clean the bath...

It didn't matter. All that mattered was that Max was beside her, holding her. So warm and safe and comfortable.

She drifted off.

When she awoke, hours later, he was gone. He'd left a note on the pillow beside her.

> *I couldn't bear to wake you.*
> *I'm going to miss you so much.*
> *Write to me?*
> *M.*

Chapter Ten

London in January was cold, muddy, and dreary. Max understood why the aristocracy tended to flee from Town this time of year. There was a stark beauty, a peace in the country that was absent from the city.

Unfortunately, Max had no choice but to remain in London through the winter. His uncle had died a fortnight ago and had left what seemed like endless work for Max. If Max hadn't felt some pride for his title, some need to do right by it, he would have said let the whole thing rot and he would have gone back to Sussex and to Olivia.

But he couldn't do that. This was out of respect for his cousins, who would have been Duke of Wakefield before him. Who would have been better dukes than he. He couldn't let them down.

So he performed his duty to the best of his ability. His uncle had been bitter and cold to the last, but he'd never-theless done as he'd promised and given Max a brief education in his personal affairs before he'd died. Despite his lingering dislike for the man, Max had given his uncle the funeral and mourning he'd requested and which his title warranted. And he hoped that the old duke was with his wife and children now, his cruel, sad life and all his bitterness forgotten.

Max managed his uncle's affairs, replied to official correspondence, met with political leaders, and tended to the ducal properties that had begun to fall into disrepair with his uncle's illness. He buried himself in the massive amount of work to be done during his transition to the title, but he thought about Olivia every day. He wrote to her, and when he found a letter from her within the piles he received, he always opened it first.

He missed her. Dreadfully. An idea had begun to form in his mind, and as the days and weeks went by and it took shape, he slowly let go of his long-standing plan never to marry. Olivia had proved to him that Max wasn't his father and would never become anything like his father. With Olivia, thoughts of betrayal or violence never surfaced within Max. He was, simply, devoted to her. He always would be.

And a duke needed a duchess, after all.

As the days went by, he formed a new plan. He'd continue to court her, and when spring came, he'd make the courtship official. He hoped he'd be able to convince her family to allow her to come to London while he sat in the Lords this spring. He'd be proper about it. God forbid he brought any scandal to his future wife's door.

He was a patient man, and he'd take the time to court her properly. He admitted to himself that he'd enjoy a spring and summer with her on his arm, presenting her beauty, grace, and goodness to all of London.

When summer came, he'd take her somewhere beautiful—somewhere he'd yet to find—and he'd walk with her. He imagined blooming summer flowers all around them, their heady fragrance surrounding them, the soft drone of insects in the air.

There, he'd go down on one knee and ask her to be his wife. He'd fantasized about the moment often—too often, perhaps. But thoughts of Olivia, of Olivia as *his,* had become his only peace in the near-frantic busyness of his new life.

Sighing, he laid down his pen. Pressing his fingertips to his throbbing temples, he looked up at the old clock on his uncle's—now his—mantel. Hell. It was late, and Max couldn't remember the last time he'd eaten. When a footman had inquired about dinner earlier, Max had just waved him away.

Now, though, his stomach was protesting that decision. Loudly.

Fortunately, the seventeenth-century London town house he'd inherited was only a few streets away from White's, and the thought of food was enough to drive him outside into the chill of the January night.

He walked briskly through the crunchy snow, his head bent against the cold, and arrived at the club in a few minutes. After handing his hat, gloves, and overcoat to the porter, he went upstairs to the dining room for a late hot supper. When he'd finished the meal and his belly was comfortably full, he retired to the club room.

As soon as he'd taken a glass of port and sat in a sumptuously upholstered chair near the fire, he heard a low voice, slurred with drink.

"Your Grace."

He looked up to see the person he least wanted to see in this world: the Marquis of Fenwicke.

He gave a sharp nod as the man sank into the seat opposite him. "Fenwicke."

Fenwicke sighed. As Max observed him more closely, he saw that the man looked quite strained and white-lipped.

"Alas," Fenwicke said bitterly, "you've won."

"I've...won?"

"Doubly."

Max had no damned idea what the man was talking about. He swallowed the last of the port, set it on the side table, and prepared to rise. But Fenwicke's next words froze him.

"Not only have you arisen to the dukedom before me, but you've succeeded in bringing Olivia Donovan to your bed."

Max pressed his lips together. His fingers curled unchecked, but he braced his legs, stopping himself from lunging up and wringing the man's neck. Instead, he asked through clenched teeth, "What, pray, gives you that idea?"

"Well, it's been all over the papers. The old Duke of Wakefield died—"

"Not that," Max snapped. "You know I'm not talking about that." He glanced to the left and right. Damn it— they were surrounded by gentlemen and servants, all of whom pretended to go about their business and not hear a word, but surely someone had heard. Surely someone was listening. Max would be damned if he'd allow Olivia's name to be slurred in public.

Fenwicke chuckled, but the sound held no humor. "Oh, I know. You do recall that we made a wager, do you not?"

Max ground his teeth. So much had happened, so much had changed, that he'd all but forgotten about that stupid wager.

"Well, I couldn't trust only my opponent's word, could I?" Fenwicke shrugged. "I employed someone to watch you."

"At Stratford's house?" Max gritted out. At his sides, Max's fists curled and uncurled.

"Indeed," Fenwicke said. "Now, then—you can see what an honest man I am. You have, indeed, gone even farther than you said you would with our Miss Donovan. You seduced her. Thoroughly. Many times."

Max shook with fury. He'd never been so angry in his life. Red spots fringed his vision. To think that someone had been watching, someone had invaded his time with Olivia, had sullied what they had together—

He was going to kill Fenwicke.

He lunged out of his chair, grabbed Fenwicke by the cravat, balled his fist tightly, and swung a punch at the man's astonished face. Fenwicke's face snapped back, and Max dropped him, already pulling his fist back for another punch. His lip curled. "You bloody bastard."

He swung, but someone grabbed his arm. Well, that was no problem. He wasn't left-handed, but he'd learned long ago how to use his left fist as a weapon. He threw a left-handed hook at Fenwicke, but before his fist reached its target, his arm was yanked backward. People shouted at him, but he didn't give a damn what they were saying. He yanked out of their grasp, only to be caught again. "Damn it," he roared, struggling to get at Fenwicke. "Let me go!"

"Calm down, man!"

He recognized the voice: Captain William Langley,

his fellow guest at Stratford's house. Langley had come to London for the winter to manage his fledgling shipping company.

He'd be an ally. He knew Olivia, knew her loveliness, her sweetness. Max was certain that he would defend her.

Fenwicke was flanked by two men—friends, obviously, because they were puffing their chests at Max as if they expected him to fear them—and holding his hand to his face. A thin line of blood was dripping from his left nostril. *Good.*

Max's lip curled, and he narrowed his eyes at Fenwicke. "You will pay for those words. No one speaks of her like that. No one."

"Damn uncalled-for response, if you ask me," Fenwicke spat at him. "You won the dukedom, *Your Grace.* You won the woman."

"I don't care about the damned bet."

"Bets. That's plural. Don't you remember our youthful bet that I'd be in possession of the title before you?"

"I don't care about any wager I made with you!" Max roared.

"Your uncle has died. You had your host's sister-in-law in your bed again and again—"

Max struggled to get to Fenwicke, to shut him up once and for all. But many hands held him back.

"Enough," Langley growled, growing red in the face.

"I'm supposed to prance about Town in my shirt-sleeves for a full day. If you'll recall, those were the terms of the first bet we made many years ago. And then there's the matter of the thousand guineas I owe you for the second." Fenwick's reptilian eyes slid from Max to Langley and back.

"I don't give a damn about the deuced thousand guineas," Max bit out. And he damn well didn't care how Fenwicke decided to prance about Town.

"Of course you don't, *duke*," Fenwicke sneered. "Now that you're the Duke of Wakefield, it's a mere pittance, I'm sure. But you'll have both your payments. The shirtsleeves tomorrow, though I daresay I'll be frozen solid before dusk. And the thousand . . ." he hesitated, his glance sliding over the assembled crowd, "soon."

That came as no surprise. It had been long rumored that Fenwicke had already spent his own fortune on women and gambling, and his father had cut off his funds long ago.

A low murmur sounded from the crowd at Fenwicke's last declaration. Hearing it, Fenwicke dropped his hand to his coat and straightened it. Max shook himself out of the grip of his captors. The moment of attack was over. At least there was some swelling on the man's cheek. Max hoped he'd sport an ugly black eye for the rest of the month. It would serve the bastard right.

"I shall take my leave, then. Good night." With a short, clumsy bow, Fenwicke turned around and strode away, his drunkenness obvious by the way he weaved through the crowd.

Slowly, the assembled people drifted off, some after having clapped Max on the back and commiserating with him about the marquis's inappropriate drunken behavior. Finally, the only man left was Langley, who was gazing at him in narrow-eyed contemplation.

"More port?" Langley asked as a servant passed behind him, carrying a tray of full glasses.

"Please."

Langley took two glasses from the tray and gestured

with his chin to the seats where Max and Fenwicke had been sitting. "There are a few things I believe we must discuss."

Max sighed. This was exactly what he had least wanted to happen: the details of his relationship with Olivia Donovan becoming public knowledge.

He took the glass and lowered himself into the open seat. "What is it, Langley?" he asked tiredly. He wanted to get away from this place and these people. A trip to Sussex and to Olivia would be ideal, but he'd have to do with his lonely town house.

"What's this about a bet between you and Fenwicke regarding Miss Donovan?"

"It was a moment of stupidity, one that I'd gladly take back."

"What did you bet?"

Max closed his eyes as his stomach churned. "I bet Fenwicke that she'd succumb to my charms before she succumbed to his."

God, if only he could take back that idiotic bet!

He opened his eyes to find Langley giving him such a frigid stare that it would certainly eviscerate him if looks had the ability to kill.

"It was before I knew her," Max said quietly. "It was before I knew any of the Donovan sisters. I promise you, I dismissed the damned bet the moment I made their acquaintance. The Donovans are special, Langley. Especially Olivia. I'd never willingly cause them hurt or embarrassment."

"Looks like you've failed there," Langley said coldly.

"I'm sorry for that. I could kill Fenwicke for that."

"How will you make it up to her, Wakefield?"

Max sighed. "My intentions toward Olivia are purely respectable, I assure you."

"Really?" Langley sipped at his port, watching him over the rim. "What Fenwicke was describing didn't sound in the least respectable."

"Fenwicke is an ass," Max said shortly.

Langley nodded. "True enough. So what are those respectable intentions?"

This was another secret he would have preferred to keep to himself. God, how he hated Fenwicke for what he'd done tonight. There would be consequences, none of which Max could predict. He knew they'd be the subject of gossip, but of what sort he wasn't certain. He had never been much interested in gossip and scandal, and he didn't know exactly how either operated.

"I plan to ask Stratford for permission to court her this spring," he answered Langley. "And in the summer, I intend to propose marriage."

Langley's dark brows rose. "You are aware that Miss Donovan has no connections? Her family isn't old—"

"I know nothing about her family, nor do I care."

"That's short-sighted, Wakefield. Have you forgotten your new position?"

Max snorted. As if he could ever forget it. Even if he did, it seemed there was always a person nearby who'd remind him every few moments. "No, I haven't. Trust me, I won't be the first duke in England's history to marry a commoner."

Surprising Max, Langley's lips cracked into a rare smile. "Well, I can't say I'm not pleased. I fear that any other answers you would have given me tonight would likely have led to a suggestion of pistols at dawn."

"So you've found satisfaction without any violence?" Max asked.

"Not satisfaction, exactly. I can't believe you made

such a wager with Fenwicke—the fact that you did so certainly calls your character into question."

Max couldn't blame Langley for feeling that way.

"I'll be watching you, Wakefield. If you don't propose to Miss Donovan by the end of summer, you'll have me to answer to."

Max raised a brow. Why was this man so invested in the Donovan sisters? "Tell me, Langley, what is the exact nature of your relationship with the Donovans?"

Langley smiled grimly. "You may recall I was once engaged to the countess."

Max shrugged. "I knew vaguely of it, but gossip of that sort doesn't interest me." He took a sip of his port. "What happened?"

"She fell in love with Stratford," Langley said simply.

"And yet you're good friends with them both. Good enough to duel for their sister's honor."

Langley chuckled softly. "It's a long and sordid story, Wakefield. If you do end up marrying Miss Donovan, perhaps you will hear it sometime. But for now, suffice it to say...the countess and I have become friends. Stratford and I remain friends. It's all that matters now."

Observing the still-raw pain in the other man's eyes, Max knew Langley was withholding a great deal. Yet, it wasn't his place to pry. Max raised his glass at Langley. "Don't worry, Captain. It's a new year. And I intend to make Olivia Donovan my wife by the end of it."

A week later, Fenwicke paced his study, hatred burning an acid hole in his chest.

Maxwell Buchanan had become a duke. Surpassed him in status and title.

Worse, infinitely worse, the man had beaten Fenwicke at his own game of seduction. He'd succeeded where Fenwicke had failed.

He'd been so certain Max would fail with Olivia Donovan, just like he had. But he hadn't. The bastard had seduced her. Had touched her, over and over again.

Fenwicke could kill Max for that alone. For touching what he'd considered solely his since the first moment he'd laid eyes on the woman.

He had always despised Maxwell Buchanan. How Max had looked down his nose at him their whole lives. Max had always thought himself better than Fenwicke. Had always thought himself not only intellectually and physically superior, but morally superior as well.

Fenwicke thought of the disdainful press of Max's lips when they'd been discussing Olivia Donovan at that ball last Season, and how he'd mentioned Beatrice, just to get a rise out of him. Fenwicke had wanted to slap that gloating look right off the man's face. He'd wanted to thrust Beatrice in front of him and shout, "Look! Look at this fat shell of a woman! How can you possibly expect me to want to bed her, much less remain faithful?"

Beatrice had been far away in Sussex, otherwise Fenwicke would have been tempted to do it.

Two years ago, Beatrice had been an ideal bride. She was from a highly admired family and came with an enormous fortune of her own. She was quiet and shy, respectable yet poised. She was in possession of a pair of strong hips, which boded well for bearing him children. And, two years ago, she had been the belle of the London Season. Everyone had wanted her.

Fenwicke loved competition, and above all, he liked to

win. He'd done everything in his power to win Beatrice, and he'd succeeded. His wedding to her, with all those titled gentlemen staring at him in glazed-eyed envy, was one of the pinnacle moments of his life.

Only after he'd married her had he realized what a bore she really was. And she was such a damned weakling it made him sick.

Max had since seen firsthand what had become of Fenwick's unfortunate wife in the past two years. Surely now he understood why Fenwicke chose courtesans and other whores over that woman. A man couldn't be blamed for seeking satisfaction elsewhere when he was shackled to such a dull lump.

Yet still Max looked upon him with a holier-than-thou countenance that made Fenwicke boil, made him want to scream in rage, made him want to wring his neck and wipe that damned superior look off his face.

And now... now this.

Fenwicke looked over at his desk. There it was. The newspaper lying on the smooth, gleaming wood.

He could see the squiggling black lines of the article that meant his demise. Some damned bastard at White's had leaked the entire tale.

In easily breakable code, it told of the bet Fenwicke had made with Max: "At a certain gentleman's club in St. James, Lord F_____ initiated a wager with Lord H_____, who has since risen to the rank of duke."

Pfft, he thought. Any simpleminded sod in London could decipher that one.

It spoke of their old bet about which one of them would ascend to a dukedom first, and it revealed the terms of their second bet, leaving out the name of the lady.

Fenwicke wished it had revealed her name. He would have liked that family—especially Olivia herself—to squirm.

Alas, he wasn't even granted that bit of satisfaction. No, it was all bad for him. In small black lettering, the article went on to say that not only had no one seen Fenwicke strutting about in shirtsleeves since his foe had risen to the title of duke, no one expected to see him thus. No one could imagine that he'd allow himself to be so disgraced on the streets of London, even to save his honor.

Translation: No one believed that he, Leonard Reece, the Marquis of Fenwicke, was honorable.

The article went on to say that Fenwicke hadn't paid the new duke for losing the wager they'd made concerning the young lady. More embarrassing, it stated that sources on the inside of Lord F_____'s household had revealed that Lord F_____ didn't have sufficient funds to pay the duke, and therefore the duke would most likely never see the money that was rightfully his.

Worst of all, the article expounded on the duke's virtues. He'd forgiven the debt from the kindness of his heart. He'd shown great restraint by not calling Lord F_____ out.

Fenwicke shook his head, snorting at the stupidity of it. Whoever had spread the story had certainly decided to offer a warped rendition of the events. What about the part where Max had slammed his fist into Fenwicke's face? The black smudge beneath his eye was still there. He hadn't left the deuced house since that night—he looked like something out of a child's nightmare.

Even after his eye healed, he couldn't leave his house. Not if he didn't want to hear the whispers, the laughter surrounding him.

He rang the bell, summoning his man. When the servant appeared in the doorway, Fenwicke said, "Pack my bags immediately. We're leaving in an hour's time."

There was no other choice. He'd return to Sussex and his insipid wife. At least until he developed some sort of reasonable plan.

Chapter Eleven

Jessica hadn't seen Beatrice in a whole week. The weather had been frightful, unlike anything Jessica had ever seen. Of course, she was only eighteen. Her family had moved to Antigua from England when she was five years old, and she remembered nothing of English weather.

But it was truly, magnificently awful. One could hardly venture outside, and if one did, one would be frozen solid within moments. Last week Jessica had made the mistake of going outdoors and she'd returned from Beatrice's house at dusk cold through to her very bones. It had taken hours, a hot bath, hot stones, warming herself before the fire, wearing every bit of wool she could find, before her teeth stopped chattering and she was warm enough to engage in a basic conversation with her sisters. Who'd laughed at her! Laughed, as if they didn't feel the same piercing coldness she did.

She liked England. She did. She liked the depth of the green during the summer, the people, the stately homes, the bustle of the city. But she hated the weather. It was enough to make her want to go home.

She laughed quietly to herself. *Almost* enough, she amended. Mother was still in Antigua. Even though Serena was sending Mother an allowance, none of the Donovan sisters wanted to return to be squashed beneath their mother's selfish, domineering thumb.

England was much better than that, despite the weather.

Today, Jessica's maid had informed her that the temperature had increased by ten degrees since yesterday, and it was a quite respectable fifty-two degrees outside.

Jessica was bored with staying inside, and she missed Beatrice terribly. She asked her sisters if they wanted to accompany her, but all three of them were playing with Margie, who had taken her first steps yesterday, a feat which delighted every single other adult in the house inordinately. Serena had actually cried over it…though Jessica harbored some suspicion that they weren't only tears of happiness. They were tears for what she had lost. For the child she had wanted so badly and now was concerned she might never have.

Phoebe and Olivia had seemed to understand, too, for they were being overly comforting and sweet toward Serena. Jessica wanted to make Serena feel better, too, but Phoebe and Olivia left her no room to do so.

So she donned her heaviest coat—for fifty-two degrees now meant it would likely be close to freezing by the time she returned home later—and her bonnet, mittens, and boots, and then she ventured outside.

There was no breeze, and the air felt balmy compared to last week's freeze. Not balmy compared to any day of the year in Antigua, though, Jessica thought grimly.

She hurried over the wet, muddy path, and her long strides brought her to Beatrice's house in less than half an hour. She went to the front door and knocked as she usually did.

No one came.

As the moments passed, Jessica's heart began to pound. Beatrice never left the house. That left two possibilities. Either her husband was at home, or Beatrice had given instructions not to open the door for her.

The first seemed the likeliest scenario. Jessica turned back and stepped down the stairs that led to the drive, and looked up at the windows on the first and second floors. All was silent. There was no movement.

There was one certain way she could tell if that awful Lord Fenwicke was in residence: by checking to see if his traveling carriage was in the stables.

Lifting her skirts, she hurried around the back of the house and to the stables. She opened the door and came face-to-face with a stable boy, who jumped back, startled, shovel in hand.

"I'm so sorry!" she exclaimed.

The boy just stared at her, wide-eyed, mouth agape. He smelled like he'd been mucking the stalls.

She gave him a broad smile. "Pray, can you tell me whether Lord Fenwicke is in residence?"

"Lord Fenwicke, miss?"

"Yes. Lord Fenwicke. Is he here?"

"Here, miss?"

"Is Lord Fenwicke here?" she repeated, her patience quickly wearing thin.

"Why, no, miss. He's gone back to London this morning."

Her heart sank. "When did he arrive?"

The boy scrunched his face up in thought. "Um... well, he arrived on Sunday when we was all at church, miss. So I b'lieve it's been four days."

Oh, good heavens. She glanced back at the house, then thanked him. The stable boy blushed and mumbled something, but she didn't hear—she had already turned and was hurrying toward the house. This time she didn't knock. She simply tried the door handle to the servants' entrance. It was, thankfully, unlocked. The cook looked up, startled, as Jessica entered the kitchen from the scullery.

The older woman dropped her spoon into whatever was boiling in the pot she stirred. "Oh! Miss Donovan, I—" She broke off abruptly, her pale face flushing.

"I'm here to see Lady Fenwicke."

Wiping her hands on her apron, the cook glanced nervously at the door leading to the outside corridor. Most of the people in this house were slaves to Lord Fenwicke's whims and possessed no loyalty whatsoever to Beatrice, but she and the cook, with their common interest, had developed a tentative friendship. Beatrice had told Jessica, however, that the older woman was still terrified of the master and that if pressed, her loyalties would sway to the man who paid her. Beatrice didn't blame her for that in the least. Jessica did, though.

"Lord Fenwicke is gone, isn't he?" she asked sharply.

"Well, yes, he—"

"Then I'm going upstairs."

"Wait!"

When Jessica turned to the older woman, she patted her bonnet nervously. "My mistress isn't at home, Miss Donovan."

Jessica gave an impatient huff. "We both know that is untrue." She strode out of the kitchen, ignoring the woman's continued protests.

Her heart thumped in her chest. The corridors were curiously quiet, emptier of servants than they usually were this time of day.

She checked the downstairs drawing room first. Finding it vacant, she hurried upstairs and looked in the salon and the library. Both were quiet and still.

Slowing her steps, Jessica walked to Beatrice's bedchamber door. Raising her hand, she knocked gently.

No answer.

She tried again, rapping a little harder this time, leaning her ear against the door. She wanted to call Beatrice's name, but if Beatrice was in there, if she had been hurt by her husband, she might not respond to Jessica's voice.

Again, Beatrice didn't respond, but Jessica heard the rustling sounds of movement inside. She cracked open the door.

The room was quiet and still, but Beatrice's dark gray bed curtains were drawn. Slowly, Jessica advanced. Slowly, she pushed open the curtain.

What she saw made her gasp out loud.

Beatrice was lying in bed, both her eyes swollen completely shut. Her mouth was swollen, too, and dried blood encrusted it. There was also a line of dried blood near her temple.

"Who is it?" she asked, her voice sharp but slurred by the swelling.

"Oh, Beatrice," Jessica whispered. She would not cry. *She. Would. Not.* But her chest was so tight with fear and grief for her friend that she felt near to bursting.

She sank down onto the edge of the bed. "Oh, my darling friend. What has he done to you?"

"Jessica?"

"What can I do, Beatrice? How can I help you?"

Beatrice's lip quivered, and she rolled away. "You can't."

"Is it..." Jessica swallowed hard. "Is it just your face... or did he hurt you elsewhere?"

After a long moment of silence, the other woman said, "He hurt me everywhere."

She dissolved into hiccuping sobs that must have pained her terribly, because she cringed with each gulping breath she took.

Jessica was terrified. More than anything, she wanted to make this better. But she didn't know how. She didn't know what to do. This was so far out of her realm. All she knew for certain was that she wanted to kill Lord Fenwicke with her bare hands. She truly wanted him dead. And if no one else would perform the deed, she would. Gladly.

She kicked off her shoes and climbed into bed beside Beatrice, holding her, smoothing her hair, kissing her temple for a long time. When the other woman's sobs diminished, Jessica left the bed and went in search of warm water, which she retrieved from the kitchens with a minimal amount of crisp words exchanged with the cook. When she returned upstairs, she asked Beatrice where all the servants were.

"I think my husband gave the household servants the week off with pay."

Jessica felt sick. "So you lie here suffering with no help, and they're rewarded?"

Beatrice didn't answer.

"Yet," Jessica said thoughtfully, "your cook is here."

"Is she?" Beatrice murmured. "I wonder why she didn't go to her family in Chichester."

Some little bit of loyalty for her mistress resided within the woman, Jessica supposed, her feelings toward the cook softening somewhat. She dipped a cloth into the warm water and proceeded to clean off the blood from Beatrice's face as gently as she could. Beatrice lay still, her eyes squeezed shut from the swelling, wincing slightly when Jessica pressed on a bruise. The subtle evidence of her friend's pain increased Jessica's anger with each passing minute, until finally, she blurted, "For God's sake, Beatrice, that bastard can't be allowed to touch you again. You must leave him!"

She stared at her friend, who lay very still as if she were as shocked by the outburst as Jessica was. After a long moment of silence, Beatrice murmured, "I can't."

Her explosion had released the heat of her anger, and now all Jessica could feel was the cold, hard lump of it, deep in her chest. She couldn't let her friend suffer like this. Never again. She could not—would not—stand by and allow it.

"He might kill you next time," she said.

"He has every right," Beatrice whispered.

"Not to kill you!"

"But to beat me . . . to punish me—"

Jessica shook her head. "No! What was the 'punishment' for this time, Beatrice? Breathing? This has nothing to do with punishment, or anything that you've done wrong. You must know that."

Ever since she'd seen Beatrice hurt that first time,

she'd been trying to drill that fact into her friend's mind. Beatrice was a sweet, kind, beautiful woman. She didn't deserve a harsh word, much less anything like this.

A fresh tear leaked from Beatrice's eye and trailed down the side of her mottled face.

"I know. It's just...he's my husband. I don't want to hate him..."

"But you do. You must."

The tears flowed faster now. "I hurt everywhere, Jessica. Inside and out. I hurt so deeply."

Jessica reached for her friend's hand and squeezed it. "Nothing you have done justifies his treatment of you, Beatrice. Nothing."

After a long silence just lying there, eyes closed and tears dripping down the sides of her face, Beatrice murmured, "I don't deserve this. I didn't do anything to provoke him this time. All I did was...greet him."

Jessica exhaled slowly. It was the first time her friend had ever made such an admission. Finally, *finally,* she was beginning to understand how horribly wrong this was.

"You must leave him."

"I can't."

"Of course you can."

"No, I cannot." Beatrice's voice was almost a wail. "He'll find me. If I leave him...if he were to find me, he truly would kill me."

Jessica shook her head firmly. "You have powerful friends. We'll keep you safe."

Beatrice squeezed her hand weakly. "Oh, Jessica, you are the best friend in the world. You are truly my only friend. But he's a powerful lord. He's going to be a duke someday. There's no way for you to protect me from him."

"Not just me, Beatrice. My sisters. My brothers-in-law. And Captain Langley and Lord Hasley became so fond of you this past autumn—"

Beatrice's lips twitched. "I think it was only my cooking that they admired."

"Nonsense," Jessica said. "And Lord Hasley is a duke now—surely that's an even more powerful position than an almost-duke."

Beatrice's expression softened. "Jessica, he's no longer Lord Hasley. Remember? Now that he's a duke, we no longer call him by his old title. He's now His Grace, the Duke of Wakefield."

"Right." Jessica frowned. Honestly, the ins and outs of the aristocracy didn't matter one whit to her. She could never remember the difference between a marquis and an earl, and she didn't really care. Mother had endlessly hammered that information into all of the sisters, but Jessica had never been able to distinguish between the ranks. It all sounded the same to her.

All she knew was that Mother wanted all the sisters to marry men with titles, so when she'd been in London during the Season, she'd paid special attention to all the men introduced with a "Lord" before their names. But honestly, most of them were terribly old, and overall, she'd found the "misters" far more attractive.

"So I shall call him 'Lord Wakefield' from now on," Jessica said to her friend.

Beatrice sighed. "No, no. It should be 'His Grace,' or 'Your Grace' if you're addressing him directly."

"Oh goodness. I'll never remember this."

Beatrice squeezed her hand again. "I'll help you."

"And I'll help *you*," Jessica said. "Along with my

family and our friends. We'll keep you safe. We simply *have* to."

With a smile, Olivia folded Max's latest letter and pushed it into the pocket of her pelisse.

She rose from the rock she'd been sitting on and stretched, reaching her fingertips to the sky. It was a warm day—well, at least in comparison to the past several days, and she felt so good. So healthy. She'd looked into the mirror this morning, and for the first time in her memory, she could see a natural flush in her cheeks. She'd gained a little weight since Max had arrived at Stratford House. She felt stronger than she ever had, and she'd discovered that she was less likely to lose her breath when walking up an incline or striding at a fast pace.

And then there was Max himself. His departure from Stratford House hadn't been the end that she'd anticipated. He'd written to her almost daily about his thoughts about his new role and his daily activities. He spoke of their time together, how much he missed her, and about his hopes that they could see each other again soon. His letters were wonderfully caring and utterly romantic.

She relaxed her arms and gazed down at the ice-encrusted spring, which was barren of Henrietta the goose and all her friends—they'd all wandered off, probably in search of warmer bodies of water to frolic in. Still, Olivia came here, the place where she'd first met Max, to read his letters whenever the weather allowed.

With one final glance at the sky, she decided she'd best head home. It was almost dusk, and Lord knew, if she arrived home a minute after sundown, her family would come together as one and have a group apoplexy.

She smiled a little as she picked her way over the rocky path.

She'd been so certain that everything would change after Max left for London. That he would think her a mere country affair or even forget about her. But from his letters, it was easy to see that wasn't the case. He was still the same man, one who was facing his new responsibilities with some frustration, a little annoyance, and always a great deal of courage.

Just thinking of his name made her smile grow wider. *Max. Max. Max.*

In the letter she'd received today, Max had talked about Jonathan's mother's upcoming visit to London. He'd hinted that the dowager countess might need a companion . . . that Olivia would perhaps want to offer up herself for that position. . . . And if she did, they might be able to see each other again very soon.

Very soon, indeed. Max didn't know this, but the dowager countess was planning to leave for London next week. Olivia couldn't wait to suggest that she accompany the older woman, and she didn't see that it would be any problem at all. She and the dowager enjoyed each other's company.

Still, what would it mean to see Max—to be with him—in London?

It wasn't over between them, that much was certain. And now that he'd given her evidence that he did care about her, that it wasn't just a fling he'd simply drop the moment he left the country, the protective walls she'd built around herself were beginning to crumble.

She just might be falling in love with him.

She couldn't think too hard about that, because if she did, she'd begin to second-guess Max's—and her own—motives. Her mind would take her in endless circles and drive her mad. For now, she'd force herself to be content with missing him and simply wanting to see him again.

As she stepped out of the shelter of the forest and the house came into view, she squinted at the end of the drive. A single figure was approaching the house from that direction—probably Jessica returning from Lady Fenwicke's house. But the figure wasn't walking at a leisurely pace; she was holding up her skirts and running.

Olivia hurried, too, hoping to intersect the person before she reached the house. As she drew closer, she saw that it was indeed Jessica, her skirts lifted so high, Olivia could see the flash of her garters as she ran.

"Olivia!" Jessica called when they were within hearing range.

"What is it, Jess?"

Jessica rushed at her, panting, her cheeks pink with exertion. When they were within a few steps of each other, she reeled to a stop, dropping her skirts and pressing her hand to her chest. She doubled over, taking sharp gulps of breath.

"Oh goodness!" Olivia exclaimed. "Are you all right? What has happened? Why did you run so?"

Jessica lifted her head. With the back of her arm, she wiped at a trail of sweat dripping down her face. "It's Beatrice," she wheezed.

Dread clenched in Olivia's chest. "What about her?"

"Oh, Olivia…Oh…" Jessica broke into a sob, mixing with her harsh breaths.

Her own heart beating wildly, Olivia put her arms around her sister. "Here, darling. Lean on me. I'll bring you inside. Calm down, Jess. It's all right. We'll go inside and have a nice cup of tea…"

She kept murmuring to her sister as they stumbled inside the house. Jessica was noisy enough that they drew the attention of first the servants, then the rest of the family. By the time they were halfway down the corridor heading toward the drawing room, Serena had arrived, a footman had been sent to fetch Sebastian and Phoebe, and Jonathan had scooped Jessica up to carry her the rest of the way. When they reached the drawing room, Jonathan set her gently on the sofa. Serena sat on one side of her, Olivia on the other. Moments later, Phoebe and Sebastian rushed in, demanding to know what had happened.

Jessica turned to Olivia, put her arms around her, and sank her damp face into her neck. Olivia murmured softly to her sister, all the while exchanging worried glances with her sisters and brothers-in-law.

Eventually, Jessica's sobs turned into whimpers and then mere sniffs. Finally, taking the handkerchief Olivia offered her, she pulled away from Olivia and seemed to try to compose herself.

"Jessica," Serena said gently, "what happened to make you so very upset?"

Jessica took a deep breath. "I need your help." She looked from one to the other of them. "All of you. Please. Help me. Help us." Her shoulders shook as she tried to contain her sobs.

"Us?" Jonathan asked. "Who?"

"Beatrice and me."

"Do you mean Lady Fenwicke?" Sebastian asked. He'd been so busy working on the Stratford House renovations that he hadn't grown to know Beatrice as well as the others had.

"Yes."

"Help you how, Jess?" Phoebe asked.

"Help me save her life. Help me to hide her from her husband."

They all stared at her, completely bewildered.

"What on earth are you talking about?" Phoebe asked.

"If we don't help her escape," Jessica said, a fresh tear sliding down her cheek, "Lord Fenwicke is going to kill her."

Chapter Twelve

Jessica told them the whole story. How she'd found Beatrice battered and bruised that first time after Lord Fenwicke had left. How this time she'd been so brutally beaten and used that when Jessica had tried to help her out of bed today, she'd been able to walk only a few steps.

"He's a horrible man," Jessica whispered. "He must be truly insane to do this to such a sweet, lovely lady."

Jonathan had been pacing during most of Jessica's explanation. Now he turned to her, his expression dark. "Jessica," he said sternly, "do you realize what you're asking us to do?"

"I'm asking you to help keep her safe," Jessica said.

"The laws aren't on her side. Technically, there's nothing we can do about this," Sebastian said. "A man has the right to discipline his wife as he sees fit."

All four women stared at Sebastian, but Phoebe was the only one to speak. "Are you mad, Sebastian? He has the right to degrade her? To blind her? To cripple her?"

"Unfortunately, yes," Jonathan said. All the ladies' gazes swung to him. "But that doesn't mean society condones such actions. Everyone knows that men who strike women are bullies and cowards."

"Well, I should hope so," Serena exclaimed.

Jonathan's voice gentled. "What did you promise her, Jessica?"

"I promised that I'd help her. And I will."

Olivia was all too familiar with the voice Jessica was using. It was that youngest-child voice. The one that let all surrounding her know that she was going to do what it was she promised, no matter what anyone thought about it.

"Of course you will," Serena soothed. "We all will." She gave Jonathan a hard look. "Won't we?"

Jonathan cocked his head at Serena. "If you think I'd allow a woman—any woman—to suffer like that under a man's hand, you don't know me very well, my love."

She rose and went to him, slipping her arms around his waist. "I knew you wouldn't." Standing on tiptoe, she kissed his cheek, and he circled his arms around her possessively.

Phoebe cocked a brow at her husband, and Sebastian rubbed a thumb over it, soothing. "I will offer her my house in Prescot. That is, if you haven't already thought of a better place for her to go."

Jessica swallowed hard. "No, I haven't. Prescot is far away, isn't it? And far from London?"

"Quite," Sebastian said dryly. "It's perhaps not quite up to a marchioness's standards, but—"

"It doesn't matter," Jessica said. "She will be happy—so happy—just to be away. To be safe. Even if it is a hovel."

"It is not a hovel," Jonathan assured her. "It's a small, sturdy dwelling. It should be adequate until we think of a more permanent arrangement. The most important thing now is to get her out of danger."

"Yes. I think…" Jessica swallowed hard, obviously trying to control her emotions. "I think she requires a doctor, Jonathan."

Jonathan's lips tightened, but he nodded. "Very well. We'll bring her here tonight. She'll stay the night, and if the doctor declares her fit, the two of you will be off to Prescot first thing in the morning." He turned to Sebastian. "Will you escort them there?"

"Of course."

Jessica rose and joined Jonathan and Serena in the middle of the room, hugging them both. She was looking at Sebastian when she said, "Thank you. Thank you so much."

At midnight, Jessica went with Sebastian and Jonathan to Brockton Hall. They parked the carriage away from the house so any of the lingering servants wouldn't hear it. They went in through the back door, Sebastian using an old skill to pick the lock.

While Sebastian kept watch downstairs, Jonathan and Jessica crept upstairs. Jessica went in to Beatrice's room first, finding her wide awake.

The swelling, which had reduced enough for Beatrice to see through eye slits before Jessica had left her earlier, had gone down even more, thanks to the cold poultices Jessica had demanded the cook prepare for her. Relief shone in Beatrice's expression when she turned her head to look at Jessica.

"You came."

"I said I would, didn't I?" Jessica held out her hand, and Beatrice reached up from the bed and took it. "Do you trust me, Beatrice?"

"I do."

"You're my friend and I love you."

"I know," Beatrice whispered. "I do want to go away from here, Jessica. Far, far away. I never want to see my husband again."

"Remember how you told me that you were happy once, when you were a little girl? How you had no worries in the world?"

"Yes."

"I want that for you again, my dear friend. I want you to be happy again."

"I want that, too," Beatrice said haltingly.

"The earl is just outside. He's going to help you to the carriage. We're going to his house. Tomorrow, you're going far away."

"Will I be alone?" Beatrice whispered.

"I wouldn't send you off alone. I'll be going with you. And my brother-in-law, Mr. Harper, will watch over us."

Beatrice nodded, her dark eyes glowing. "Thank you. I don't...I don't think I could do this without you."

Someday, Beatrice would be strong enough to do something like this on her own. She'd been so beaten down by Lord Fenwicke for so long, she was like a piece of shattered glass. Jessica would stay by her side and help her glue every last shard back into place. Hopefully, when they were finished, Beatrice would be stronger than she'd ever been before.

But now... Well, now was the low point. Beatrice was broken, and she needed to lean heavily on others.

Jessica was fully aware that she was young, and she'd lived the vast majority of her life on a small island far away from society. Nevertheless, she intended to be a rock for Beatrice for as long as she needed one.

She went into her friend's dressing room, and with Beatrice's help, she gathered the basic necessities: several changes of undergarments, hairpins, shoes, and a few dresses. She found a valise where Beatrice had said it would be, in her husband's closet through the doors adjoining their bedrooms, and stuffed the clothes into it.

Finally, she went to Beatrice's door, where Jonathan was waiting, and told him they were ready.

He came into the bedchamber. Jessica watched him carefully and observed the twitch in his jaw when he saw how terribly Beatrice had been beaten.

Not all men were bad, Jessica thought. Some, like her brothers-in-law, were very, very good.

Beatrice averted her eyes as Jonathan very gently lifted her into his arms. "Am I hurting you?" he murmured.

"No, sir."

Cradling her gently in his arms, Jonathan passed Jessica and headed toward the door. Carrying the packed valise, she followed them down the stairs. When they reached the bottom, Sebastian joined them, relieving Jessica of the valise. Locking the door, they stealthily left the house. As they walked toward the carriage, Beatrice looked over her shoulder. "I'll never go back there."

"No, never," Sebastian agreed. "Not if you don't want to."

"I don't," Beatrice said. And she didn't say any more.

They drove home in silence. When they arrived, the doctor was waiting. Sebastian carried Beatrice upstairs to a guest room near Jessica's room, and when he laid her in the bed, she reached up and grabbed his arm. "Please," she begged. "I don't..."

Jessica hurried up behind Sebastian. "What's wrong, Beatrice?"

Beatrice flashed her a desperate look. "I don't want to see the doctor."

"Why?"

She swallowed hard. "He is from the village. He might tell Lord Fenwicke—"

Sebastian squeezed Beatrice's hand. "It's all right, my lady. Jonathan already spoke to him. We have his assurance, as a man of honor, that he won't reveal your presence here. No one outside this house will hear of it."

"Are you sure?" she whispered.

He nodded solemnly, and she relaxed back into the sheets, closing her eyes. "Very well."

She insisted that even Jessica leave, though, while the doctor saw her. So Jessica joined the others in the drawing room, pacing and wringing her hands in worry.

An hour later, the doctor knocked on the drawing room door and entered to a roomful of anxious Donovan sisters and two husbands. "Well," he said. "She is well enough to travel, but barely. And I daresay it'll be rather painful for her, with the roads in the condition they're in this time of year. She has at least three broken ribs."

Jonathan made a sound that resembled a low growl.

"Other than that, she's quite bruised, from head to foot. However, there are no other serious internal injuries that I can find." The doctor hesitated, then lowered his head. When he spoke again, he seemed to be speaking to the floor. "She was not only beaten, but used quite brutally."

No one spoke. Tears slipped unchecked from Jessica's eyes. On top of everything else, that evil man had raped her. Jessica had suspected it, but to hear the confirmation wrenched her heart wide open. How she hated that man.

There was a long silence. Finally, Sebastian stepped forward. "Thank you, doctor."

"I've bound her ribs to help with the pain, and left some laudanum. She was drowsy when I left her and probably sound asleep by now. I'll leave direction on the treatment of her wounds while on the journey."

Jessica wiped away her tears, impatient with them, and strode to the writing desk by the tall window looking out over the driveway below. "Here is some paper and a pen, doctor. If you'd be so kind as to write the instructions out for me?"

"Of course." The doctor dipped the pen in the ink and scrawled a few lines while the family waited in silence, then pushed the paper across the desk toward Jessica. "Here you are, miss."

"Thank you."

As Sebastian went to escort the doctor out, Serena said, "It's near dawn. We should all get some rest. Especially you, Jessica. You've a long journey ahead."

"Yes," Jessica said dully.

Olivia slipped her hand in hers and tugged. "I'll walk you to your room."

Jessica was silent as she walked with Olivia upstairs. It

seemed all her emotion and anger and urgency had been driven away by the doctor's diagnosis. All she felt now was utterly numb.

At her door, Olivia embraced her. "You're such a good friend, Jessica. Out of all the people in the world, I would choose you to be my closest friend. Beatrice is lucky to have you."

She didn't answer. She kissed her sister, went into her room, and tumbled into a fretful sleep. Morning seemed to come within minutes, and she was being shaken awake by Serena. "It's time to go, Jess. You've time for a quick breakfast, but then you must be on your way."

At noon, they were in a carriage rattling over pitted roads on their way northward, to Prescot.

Fenwicke returned to London feeling much stronger. He'd proved his superiority over his wife. True, she was a sniveling, cowering thing, but the way he'd so utterly mastered her reminded him of how strong he really was. He was a powerful man, and he could use that power to finally master the Duke of Wakefield.

He'd succeed this time. He knew it. No longer would Max Buchanan look down that aristocratic nose at him. No, he'd beg for mercy, just like Beatrice had.

Nothing would be better. Not only would it prove, once and for all, that Fenwicke was the superior man, but he'd finally rid himself of the man who just wouldn't stop pestering him. He would finally move forward with his life with a clean slate, finally free from Max's tenacious hold on his self-confidence. His long-time nemesis wouldn't know what had hit him.

Fenwicke dismissed his man with a flick of the wrist,

but he didn't leave his dressing room chair. He studied himself for a long time in the looking glass, pressing on the light wrinkles that had spread across his forehead in the past months. They weren't so bad. And his eyes still held a dark glint of wickedness. A promise of . . . *more* that he knew the ladies couldn't resist.

He smiled at himself in the mirror. He was still a handsome devil, if he did say so himself.

He rose, adjusted a soft wrinkle in his banyan, and wandered downstairs. He entered his morning room, finding his steaming coffee placed to the left of the morning correspondence, which was to the left of today's *Times,* which was to the left of his boiled egg. Everything was as it should be.

He seated himself, spread his napkin carefully across his lap, and smoothed all the wrinkles from it. Then he drank half of his coffee, and when he began to feel it work through him, he filtered through his correspondence. There were only two letters today. One was from his father—the old man who refused to die—and the other was from Brockton Hall.

That was fast. Frowning, he broke the seal and read the childish, nearly indecipherable handwriting of his cook.

My lord,

My mistress left last night. I do not know where she went.

However, Miss Jessica D_____ came to the house yesterday. She broke in and saw my mistress, though I threatened her with dire consequences which she wholeheartedly ignored.

> *But my mistress is gone, to where I do not know.*
> *I can only guess that she has gone off with Miss*
> *D_____.*
> *Please forgive me, my lord.*

Fenwicke stared at the letter for a very long time. At first, he couldn't believe it. Beatrice couldn't have left Brockton Hall. He'd forbidden her to. She always obeyed his orders, because she knew very well the severity of the consequences if she didn't.

Yet the cook wouldn't have written this letter to him if it weren't true.

Well, well, well.

It seemed his wife had grown a rebellious streak. When he found her, the punishment would be severe indeed.

Damn the Donovan sisters. Damn them all to hell. They'd done this. They'd caused Beatrice to misbehave in a way that had the potential to cause him a great deal of trouble. Those sisters had caused him nothing but difficulty ever since their arrival in England.

His fury mounted, and he crushed the letter in his hand and tossed it into the fire.

Beatrice certainly hadn't kept her simpering little mouth shut. She'd probably told those Donovan sisters all manner of lies. And the Donovans had probably told Stratford. Stratford was someone Fenwicke had once admired—they'd gone carousing together many times over the years. Ever since he'd married the eldest Donovan sister, however, he'd become quite dull.

Fenwicke clenched his teeth. Was Stratford involved in Beatrice's disappearance? If so, this could become extremely complicated. Difficult, even. Stratford was a powerful man, with powerful connections.

Not as powerful as me, Fenwicke reminded himself. His title, though only the courtesy title for his father's heir, was higher than Stratford's. He held precedence over the man. He always would.

Maybe Stratford had some plan to ruin him. To steal his home in Sussex. To steal his wife.

Fenwicke hissed through his teeth.

He blinked hard and stared down at his hands clenched in his lap. If he was to beat them—beat them all—he must focus.

He spent the afternoon at Tattersall's, dreaming, thinking of all the horseflesh he'd keep in his stables once his father was dead. After he grew bored of that—because thinking of all the things he'd do once his father was dead sometimes started to grow into thinking of ways to kill the man—he went home and changed his clothes, and then he took his carriage to White's.

As soon as he walked into the card room, a hush fell over the room as, one by one, the men looked up at him. Every single expression was full of antipathy. Of *disgust.*

He wound through the tables, feeling eyes on him, and joined a group of men at a table.

"May I join you, gentlemen?" he asked, sliding into the empty chair.

No one spoke. No one looked at him. Instead, they collected their winnings, stood, and walked away from the table, leaving him alone. As the last departing man walked past him, Fenwicke heard the slicing accusation like a razor across his throat.

"Wife beater."

Fenwicke stood. Keeping his chin high and his back straight, he left White's. He summoned his coachman and went straight home and into his drawing room, where he put out all the lights and sat on his most comfortable chair facing the fire.

He really preferred his London house to his home in Sussex. It was a large, stately home situated in Mayfair on an enormous piece of property—well, enormous for a private dwelling within London and considering its proximity to everything important.

He stared into his drawing room fire—the only supplier of light in the room—for a long while, but the flames died down until there were only a few glowing coals. Then those went black, and still he sat.

Where had this newest scathing gossip come from? His first thought had been that it must be Beatrice spreading filth about him. But surely not. She didn't have the gumption.

It had to be someone else. Someone who hated him. The Earl of Stratford wasn't in Town, and neither was his wife and her damnable sisters.

That left one man. One person in the world who was always trying to better him, who hated him. Who liked to pretend to be an innocent but had obviously been plotting to destroy him from the beginning.

Maxwell Buchanan.

The duke had buried his dagger deep. Now he'd twisted it by spreading these rumors about Beatrice.

Fenwicke wasn't about to roll over and die, however. Not yet. Not for a very, very long time. Wakefield would be dead long before he was.

With this blow, the duke thought he'd won for good.

Fenwicke's reputation probably would never recover from this scandal. Max was probably in his new ducal lodgings congratulating himself on the fool he'd made of Fenwicke, three times over. He'd become a duke. He'd seduced the slut Olivia Donovan. Now, he'd destroyed Fenwicke's reputation among his peers.

But he hadn't won. Not by a long shot. Because Fenwicke had plans of his own. Plans of vengeance that couldn't fail. Wouldn't fail. Because Leonard Reece, the Marquis of Fenwicke, was no fool. He was a careful planner, and this time, he'd make certain he did things right.

He couldn't see his timepiece, but it was probably about three o'clock in the morning by now. The perfect time to find just the right kind of man to perform the task he had in mind.

He rose and went to awaken his coachman.

Chapter Thirteen

Dearest Miss Donovan,

Will you join me at the theater on Thursday? A production of the new opera, Ninetta, *is performing at Covent Garden, and I think you will enjoy it. I shall fetch you and Lady Stratford early in the evening and escort you there.*

> *Yours fondly,*
> *Wakefield*

Olivia glanced across the small drawing room at the dowager Lady Stratford, who had looked up from her tea and was gazing with interest at the letter in Olivia's hand. The dowager's mother, a crotchety old woman, was still upstairs taking her afternoon nap.

"Would you like to go to the opera tomorrow night, my lady?" Olivia asked.

"The opera? Goodness me. I haven't been to the opera in years."

"The Duke of Wakefield has invited us."

At that, the countess broke into a wide smile. "Did he? What a lovely gentleman he is. How good of him not to have forgotten all about us lowly beings despite his lofty new title."

Olivia smiled down at the letter.

"However," the dowager continued, "my mother will have a tantrum if I leave her so soon. She wishes to monopolize my nights."

"Perhaps we shouldn't go, then," Olivia said.

"Nonsense! Of course we shall go. It is an honor to be invited to a duke's box, my dear. I'm sure many people are clamoring for an invitation like that." Her smile turned sly. "Olivia, I do believe His Grace might have a tendre for you. And it seems to me that this is a sign of his intentions."

Olivia had been steadfastly avoiding thoughts about Max's intentions, because Max's words were so different from his actions. Trying to predict the man's motives would only drive her to madness. Yet maybe the dowager had insight she did not. She cocked her head at the countess. "How do you mean, my lady?"

The countess gave her an assessing look, then a sharp nod. "You've married sisters, so I feel I can be frank with you."

"By all means, please do."

"Well, my dear, the duke has been writing you nonstop since he left Sussex, and now he's inviting you to the theater in a very public gesture. I do believe he's sending the clear message that he wants you."

"As...his mistress?" Olivia asked, suddenly full of dread. Had she allowed her hopes to build too high? Would Max really flaunt her as his mistress? He'd wanted to be discreet about their relationship in Sussex—as much as he'd teased her about it, he'd ultimately seemed to have valued discretion as much as she had. And while he hadn't treated her like a mistress, he'd also made it clear that he never intended to ask for anything more from any woman.

The countess laughed. "Oh no, of course not. No, I mean that perhaps he is considering marriage."

Olivia released the breath she'd been holding. "I see."

Of course, the dowager hadn't heard about his intention never to marry. She couldn't know of Max's fear of becoming like his father.

If Olivia dared hope that he had changed his mind about marriage... Well, what if she was wrong? What if he didn't want that from her? There was more at stake now than that day at the goose spring. If she believed he wanted her on a permanent basis, she'd drop those flimsy remaining walls protecting her heart, and she'd fall quickly. She'd build up so much hope, thinking of Max waking beside her every day, thinking of being his wife and of sharing a life with him, that she'd be setting herself up for a very long, very brutal fall.

Socially, she was still far beneath him. Goodness, it was possible that she couldn't even give him the heirs he would certainly need.

Oh, she wished the countess hadn't told her that. Because the older woman's words further crumbled Olivia's walls of defense.

Olivia wanted it—wanted him—badly. She wanted him, and she wanted it to be forever.

She couldn't wait to see him. She'd count the hours until he came to escort her to the theater.

That night, Max went to his club. Last night he'd eaten dinner alone, but tonight he felt like company and pleasant conversation.

His time at White's was made all the more pleasurable by his knowledge that Olivia had arrived in Town today. He was itching to see her, but he hadn't wanted to call on her and the dowager when they were exhausted from travel. He hardly knew how he'd contain himself until tomorrow evening when he went to fetch them to the theater.

So instead he tried to focus on the men surrounding him, on politics and sport, on his food and drink, when he saw Captain Langley, who approached him with a furrowed brow.

"Good evening, Langley."

"Wakefield." Langley's dark eyes scanned the room, and then he gestured to a dimly lit corner. "Can you spare a few moments? There's something I must speak with you about."

"Of course." But Max's gut clenched. God, had something happened to Olivia? Another fever? He sure as hell hoped not. She'd said there were lengthy intervals between her fevers—surely it was too soon.

He sat in one of the seats. Langley pulled a chair closer before lowering himself in it, and he leaned forward. "I was hoping I'd see you here tonight. If you didn't come, I intended to call on you later."

"Tell me what it is." Max swallowed past the sudden lump that had formed in his throat. "Has Olivia...?"

Langley raised his hand. "Olivia is well, as far as I know. In fact, Stratford has sent me a letter saying she's come to London with the dowager. He asked me to keep an eye on them."

Max released a breath of relief.

"But what I have to say concerns the Donovans as well as your friend, Fenwicke."

Not Fenwicke again. "He's not my friend," Max said through clenched teeth.

"That's good to hear, because rumors have been flying, and I just received verification of their veracity from Stratford."

"Rumors about what?"

"Fenwicke has been beating his wife."

Max's eyelids sank shut. But he couldn't even bring himself to be surprised. He'd seen Beatrice enough when he was at Stratford House to know that something must have happened to change her from the bright, happy debutante she'd once been. He just hadn't made the connection. Now, it all made sense. "Good God. Is she...?"

"After your last meeting here at the club, he returned to Sussex and beat her quite soundly."

Max clenched his fists. He had been responsible for Fenwicke's anger, so the responsibility for the beating lay squarely on him.

"The reports originated from a doctor who saw her in Sussex. He was appalled by the brutality of the beating and immediately set about destroying Fenwicke's reputation."

"Without a thought for the young woman's safety?"

"She has run off." Langley leaned closer to him and lowered his voice. "This part isn't public knowledge. The doctor didn't reveal any link between Lady Fenwicke and the Donovan sisters—apparently he had given his word that he wouldn't—but you and I both know that Miss Jessica and Lady Fenwicke are bosom friends. Stratford informed me that it was Jessica who convinced the lady to run away."

Max just stared at Langley. Brave Jessica. He wasn't surprised by this either—he could easily envision the youngest Donovan sister as a stubborn protector of anyone she held dear.

"They're both gone," Langley said in a low voice. "Stratford didn't reveal where they have gone, which is probably for the best. I know you've been locked up working, Wakefield, but everyone has heard the story by now. Fenwicke is back in Town, and he came here to White's last night."

"What happened?" Max asked.

"He was cut."

"Good," Max bit out.

"If what Stratford says is true—and he's not the kind of man to exaggerate such a serious charge—the young lady is in risk of losing her life to Fenwicke's violence. And, yes, he deserves to be cut."

"And more," Max said.

"And more," Langley agreed. "But I thought you should know, since you're—well, not his friend, but it appears you and Fenwicke have had a frequent association."

"Not by my choice." Max leaned back in the chair. The information he'd just received drained away the excitement that had been bubbling up within him all night. He still wanted to see Olivia—perhaps even more than he had a few minutes ago—but he wanted to see her in private. He wanted to hold her, to make gentle love to her. To worship her perfect body and drink in her sweetness.

To obliterate from his mind the fact that Fenwicke had taken out his anger at Max on his innocent wife.

Max swiped a hand over his brow, wiping away beads of sweat that had formed there. He rose on unsteady feet.

"I think I'll go home."

Langley rose, too, and clapped him on the shoulder. "I'm sorry I had to be the bearer of that news."

"I'm glad I heard the accurate version from a friend," Max said. "Far better than an exaggerated version from an acquaintance, or the gossip that I'm bound to hear soon enough."

Pressing his lips together, Langley nodded.

Max made his good-byes and went downstairs, took his heavy greatcoat—there was ice in the air tonight—and hat from the porter, and left White's. He turned right and took St. James's Street and hooked across Piccadilly to Dover Street, dark at this time of night but for the streetlamps burning, casting a cold light over the street—just enough that Max could see where he placed his feet. He liked how close the house was to White's—he imagined within a few months, he'd know every step of this path.

As a silence descended over the street that would be bustling in a few hours, he paused to study the heavens. There was no moon tonight, nor any stars. The soft glow of the streetlamps lent a gloomy, otherworldly glow to the mist swirling about the edges of the buildings across the street.

He continued down the road as the clomping and rattling of a carriage sounded behind him. As it neared, the driver slowed the horses until they walked at Max's speed, a few steps behind.

He scowled over his shoulder. The silhouette of dark-colored horses and the sleek, black carriage emerged from the fog. From its elegant lines and the flashes of polish on its finish, he determined it was a regal affair and not someone out to rob him.

Was it someone he knew?

A blast of cold wind slapped him in the face as he turned back toward Hay Hill and his destination. He picked up his pace, striding through the mist created by his breath. Whoever they were, whatever they wanted, he was not in the mood. He wanted to be with Olivia. Since that wasn't an option right now, he wanted to be home. Alone. He didn't want to see anyone else.

Max turned onto Hay Hill, and the carriage drew to a halt behind him. A harsh, gritty voice came from close behind him. "Your Grace?"

Had the man come out of the carriage? Max reeled to a halt, pinching his lips together in annoyance. Heaving an exasperated sigh, he turned.

Pain exploded in his face. He reeled backward, pinpricks of light bursting in his vision.

"Bloody hell!" He clutched his nose. His fingers slid over hot, slick blood. Blinking rapidly, he made out the shadows of at least four men in dark coats.

So they were out to rob him, after all.

Max made a quick assessment of the enemy. The one in the front was the tallest by far—probably half a foot taller than Max, who had always been considered rather enormous at just over six feet tall—and his fists were clenched, ready to fight. Max spread his legs, adopting a battle stance. If he wanted any chance of getting out of this, he'd have to fight through this man first.

His waistcoat and tailcoat were too tight to give him a decent range of motion, but he doubted the giant would allow him to prepare properly. His valet would be highly inconvenienced by this, but there was no way around it.

Max gave a hoarse yell and attacked, balling his hand just before his punch met its target. His greatcoat remained intact, but buttons popped on his waistcoat, and his tailcoat screeched in protest, ripping along the side seam.

Max's fist met solid flesh, and the large man let out a strangled "Oomph!" and staggered backward.

It was then that the other men closed on him.

Max fought. He was a good fighter—he'd done his share of sparring in the boxing ring. But these men were coarse—he could tell from their smell, from their muttered grunts and curses, from their shabby clothes—and they didn't follow the rules of gentlemanly conduct in a fight. They hit him below the waist, anywhere their fists could make contact with his flesh.

Two of them managed to yank his hands behind him, and someone twined rough rope around his wrists. He strained hard, nearly twisting free, but one of the men wrapped his arms around Max, holding him in a headlock as the others finished their job.

Well, if they wouldn't fight like gentlemen, neither would he. He swung his knee upward, striking the man who held his head in the ballocks. With a yowl, the man let him go, his hands flying to his crotch as he sank to his knees.

Max lunged away, but his movements slowed without

the use of his arms. He'd taken only a few steps before one man hooked his hand between Max's wrists, using the rope to yank him backward. He stumbled, trying to keep his footing on the slick, icy ground, but hands seemed to be everywhere, thrusting him down. He kicked, skidded, and finally lost his balance.

The last thing he heard was the sound of his head hitting the pavement with a *crack*.

Chapter Fourteen

Some time later, a loud screech awoke Max. Damn, but he was cold. And deuced uncomfortable, to boot. It felt like blunt fingers were poking into his brain.

He opened his eyes to a blinding light, and pain slashed through his head. He closed his eyes with a low groan and shifted, trying to get more comfortable on the hard surface he was lying on. Just as he realized his range of motion was limited—that he couldn't move his arms—he heard voices. Memories streamed through him, and he froze.

He squinted toward the sound of the noise. A blurred figure of a man was approaching him.

"Good morning."

The voice spurred Max into action. He knew this man. He despised this man. This was the man who'd beaten an innocent woman.

Fenwicke.

His wrists were still tied behind his back, so he stumbled awkwardly to his feet, blinking hard to focus on his adversary and to try to dispel the dizziness that made his head swim.

The first thing that snapped into focus was the gun aimed at him. Again, he froze.

"You might wish to sit, Wakefield."

Slowly, the figure of Lord Fenwicke cleared as, keeping the gun solidly aimed at Max, he knelt to lower a lantern onto the floor. The figures behind Fenwicke emerged, too. Their sizes and shapes matched those of the four brutes who had accosted him on the street... was it last night? They clustered beyond the door's threshold, glowering at him with threatening expressions.

"I do not wish to sit," Max answered, his voice hoarse. "What the hell is going on, Fenwicke? Where am I? Why are you pointing a damned pistol at me?"

Fenwicke raised his dark brows. "It isn't necessary to play stupid."

"I don't know what you're talking about," Max ground out.

"You're in my cellar."

For the first time, Max glanced at the room. It was small and windowless, with gray-tinged cement walls and a rutted wood floor. The only piece of furniture was the moth-eaten faded blue chaise longue that he'd been lying on moments before.

Pressing his lips together, Max gave a sharp nod. "Very well. I'm in your cellar. My hands are tied behind my back, and you're pointing a weapon at me. I understand all that. What I don't understand is, why?"

"Because I wish to speak with you."

"If you wished to speak with me you could have met me at White's or come to call on me at my house."

Eyeing him over the gun, Fenwicke chuckled, an evil sound that raised the hairs across the back of Max's neck. He'd never heard Fenwicke laugh like that before.

"If I'd thought I had any chance of you granting me my just due by simply calling on you, Wakefield, I would have done so, but alas, these lengths were necessary."

"What do you mean by your just due?" Max asked.

Holding the gun steady with one hand, Fenwicke reached into the pocket of his coat and pulled out a folded sheet of stationery. "It's all here." He reached forward as if to hand Max the note and then chuckled again. "Oh, that's right. I forgot. You're having some difficulties with your hands at present." He dropped the sheet, and it fluttered to the dirty floor. "I'll leave it to you to open it and read it, Your Grace. Adieu."

Keeping the gun trained on Max, he backed through the door. As he stepped into the corridor, Max said, "Wait."

Fenwicke stopped.

"Once I read that"—Max gestured with his chin to the folded piece of paper on the floor—"what then?"

"Then," Fenwicke said pleasantly, "I shall return with pen and ink, and you will sign it."

He snapped the door shut, and Max heard the scrape and thud of a heavy bolt being drawn into place. He stared at the door for a long moment, still too stunned to consider how he should be reacting to this.

Fenwicke had kidnapped him? Had locked him, hands bound, in his cellar, and aimed a gun at him?

Max broke his stare from the door, shaking his head in complete confusion. His gaze snagged on the sheet of stationery on the floor. Maybe that would contain the answers.

It was a little more complicated than simply picking it up and reading it. With a sigh, he sat on the floor, turning his back to the note and moving his fingers until he had a firm grasp on it. Clumsily, he broke the seal, folded the sheet open, and smoothed it flat. He turned around to read it, using his boot to nudge it closer to the lantern Fenwicke had left.

I, Maxwell Buchanan, Duke of Wakefield, do hereby declare the following:

As a product of my personal spite and malice directed at the humble and deserving Leonard Reece, the Marquis of Fenwicke, I have intentionally blackened his name throughout Britain. I've done so by spreading false rumors that he has abused his wife—an accusation that is an utter lie and the opposite of the truth.

This is my letter of confession, for I can no longer bear the heaviness of the leaden guilt upon my soul. I was the one who used the marchioness with an evil brutality beyond what most respectable people can possibly imagine.

I, the Duke of Wakefield, am guilty of misusing a lady, a wife of a man who has always treated me with the utmost respect and admiration.

The Marquis of Fenwicke greatly admires his wife and protects her with the full power of his name and position. I denounce anyone who would label him as anything other than a perfect gentleman and a doting husband.

I hereby swear that everything in this statement is the unqualified truth.

There was no signature, of course. Simply a blank area where Max was expected to sign.

Max stared at the letter for a long time.

God, was this some kind of a joke? Could Fenwicke possibly be serious? If he was, the man was mad as a March hare.

As he gazed at the sheet of paper, a sick feeling tightened in Max's gut.

This wasn't a joke. Fenwicke was not the kind of man to perform elaborate jokes. Especially not about as serious a matter as beating his wife.

There was no way Max would ever sign this letter. No way in hell. Fenwicke could take his body apart, piece by piece. He could flay him or stretch him on the rack, but Max would never allow his name to go on this piece of rubbish.

Never.

He rose to his feet and paced the room for what seemed like hours. He tried to extricate himself from the thin, rough ropes digging into the flesh of his wrists, to no avail. Whoever the hell had tied him up must have been a sailor.

His mouth was dry and his stomach was empty, and he needed to relieve his bladder, but he ignored all those inconveniences and focused on what he was going to do.

The only way out was through the door, but upon clumsily rattling the handle, he found that it was indeed bolted from the outside, and quite sturdily, too.

He might have tried lunging at Fenwicke and knocking the gun out of his hand if the men hadn't been behind him. God help the marquis if he ever came to Max alone.

If Max pretended to sign the letter, perhaps he could fool Fenwicke into releasing him somehow.

Was Fenwicke fool enough, however, to believe that Max would admit to such a falsehood and then slink away with his tail between his legs like a defeated pup? Surely the marquis knew him better than that.

Max lowered himself onto the chaise longue, rolling his shoulders. His arms, frozen in this position for God knew how long, had grown stiff and sore.

No, Fenwicke knew very well that Max wouldn't tip-toe humbly away.

There was only one reasonable assessment of Fenwicke's intentions. He planned to force Max to sign the incriminating letter. Then he planned to kill him.

Dressed in her new red satin opera gown, Olivia parted the curtains and looked through the window up and down the empty street. It was nearly ten o'clock. Blinking hard, she turned back to Lady Stratford.

"He's not going to come, is he?" she whispered.

"No," the dowager said in a kindly voice. She rose and, walking forward, took Olivia's hands in her own. "I'm sure there's a very good explanation."

"He must have changed his mind. Decided he didn't want to go to the theater tonight."

"Nonsense. If that were the case, he would have sent us a message saying so."

"Are you sure? I know he's very busy. Perhaps he was caught up in work and forgot our plans."

The dowager shook her head. "I doubt it, my dear. It's unlike a gentleman to simply forget his theater plans with a beautiful young lady."

"I'm not—" Olivia stopped herself from finishing. Jessica was the beautiful one. Phoebe was nearly as beautiful as their youngest sister. The twins Meg and Serena had always had a loveliness about them nobody could deny. But Olivia was thin and sallow, and too small and flat-chested to capture anyone's notice. Except Max's, that was.

But tonight, he'd forgotten about her.

She took a deep breath and looked into the lady's kind blue eyes. "I shouldn't jump to conclusions, should I?"

"No, my dear."

"What should I do?"

"Well—" The dowager hesitated. "Propriety would dictate that you ignore the slight, Olivia. But the extent to which you adhere to propriety should be decided by you alone and should depend on how you and the Duke of Wakefield have communicated in the past." Gently, she released one of Olivia's hands. "I saw that you often walked the grounds together at Stratford House. I assume you and the duke had become quite…" She hesitated, then punctuated the word with far more meaning than it would have otherwise implied. "Intimate."

The blush rose quickly, burning Olivia's cheeks. She couldn't look the countess in the eyes, so she whispered, "Yes."

"I thought so." The older woman squeezed Olivia's hand. "In that case, I think you should be honest with him. Simply say that you waited and he did not show."

"If I do that, I will sound desperate." Olivia's mind was reeling. What if he'd decided that being seen with her publicly in London wasn't a good idea? What if he was embarrassed to be seen with her? What if he'd suddenly lost interest in seeing her again?

She took a deep breath. She wasn't being rational. She

was being a simpering fool. She needed to gather her strength and stop herself from having all these baseless thoughts.

Smiling at the countess, she murmured, "Do you need anything more tonight, my lady? I suppose...If you don't mind very much, I should like to go to bed."

With a final squeeze of her hand, the dowager released her. "Of course, my dear. And please don't feel so sad. I can read your face as clearly as a book. As I said before, I'm sure there's a very good explanation." She smiled. "Would you care to go to the theater day after tomorrow? I know you were looking forward to seeing your first opera. We'll use Stratford's box. And"—she glanced up in the general direction of her mother's bedchamber—"it will force Mama to have another early night. I've always believed that she keeps in a much better humor if she goes to bed early."

"That would be lovely," Olivia murmured. "Thank you, my lady."

With the dowager's kind smile blurring in her vision, Olivia turned and hurried from the room.

Chapter Fifteen

Two nights later, Fenwicke stood in his box at the theater, his mind churning as he stared into his opera glasses. So it was true. There she was, as lovely and composed as ever.

The slut.

Olivia Donovan was back in Town and at the theater, sitting primly in her seat in Stratford's box, her hands folded in her lap and her gaze turned downward, never straying from the stage.

Why had she come back to London?

Well, the reasons for her sudden arrival didn't really matter at all, did they? The point was that Max wasn't signing the damned confession. Fenwicke had stricken the man of every creature comfort, had threatened him with dire consequences, and still he steadfastly refused to sign. The bastard was being more difficult than Fenwicke had anticipated.

Perhaps little Miss Donovan could be of assistance.

Not to mention the fact that it would be very satisfying to finally see her receive her just due for having chosen the Duke of Wakefield over him.

The plan struck him like a bolt of lightning. A bolt of genius.

It was brilliant, really. A way to kill two birds with one stone. *Literally.*

Fenwicke lowered his opera glasses, a smile of victory curving the corners of his lips. He gazed at the massive cut glass chandelier hanging from the center of the ceiling overhead.

Olivia Donovan was a solitary sort of girl, always wandering off on her own at parties and balls. That was why no one had questioned her absence for the short time he'd had her alone the night he'd met her for the first time.

He'd wait until she was alone, and then he would strike. When it came to Max Buchanan and his warped sense of honor, a woman would serve as a more powerful weapon than any pistol.

Fenwicke raised his opera glasses again. *Soon, little Miss Donovan, you will be mine.*

The opportunity came far sooner than he expected.

Olivia watched the opera, but she wasn't really paying attention. It was a lovely opportunity, and it had been so kind of Lady Stratford to invite her, but as much as she tried, Olivia couldn't stay focused on what was happening on the enormous stage directly below Jonathan's opulent third-level box.

All she could think about—all that had occupied her mind for the last two days—was the fact that she had received no response to her letter to Max. She was devastated. She kept trying to convince herself that he must be managing some horrible emergency pertaining to his new title, but she didn't really believe that. No, if Max wanted to see her, wanted to talk to her, he would have contacted her by now. He wouldn't ignore her.

She was angry, but more than that, she was confused by the wildly disparate signals he was sending her.

Admittedly, she was highly inexperienced when it came to men. Maybe this was how London rakes lured their prey: They pretended true affection, true passion, and then, once they'd captured their quarry and taken what they wanted, they simply turned away. Olivia had heard rumors and warnings, as all ladies did, about men engaging in such behavior, but she'd never thought it possible that she'd fall victim to it.

In any case, it didn't make sense. Why send her all those letters from London if he was finished with her? Why bother to invite her to the theater if he didn't intend to show?

In the end, she still trusted in all the time she and Max had spent together. It couldn't all have been a lie. When she closed her eyes, she could see that look of sweet tenderness in Max's eyes when he'd touched her. How could that possibly have been counterfeit? She couldn't believe it.

And yet, the evidence was there, staring her in the face. He was ignoring her.

She was so confused. She'd never felt this way before, and right now more than she'd ever thought possible, she longed for her sisters. They would help her to understand Max's behavior. But Serena and Phoebe were far away in Sussex, and Jessica was even farther, in Lancashire with Lady Fenwicke.

And Olivia had promised to stay in London with Lady Stratford, at least for a few weeks. It wasn't that she disliked Lady Stratford—on the contrary, she grew to like the sweet older woman more every day. She'd seemed a bit of a flibbertigibbet in Sussex, but in London she'd honed in on Olivia's exact feelings, and, more important, she was sympathetic rather than judgmental.

Intermission came, and Olivia rose from her richly upholstered chair to stretch her legs. Several ladies came in to speak with Lady Stratford, and Olivia stood there awkwardly, smiling at the older ladies when spoken to but otherwise staying quiet.

One of them, Lady Bright, was about Lady Stratford's age but possessed none of her kind features. Lady Bright had thin lips, a sharp nose, and narrowed eyes, and she seemed to look at the world as though she were searching for fault with it.

She leaned forward, her lips moving just above the top edge of her fan. "Have you heard the latest, Lady Stratford?"

"The latest? Why . . . no, I don't believe so."

Lady Bright's eyes lit up—it was moments like this that ladies of the *ton* lived for, Olivia realized.

"Do you know the new Duke of Wakefield?"

Lady Stratford's eyes flicked toward Olivia then away—quickly enough so that no one except Olivia noticed. Olivia lowered her gaze to the red carpet.

Another lady elbowed Lady Bright in the ribs. "Of course she must know the duke. He was at your son's house party this autumn, Lady Stratford, wasn't he?"

"Why yes, he was."

Olivia tried to stand very still, to not give herself away.

Truthfully, she wasn't sure if she could endure gossip about Max right now. Especially if it had anything to do with his private life.

"Well"—Lady Bright paused significantly—"he's gone missing."

At first Olivia's mind didn't register what the woman had said. Then she stopped breathing. *Gone missing?*

"Missing?" Lady Stratford repeated. "Why, what on earth do you mean?"

"I mean that he went out to his club—two nights ago?" She looked at one of the other ladies, who nodded in confirmation. "And he never returned home, though he'd informed his staff he'd return later in the evening." Lady Bright laughed. "Of course, a young duke given to carousing might have spent a night away, but after two nights with no contact with anyone in his household, his valet officially raised the alarm. Absolutely no one has seen him. The authorities are speculating that he was abducted or possibly . . . murdered by footpads."

Olivia gasped, and all the ladies turned to her.

Lady Stratford wrenched their attention back to her with a loud exclamation. "But how can that be? Wasn't someone with him?"

"He left his club alone," Lady Bright said.

"But surely someone must know something. Did anyone see him disappear?"

"It is a great mystery. No one knows a thing. By tomorrow morning, I'm certain it'll be the talk of London."

"I'm so sorry. . . . please excuse me." Olivia mumbled something about going out for some air.

"I'll join you," Lady Stratford said in her kindly voice.

"No, no." She attempted a smile. All she really

wanted—needed—was to be alone. "I'll return shortly, my lady."

The dowager seemed to understand the pleading in Olivia's expression, for she acquiesced. "Be back soon, dear. The play is going to start in a few minutes."

Clutching her reticule to her chest, Olivia slipped out into the corridor, breathing heavily, looking this way and that.

Max. Missing. Murdered?

No, no, no... She walked blindly, pushing through the crowd. They all looked the same to her, closing in on her, surrounding her. She did need fresh air. The stale air inside the theater was choking her. Stifling her.

She hurried down flights of richly carpeted stairs, brushing past people going down, dodging people coming up. In the gilded saloon, she turned wildly, searching for the exit, her heart feeling like it was going to pound right out of her chest. And then she found one of the doors leading outside.

She burst out under the portico and took several gulping breaths of fresh air. She hurried to the corner and turned down the street edging the side of the theater—there were fewer people to witness her odd behavior on this narrow street—and sagged against the outside wall of the theater behind one of the columns.

She sank her face into her hands.

Max wasn't ignoring her at all. It was far worse. He was *missing*. He could be...dead.

She shook uncontrollably. Her fingers grew wet from tears.

"Miss Donovan?"

Startled, she jerked her face out of her hands. The man

standing across from her didn't seem to see the tears flowing down her face, but that didn't surprise her. This was a man who beat his wife—and poor Lady Fenwicke had shed many a tear without affecting him in the least.

Olivia's distress transformed instantly into fear. Lord Fenwicke was a dangerous man, and she was alone, outside, at night, on a nearly deserted street.

Fenwicke smiled at her, but it didn't reach his eyes. "Why, it's so lovely to see you again. I understand you've spent the past several months in Sussex with your sisters."

"Yes . . . that's right," she murmured.

He nodded. "What brought you back to London? And at this time of year?"

"I've . . ." She swallowed hard. She would be polite and then she'd escape from this man's company as quickly as possible. "I've come with the dowager countess." She began to sidle along the edge of the wall, her only means of escape since he was standing directly in front of her and the wall was behind her. "If you'll excuse me, my lord, I should be returning to the performance."

But as she stepped away, he grasped her wrist. "Wait, Miss Donovan."

She looked desperately toward the front doors. People were heading back inside en masse now, but nobody was looking in their direction.

"I'm sorry, my lord, but I really should be—"

"I believe we have some unfinished business."

"Unfinished—?"

"I think you should come with me."

He gripped her arm hard and yanked her to the back corner of the building to the lane where the mews were located.

"Lord Fenwicke!" she managed as she stumbled along, trying to keep her footing while twisting her arm to loosen his hold on her. "Let go of me!"

Her efforts were useless. He wrapped an arm around her waist and lifted her until only her toes were dragging on the pavement. "Hush," he commanded her. "I have ways to silence you, Olivia, and I'm sure you'll agree it's best if I don't use them."

Goodness, he'd called her by her given name. "Ways? What do you mean—?"

He slapped her, a blow that made her head snap back and stars swim in her vision.

"Ways like that," he said pleasantly. "And that was just the beginning. The first of many."

They passed a few vehicles waiting quietly for theater patrons to exit. Without releasing her, Fenwicke opened the door of a black, elegant carriage. "Get inside."

"No, I—"

He lifted her by the waist and shoved her inside the carriage. She landed in a heap, half on the front-facing seat and half on the floor. He came in behind her, pushed her aside to make room for himself, slammed the door behind him, then used his knuckles to rap on the ceiling.

The carriage lurched into movement as Olivia cowered in the corner, as far away from Lord Fenwicke as she could possibly get. She held her hand to her smarting cheek and glared at him. "What are you doing, Lord Fenwicke?"

"Taking you to my home."

She struggled to choke down the enormous lump of fear rising in her throat. "Why? What do you want from me?"

With that, he broke into a real smile. "Oh, Olivia. Don't you remember? I want you." His eyes raked up and down her body. "*All* of you."

The fear hardened into anger. *You'll never have me,* she thought. But as much as she wanted to say it, to spit it at him, her throat closed, refusing to allow the words to emerge.

It was probably for the best. Let him think her a frightened weakling. She *was* frightened—more than she'd ever been in her life. But everyone underestimated her. She'd always known she was stronger than people assumed, but in the past several months, ever since she'd met Max, she'd grown even stronger.

Fenwicke settled back against the cushion and folded his hands in his lap. As if he were alone in the carriage, he faced forward and ignored her cowering on the floor.

The door handle was pressing into her back. Ever so slowly, she reached behind her. She might be able to escape, but she'd have to be quick. Open the door and fly out before he could catch her, not worrying about how she might hurt herself when she landed.

She took her time, thinking they were most likely headed toward Mayfair—she was fairly certain his house was located there. The closer they were to Mayfair, the more likely it would be that she'd know someone close by. She'd run to the safety of the closest house....

Her thoughts spinning, she kept edging her hand higher up the door until her fingers brushed the handle. She took a long, slow breath, and as soon as the carriage slowed at the next turn, she grabbed the handle and turned it, simultaneously thrusting open the door and throwing her body out of the carriage.

Lord Fenwicke was faster than she ever would have imagined. When half her body was free of the carriage, he hooked one arm about her waist, dragged her back inside, and grabbed the open door and slammed it shut.

He thumped back onto the seat. She felt his hard, bony legs beneath her bottom, and she realized he'd pulled her onto his lap. She writhed, trying to get away from him, from his touch, but his arm looped around her in an iron grip.

"Let me go!" she cried.

"And allow you to throw yourself out of my carriage?" He didn't seem angry. Only mildly amused, which scared her even more. "Of course I won't. Sweetheart."

She froze at his use of the endearment Max always used for her. Terror scurried over her skin like a thousand ants. She stared at him, absolutely still only because she couldn't move.

He pushed a finger to the tip of her nose, as if he were a friendly papa tweaking the nose of a child. "That calmed you down, didn't it? You liked that, didn't you, sweetheart?"

She'd begun to shake all over. She was an autumn leaf trembling in a windstorm, fighting to stay connected to the branch.

Don't fall apart, Olivia. Fight!

But she couldn't move. His arm squeezed around her even more tightly, and he leaned down, pushing his nose into her hair, and nuzzled her ear. Her eyes closed in utter horror. She'd never be able to wash his touch off.

"You smell so sweet, Olivia. So sweet and fresh and delicious. Wakefield might have soiled you, and, knowing that, most men wouldn't give you a second chance. But

I will, Olivia. I'll still have you...because even though you're ruined, I still want you."

How on earth did he know about her and Max? What was this about? Had Max told him about their liaison? Surely he wouldn't do such a thing!

She couldn't bear his touch a second longer. She lurched into battle, kicking and scratching and flailing out at him. Something caught on her skirt and she heard the screech as the expensive silk tore, but she ignored it. She couldn't abide him touching her.

She scored his cheek with her nails, and he caught her wrist, wrenching her arm away with a curse. "Damn you, you little witch. Stop it!"

But she didn't stop. Not until she was beneath him, pinned down on the seat, his heavy weight resting on her body, so heavy she had to gasp for air. He held both of her wrists in one hand. "Stupid little slut," he hissed down at her. "I'm bleeding!"

He was, and she was glad for it. Three parallel lines of red slashed across his cheek where she'd scratched him.

He patted his oily dark hair, and then he lowered his hand to her neck, applying enough pressure to make her cough.

"Pay attention." The sharp edge in his words carried a promise of violence. The smell of pomade and wax washed over her. He applied more pressure to her throat until she was choking, trying to breathe, failing. Panic swarmed over her, crushing and powerful.

"I can kill you," he said in a matter-of-fact voice. "Easily."

And she knew he could.

"But not yet." He eased the pressure. "I want to see the look on your face when I take you first. I want to hear you admit that I'm better than Maxwell Buchanan will ever be." He looked up at the carriage window, and his voice lightened. "Ah, we're home."

Home. Lord Fenwicke's home. It was somewhere in Mayfair, though she had no idea of its exact location. Still, if she could get onto the street, she'd be able to make her way to Lady Stratford's town house or her aunt Geraldine's house.

Lord Fenwicke was smiling down at her. "Won't you come inside?"

He was truly, utterly mad. Her panic had receded a little with his grip on her throat, and now he pulled away from her, reaching out his hand to help her up. She didn't take it. Instead, she held her neck and took in great, gulping breaths of the fresh, cold night air.

He watched her for a few moments, then slipped out of the carriage, straightening his coat and once again reaching forward to help her down. As if he were a gentleman.

"You're no gentleman," she grated out, her voice harsh and painful. "So stop pretending to be one."

"On the contrary, " Fenwicke said smoothly. "I am far more than a gentleman. I am a marquis and the heir to a dukedom."

You're evil, she wanted to say, but she didn't dare. He was crazy. She didn't know how he'd react to that accusation.

He curled his fingers to her in a summoning gesture. "Come along, sweetheart."

She flinched. "Don't call me that."

"I heard you liked it well enough when Wakefield called you that."

"You're ... not ... him," she choked.

His dark eyes narrowed. He reached into the carriage and simply plucked her out, setting her down hard on her feet. She felt a weight on her arm and looked down in shock. Her reticule had been hanging from her wrist since she'd left her box at the theater. She hadn't even noticed it was still there until now.

Fenwicke held her arm with one hand and pressed the other into the small of her back. "Come along."

He half pulled, half pushed her up the stairs leading to his front door. A tall, thin man opened the door. She recognized him—he was the servant who'd answered the door to her and her family when Fenwicke had come to Brockton Hall that first time. He appeared not at all perturbed to see his master dragging an unwilling woman into the house.

"I think," Fenwicke mused as he muscled her down a dimly lit corridor, "that all we need is a comfortable bed. What do you think, sweetheart?"

"I must return home," she said, but her voice was weak. He wasn't going to be allowing her to go home tonight—that much she knew. But...oh God, he'd made it clear that he wanted her....

Good Lord, he intended to rape her.

Black tinged the edges of her vision. She was familiar with the sensation. The malaria made her susceptible to fainting fits, and though she hadn't fainted since she'd come to England, she had lost consciousness on occasion in Antigua. She'd done so often enough in her life that she'd grown familiar with the symptoms preceding the faint and could usually make her way to a sofa or bed before it happened. Sometimes, if she sat very still and concentrated, she was even able to stave it off.

Should she do that now? Something told her, deep in her mind, as the black spots began to overwhelm her vision, that she *should* faint right now. That a man like Fenwicke wouldn't touch an unconscious woman. He wanted her awake and screaming. He wanted to take strength from her fear.

She allowed the blackness to claim her—for once welcoming it with open arms. The last thing she remembered was her knees buckling as she crumpled to the floor.

Chapter Sixteen

Olivia awoke in a comfortable bed with gentle bands of sunlight streaming over the covers. She turned over with a soft "mmm," and closed her eyes.

Then she remembered. Her eyes popped open, and she scrambled to a sitting position, noticing about a dozen things at once. She was dressed only in her chemise. She was in a strange, sunny bedroom, and there was a woman—a maid—sitting in a chair by the bed smiling pleasantly at her.

Olivia yanked the blanket to her chest, hiding her near nakedness. "Where am I?" she squeaked.

"Why, you're in London, ma'am."

"But where?"

"In Lord Fenwicke's house."

She looked around the room frantically. "Where are my clothes?"

"They're in the clothes press, ma'am. I'm to help you dress for breakfast." The woman stood and disappeared into a small closet, emerging after a moment with the dress

Olivia had been wearing last night. "It had a wretched tear in it, but I've mended it for you."

Olivia was too stunned to thank the woman, who was grinning at her. One of her front teeth was missing. She laid the dress across the foot of the bed and went to fetch Olivia's petticoats and stays as Olivia sat, frozen. This felt...unreal. Like she was in someone else's dream. This wasn't really happening, was it?

"Come along then." The woman gazed at her expectantly.

Warily, Olivia slipped out of bed and walked toward the maid. She was silent but tense as the woman helped her to dress.

Fenwicke would be here somewhere. He wanted something from her...besides her body, perhaps. Why her, when he could have his choice of willing women? She'd noticed how other ladies gaped and batted their eyelashes at him. He was widely considered a desirable man.

Then why her? Could it have something to do with Lady Fenwicke's escape to Lancashire?

Or, perhaps, Max's disappearance? Fenwicke clearly knew far more about her relationship with Max than was appropriate.

The maid had led her to a chair before a dressing table and, with efficient strokes, began to comb and style her hair. Olivia sat still, scanning the items on the dressing table—all the items she'd had in her possession last night, including her reticule and jewelry—as she tried not to stare at the ugly bruise marks on her neck in the mirror. Fortunately, while the neckline of her red satin opera dress was very low, the maid arranged Olivia's lace shawl to cover most of the marks.

Acquiescing to the maid's ministrations was a practical decision—if there was one thing the three eldest Donovan sisters had in common, it was practicality. She had a much better chance of escaping if she was fully clothed, after all. She couldn't be running about in London in winter clad only in a shift. Either she'd freeze to death or be caught, deemed a lunatic, and sent to Bedlam.

"There you are, ma'am. You'll be looking fresh and pure for the master, won't you?" The maid gave her a friendly pat on the shoulder.

Olivia looked in the mirror to see the woman giving her that gap-toothed smile. "May I go outside? I require some air. I . . . I tend to faint—like I did last night—if I am kept indoors for too long."

"Aye, well, you'll have to take that up with the master. He's waiting for you in the breakfast room."

"I see," Olivia said, her voice breathy with fear. Perhaps, though, she'd find a way to escape between this room and the breakfast room.

That thought was quashed, however, as soon as the maid opened the door. There was a burly, frightening-looking guard standing just outside the room, and when the maid turned to lead her down the corridor, Olivia saw another enormous man standing at its end. She had no doubt they'd been posted for her benefit. To prevent her from trying to run away.

Her knees felt weak and wobbly, but she squared her shoulders and stood tall and walked with as much strength as she could toward her fear.

A part of her assured her nothing bad would happen. She'd had enough bad things happen to her in her life. There was her father's death, her illness, her sister's drowning. She'd had absolutely no control over any of those events. But something told her that although she might not hold the lion's share of control in this situation, she held a little. A mouse's share, perhaps. Mice weren't powerful, but they held just enough to run... and sometimes to escape.

That thought made her straighten her spine, made her keep walking with a little more determination.

The maid led her into a small, dim, but perfectly presentable breakfast room. Lord Fenwicke was sitting at one end of the small table, and there was a place set—obviously for her—on the other.

Fenwicke rose. "Ah, good morning, Miss Donovan. Please sit down. May I offer you some chocolate?"

The maid ushered her to the chair and firmly pressed her into it.

She looked up at Fenwicke, who was still standing, his brows raised as he awaited her answer.

"No chocolate, thank you," she murmured.

She went through the motion of smoothing her napkin over her lap, because it was something to do other than acknowledge Fenwicke. However, when she looked down at the elegant plate of food a footman laid in front of her, her stomach churned violently. There was no way she'd be able to eat.

She gazed at the plate bleakly, swallowing hard against nausea, wondering if she looked as green as she felt.

Fenwicke, however, dug right into his food. "You slept well, I hope?" he asked between bites.

Slowly, she raised her head until her gaze clashed with his. His expression seemed jovial this morning, but there was an assessing, calculating darkness in his eyes that made her want to leap out of the chair and sprint out of this room.

"I slept," she said flatly.

He nodded and took another bite, then chased it with what looked and smelled like coffee. He eyed her over the rim of his cup. "I heard you have only recently come to Town."

"Correct," she said in a clipped voice.

"I don't suppose you heard from my wife before you left Stratford House?"

She hesitated, but then the lie flowed out easily. "No. In fact, I hadn't seen her for several weeks."

"Really? Ah, well that's unfortunate." Fenwicke set his coffee cup down. "I asked you to join me for breakfast because I'd like to strike a bargain with you."

"A bargain?" she repeated, her voice sounding dull and hollow. Perhaps he was going to try to force her to tell him where Lady Fenwicke was. But she wouldn't tell him that—she couldn't. If Fenwicke found Lady Fenwicke and Jessica . . . *no.* The thought of what he might do to them made her shudder. She couldn't give them away, even to save herself.

"Don't fret so, my dear. I can see the panic written on your face. Don't worry—we needn't discuss Lady Fenwicke any further. Rest assured, I have other means of locating my darling wife." He smiled, and nothing had ever struck her as sinister as the curve of his thin, pale lips. "But I do find myself in possession of something that you want. Something that might surprise you."

"I doubt that."

He laughed. "Have faith, Olivia. I happen to know it's something you want."

"What is it?"

Fenwicke took his time. He took a bite, chewed it in a leisurely fashion, took several sips of his drink, then set his cup down again.

Finally, he said, "Maxwell Buchanan, the Duke of Wakefield."

"I don't understand."

"I have him." Fenwicke took a bite, a sip, and patted his napkin over his mouth. "Completely at my mercy. And you, sweetheart, are to determine his fate."

Oh, God! She'd been right—the evil man had something to do with Max's disappearance! She struggled to maintain her composure. "Is he well?" Her voice, miraculously, sounded calm. Even serene.

"Yes, he is quite well." Fenwicke smirked. "Though he is doing his best to provoke me to change that."

"Where is he?"

"Close," Fenwicke responded easily. "In fact, he's here. In this very house."

Olivia swallowed hard. She was gripping her legs so tightly that she was certain her thighs would be covered with bruises.

Max was alive. He was here. If they could join together against Fenwicke...Together, they could do anything. They could escape from this madman.

Fenwicke laid his fork down and leaned forward. "He's in a less comfortable position than you." He smiled. "I like him less than I like you, you see. I tend to spoil those I like."

Olivia stared blandly at him. She wanted to claw his eyes out. She had never truly hated anyone, until now.

"I have him locked tight somewhere. Trussed up, in a

cold, dark room in my cellar. I've denied him the modern conveniences as well as food and water. This afternoon, I am going to ask him for something, and if I know him well—and I do, mind—he'll refuse yet again. Then, I'm afraid I'm going to have no choice but to resort to even more unpleasant consequences."

She glanced over her shoulder at the closed door. Even if she ran—even if she escaped from this horrible place— she'd be leaving Max behind.

No. She wouldn't go anywhere without him. Not now.

"Don't worry about that. I have a guard posted, Olivia. If you run away, he'll just sit you right back down. So . . . no reason to waste your time trying, hmm?"

She turned back, staring at her lap, at her hands clenched over her thighs.

"Look at me."

Her heart raced. She didn't look at him—couldn't, not without retching.

"He's angered me greatly. For so many reasons, but I won't get into those now—except for the one that upsets me the most." Fenwicke's voice was quiet and grave. "He stole you from me, Olivia. I shall never, ever forgive him for that. And I think he needs to pay a very, very high price for distressing me so thoroughly, don't you?"

Olivia swallowed hard. She gripped her legs and focused on breathing. She heard Fenwicke's words and understood them, even though each one twisted her insides tighter and pushed her closer to the edge of her control.

"Don't you want to hear the bargain I wish to make with you? Don't you want to save your handsome duke?"

She squeezed her eyes shut.

"Look at me."

She pried her eyes open and slowly raised her chin until she faced him. His figure swam and danced in her blurry vision.

"It's very simple, sweetheart," he said in a smooth, low voice. "Spend one night with me, and I'll release your duke."

Her mind worked frantically.

Fenwicke grinned. "I want you willing. I think it'll be more fun that way, don't you?"

She couldn't look at him a second longer. She closed her eyes again.

"I want you in my bed, lovely Miss Olivia Donovan. I've wanted you for a long time. You know that."

She tried to breathe, tried to calm her racing heart.

"Can you deny wanting me? You were affected by me, when we first met, weren't you? Admit it."

She dug her nails deep into the muscles in her thighs.

"One night with me, Olivia. One night of pleasure that will surpass anything you could ever dream of experiencing with Wakefield. One night, and then you'll both be free."

"One night..." The blackness edged her vision again, but this time she fought against it. She needed to think, to reason. She needed to save Max.

"Yes. One night. With you naked under me, taking me, crying out my name—"

She took a deep, strengthening breath. Then she raised her chin and stared at him with narrowed eyes.

"I'll do it. If it means you'll free Max, I'll do anything you want."

Chapter Seventeen

Max's mouth felt like it was full of cotton. His wrists had begun to bleed—he could feel the stickiness of the blood as it oozed onto his hands.

His stomach growled, he was growing a scruffy beard, and he stank, but those were the least of his problems. He'd go mad if he was forced to stay in here much longer. There was nothing to do. Nowhere to go. The room was small and cold. There was nothing beyond the steady burn of the lantern, and the chaise longue, and the musty, enclosed odor of the place.

One could only think of how many ways to kill someone for so long. It felt like he'd been imprisoned for years, but Max guessed this was only the fourth day...or night. It was difficult to be certain—there was no distinction between day and night down here. The sounds of the house above him gave him the only clues as to the time of day. Everything became quiet and peaceful in the latest hours of night.

He heard the scraping sound of the bolt being drawn, and though his heart pulsed, speeding up the sluggish blood through his veins, he didn't move from his slumped position on the chaise longue.

It was probably Fenwicke come to taunt him again. God help him, but even that sounded far more appealing than sitting here alone for hours on end, with nothing but one's own increasingly violent thoughts for company.

It was Fenwicke, unsurprisingly. Also unsurprising, his hired brutes hovered in the doorway.

Max didn't bother to look at the man. "What do you want this time?"

"How rude."

Max glanced up, raising a brow. "I'd kill you with my bare hands if I had the use of them."

It was then that he noticed the odd scratch marks on Fenwicke's cheek. It looked like the man had been attacked by an angry cat. It wouldn't surprise Max that a cat would dislike Fenwicke. Animals seemed to sense the evil in things.

"Well, I have news for you," Fenwicke said, "but if you're going to be so disagreeable, perhaps I should save it for another time."

Perhaps Fenwicke had purchased some instrument of torture he planned to try on him to induce him to sign the counterfeit confession. That was the next step, Max was sure of it. He gave Fenwicke a nonchalant shrug, as if he didn't care whether the man came or went.

Fenwicke clasped his hands together. "Well, I might be too eager, but I've a lovely surprise for you."

Max was certain he wouldn't be surprised. Still, he braced himself.

"In the form of a lithe, lovely young thing."

"A woman," Max said flatly. What the hell?

"Not just any woman, my friend." Fenwicke's lips curled. "Miss Olivia Donovan."

Max jumped to his feet. "Where? Is she here?"

God, please let her not be here. Please let her be safe... shopping on Regent Street with Lady Stratford, perhaps, or tucked into an armchair reading, or sipping tea with her aunt...

"She is here." Fenwicke's smile broadened. "And she knows you're here, too."

The thoughts roiling in Max's brain instantly calmed. He took a menacing step toward Fenwicke, noting that his men came to instant attention. These weren't dolts. If he attacked, they'd be on him in a second.

"What did you tell her?" he growled.

"That you're in dire circumstances."

Max narrowed his eyes.

"That I just might kill you."

Max let out a hissing breath.

"That she is the only one in the world who can save you." Fenwicke chuckled. "Such a biddable girl, isn't she?"

"Shut your mouth, Fenwicke."

Fenwicke didn't fear Max like he should, though. He didn't shut his damn fool of a mouth. "So very pretty. And delicate, isn't she? Like a bird. I could snap her bones as easily as I could break a toothpick."

That was it. Max lunged, aiming to wipe that sneer off Fenwicke's face. Without the use of his fists, he head-butted Fenwicke, landing a hard blow right on Fenwicke's cheek. Fenwicke's head snapped to the side and back, and Max was tossed backward by God knew how many men.

He struggled. Kicked and fought, and he fought dirty like they'd taught him. He managed to knee one of the men between the legs, taking him out of commission, but another came to take his place, pinning Max's arms down.

Heavy force threw him on the cement floor. He went down with an *umph,* the impact sucking the breath from his lungs. And then they pinned him, four men at his shoulders and legs. As much as he struggled, he couldn't move. Clenching his teeth, he looked up at Fenwicke, who hovered over him, holding his damaged cheek, blood dripping from between his fingers. Max had no idea if he'd caused a new wound or reopened the scratches that had already been there.

It suddenly hit him: the scratches…those were Olivia's work.

God, if Fenwicke had hurt her, he'd kill the man, no matter what it took.

"You'll regret that, Wakefield," Fenwicke said from between clenched teeth.

Max didn't respond.

"Your pretty little lady is prepared to do anything to help you out of here, did you know that? So she and I made a little bargain. She's upstairs right now, preparing."

"For what?" Max growled.

"I've provided her with some provocative garments for our upcoming night together," Fenwicke said simply. "In my bed."

Fury, hot and sharp, and unlike anything Max had ever known, arced through him. He twisted, breaking free from the men grasping his shoulders, and wrenched his legs out of the other men's holds. He fumbled for balance, managed to get himself into a lunging position, and once again went for Fenwicke, this time for his gut.

He barreled into Fenwicke's stomach with all the force and power of his anger, and Fenwicke, taken completely off guard, went flying. His back slammed against the cellar wall and he crumpled to the floor.

But the other men were on Max again. He fought with everything he had, but his opponents were four strong and well-fed men, and he didn't have the use of his hands.

It took them a while, and by the time it was over, they were all sweaty and bruised. One of the brutes' eyes was already swollen shut, and blood was running down Max's chin from a cut in his lip. His wrists screamed in agony from the stress he'd put on them during the fight, and blood flowed freely to his fingertips, hot and wet.

They trussed him like a Christmas turkey, tying his ankles in much the same fashion as his wrists were tied. But Fenwicke was still in the room. If Max didn't have the use of his body, he still had the use of his voice.

"If you so much as touch her, Fenwicke, I'll kill you." Through his rage, the words came out icy and calm. "If you lay a hand on her, that's the hand I'll be cutting off. If you—"

"Gag him," Fenwicke snapped.

Quickly, the men did as they were told, as if they'd been prepared for this inevitability. Within seconds, he was choking on the cloth they'd stuffed into his mouth, trying to spit it out. But they tied a strip of muslin around his mouth, holding the cloth in place, and he could do nothing but breathe angrily through his nose.

Fenwicke stood at the door, watching him. Max saw the anger in the tightness of his cheeks and the flat press of his pale lips.

God…oh God, he might have just made it worse for her.

This was his worst nightmare come to life. This couldn't be happening. He wanted to pound his head against the floor in frustration…in total failure and defeat.

"I'm going to be busy tonight, Wakefield," Fenwicke said quietly. "We're going to leave you right where you are, as you are, so you can spend the night thinking about the folly of your ways while I"—his lips cracked into a smile—"plant my seed inside your pretty little whore."

Olivia stumbled into the drawing room, but she didn't turn around as the maid snapped the door closed behind her.

Even though it appeared as though he'd somehow reopened the marks she'd made on his face, Fenwicke smiled in pleasure. Olivia glared at him. He thought he'd won, the bastard.

The harsh word spoken in her mind didn't even make Olivia flinch. She'd scream it out loud, a hundred times, in front of all of London: *Lord Fenwicke is a bastard.*

Then his expression softened until, if she didn't know better, she'd say his face was awash with sympathy. With compassion. She did know better, though.

"Alas," he said sadly. "I am an honest man. I feel it is my duty to warn you of something before we begin. Something that might change your mind about your beloved duke. And, sadly, it might affect the bargain we made earlier."

"Nothing will change my mind." She looked Fenwicke in the eye. Her hatred made her strong. Once she might've wilted like a flower being at this man's mercy, but with every minute that had passed since she'd learned Max was here, she'd grown stronger. She knew what the stakes were now. She knew what to fight for, and she knew she *could* fight.

He gave her a gentle smile, and sighed deeply. "I feel I must tell you this. For your own protection. You see, the Duke of Wakefield isn't exactly who he seems."

"What are you talking about?"

He tilted his head at her. "He's not a very good man, Olivia."

She made a scoffing noise. This man, telling her that Max wasn't very good? Laughable.

"Oh, I do dislike having to be the bearer of this news...."

She stared at him, her lips set. She challenged him with her eyes, daring him to tell her something that would change her mind about Max, confident that it couldn't be done.

Fenwicke drummed his fingers on his chin. "Would you like to see him before you make your final decision?"

"Yes!" The exclamation burst out from her before Olivia had the chance to modulate it.

Fenwicke stepped toward the door, a sly smile spreading over his lips. "Very well, my dear. This way."

Gesturing at the two men stationed at the drawing room door to follow them, he led her down a long, opulent corridor lined with damask wallpaper and gilded wall sconces and into a spotless kitchen. A tall, narrow door in the wall led to even narrower stairs. At the bottom, they turned down another long corridor, this one bare, with white plaster walls and a cement floor. Two more of Fenwicke's burly guards were stationed in front of a door halfway down the corridor.

Olivia swallowed hard. Her heart felt like it was going to beat its way out of her chest.

Max ... she was going to see him, make sure he was all right, talk to him ...

At the door, Fenwicke hesitated. "Now, Olivia, love, I'd prefer it if my men weren't forced to touch you, but they will do whatever it takes to ensure that you behave. Here's how it will go: I will walk into the room. You will stop at the threshold. You may speak to the duke, but if I were you, I wouldn't expect any answers. I'll give you the proof that the Duke of Wakefield isn't the man he's feigned to be, and if your duke has any sense at all, he will corroborate the evidence I will offer you."

Olivia glanced from Fenwicke to the door. She was so distracted by her proximity to Max that she hardly heard what the marquis was telling her.

He nodded at the guard closest to him, and the man drew the bolt and turned the handle.

"Wait," Fenwicke hissed to her as she began to step forward. The tallest of the men situated himself just behind her, ready to grab at her if she lunged inside.

The three other guards went in first, and Olivia heard a scuffling noise. When the sounds diminished, Fenwicke glanced into the room, then gave her a crisp nod. "They're ready for us. Come along, my dear."

Turning, he went through the doorway. Just inside, Fenwicke paused, and then he stepped aside so she could see into the tiny room.

Max was sitting on a chaise longue in the center of the room, looking at the door with narrowed, angry eyes. When he saw her, he lunged up, but Fenwicke's men were ready for that. They grabbed his upper arms, preventing him from moving toward her.

Not that he could have moved toward her, anyhow. His

ankles were bound with a rough rope and his hands were behind his back, probably bound in similar fashion.

He looked terrible. A gag was tied tight around his mouth, and a line of dried blood descended from the corner of one of his eyes to the gag, staining the side of the dirty rag reddish brown. His other eye was swollen and bruised. His chin was covered in blood. His clothes were dirty, wrinkled, and torn.

Olivia gave a jagged cry. "Max!" Her feet propelled her forward.

The guard standing behind Olivia grabbed her arm and jerked her to a painful halt. She gasped.

Max made a noise of rage and fought against the men, but he was ineffective against them without the use of his arms and legs. He was shouting behind the gag, something that sounded like, "Let her go, damn you!"

She tried to move forward, to get to him, but the hand curled around her arm was like a shackle. She couldn't move any closer.

"I love reunions," Fenwicke murmured.

Both she and Max turned furious gazes on him. "How could you do this to him?" Olivia blurted. "Are you mad?"

Fenwicke appeared to think about this for a moment, then he shook his head. "I don't think so, my dear. It's just that my enemy has driven me to extreme measures."

"Nothing could possibly be this extreme!" she exclaimed.

Fenwicke shrugged. "You have spent many years away from London, Olivia. You cannot understand the effects of his slights and slander on my reputation. On my family's status and well-being. And now I want to show you proof that you have fallen victim to this man's conniving nature as well." His expression gentled. "You see, Olivia, you were nothing but a wager to him."

Olivia snorted like Phoebe might have. "That's a lie."

"Sorry. It isn't. I was at Lord Hertford's ball the night the duke saw you for the first time. I watched him watch you, then I took him into the gentleman's parlor, and I made a wager with him. I bet him a thousand guineas that he wouldn't be able to seduce you."

Olivia stood very still, staring at him. What nonsense.

"He readily agreed, then set out to Sussex in hopes of luring you into his bed under your brother-in-law's roof."

No. No, no, no. Impossible. She glanced at Max, who was standing very still, his green eyes pleading.

"No, Olivia—" He continued trying to speak, but she didn't understand the words through the gag. She did understand Fenwicke's, however.

"And…" Fenwicke held up his hands. "He succeeded entirely. In fact, he informs me that he took you to bed more than once…perhaps…a dozen times?"

A slow burn began to crawl across Olivia's face. Her ears felt like they were on fire. Still, she didn't move.

He tilted his head at her, his eyes dark with what he pretended was sympathy but was probably something more like glee at imparting this devastating information to her…and in front of Max.

No, it was not devastating. It was complete nonsense. She glanced at Max again, searching for verification that Fenwicke was lying, but the expression of utter defeat on his face made panic flood into her gut, sickening and overwhelming.

It had to be a lie. It simply couldn't be true! If it was…

Olivia shoved away the panic. She simply wouldn't believe Fenwicke. She had no reason to believe him... even though he somehow knew about the number of times she'd met with Max in his bedchamber. *How?* Surely Max wouldn't have told him all this.

And Max couldn't defend himself right now—not with the gag. She couldn't condemn him based on Fenwicke's words and the look on his face!

"After the duke succeeded thoroughly with you and was called back to London on account of his uncle's impending death, he came to me. He told me of his conquest of you. I, naturally, conceded the win to him." Fenwicke leaned toward her, clasping his hands together in front of him as if in prayer. "But I thought you should know the lengths a bored London aristocrat will go to for a little fun, Olivia. You're an innocent miss, sheltered from the hard reality of the *ton*. You were a simple target for a man like Wakefield. You probably believed every bit of flattery he whispered at you." Fenwicke shook his head sadly. "Poor dear."

"You're lying," Olivia gritted out.

"No, my dear. I'm not."

She blinked hard against her stinging eyes. "Well, I don't believe you."

She gazed at Max, pleading with him to assure her somehow that none of this was true. But all he did was give Fenwicke such a look of hatred, it sent an icy shudder through her body.

She turned back to Fenwicke. "If you think I'd believe your word over His Grace's, my lord, you are sorely mistaken." She gestured at Max. "And I'm even more convinced that you are lying since you aren't giving His Grace the opportunity to defend himself."

Fenwicke sighed. "He's prone to ranting when I take off his muzzle. It tends to give splitting headaches to anyone in his proximity. I decided to save you the trouble, my dear. In any case, of course I don't expect you to believe my word over his. You fancy yourself in love with the man, after all." He gave a small grimace. "I've encountered ladies who thought they were in love before, who've lost all sense. However..." He reached into a pocket sewn on the inside of his coat. "...I have proof."

He pulled out a folded piece of stationery. "You see, I'm a careful gambler. I wrote down the details of the wager, and both of us signed it before he left London. As you will see for yourself."

He held out the paper to Olivia, and as she took it from him, she heard Max give a muffled curse from behind his gag.

Lord Fenwicke bets Lord Hasley a thousand guineas that he shall find it impossible to seduce Miss Olivia Donovan on or before the 1st January next. 14th August, 1829.

At the bottom were two unreadable, scrawled signatures. The unfamiliar one was undoubtedly Lord Fenwicke's. The other...Well, she knew it well from the letters he'd written to her before his uncle died and he'd still signed his correspondence as "Hasley." It was Max's.

She glanced up at Max. They stared at each other for a long moment. She didn't breathe. And then, very slowly, Max's eyes closed and he bent his head.

Yes, he was saying. *It was me. I signed that wager.*

Unbidden, a tear crested and slipped down her cheek. Without wiping it away, she looked up at Fenwicke and handed the paper back to him.

"I'm so sorry to be the bearer of this news."

"No you're not."

He was gloating. She could sense his joy. This was a coup for him, and she hated him even more for it.

Fenwicke *enjoyed* hurting people. He'd enjoyed every single second of this horrible scene.

"I only thought it fair to inform you of what kind of a man you were choosing to give your body up for. Again."

Did this information change how she felt about Max? He'd betrayed her, but did that mean she'd leave him to the insanity of Lord Fenwicke?

"What will you do with His Grace if I refuse you?" she asked softly. "What will you do with me?"

The evil glint returned to Fenwicke's obsidian eyes. "You are welcome to return to whatever you were doing before I interrupted the course of your life in such an ungentlemanly fashion."

She didn't believe him for an instant. "And Max?"

"Max," Fenwicke repeated, making the consonants in the word sound hard and unforgiving. "Well, he and I have several outstanding scores, you see. I cannot release him until those scores have been settled."

Max's head remained bowed.

"And when will that be?" Olivia asked.

"Your duke is a very stubborn man," Fenwicke said. "So"—he shrugged—"perhaps never."

"So you'll keep him here until he starves to death?"

Fenwicke didn't hesitate. "Perhaps. I have many options, and that is certainly one of them. But if that did come to pass, wouldn't you consider it adequate remuneration for the wrongs he's committed upon you, Olivia? Doesn't he deserve whatever fate shall befall him at my hands?"

"I don't know."

No, that wasn't right. She did know, to her bones, what she must do.

"Well?" Fenwicke looked at her earnestly. "What say you? Will you walk away from our bargain? From our devilish duke?"

Max's head moved up, and somehow, though his shout was still muffled, she understood every word. "Yes! Walk away, Olivia! Go!"

Meeting Fenwicke's cold black eyes, she shook her head.

"No, I won't," she murmured. "Our bargain still stands."

Chapter Eighteen

A few hours later, the gap-toothed maid declared Olivia nearly ready for her "dinner" with Lord Fenwicke. When the woman left the room to fetch a few more hairpins, Olivia withdrew her packet of medicinal quinine from her reticule and tucked the folded paper into the bodice of the single-layer silk garment Fenwicke had insisted she wear.

Usually, she'd be appalled about wearing such a thing, for it was red and tawdry, and revealed far too much skin. Yet tonight she had allowed the maid to put it on her without complaint, observing how horrid, how pale and thin, she appeared in the looking glass.

Calmness had taken over her. She was no longer shaking, no longer at risk of fainting. She had a plan, and no matter what, she was going to make it work. This would be over soon. After tonight, she and Max would be gone from this place, and she'd hopefully never have to lay eyes upon Lord Fenwicke ever again.

The maid bustled back inside, and Olivia quickly returned to the dressing chair she'd been seated in before.

"There, now," the woman murmured. "That should be enough for me to do your hair just the way the master likes it."

Olivia bit back the sarcastic retort on the tip of her tongue and forced a smile instead.

Sarcasm... goodness, she was becoming more like her sisters with every moment that she passed in Lord Fenwicke's home.

They must know she was missing by now. Lady Stratford must be out of her mind with worry. The poor woman.

"Excuse me?" Olivia said.

"Yes, ma'am?"

"Is there a way I might get a message to a friend? She doesn't know I'm here, and I fear she might be quite worried about me."

"Oh, yes, ma'am. Of course, Lord Fenwicke must read the letter first. The master approves all correspondence that leaves the house."

"I see." Olivia fell back into silence. Lord Fenwicke appeared to have complete control over his household and servants. How had he done it? Had he struck fear into these poor people? She watched the maid in the mirror. The woman held pins between her lips as she wrapped strands of Olivia's hair. Olivia thought of her absolute dedication to not breaking any of her master's rules. Of her missing tooth—had Fenwicke knocked that tooth out with a blow?

The mere thought made Olivia cringe, and the maid dropped one of the pins. "Oh dear me!" she cried before bending down to retrieve it.

It was horrid to abuse anyone—a wife, a servant. Fenwicke had to be stopped. But how? He was a marquis and would be a duke someday, for heaven's sake. He wasn't quite above the law, but nearly so. Enough that it would make it nearly impossible to prosecute him. Or for Lady Fenwicke to divorce him.

She smiled at the maid as she rose with the hairpin in her hand, but the woman didn't meet her eyes, just continued on with the task of doing her hair "just the way the master likes it."

When she had finished, the woman spread something over Olivia's bruises to hide them. Then she swiped rouge on her cheeks and paint on her lips. "There now, that makes you look more lively, I think. Don't you, ma'am?"

Olivia looked in the mirror and decided she'd rather look pale than hideous. "Mmm," she murmured.

The maid helped her up, smoothed out some of the wrinkles in her dress, and then beamed at her. "I think the master will be very happy."

Olivia didn't respond. How could she? She didn't want Fenwicke to hurt this woman for failing to please him, but she didn't want to appeal to him in any way, either.

So she just followed the maid down the corridor and into a large, stern-looking bedchamber bedecked in masculine-colored silks and velvets.

When she stepped inside the room and saw Lord Fenwicke, it took all her willpower to not turn on her heel and try to flee.

Fenwicke was dressed in an elaborately embroidered silk banyan that was tied around his waist in such a way that it revealed a big vee of the skin of his chest, dappled with black hair.

Besides Max, Olivia had never seen a man in such a state of undress. And of all the men in the world, this was the one she least wanted to see that way.

Be strong, Olivia. She could do this. She would do it.

Fenwicke rose from his chair at a small, intimate table and held his hand out to her. "Welcome, Olivia. You look…" His cold, silvery eyes swiped over her from her coiffure to the red slippers on her feet. "Fetching."

She stopped in the middle of the room. She simply couldn't force her body to take another step toward him.

He came to her, though, reaching for her hand and tugging her toward the table, where he pulled her chair out for her and pressed her into it.

She stared down at the food and had to admit that it looked—and smelled—delicious. Her stomach growled in response to the aromas of roasted meat and savory sauces. She had refused breakfast and hadn't been offered food since. She was hungry, and when she didn't eat, she became weak quickly—she knew that from her experiences with the fevers.

Off to the side, a smaller table held additional dishes and an assortment of bottles of wine and other spirits, along with glasses. Goodness, how much drink did he intend to get into her tonight?

Fenwicke smiled down at her. "Would you like some wine?"

"Yes, please."

Fenwicke went to the side table and proceeded to open one of the bottles.

His back turned toward her as he uncorked the bottle. Now might be her only chance. With shaking fingers, she yanked the packet from her bodice and tore the corner.

She tapped it over Fenwicke's plate, watching his food swallow the grains of quinine, and then, as he poured wine into two glasses, she shoved the packet back into her dress.

After Fenwicke sat in the chair across from her, she began to eat. The food was good. Meat slathered with a flavorful sauce, stuffed dumplings, potatoes. She hardly recognized what she ate, but she swallowed every bite, even though her stomach roiled and complained. She needed the nourishment it would give her.

She sipped at her wine, and for the first time, looked at Fenwicke over the rim.

He'd hardly touched his food. This was what she'd been afraid of. She knew the taste of quinine very well. She took a small dose every month or two and a larger dose daily when she had a fever.

Quinine tasted awful. Bitter, with a horrid aftertaste.

"The meat is very good," she said.

He frowned down at it, but when he looked back up, he was smiling. "Indeed." He took a bite, and she could see the confusion on his face. He'd probably tasted nothing like the quinine before and was wondering what on earth the cook could have done to give his meat such a bitter flavor.

She slowed her own eating, realizing that if she finished before him, he would simply not finish his food... and the quinine wouldn't do its job.

Please, she prayed silently, *please eat.*

But after a while, he rose, taking his plate with him. He went to the side table, carrying his half-empty plate. As soon as he turned away, Olivia plucked the packet from her bodice and tapped several grains into his wine.

He returned in a few moments with a plate of fruits and cheeses, abandoning his main course at the other table. He'd given up on it. Hopefully he'd taken at least some of the quinine. Hopefully he'd drink the wine.

He did drink all the wine—in one long swallow, though his mouth puckered when he lowered his glass.

Olivia released a breath. At least ten grains had been in there. Now, if he'd had another ten with his meal...

He rose twice more, and Olivia managed to pour the rest of the quinine into his wine and onto his food. The final time, he turned toward her just as she was tucking the packet into her bodice.

He frowned at her. "What is that?"

Her heart pounded. She held the packet out, staring at it as if she'd never seen it before. "This?"

"Yes, that," Fenwicke said dryly. He snatched it from her hand and opened it.

Please, oh please, let there not be any additional grains of quinine.... She flinched when a fine mist of powder fell from the paper.

But he didn't seem to see it. He looked from the open, blank paper up to her, his dark brows knitted. "What is this?"

"A...sheet of paper?"

"I see that," he said dryly. "Why did you have a sheet of paper by your bosom?"

"I..." Good heavens. She couldn't think of a single acceptable reason she'd have it. She prayed he didn't put two and two together and figure out that was why his food had tasted so odd this evening.

She bit her lower lip.

A muscle in his jaw twitched. "You intended to send a message to your duke, didn't you?" His voice was hard.

"I did," she whispered.

Silence. She didn't dare look up.

"Well? How did it end up stuffed in your bodice?"

"I...I..." She swallowed hard. "The maid...she is so devoted to you. She walked in, and I was holding the paper, preparing to write...and I was panicked. I...I thought she'd tell you."

"Well, of course she would. She informs me of everything that goes on in my house."

"I...I know that. So I tucked the sheet into my bodice before she could see it."

She glanced up to see him curling his lip into a sneer. "Stupid little chit. You were foolish enough to bring this to dinner with me."

She didn't respond. What could she say to that? Instead she bowed her head, managing to look contrite and afraid. The fear, at least, wasn't contrived.

She felt the weight of his hand on her shoulder and tried not to cringe away from it. He squeezed, so hard she released a little yelp.

"Don't worry," he murmured. "After tonight, you'll never have to worry about such things again. I'm going to wipe every trace of the Duke of Wakefield from your memory." His hand slid across her back and down her spine. "And from your body."

She swallowed hard against the sudden, nearly overwhelming nausea.

Slowly, she raised her head until she was looking up at him looming over her. With a sweep of his hand, he slapped her, hard, across the cheek. Her face snapped to the side, and she raised her hand to cover the sting, her eyes watering.

"Get up," he said. When she didn't move, he snapped, "Now."

His tone was dark and angry, and she knew if she didn't respond to his command, he'd hit her again. So she rose on shaking, watery legs.

Why wasn't the quinine working? Surely he'd ingested twenty or thirty grains by now.

"Come here."

He took her by the shoulders and yanked her against him, smashing his lips against hers.

Oh, Lord. Oh, no. She could feel his arousal beneath the two flimsy layers of silk separating them.

She stood rigidly as his mouth moved over hers. He wrapped his arm around her, pushed his pelvis against her, and thrust his tongue into her mouth.

No! Her body cried out in panic, in utter terror at this unwelcome invasion. She jerked away, but he yanked her even closer and pushed his disgusting tongue into her mouth again.

Then he stumbled away, making a gagging noise.

Frozen in her spot, she looked at him, terrified, her heart threatening to beat out of her chest. His face had turned pale—almost yellow—and his expression was drawn tight.

He took two staggering steps backward, blinking hard at her.

"Ah...excuse me." Covering his mouth with both hands, he turned and lurched out of the room, leaving her staring after him.

Chapter Nineteen

Olivia gazed after Fenwicke for a long while, wondering if he'd return. She knew something of what he must be feeling by now. She'd accidentally taken double her highest dosage of ten grains once at the end of a bout of fever, and she'd vomited for a week.

She slowly walked toward the door, and opening it, peered into the corridor. Most of the servants were abed, and she'd noticed only one man on guard in the passageway when she'd come to Lord Fenwicke's room earlier this evening. Now, the passageway was empty.

On tiptoe, she approached the stairs in the dim light of a single burning wall sconce. Hearing no sounds coming from the stairs, she descended quietly.

At the bottom, she turned to the right and hurried toward the kitchen.

She heard a long, low moan coming from behind her. And then a panicked shout. "Do something, damn you! Do something!"

It was Fenwicke's voice, raw with pain and panic.

"But what, sir?" She recognized the voice of one of the guards.

"I don't know," Fenwicke roared. "Get someone. Anyone! I can't see, damn you!"

Oh, heavens. Olivia had heard blindness was one of the symptoms of serious quinine poisoning. Had she given him enough to kill him?

She closed her eyes briefly, but the sound of footsteps in the passageway behind her made her lunge toward the kitchen door. She slipped inside and closed it behind her before looking around in the dimness. There was a great stone hearth and bread ovens, along with shelves packed full of unidentifiable items and rows of shadowy pots and pans hanging from hooks on the ceiling.

She opened the tall, narrow door and looked down into the darkened cellar. She'd have to make her way carefully—it'd be stupid to rush and fall down the stairs when she'd come so far.

Suddenly, the kitchen door opened behind her. She slipped behind the door leading to the cellar stairs.

Heavy footsteps approached, then stopped, right on the other side of the door. Lantern light leaked around the edges of the door. Olivia held her breath as the man bellowed down, "Charlie?"

Dimly, she heard the response. "Eh?"

"Come up here. There's some trouble with his lordship."

Unintelligible words wafted from below.

"I don't think he gives a damn about that no more, Charlie! He's sick. Get up here, I say! And hurry up about it!"

She heard Charlie's thin voice again. "If 'e's sick, fetch a bloody doctor."

The man began to stomp down the stairs but Charlie evidently met him halfway, because he cried, "Come on with you! You've got to help us get him into his bed. Hurry!"

The men hurried past the door and out of the kitchen, oblivious to her.

As soon as they were gone, she slipped out from behind the door and made her way down the narrow cellar stairs and down the corridor. With shaking hands, Olivia slid the heavy bolt and opened the door to Max's prison.

A lantern flickered in the corner of the room. Max lay on the chaise longue, his wild green eyes staring at her above the gag.

She rushed to him, knelt down, and fumbled at the tie on the gag.

It seemed to take forever, but finally she unwound the dirty strip of cloth. It left deep parallel lines of chafing across his cheeks and jaw.

He coughed, spitting out the balled rag that had been stuffed into his mouth. "Olivia," he said through dry lips, his voice cracking. "Why didn't you go? Why didn't you leave here when he gave you the chance?"

"I couldn't leave you," she choked out. "Even though... I couldn't."

Max's body was trembling all over. "Did he touch you? If he touched you, I swear to God, I'll—"

She cupped his cheeks in her hands, the growth of his beard rough against her palms. "I'm all right. But we have to get out of here before they discover we're gone. Now let me untie your wrists."

Again, it seemed to take hours before she could get the tight knots binding his wrists undone. This task was made even more difficult by all the dried and sticky blood caking the ropes. His wrists must hurt terribly. By the time Olivia unwound the rope, peeling it from Max's raw and oozing skin, she was shaking like a leaf.

Finally, she tossed the rope aside. She stared down at her hands—they were covered with fresh blood.

He pulled her into his arms, his movements rough and jerky. "Oh, sweetheart." The endearment made her freeze. She let him hold her, but her arms felt heavy, and she let them hang at her sides. She felt like a part of her had been flayed open and was now raw and exposed. "I'm sorry," he choked. "I'm so sorry. This is my fault."

She blinked her eyes hard so she could focus on the task at hand. Now wasn't the time for explanations and apologies. They needed to *go*.

His ankles weren't as damaged as his wrists, and with his help, untying them didn't take much time at all. Finally free, Max stumbled to his feet and drew her against him once again.

"Did he hurt you? God, Olivia. Please tell me he didn't hurt you. Please," he whispered, burying his face into her hair.

"He...no. He wanted to. He hit me...kissed me." She felt Max's arms tense around her as the air left his chest in a hiss. "But it could have been...worse." So much worse.

"How did you get down here?"

"I poisoned him with quinine. The medicine I use for my malaria. I gave him all the medicine I had. I think..." She swallowed down a heaving sob of a breath. "I think I might have killed him."

"Is he upstairs?"

"Yes."

"Conscious?"

"Yes."

"Who else is there with him?"

"At least two of those big guards he has. And they were talking about calling a doctor."

"The servants?"

"I think they're all in bed, but given how loudly he's shouting, they'll be down soon."

He held her shoulders gently, over the place where Fenwicke had bruised her earlier, and he looked into her face. "Do you know how to get out of the house?"

"I think I saw a door leading outside from the kitchen. The cellar stairs come up right near it."

"Good." He frowned down at her. "You shouldn't have risked this, Olivia. You should have gone before he—"

She simply shook her head. "Let's go, Max."

He took her hand and led her outside and down the corridor. They hurried up the stairs. At the top, she pointed to the door she had thought must lead outside.

Beyond the kitchen door, there was even more noise now. The sounds of shouting, talking, worried murmurs, running feet. Above it all was the sound of Fenwicke's shouting, loud with panic.

Max pulled her to the door at a near run. He worked the latch, but just as he opened the door, the kitchen door behind them swung open.

"Go!" Max murmured, pushing her outside. She stumbled forward and turned to see Max facing one of the guards.

"How'd you get out?" the man growled. Then he saw Olivia and sneered. "The slut got to you, did she?"

Max lunged forward, his fist slamming into the guard's stomach. The guard doubled over with an *oomph,* but he recovered quickly, swinging a punch that Max dodged before landing a blow to the guard's kidney.

The brute grunted, and then the men moved so quickly that for a few seconds, Olivia couldn't tell which fists belonged to whom. Finally, Max stepped back, leveled a hard second blow at the man's stomach, and the man crumpled to the floor.

Turning, Max saw Olivia. Pressing his lips together, he hurried outside, kicking the door shut behind them. Once again, he took her hand.

"Let's go."

As soon as they emerged onto the street, Max took off his torn coat and covered her shoulders with it as best he could. "I don't want anyone seeing you like this," he murmured. "We'll go to my house first—it's closer. After we're both clean and presentable, I'll take you to Lady Stratford."

Too numb to respond, she simply nodded. The night was frigid, and even wearing Max's coat, she was shuddering. The ice on the ground seeped all the way through her slippers and deep into her feet.

After a few blocks, she stumbled, and Max swept her up into his arms. "Put your arms around me, Olivia," he murmured. "That's right. We're almost there, sweetheart."

"You say 'sweetheart' so differently than he does," she murmured.

Max's step faltered. "Fenwicke called you that?"

"Only because he wanted to mock me."

"I won't call you that anymore," he said firmly. "Not if it will remind you of him."

Remembering his betrayal, his bet, his lies, she didn't answer him. It was probably best he didn't call her sweetheart anymore.

But for now, his body was warm and he held her so tightly, so comfortingly against him that she couldn't fathom doing anything but resting her head against his shoulder.

Fenwicke had been right about one thing—Max wasn't the man she thought he was. She'd have to distance herself from him.

But not tonight. Not now.

Tomorrow, maybe.

Max took her home to the town house that had belonged to his uncle. At the front stoop, he pounded on the door for several minutes before a disheveled butler answered. The man's eyes widened when he saw Max carrying Olivia.

"Oh . . . Your Grace! You're home. And thank God—"

Max brushed past him and headed toward the drawing room. "Fetch a maid to help the lady, and someone to light and heat the drawing room."

"Why, yes, sir, of course, sir." The man hurried off.

Inside his uncle's dark drawing room, Max carefully laid Olivia on the leather sofa. He saw the glint of her blue eyes as she looked up at him. He knelt at the edge of the sofa and stroked a finger down her cheek, reveling in the softness of her skin. "Where did he hit you, Olivia?"

"He slapped me," she whispered. "It wasn't too bad. I'm all right."

"Are you sure?"

He saw the movement in the dimness as she nodded. He couldn't bring himself to ask her about the forced kiss.

Someone knocked on the door, and Max answered it to discover one of his housemaids. He murmured a few instructions to her and she scampered off, returning moments later with a blanket for Olivia. Max directed her to go warm some milk for the lady. Within a few minutes, another servant had come in to light the lamps and stoke the fire.

In the flickering light, he assessed Olivia's condition. Except for her state of undress, he didn't see anything at first, but then he noticed the dark purple bruises around her neck, mottled by what looked like some kind of concealing body paint.

The rage was too powerful, too overwhelming. He lurched away to lean his head and palms against the wall and take deep breaths. He'd seen his mother with purple bands around her neck. He'd been a little boy, and she'd worn a high collar to hide them, but he'd been sitting on her lap and had seen a hint of purple and had pulled her collar down before she could stop him. Even then, he'd known that his father had been responsible.

And now Olivia. God damn it. Why was he so incapable of protecting the women he loved?

When he'd contained himself enough to turn back to Olivia, Max saw that she'd scrambled up to a sitting position on the sofa. She'd wrapped the blanket around her—probably both for warmth and to hide her state of undress from the servant. And to hide the bruises.

"Max?"

He walked back to her in slow, measured steps, and sat beside her on the sofa. Turning toward her, he brushed his fingers over the material of the blanket at her neck. "You didn't tell me about this."

"Oh..." She swallowed hard, and as the man lit another lamp, he saw the gray shadows beneath her eyes. He couldn't push her tonight. She wasn't only exhausted, she was terrified from the ordeal she'd just gone through.

"It seems so long ago, but it was yesterday." She looked at him, her blue eyes searching his face. "He did it to make a point. To say that he was all-powerful. That he was in charge and he possessed all the control. That he could kill me...easily."

Max gave a sharp nod.

"I thought he meant to strangle me...but he stopped before he did any real damage," she whispered. "His intention was to make a point rather than really harm me. Unlike what he did to Beatrice."

Max closed his eyes and bent his head down, rubbing the bridge of his nose between two fingers. "She's safe now, isn't she? Stratford made sure she's somewhere he can't get to her?"

"Yes. She's safe. Thank God. That poor girl."

He took Olivia's hand and laced her fingers with his. "You're safe, too. I'm not going to let him touch you. Ever again."

Her lips twitched in an attempted smile that didn't reach her eyes. "Will you take me to Lady Stratford's house? She's probably worried sick."

"Yes." He took a breath. "I haven't any appropriate clothing for you. Perhaps one of the maids will have something."

She shook her head. "No, that's all right. Lady Stratford will understand, and I'll get into my own clothes and burn this dress as soon as I can."

The maid walked in with a silver salver bearing two

China cups steaming with warm milk. "Set it down over there." Max gestured to the side table.

"Yes, Your Grace."

She deposited the tray and stood awaiting further instructions.

"I don't want to leave you," Max said. "But I smell and I look like a barbarian. I think it'll be better if I take you to Lady Stratford shaved and properly dressed."

"Yes, of course," Olivia said.

"Are you sure it's all right if I leave you here with…" He glanced up at the maid, his brows raised. He'd only been here a few weeks, and he didn't know the names of all the servants yet.

"Sally, Your Grace," she said.

"With Sally?"

She squeezed his hand reassuringly. "Of course. Go. I'll wait right here for you."

He stood and went to the sideboard. Pulling the stopper from a decanter of brandy, he poured a healthy dollop into one of the cups of milk and took it over to her.

"Here's some warm milk." When she took it from him, he added, "With a little brandy."

She sniffed it. "Smells like a lot of brandy."

He needed to touch her. To make some connection to reassure him that she was all right. Cupping her cheek in his palm, feeling the warm supple skin against his own, he told her, "I'll be back in a few minutes. Send for me if you need anything."

"I will." She smiled, but once again it didn't reach her eyes. "I won't need anything, though."

With a tight nod, he dropped his hand and left the room. He ascended the stairs at a near run, threw open his closet, and rooted through his clothes until he found something acceptable to wear. Turning, he saw Gardner, dressed in a crisp white nightgown and matching cap, hovering in his doorway. As usual, the man's primary concern was for the clothes.

"Welcome home, sir. But I really must advise you against carrying the garments in such a fashion. It will create unseemly wrinkles."

Max tossed the clothes onto his bed. "Can't be helped."

As Gardner rushed forward to rescue the clothes, Max peeled off the clothing he was wearing, which was rank with days of sweat and blood. He went to his basin, and using a washcloth, he quickly wiped down his body. Then, taking each item Gardner handed him, he yanked his clothes on. Gardner brushed his hands down the front of Max's trousers, muttering about the wrinkles and how he'd never be able to show his face in Town again if his master went outside looking like this, even in the middle of the night.

Max raised a bemused brow. "What about the clothes I just arrived in?"

Gardner looked down at them, his lips pursing with disgust. "Of course everyone will know I had naught to do with their unconscionable state. I shall burn them as soon as possible."

"Please do," Max said grimly.

Max turned to the basin and splashed water over his face, then had Gardner shave the annoying several-days' worth of growth from his face. By the time he returned downstairs, Gardner fretting at his heels, less than a quarter of an hour had passed. Still, it was almost two o'clock in the morning.

At the door to the drawing room, he told Gardner to go to bed. As the valet reluctantly left him, Max slipped inside the room.

She was sitting where he'd left her. She had a towel in her hand and was wiping away the tawdry face paint that Fenwicke had obviously demanded she wear.

He told the maid to inform the butler to have his carriage readied, and as she left the room, he sat beside Olivia again. The rough swipes of the towel were reddening her skin, but the face paint had smeared down to her jaw.

"May I help?"

She hesitated, then nodded, handing him the damp towel.

He was gentle about it. Maybe too gentle, because after several minutes of wiping at the persistent stripes of red, he could sense her impatience.

"I don't want to hurt you," he murmured. God knew, she'd been hurt enough.

"You're not hurting me, Max."

"Almost finished."

He cleaned along her jaw, then brushed the towel over her lips. He far preferred the natural pink of her lips to this garish red paint.

When he was finished he brushed his thumb over her lips. Soft and warm. Olivia's lips. Longing struck him hard. How he wanted to take her to bed, curl his body around her, make gentle love to her, and hold her for the remainder of the night.

But she was too anxious to get back to Lady Stratford, and for good reason. The dowager had probably alerted the entire city that her companion had gone missing.

"I wish you could stay," he murmured.

"I…" She looked away from him. "I can't."

"Do you want to go now?"

"Yes. We should."

He nodded. "Can you walk?"

"Yes."

He stood and helped her up, wrapped the blanket more securely around her, then led her to the front of the house where his carriage awaited. He handed her in, then gave the coachman instructions.

At this time of night, because there was no traffic, Lady Stratford's house was only a few minutes away. Olivia sat beside him, quiet and still, while his mind churned with all the ways he could ask her forgiveness for the wager he'd made with Fenwicke.

Finally, he looked up at her. Gathering her hands into his, he kissed them gently. Reverently.

"The wager, Olivia. It was stupid. It meant nothing. It has no bearing on how I feel about you now."

She blinked hard and turned to look out her window. The carriage was drawing to a halt.

"The lights are on," she murmured.

It was true—the windows of the house glowed with bright lights. He descended from the carriage and went around to Olivia's side. Opening the door, he swept her into his arms.

"I can walk."

"You haven't any shoes." He'd seen her little toes poking out from under the blanket and had realized she'd walked out into the icy street in her bare feet to get into the carriage. "I'll carry you inside. I promise I'll set you down the moment you're on a clean floor."

With a sigh, she acquiesced. Max carried her to the

door, which was opened just a few seconds after he knocked. The butler's eyes widened. "Miss Donovan!"

Reaching out, the man physically pulled Max inside with Olivia in his arms. "Come in, come in."

Max stepped inside and lowered Olivia onto her bare feet.

As the butler hurriedly closed the door, Max heard a feminine squeal. "Olivia!"

Her sister Phoebe rushed toward them from the passageway leading to the drawing room. Seconds later, the door to the drawing room opened, and Stratford and his wife, the dowager, Captain Langley, and Sebastian Harper all poured out of the room at Phoebe's heels.

Phoebe reached Olivia first. She threw her arms around her sister and burst into tears. "Oh, God, Olivia, we were so worried. I thought I'd never see you again."

The others reached them, crowding around. Pandemonium reigned for several moments. The questions and exclamations from Olivia's family were so fierce, Olivia was scarcely able to get a word in edgewise. Max tamped down his urge to protect her from their bombardment, reminding himself that this was her family; they wouldn't hurt her. She looked exhausted and on the verge of falling apart, but she returned their embraces, paying no attention whatsoever to him.

"Oh my dear, my dear," the dowager exclaimed, soothing her hand over Olivia's tangled hair. "We've all been so terribly worried about you. Kidnapped from the theater! A worse thing has never happened in the history of the world, I'm sure of it."

How had her family arrived in London so quickly? The dowager must have sent for them right away once

Olivia had gone missing, and they'd dashed to Town in record time.

The ladies crowded around Olivia, crooning, holding her, making exclamations of horror when Olivia whispered the words, "Lord Fenwicke."

Of course, thought Max, they all knew what a bastard Fenwicke was...young Jessica had been the one who'd discovered how brutally he was treating his wife.

Turning from his sister-in-law, Stratford caught Max's eye. His face hardened and he gestured toward the corridor. "Come with me, Wakefield."

With one last glance at Olivia to ensure she was all right, Max followed Stratford into an alcove off the corridor.

The man turned on him, his expression tight. "Explain," he said in a clipped voice, "and you'd best convince me that you had nothing to do with her disappearance, or you'll be wishing you'd never met the Donovans."

"For God's sake, Stratford," he bit out. "I had nothing to do with it. Lord Fenwicke abducted both of us. The man has lost his mind."

Stratford narrowed his eyes. "Langley wrote to us and told us that Fenwicke had employed a spy within our household to watch you and Olivia, but why in hell would he kidnap the two of you? It makes no sense."

"He bears a long-standing grudge against me," Max said tightly. "He took Olivia to get to me. And I'm damned sorry she was involved."

Stratford eyed him. "Did he hurt her?"

Max grimaced. "He hurt her enough to ensure I'll kill that bastard the next time I see him."

"Does she need a doctor?"

God, his gut felt hard as stone. Red tinged his vision. It was difficult to concentrate on anything besides beating Fenwicke to a pulp.

He swallowed hard. "It's probably best to call one just in case," he managed to grind out.

"How did you get away? Does he know where you are?"

"Olivia orchestrated it—she said she gave Fenwicke some of the medicine she uses for her malaria. Qu... qui—"

Stratford raised a brow. "How much quinine did she give him?"

"I don't know. She thinks she might have killed him. She said he lost his vision."

"Quinine can blind a man if the dose is too high."

"Permanently?"

"Sometimes."

"Could it kill him?" Max asked.

"It's possible."

They stood for a moment in silence, both of them watching the crowd of Olivia's family as they passed by, bustling her toward the staircase. Then Stratford turned back to Max. "I will call the doctor."

Max reached out and grasped the other man's arm. "Make sure he's gentle with her. She's been through a terrible ordeal."

His shirt and coat sleeves pulled back, exposing the bloody rings around his wrist that he hadn't had the time to clean and dress properly.

"You can trust that I'll ensure my sister-in-law will be properly looked after," Stratford said, somewhat coldly. Then he looked from Max's wrist to his face. "Looks like you need a doctor, too, Wakefield."

Max grunted. "I'm fine."

Stratford turned fully back to him. "Go home, get your wounds seen to, and get some rest. You look damn exhausted. We need to take care of Olivia, and it's probably best that the whole world doesn't find out that you and she were together in this debacle."

Max took a breath, then glanced toward the crowd of people disappearing up the stairs. Stratford was right, but he didn't want to leave her. Not now, when she was hurt and fragile. "I'm worried about her."

"We'll take good care of her."

God, he hated to go. But this was her family. She'd be safe with them, at least for the rest of the night. He gave a tight nod and left the house, promising himself that he'd see her tomorrow.

Chapter Twenty

The next day dawned gray and rainy. Smithson was nowhere to be found; instead, a different maid from Stratford House, Cora, came to help Olivia dress.

Olivia went downstairs for breakfast, and at the table she learned that Jonathan had inquired about Lord Fenwicke. The marquis lived, but he was very ill. The word about Town was that the doctor had attributed Fenwicke's illness to rotten meat and thought he would survive, but he was to be confined to his bed for an indeterminate amount of time.

Serena had told her the latest news about Jessica and Lady Fenwicke. Sebastian, Phoebe's husband, had returned from Prescot with the news that the ladies had settled in very well, and Lady Fenwicke's wounds—internal and external—were slowly healing.

With Olivia's blessing, Phoebe and Sebastian left early in the afternoon to get back to Margie. Olivia saw them off to Sussex with a kiss and a hug for her little niece.

Afterward, she went back inside and made good on her promise to burn the tawdry red dress.

Serena watched her as she ripped the fabric and fed the pieces to the flames. "Olivia, there's something I have to tell you."

Olivia kept her eyes on the flames. "What is it?"

"We received a letter from Captain Langley a few days ago. He said Lord Fenwicke had employed a spy within our household to feed him information about your liaisons with Max."

Olivia sucked in a breath. So that was how Fenwicke had known so much. He'd lied when he'd claimed Max had told him everything.

Serena continued, "Jonathan was furious. He questioned every single member of the household, from the scullery maids to the butler."

"Did you discover who it was?" Olivia asked, pushing the words out through her tight chest. She tossed another wad of fabric into the fire and watched it burn.

"It was your maid, Liv. Smithson."

Olivia closed her eyes against the well of betrayal. "Are you sure?" she choked out.

Serena sighed. "Yes. Cora, who shared a room with Smithson, saw her writing letters every day. Thinking the letters were romantic missives between Smithson and a suitor, she peeked at one of them. She was confused about why Smithson would be writing to a Lord F. about the goings-on at Stratford House, but she dismissed the matter from her mind and didn't think of it again until we questioned her."

"And Smithson?"

"As soon as we arrived in London yesterday, Jonathan

pressed her for the truth, and she admitted to all of it. She said Fenwicke paid her ten pounds to betray you. Jonathan dismissed her soundly. She's never to show her face in London, or in Sussex, again."

Olivia scrubbed away a tear threatening to fall. She gathered her composure. "Thank you, Serena. I mean... Meg."

Serena slipped her arms around Olivia's shoulders. "Forgive me, Liv. I can't believe I hired a maid who would betray you so horribly. I feel terrible about it."

"It's not your fault." Olivia sighed. "Ten pounds is a large sum. I'm sure anyone in Smithson's position would be lured by that amount."

Serena pulled back. Cupping Olivia's cheeks in her hands, she asked, "Are you really all right, Olivia?"

"Yes." She was better than she could ever have expected to be after such an ordeal, she thought. She felt absolutely calm.

"But you seem terribly..." Serena's brows knitted, and she dropped her hands. "Sad," she finished.

Olivia tossed the remnants of the dress into the fire, watched it catch, and then turned back to her sister. "I made a mistake, Serena."

Serena's frown deepened. "What do you mean?"

"With Max." Blinking hard, she looked away. She would not cry over him. God forbid.

"How do you mean? He seemed so worried about you last night."

"Yes. He did. But I found out..." She sighed. "Well, the truth is that when it came to Max, I didn't heed your warnings. I didn't protect my heart."

"What happened?"

"Fenwicke gave me a few insights into Max's character, and it's not as solid as I'd thought."

"For God's sake, how could you trust the word of such a madman?"

Olivia bit her lip. "He showed me—in writing—a wager he'd made with Max. Max bet him a thousand guineas that he could seduce me."

Serena gasped. "No."

"Yes."

"I can't believe it. It must have been forged!"

"It wasn't, Serena. I know his signature. And Max was there. The expression on his face confirmed that it was true. It also explains why Fenwicke paid Smithson to watch us. He wanted to make sure that Max was telling the truth when he came back to London claiming he'd succeeded in the seduction of the frigid Miss Olivia Donovan." Her voice cracked on the last few words.

"Oh, Olivia," Serena murmured. "I'm so sorry. This... this is devastating news."

Olivia gave her a faltering smile. "I should have known better than to let my heart become involved. I've been a fool."

"It's not your fault. He's been so..." Serena shook her head. "Well, I believed he was utterly taken with you. The way his eyes follow you across a room... Well, seeing the way he looks at you always gives me shivers."

"Me too," Olivia murmured.

Serena's arms encircled Olivia in a tight hug, and in the comfort of her older sister's embrace, Olivia released her anguish and allowed the tears to flow. Tears for all the fear and horror that she'd endured in Fenwicke's house. Tears for the loss of Max... and the loss of the part of her that had believed she was in love with him.

• • •

Max came to see her late in the afternoon. Knowing she needed to see him, to explain that she must distance herself from him, Olivia asked her sister and brother-in-law to give them time alone together.

She'd been standing at the window, staring at the gray world, at the rain falling in sheets outside, when he was announced. She turned to greet him as he walked into the room. "Good afternoon, Your Grace."

He smiled. "What do you think of my new title?"

"I think it suits you."

"Do you? It still feels strange to me."

"Maxwell Buchanan, the Duke of Wakefield," she murmured. "Do you like it?"

"Being the Duke of Wakefield?"

"Yes."

He met her eyes and held them a beat before answering. "No, I haven't liked it very much at all. It has kept me away from you."

Something in her chest tightened. She gestured to the sofa. "Let's sit down, Max."

He waited until she sat and then he lowered himself beside her, gathering her hand in his own. Olivia had thought she'd cried all her tears with Serena earlier, but she could feel them welling in her throat again now, and it took her several moments to gather her composure.

"There's something we need to talk about."

He nodded, keeping his gaze fixed on her.

She took a deep breath. "You and I—we are very different. We're from different worlds, and we're going different places."

"No," he said firmly. "We're not from entirely different worlds. You are an English lady as much as any lady born and bred in England. And as for us going different places—not if I have anything to say about it."

"Please, Max. Please don't make this more difficult for me than it already is." She tried to keep her voice steady. "You're not the man I thought you were."

Max clenched his teeth. "Listen to me, Olivia. I once told you there was a part of me I never wished for you to see. That damned bet came from that part of me, and I regret it. It was a stupid, foolish thing for me to do."

She sighed. "Why did you agree to it, then? Why did you sign it?"

He released her hand but he didn't draw his gaze away from her. "Fenwicke and I have a long and complicated history. The man has always brought out the parts of me that are most like my father. That night I first saw you, Fenwicke was boasting about his ability to conquer women. He assumed that since you didn't succumb to his advances, then you wouldn't succumb to mine. I wanted to prove him wrong." Finally, Max broke his gaze away from her. "I was angry. Angry at his arrogance, at his easy willingness to betray his wife. I *wanted* to beat him. Wanted to show him once and for all that he wasn't better than me. I agreed to the bet, I signed the damned wager, and I planned to come to Sussex. But once I arrived at Stratford House I didn't think of the bet once, except to consider what a foolish thing it had been for me to agree to it, and then to dismiss it once and for all."

"Yet you came to Sussex with plans to seduce me," she murmured. "Before you'd even met me." She pressed her palm over her eye so the threatening tear wouldn't fall.

Gripping the arms of his chair, he said, "There has

always been a competition between Fenwicke and me. Ever since we were schoolboys, he's been trying to best me. There have been many times I've wanted to wipe that superior sneer from his face, so I've made many wagers with him, always thinking 'this is the one that will put the ass in his place.' And I always win, but he always keeps coming back for more. It's a compulsion for him...the never-ending need to best me."

"And your never-ending need to prove to him that he can't," Olivia said softly.

Max sighed and looked away from her, but he didn't disagree with her. "When I saw you at Lord Hertford's ball, I couldn't take my eyes off you. He saw me watching you, and the competition began once more."

Olivia's heart felt fragmented, like delicate crystal in the instant before it shattered. "You gave in to his need for competition, because you have that same need—you want to best him. You enjoy proving, over and over, that you are superior. So in the end, it was all a game to you. A silly, childish competition to see which immature, insecure *boy* would win the race. At the expense of my virtue. At *my* expense."

"God, no." He leaned closer to her, and she had to fight to keep from drawing away from him. "I was intrigued by you that night at Hertford's ball, but when I went to Stratford House and grew to know you better..." He shook his head. "I didn't give a damn about the bet. I didn't want to share anything of my experience with you with Fenwicke. I didn't want to soil it like that. My need to best him seemed stupid and meaningless. I intended to pay him his one thousand guineas to make him go away."

She stared at him, not knowing what to make of all of

this. If she didn't believe him now, then that meant all their time together at Stratford House, and all the letters he'd sent since he'd left, were false. And that didn't make any sense either. If he'd already had the proof that he'd compromised her, then why send her so many letters? Why invite her to the public venue of the opera once she arrived in London? And last but not least, why on earth had Lord Fenwicke made so many threats against them both?

Once it might have been farfetched to think that Lord Fenwicke was as crazy as a loon, but she'd seen the truth of that firsthand.

"Our dealings have been similar to my father and uncle's dealings: based on bitterness and competition." Looking away from her, Max pushed a harsh hand through his hair, making his dark curls fly. He closed his eyes. "But I don't want to live like that. I never have. God knows I don't want to be anything like my father, but there is a weakness in me—that damned darkness—and Fenwicke kept sucking me back in. I was a fool to let it go on for as long as it has." He gazed at her, his green eyes pleading. "I want out. I don't want the darkness anymore. I don't want anything to do with Fenwicke. I'm done with it . . . with him."

She stared at him for a long moment, then bent her head down and rested her face in her hands. "I don't know what to think."

"I do," Max said firmly. "Forget about him. Forget about the wager. Believe me when I say I'm never going to be associating with that man, or anyone like him, ever again."

She looked back up at him, feeling utterly hopeless. "I can't forget, Max."

His lips tightened. "Why?"

"Because . . . I don't think I can come to terms with the

fact that our meetings didn't begin innocently. I was little more to you than a desire to best a rival. That day you met me at the spring—that wasn't by chance, was it? You knew I'd been going there. You engineered that meeting."

Max blew out a harsh breath. "I wanted to meet you. I would have been there waiting for you even if the wager had never been made."

"But you wouldn't have been at Jonathan's house, would you? My brother-in-law spoke of how you turned down his invitation at first—you laughed and said that you weren't interested in hunting."

He frowned. "Regardless of the wager, I was intrigued by you and I wanted to know you." He leaned forward. "Listen, Olivia. Your intentions towards me have changed as well, and more than once. You went from wanting friendship, to wanting me in your bed, to…whatever it is you feel for me now. Does the fact that you wanted only friendship from me once make your current feelings for me any less real? Your feelings for me grew and changed, just like my feelings for you."

She wrapped her arms around herself. "I don't think that makes me see this any differently. Yes, my feelings for you have grown, and I would like to believe that yours have, too. But I still feel as though I've been used. Like a pawn in a child's game. The foundation of what we've built between us is unsteady."

"That's not true!"

"I can't see it any other way."

"I still want to be with you."

"I can't, Max. Not now. I need time…to work this out."

She watched his entire face tighten, his expression harden. "Time?"

"Yes. Time away from you." She rose on unsteady legs. "I need to reassess my priorities. I've been flying so high with you, but learning this has clipped my wings. I have to decide what I want, what's right for me."

"*I'm* right for you. Let me prove that to you."

She couldn't meet his gaze. She was so confused. One part of her was screaming that he'd used her simply to make a childish point; the other was shouting that she should—she *must*—give him a chance to prove himself. She had no idea which one to listen to.

"Please," she murmured. "Give me time."

"How much time?"

"I don't know. I just need...space. Please."

She heard him rising beside her, but she didn't turn to face him. "Very well. I'll give you time to think, Olivia. But understand—I'm not letting you go."

He rested his hand on her shoulder. The possessive weight of his touch sent a clear signal that while he might be capitulating now, he had no intention of making their separation permanent. Without another word, he let go, turned, and left the drawing room, closing the door softly behind him.

She sank back onto the sofa and lowered her face into her hands. "You're doing the right thing, Olivia," she whispered to herself. "It's safer this way."

But she felt the damp of tears on her fingertips, and an enormous part of her wanted to rush after him and throw herself into his arms.

Max kept himself apprised of Lord Fenwicke's condition as well as Olivia's movements in Town. A few days after Olivia returned to the safety of her family, Lord and

Lady Stratford left London, but Olivia, surprisingly, had remained with the dowager.

The potentially enormous scandal of what had happened between Max, Olivia, and Fenwicke never developed into anything. Stratford and the Donovans didn't speak a word of Fenwicke's villainy to anyone—it was still unclear whether Fenwicke would recover, and the family had determined that it wouldn't do Olivia any good to suffer through a long and draining legal battle against the heir to a dukedom. It wasn't fair, and justice would never truly be served, but the fact that a select few could remain above the law was a fact of life they were forced to face.

Max had no intention of talking about it either, because despite the fact that Olivia was a victim, the incident would damage her reputation far more than it would his or Fenwicke's. The word about Town was that Max had left for a few days without telling a soul. And Olivia had been at her aunt Geraldine's house, and Lady Stratford had made such a fuss due to a simple miscommunication.

Not a word came from Fenwicke's quarter...which worried Max more than anything else.

Did he know that Olivia had poisoned him? Was he planning revenge?

For this reason, Max had hired two men—one to watch covertly over Olivia and the other to watch every move Fenwicke made. If the man took a step toward Olivia, Max would know about it, and he'd stop him.

As for Olivia and her desire for him to stay away from her—he'd give her the time she'd requested. He was a patient man, but his patience wouldn't last forever. Every day he spent without her intensified his desire to make her his in a permanent way.

A knock on his study door made him look up from the papers he was sorting. "Yes?"

The door opened to his implacable butler. "Your Grace, Mr. Childress is here to see you."

Max sat straighter. Childress was the man he'd hired to keep an eye on Fenwicke. "Please show him in."

The man was ushered into his study, and Max stood to shake his hand. "What news?"

"Lord Fenwicke remains abed, sir. It appears as though he's too ill to be removed from it any time soon."

"I see." *Good.* "Is he out of danger?"

"I believe so, sir. The doctor believes that the bad humors will take several more days to clear themselves from his body."

"And his vision?" Last week, Childress had reported that Fenwicke's sight had been improving.

"Completely restored now," Childress said.

"I see." Max tapped his fingertips on the sleek mahogany of his new desk, thinking. "Keep watching him as you have been. And please gather a list of all his properties in the United Kingdom for me." When Fenwicke recovered, Max had the impression that he'd leave London. And Max wanted a good idea of where the man was at all times, because that was information he needed to know if he was to keep Olivia safe.

"Yes, sir." Childress saluted and left.

Max stared after the man, a sense of foreboding tightening in his gut.

Two days later, that sense grew when Mr. Tanner, the man he'd hired to watch over Olivia, came to see him just after he'd had his morning coffee and was in his study reading the *Times.*

"Miss Donovan left town yesterday, Your Grace," Tanner said. "She left quietly, and I didn't discover she'd gone until I'd spoken with the dowager countess's coachman this morning."

So she's returned to Stratford House, Max thought grimly. Knowing that she would be miles away from him seemed to open a gaping hole deep inside his chest. Not to mention the fear that lodged like a lump in his throat when he thought of how difficult it would be to protect her when she was so far away.

He took a breath. She'd needed time, and he'd given her that. Fenwicke was safely in bed in London, so he didn't have to worry for her on that account.

He'd give her the short month of February, and then he'd be back.

"Looks like a trip to Sussex for me next month," he murmured to himself.

"Sussex, Your Grace?"

Max raised a brow. "Yes. Sussex."

"Oh!" Tanner's brown eyes widened. "You mean to follow after the lady. But she wasn't heading toward Sussex. The coachman said she was traveling north."

Max frowned. "Why north?"

"Well, I couldn't quite say—"

The man hurried after Max as he went into the corridor, bellowing for his horse to be saddled. Turning on Tanner, he pointed at the study. "Stay put until I return."

The man nodded, and a few minutes later, Max was heading toward the dowager's house in Bedford Square. When he strode into her drawing room, two ladies stood to greet him. One was the dowager Lady Stratford. The older one, a thin, wrinkled woman with a pinched face, scowled at him. She was, of course, Lady Stratford's mother, Lady Pierce.

Lady Stratford hurried toward him, her hands outstretched. "My goodness, Your Grace. What on earth brings you here at this hour?"

Max realized it was early—in fact it was earlier than most Londoners awoke. It was extremely rude and uncouth to go on a social visit at this time of day.

He managed a stiff bow. "Forgive me, ladies."

"Well, of course." Lady Stratford led him to a chair. Max supposed there were some advantages of being a duke—one being that intruding into an acquaintance's house at an unreasonable hour didn't necessarily result in immediate banishment from the premises. "Can I offer you some tea?"

He glanced at Lady Pierce, who was gazing at him through a quizzing glass. "I doubt the duke came here for a hot drink, Sarah."

Lady Stratford stepped back from him, wringing her hands. "Oh, you are making me quite agitated, Your Grace. Do tell us the reason for your visit."

"I need to know where Miss Donovan has gone," he said. "I know she didn't return to Sussex."

Lady Stratford's brows rose. "Oh, well, she went to visit her sister, Miss Jessica, in Lancashire. She was only planning to be gone for a few weeks—she wanted to be back soon, before you..."

Max frowned. "Before I... what?"

The lady's blue eyes twinkled. "Well, she thought if she stayed away too long, you might come after her."

Despite himself, Max released a short chuckle. Olivia knew him well. "So... that's where Miss Jessica and Lady Fenwicke are? In Lancashire?"

"Yes, indeed. Mr. Harper has a house there, and that is where they are staying until they determine the best course of action to take." She leaned toward him. "To keep Lady Fenwicke safe, you know."

"Where is the house located in Lancashire?"

"I believe it is outside of Prescot," Lady Pierce supplied.

"And Olivia was traveling alone?" Max realized belatedly that he'd called her Olivia and not Miss Donovan.

"Well, she had a maid with her, of course," Lady Stratford said.

For a moment, Max rested his forehead in his palm. He should feel relieved. Surely Olivia was safe with her sister and Lady Fenwicke. Yet this news hadn't placated the foreboding feeling within him at all. He rose from his chair. "Thank you, ladies."

Lady Stratford rose, too, and hurried toward him. "Oh, Your Grace, what is the matter? Is it that awful Lord Fenwicke? I should send word to Stratford—"

He placed a calming hand on her arm. "Fenwicke is still very ill, and as far as anyone knows, he isn't aware of his wife's location. I'm sure the ladies are perfectly safe." Lady Stratford released a breath of relief as he continued. "There's no reason to contact Lord Stratford." He bowed at the older women. "I'm sorry to have disturbed your morning, ladies."

"I assume you're on your way to Prescot, then," Lady Pierce said.

He turned to her. He'd known Lady Pierce all his life—she'd been friends with his aunt. He'd always known she was an intelligent woman. Yet in this case, she'd deciphered his intent before it had even solidified in his mind. However, as he stood there staring at her, he realized that she was right. He was going to Prescot, without delay.

"Yes, I am. Just to make sure all is well." He offered them a smile of reassurance.

He hurriedly took his leave of the ladies and returned to his house in Hay Hill. That afternoon, armed with descriptions of Fenwicke's properties throughout the kingdom and the exact location of the house in Prescot, Max left London, heading north.

Although Lady Stratford had pleaded with Olivia to take her carriage, she couldn't accept such a generous offer, so she'd traveled to Prescot by stagecoach. The journey was longer than Olivia had anticipated—England was much more vast than the small islands she was more familiar with. By the time the coach approached Prescot a few days after their departure from London, Olivia was exhausted.

And she was worried. Throughout the day, she had been experiencing the symptoms of a fever coming on. Cora wasn't familiar with Olivia's fevers. Worse, Olivia still hadn't replenished her supply of quinine. It was so soon after the last fever, and she'd never had two fevers closer than half a year apart, so she'd thought it unnecessary to buy quinine until she could return to Stratford House and ask Serena to order her some.

She sat in the crowded stagecoach, miserable, achy, and feverish. All she needed to do was get to Sebastian's house. Out of all the people in the world, Jessica was the most experienced and competent when it came to Olivia's malarial fevers. She would know what to do.

The stagecoach stopped at the only coaching inn in

Prescot. Olivia disembarked along with Cora, and they looked around the unfamiliar area.

The town was quiet, with hardly any traffic on the street. She looked at her maid. "Go inside and see if you can find someone we can hire to take us to the house."

Cora's brows knitted—to this point, Olivia hadn't asked her to go anywhere without her—but Olivia knew she needed to conserve her strength. She leaned heavily against a maple tree trunk and awaited her maid's return. Several minutes later, Cora came back, frowning.

"I couldn't find a soul, miss."

Olivia took a deep, stabilizing breath. "Very well. We'll leave our luggage at the inn and walk, then. It's only a mile."

"Yes, miss." Cora took their valises into the inn, emerging a few minutes later saying the innkeeper would watch the luggage for them until someone came to fetch it.

A mile was nothing compared to Olivia's daily walks. But she was feeling weaker by the minute.

She squared her shoulders. All she needed to do was walk a mile. A mile wasn't very far at all. When she arrived, Jessica would be there. Jessica would know what to do.

Side by side, Olivia and Cora walked. Every step was more difficult to make. Blurriness gradually began to overtake her vision, and she alternately shuddered from cold and wanted to rip the clothes off her burning skin. Her muscles—every one of them—ached, and her legs screamed in protest, taking offense at being forced to hold up her body.

"One step forward," Olivia murmured. "Just a few steps more."

She hardly noticed Cora's concerned looks. She couldn't spare a glance at the maid—all she could focus on were the steps ahead.

"That must be the house, Miss Donovan," Cora finally exclaimed.

She saw it—a white, block-shaped structure. "Not too far," she murmured, blinking hard to keep it in focus.

"Not at all," Cora said. "It's close as can be."

Olivia stumbled and felt the maid's sturdy arms encircle her.

"Just a little more then, Miss Donovan." Cora kept whispering encouraging words into Olivia's ear, but they all merged together. It didn't matter. All that was important was that she get to the white house before she lost consciousness.

"Miss Jessica!" Cora called. "Lady Fenwicke?"

Olivia turned, fighting against the pull of her stiff neck muscles, to look at the maid, but Cora was gazing toward the house. Calling for help, Olivia realized.

"Jessica," she called, but her voice emerged scratchy and weak.

There was no movement from the house. No one had heard them.

"Anyone here?" Cora sounded more desperate now as Olivia rested more of her weight on the maid.

Still . . . no movement except for the breeze that rustled over the overgrown hedges of yew lining the path leading from the road to the front stoop. Olivia wondered vaguely what it would be like to sleep in a yew bush.

"Is anyone home?" Cora yelled. The sound was so loud, so frantic. It hurt Olivia's ears.

She stopped suddenly, blinking at the still house. It might as well have been a hundred miles away. "I can't," she whispered.

The yew bushes swallowed her, and everything faded to black.

Chapter Twenty-one

Max was surprised he hadn't caught up with Olivia and her maid by now. Perhaps they'd traveled through the nights via stagecoach or mail coach. He'd made the assumption that they'd spend the nights at inns along the way, but no inn he'd inquired at had seen any trace of a slight young blond woman and her maid.

On the other hand, Max had made the foolish decision to ride. While it was easy enough to exchange his horse for a fresh mount every once in a while, it was physically impossible for him to ride twenty-four hours a day—even though he attempted to do so. Once in a while, it became necessary for him to rest.

He didn't arrive in Prescot until late in the afternoon on the third day. He went into the Legs-of-Man and Swan Inn, where he discovered that a stagecoach had arrived an hour before. The innkeeper was eager to offer him the finest room in the establishment, and as soon as the man gave him directions to Harper's house on the outskirts of the town, Max set off, his heart pounding.

He'd reunite with Olivia soon. He'd make sure she was all right, and he'd see her safely home as soon as she was ready to return.

The drizzle and rain he'd been forging through for the past few days had finally abated, leaving the air cool and fresh, while droplets of water sparkled in the sun like diamonds over the fields.

Within a few minutes, he saw the house—a small, square cottage painted a stark white, with a door in the center offset by two windows on either side. The lane leading up to the front stoop was lined with hedges of yew, and someone was on the lane. It looked as though she was bending to retrieve something.

As he drew closer, Max frowned. There was something on the ground, between the hedges. A person, dressed in white, with reddish blond hair escaping from her bonnet.

"Oh, God," he choked. "Olivia?"

He urged the horse into a run, then reined in sharply at the head of the path. He swung off his mount, and leaving the horse standing, he rushed toward Olivia and the woman he recognized as one of the maids from Stratford House.

"Olivia?" he shouted.

She didn't respond, but the maid was looking at him with wide, doe-like eyes. "Oh, sir. I'm so glad you've come. Miss Donovan…she's so feverish, and she fainted, and—"

Max sank down beside Olivia's limp form and scooped her against him. "Why didn't you take her inside?" he snapped.

"I can't," the maid said. "I've called and called, but there's no one home, and the door is locked. I've only just managed to get her out of the bush."

"When did you arrive?"

"I don't know, sir. It's probably been a good half hour. We walked from town…"

God. Olivia burned against him, her skin heating through all their layers of clothing. She was so pale he could see the thin blue lines of her veins through her skin.

"She walked in this condition?"

"She didn't tell me she was ill, sir."

Max gritted his teeth. He was furious, but as tempting as it was, he couldn't take it out on the maid. Lifting Olivia, he stood and strode toward the door of the house.

Holding her close against his body, he banged on the door. "Is anyone home?"

Though he was shouting, Olivia didn't budge in his arms.

Nothing but dead silence came from inside the house. Quickly, Max assessed his options. He could take her back to Prescot or he could break in to Harper's house. He knew Harper wouldn't care about that—God knew he'd want his sister-in-law to have access to the house, especially if she was in the throes of fever. If Max returned her to Prescot, there would likely be a doctor on hand, but she'd be relegated to staying in one of the inn's small rooms, which wouldn't be as comfortable as a bedroom in the house.

He glanced back at the maid. "We're going inside. If we can't find a way to get in easily, I'll break down the door."

She wrung her hands. "Yes, sir."

He probably should relinquish Olivia to the maid, but his body simply didn't want to. He found himself drawing her closer against him. He stepped back and circled the house, directing the maid to try each of the windows before he did. He confirmed that they were all locked. The back door was locked as well, and the door leading outside from the kitchen pantry. Max assessed all three entrances to the house, then determined that the pantry door would be the easiest to break down.

He shrugged out of his coat awkwardly and instructed the maid to lay it over a patch of grass that had survived the winter freezes and was somewhat soft-looking. After she smoothed it over the grass, he gently laid Olivia upon it.

He stood, staring down at her for a second. Panic welled, like a swirling hole of darkness, inside him. She looked so helpless, so colorless and weak. So sick.

Swallowing hard, he turned away. He needed to focus. She needed shelter. She needed a doctor. She needed a bed, food, clean clothing, warm blankets.

He stared at the door for a second, then kicked it in, splintering the area around the latch.

He returned to Olivia and scooped her once again into his arms. The maid retrieved his coat and quietly followed him inside.

He carried her through the pantry and kitchen, finding himself in a dining room separated from a parlor by a small entry hall and a set of stairs. He climbed the stairs to find two bedrooms off the landing. He went into the larger room, which was well furnished with a large bed, a clothes press, two comfortable-looking chairs, and a dressing alcove.

Instructing the maid to start a fire, he gently laid

Olivia on the bed and sat beside her, placing his palm on her burning forehead.

"Olivia?" he murmured. "Sweetheart? Can you wake up?"

She made a small moaning noise, and she shifted slightly, but she didn't wake. Max stared at her for a moment longer, then turned to the maid, who was standing behind him, waiting for instruction.

God knew he didn't want to leave Olivia. But it was almost dark, and he wouldn't send a young woman into a town unknown to her at this time of day.

"I need you to stay with your mistress. If she wakes, tell her I'm here, and that I'm taking care of her."

"Yes, sir."

"Don't leave her side. I'm going to Prescot to find a doctor. I'll return shortly."

The maid nodded.

Max turned back to Olivia. He bent down to her and brushed his lips over her earlobe. "I'll be back soon, sweetheart."

Grabbing his coat, he hurried downstairs, unlocked the front door, and found his horse wandering a ways down the lane. Poor creature was tired from the day's ride and needed a brush-down, but that would have to wait.

In Prescot, he returned to the inn first, which, at dusk, seemed to be the center of activity in the town. He burst into the downstairs tavern, causing curious faces to turn in his direction.

"I need a doctor," he announced. "Does anyone know where I might find one?"

The patrons of the tavern passed curious looks back

and forth, but no one answered until the innkeeper he'd met earlier came hurrying up to him.

"Your Grace," he said. The announcement of Max's title caused the onlookers' eyes to widen. "How can I help you?"

"There's a lady who's very ill with malaria—"

"Malaria?" The innkeeper frowned, as if he'd never heard the word before. Perhaps he hadn't.

"And she requires a doctor. Immediately," Max added.

A line appeared between the innkeeper's silver-frosted brows. "Well, sir, we have a doctor, but I believe he's gone to Liverpool to visit with family—"

"You have *a* doctor? One doctor?"

"Yes, sir."

"Only one?"

"Yes, sir. Prescot isn't a very large town, you see."

Max pressed his lips together. "I require a rider to carry a message to Liverpool. I need the best doctor in Liverpool here by midnight. At the latest."

No one responded until he pulled his purse from the inside of his coat pocket, stood beside an empty table, and started pouring coins onto the wooden surface. In his periphery, he saw figures rising, walking toward him.

"I can do it, sir."

Max turned, narrowing his eyes to assess the man who'd approached him. He was short and stocky, with a round face and an honest look about him. "Your name?"

"Peebles, sir. Wat Peebles."

"Very well, Mr. Peebles." He gestured to the chair opposite him. "Have a seat."

Peebles sat, and so did Max, although he didn't want to be sitting. He wanted to be rushing back to Olivia. The serving girl came by, and he ordered Peebles some ale, then gave the man his instructions. "When you locate the doctor, tell him that the lady suffers from malaria, and to bring…" He hesitated, hoping to hell that he'd get the name of her medication right. "Quinine."

"Quin-ine," Peebles repeated.

"Will you remember that?"

"Yes, sir."

Max gazed at him, assessing. He believed him, but he called for a pen and ink and wrote it down for the man just in case. He also penned a quick letter to the doctor. Max had never thrown around his new title before, but he knew the weight of it would mean something, would induce people to move faster than they usually would, so he signed the letter with his full title.

As he handed the letter to Peebles, he said, "Tell him that the Duke of Wakefield has sent for him and will reward him handsomely if he has a hand in contributing to the lady's recovery."

"Aye, sir. I'll tell him, sir."

"Good." He rose with final instructions for Peebles to bring the doctor to Harper's house on the outskirts of the town. He gave the man a generous portion of the agreed-upon sum, promising the remainder upon his return to the house before midnight.

Together, Max and Peebles left the tavern and went into the stables. Max wanted a look at Peebles's horse, to make sure the animal was up for heavy night riding.

"He's a young gelding, sir," Peebles assured him. "Strong as can be, and he's had a full day's rest since I arrived in Prescot yesterday."

Max checked the animal over, finding him more than

acceptable. Certainly more able to perform the feat of riding hard than his own mount would be tonight.

He instructed the stable master to see Peebles off, then stabled his own horse to rest for the evening and borrowed one of the inn's horses for the return ride out to Harper's house.

It was full dark now, and though he carried a lantern, he couldn't ride as fast as he would have liked. The road was rutted and uneven from the winter storms of the past months, but the horse seemed to sense his anxiousness, and held a pace faster than Max would have chosen at any other time.

He arrived at Harper's house in a few minutes. Behind the house was a small stable, where he put the horse, quickly unsaddling it before leaving it for the evening and rushing inside, taking the stairs two at a time in the dark house.

He slowed when he saw the soft light glowing from beneath the door of the room where he'd left Olivia. Taking a deep breath, he pushed the door open.

The maid, who was sitting in the armchair nearest the bed, jumped up in surprise. "Oh, sir, it's you!"

But he was looking at Olivia's still figure, relieved to see the blankets move in just the faintest rise and fall with her breath. "Did she wake?" he asked in a low voice.

"No, sir. She's been fast asleep." She frowned in Olivia's direction. "She's still burning with fever, but she's started trembling. As if she's frozen cold."

Max strode to the side of the bed. Olivia lay on her side, clutching her knees to her chest. The maid had stripped off her pelisse, dress, and petticoats, and she was clothed only in her chemise. The room was warm—the fireplace coals glowed with heat—but gooseflesh rippled over Olivia's exposed arm.

Hell, Max knew nothing about doctoring. Besides a few mild colds, he'd never been sick in his life. But if he were Olivia, he imagined that it would be comforting to feel warm. "See if you can find a brick to heat downstairs. And assess what food is in the house. If there's any broth, or anything you might be able to heat to give her, do that. Otherwise, send up some wine or brandy." He realized he'd probably have to send for food from the inn and cursed himself for not having thought of that when he'd been in town. They didn't have a cook here, and Olivia's maid couldn't be expected to do everything.

"Yes, sir." Taking one of the candles she'd lit, the maid turned to exit the room.

"Thank you," he said after her. She closed the door, and Max turned back to Olivia to finding her shaking visibly now.

Max pulled off his boots, his coat, and his shirt. Clad only in his trousers, he climbed in beside Olivia and drew her close. "Here, sweetheart," he murmured, pulling her back against his chest. "Let me warm you."

She seemed to sink into him, relaxing a little in her sleep, murmuring something unintelligible. He stroked her coppery hair back from her face, feeling the hot, dry burn of her skin under his fingertips.

Don't die, Olivia. Please don't die. He nuzzled his lips into her hair and closed his eyes.

He hated this—this feeling of helplessness, of terror. Would she ever wake up?

Where was the damned doctor?

It would be a few hours yet, certainly. There was nothing to do but wait ... and hope she didn't get any worse.

• • •

Olivia shifted. She hurt all over. And she couldn't determine whether she was hot or cold.

Hot, she decided. She began to kick off the heavy blankets covering her and the solid lump—a brick?—burning at her feet.

"Olivia?" The voice at her ear was warm, reassuring...and masculine.

Still half asleep, she tried to smile. "Max," she murmured. Just the thought of him made her smile. If he was nearby, he'd take care of her.

She blinked, opening her eyes, remembering. She wasn't anywhere near Max. She was in Prescot with her maid, on the walk leading to the house where her sister and Lady Fenwicke were staying. And the last thing she remembered was her vision blurring as she'd realized no one was coming to help.

Yet here she was, in a comfortable bed, in a warm room. She struggled to turn over.

"Careful, now."

It was Max's voice. She was certain of it. Moving her head felt like she was moving a lump of painful, solid granite, but she turned anyhow.

Max lay beside her, gazing at her with concern etched in deep lines across his forehead. She reached her heavy arm and touched his skin to smooth out the lines.

"Max?" she whispered, her voice emerging sounding grating and strange. "Is it really you? Are you really here?"

"Yes, I'm here."

"How...How did you...Did you follow me?" She winced and swallowed. Her throat hurt. *She* hurt.

"I heard you left London." He brushed a knuckle over her cheek. How was it that his touch felt so good when the rest of her felt so terrible? "I wanted to make sure you were all right."

"I'm glad you came," she said. Then she remembered where she was. "Where are Jessica and Lady Fenwicke?"

"I don't know, sweetheart. There was no one here but you and your maid when I arrived."

"That's odd."

"Perhaps they returned to Sussex?"

"Perhaps," she said, but something niggled inside her, something she couldn't bring into clear focus.

"We'll find out where they've gone," Max said. "As soon as you're better."

"I'm having a fever from the malaria."

"I know, sweetheart."

Panic rushed over her all of a sudden, and she grabbed his arm. "I don't have any quinine. I gave all that I had to Lord Fenwicke."

"It's all right," he said soothingly. "The doctor should be here soon. I told him to bring some medicine for you."

She relaxed, smiling at him. Even the small motion of holding his arm had left her breathless. "Thank you."

She heard the click of an opening door, and Max turned. It was Cora.

"I found some eggs, so I made an egg soup," the maid said. "And some wine."

Max looked back at Olivia. "Will you have a little soup?"

The mere thought of eating anything, as always when she was suffering from one of the fevers, made her nauseous, but she nodded gamely.

He smiled at her. "Good."

He helped her up until she was sitting against the wood slats of the headboard, and Cora brought her a tray. She looked down at the frothy, steaming yellow concoction and tried to steel her stomach against revolting.

"My mum used to make it for me whenever I had a bit of fever."

"Thank you, Cora." She picked up the spoon, but her hand was shaking, and she spilled the soup out of it before she was able to get it into her mouth.

Max took the spoon from her. He scooped out a bit, blew on it, then held it to her lips. He continued to feed her at a slow pace until she'd finished about a third of the bowl.

The next spoonful Max offered her, she shook her head. "Enough?" he asked.

"Yes. Can I lie down?"

He whisked the tray away, gave it to Cora, then helped Olivia to lie back down. Keeping her eyes open was beginning to be a struggle, and the blackness was once again taking over.

He smoothed his hand over her forehead. "The doctor will be here soon, Olivia. Rest."

Comforted by his touch, she let oblivion take her.

Peebles arrived with the doctor from Liverpool just before midnight. After questioning the doctor, a Mr. Grubb, on his credentials, Max paid Peebles and sent him on his way while Grubb examined Olivia.

As soon as Peebles left, Max hurried back inside, meaning to talk to the doctor. As he walked in, though, he found Cora coming from the kitchen. "Sir?"

"What is it, Cora?"

"Well, I didn't want to say so in front of Miss Donovan, but I found something a mite odd while I was making up the egg soup."

"What was that?"

"Well, you know how the house was closed up, all nice and tight? How the beds were made, there was no clutter, and the doors were locked, just as though Lady Fenwicke and Miss Jessica and their servants had deliberately and carefully left?"

"Yes?" He tried not to sound impatient, but his toes itched with the need to get back to Olivia.

"Well, there was a pitcher of curdled milk on the kitchen table." She frowned, then looked up at him and shrugged. "It just struck me as odd is all, sir. If they planned to leave, why would they leave a pitcher of milk out? Why would they have it in the kitchen at all? There are no cows here, so why would they have gone through the trouble of purchasing the milk if they were intending to leave?"

"They could simply have forgotten it," Max said.

"I suppose so." She gave him a shy smile. "I'm sure it's nothing, Your Grace. Please forgive me for mentioning it."

"No, I'm glad you did. And please be sure to tell me if you find anything else that strikes you as odd."

"Yes, sir."

Cora walked away, and he stared after her a moment. God, he didn't want to think what it could mean.... He didn't want to consider the idea that the young ladies might have been taken from the house against their will, that the person who'd taken them had made it look like they'd left deliberately, but in the rush had forgotten the milk on the table.

No. He couldn't let his thoughts turn in that direction. Not now. He needed to think of Olivia. He hurried upstairs, opening the door to the bedchamber to hear Olivia murmuring in her scratchy fever-affected voice. She sounded agitated.

"What's wrong?" Max asked.

She turned toward him. She was completely white except for the two splashes of scarlet on her cheeks and the bright blue of her eyes. She looked terrified.

"He hasn't any quinine."

"What?" Max turned to the doctor for clarification. "I instructed you to bring quinine in my letter."

"Forgive me, Your Grace, but quinine is a rare and expensive medicine. Furthermore, malaria is not a common ailment in Liverpool. I'm afraid you'll have to send for some from London."

"I see," Max said through gritted teeth. "Miss Donovan, will you excuse us for a moment?"

"Yes," she said, closing her eyes. It looked like it hurt her to keep them open. Max was going to go mad if he couldn't provide her some relief soon.

He gestured to the door, and the doctor followed him outside.

"All right," Max said, "what other ways are there to relieve the symptoms of an attack of malaria?"

"Nothing is known to be as effective as quinine, sir."

Max ground his teeth. He took a deep, steadying breath. "Surely there must be something."

"Well, I could treat her as I would anyone with a high fever. Or"—the doctor's bushy brows drew together—"there is one other option—said to be some-what efficacious for malarial fevers."

"What is it?"

"Arsenic."

Max raised his brows. "Arsenic? Isn't that poisonous?"

"It can be, but not usually in medicinal dosing."

Max gazed at the doctor skeptically, not liking the use of the word "usually."

"I would suggest that we try the usual treatment for a high fever. I've bled her and doused her, and I'll continue to use all the proven methods to reduce the fever. If that doesn't work within the space of a day, we should try the arsenic."

"I'd rather send for the quinine from London."

The doctor's brows rose. "Well, yes, you could try doing that. However, from here to London and back—that's four days at the least. Her fever is quite high, and I'm very uncertain we can keep her stable for that long." Seeing Max's face transform, he quickly added, "But it is certainly worth a try."

Max grabbed the man by the shoulders and tried not to shake the wits out of him—he needed those wits if he were to have any hope of helping Olivia. So instead of shaking him, he just gripped him tightly. "Go in there," he said, "and do whatever you can to help her. I'm sending to London for quinine. You'll either cure her entirely or keep her stable until it arrives."

The man's pale blue eyes stared up at him, wide and fearful. "Yes, Your Grace, I'll do my best. I promise you."

Max released him. "Good." It was all he could ask for. Why, then, did he feel like it wasn't enough?

Chapter Twenty-two

By dawn, Max had managed to rehire Peebles, this time for the much longer and potentially more profitable trip to London for quinine. Peebles would be on the mail coach heading for London later this morning. That was all that mattered.

Max returned to the house, stripped off his clothes, and tucked himself beside Olivia. It was cold outside—below freezing, and the coldness of his skin made her shift and then awaken with a sigh.

"Max?"

"I'm sorry to wake you. Go back to sleep."

"It's getting worse. It hurts. It's difficult to think."

He tried not to let the jerk of his reaction register through his body. "Oh, sweetheart," he murmured. "What can I do to help?"

"Hold me," she murmured. "You feel good. So cool. I'm so hot…"

"I'll hold you," he whispered. "For as long as you need me here."

"And don't let that doctor come back, Max."

His eyes popped open. "What?"

"He's..." Her voice drifted off.

He lifted himself up on one elbow and shook her gently. "Olivia, wake up. I need to know why you don't like Dr. Grubb."

"Hm?" Her eyelids fluttered. She didn't move though. He'd noticed she moved less as time went on. The fever was sapping her strength.

"What's wrong with the doctor, Olivia?" he said firmly. He needed to know. "Why don't you want him to help you?"

"I do," she murmured.

"But?"

"He doesn't have my medicine."

"I know that. We're going to get some to you soon."

"Only quinine helps."

Max blew out a breath. He hated this feeling of total helplessness like he'd never hated anything in his life.

"I don't like leeches. Don't like being bled. Don't like being cold."

"But he says all that will help reduce your fever."

"Only...quinine..."

"He'll give you arsenic if the bleeding doesn't work. That's supposed to help cure malaria."

Her eyelids fluttered again, but she didn't respond.

Max looked down at her, taking deep breaths to calm himself. She was so lovely lying there, like a porcelain doll, so beautiful and perfect.

But when he closed his eyes, he remembered her laughing up at him as she did so often when they'd walked together, her blue eyes sparkling, the lightest rose blush coloring her cheeks. He wanted that again.

"Olivia," he murmured. "You need to get better. Please."

She didn't move. He pulled her closer, feeling the burn of her skin against the cool of his body. Finally, he fell into a fretful sleep.

It was late in the afternoon when a knock on the door woke Max. He turned to check on Olivia, finding that her breathing had gotten shaky and there was a bluish tint to her skin that hadn't been there yesterday. Gently, he touched her cheek. It was burning.

Hell.

"Your Grace?" It was the maid outside the door. "The doctor has come."

"Yes, yes," Max said crossly. "Show him up."

He'd spoken loudly, but Olivia didn't budge.

Dr. Grubb entered a few moments later, just as Max was buttoning his coat.

"Good morning, Your Grace." The doctor seemed to deliberately ignore the fact that it was obvious Max had spent the night in Olivia's bed. Even though he probably knew that Max wouldn't be destroying her innocence in her state, sleeping with a lady like Olivia in any circumstance was not only fodder for gossip, it could ruin her reputation.

Max would count on the man's discretion. He could do no more. He looked from the doctor to Olivia, remembering what she'd told him before he'd fallen asleep this morning. He sighed. "There is to be no more bleeding. And no cold baths. They won't help her. She's getting worse. She feels hotter this morning."

The doctor raised his brows but nodded. "Very well.

I've thought on the arsenic. Since she's so slight, I'll prescribe a sixth of a grain in sugar water, three times daily. If she manages that well, we'll increase the dose." Grubb gave him a reassuring smile. "Have faith, Your Grace. I have confidence the arsenic will work wonders."

But it didn't work wonders. Late the next night, after two full days on the arsenic, Olivia grew delirious. She couldn't keep anything down, her fever was as high as ever, and the area beneath her eyes had turned a ghastly blue.

The doctor finally admitted she wasn't responding well to the arsenic and he wasn't inclined to give her any more. He said that all that was left to do was pray that the quinine arrived in time, but he doubted it would.

Max wanted to put his fist through the wall.

He wanted to wrap his hands around the useless doctor's neck.

He was pacing the room like a caged tiger when the maid came in, carrying a basin.

Max frowned at it. "What's that for?"

"I thought I'd give my mistress a bit of a bath."

Max stopped walking. "I'll do it."

"Yes, sir."

The girl set the basin on the table beside the bed. "I added some lavender and calendula to the water to soften her skin."

She left with a curtsy. Max went to the bedside and dipped the towel into the lukewarm water.

"I hope this feels good," he murmured, remembering how sensitive his skin had felt once when he'd had a mild fever as a boy. He was very gentle as he stroked the damp cloth over her.

At first she lay utterly still, limp as a rag doll. But then her eyelids began to flutter, and she awoke.

"What...what are you doing, Max?"

He closed his eyes for a second, just happy to hear her lucid after so many hours.

"I'm giving you a bath...of sorts."

"Like at Stratford House."

He smiled, remembering. It seemed so long ago that he'd bathed her in her room at Stratford House. "Yes."

"It feels...nice."

"Good. I want you to feel good."

She looked up at him with shining, clear eyes. "Max, why haven't we heard from my sisters? I'm worried about them."

He was, too. He'd written to Stratford House but hadn't received a response yet. Had the young women gone back to Sussex, or had they gone somewhere else? Or, God forbid, had Fenwicke learned about their location and sent his minions after them?

"I'm sure they're all right," Max murmured. He didn't want to make things worse for Olivia's recovery by causing her undue anxiety. "I've sent out some letters. I'm sure we'll find out where they are in the next few days."

"I hope so."

She was quiet for a second as he continued washing down the length of her pale leg.

"Max?"

"Hm?"

"It's not working. The medicine he's giving me. I'm getting sicker."

He dropped his hand and looked at her face. She was watching him with a fearful—but perfectly lucid—gaze.

He shook his head, blinking hard. "No, Olivia. I'm not

going to let this happen. The quinine is coming. In just a few days."

"I can't, Max. I can feel it sucking me under. A great weight. I'm struggling to stay above it, but it would be so easy, so comforting to sink."

"No!"

"I don't want to leave you," she whispered.

"You can't, Olivia. I need you."

"Maybe the lotion will help."

"Lotion?" he repeated dumbly.

"In...my luggage...I left it at the inn in Prescot."

"Your maid had the luggage delivered. It's here."

"In my cosmetics, there's a pink lotion in a glass jar. It's an ointment made from Peruvian bark. It was given to me by someone who also had malaria...she said it felt nice when her skin had dried out from a fever. She said it made her feel better."

Max had already slid off the bed and was heading to the dressing table where the maid had set out Olivia's cosmetics. The tiny jar was sitting there beside her hairbrush, visible from the bed. He could see the pink-tinted ointment inside it. He grabbed it and hurried back to her.

"Here it is. Tell me what to do."

She shook her head weakly, and her eyelids fluttered. "I'm so tired, Max. Just want to sleep."

"Olivia," he said sharply. "What do I do with this lotion?"

"Spread it...all over me," she murmured. As her eyelids slipped shut, he saw that her eyes had rolled back in her head.

"She's only fainted," he murmured. Still he reached for her neck to find her reassuring pulse. It was there—thready and fast, but there.

Put it on her? He opened the jar and sniffed it—it

didn't smell bad at all—then dipped his index finger and felt the stuff between his thumb and finger. It was thick and somewhat greasy.

Lifting her hand, he smoothed it over her dry, pale skin, rubbing it in until it disappeared, leaving her hand smooth and supple. He continued, rubbing the lotion up one arm and down the other. He massaged it into her chest, breasts and stomach, and down her legs. He rubbed it into her feet, between each of her toes.

When he'd finished she looked dewy and soft, and he was probably imagining it, but her face didn't look as yellow-pale as it had earlier. There was a bit left in the jar, so he gently turned her and rubbed it over her back.

He'd used every bit of the creamy ointment. He hoped that was what she'd meant for him to do.

He slid off the bed to put the jar away, and looking up at the clock, saw that it was nearly midnight. He slid into the chair beside the bed and watched her limp form as she struggled for every breath.

"I love her," he murmured out loud. And he didn't know what the hell he'd do if he lost her.

Olivia woke, sore but comfortable, but when she swallowed her throat was painfully dry.

"Thirsty," she whispered. Her voice came out in a grating croak.

Immediately, a hand was supporting her neck, lifting her enough that she could drink from the glass pressed against her lips.

The water was smooth, cool, and crisp. It seemed to cleanse her mouth and throat as it went down. She swallowed one refreshing gulp, and then several more.

"Thank you, Max," she murmured as he laid her back onto the pillow.

"How did you know it was me?"

His low voice was just as much of a balm as his touch. She smiled. It was the way he touched her. The way he was just... there. It seemed he'd been there forever. She wondered how long it had been since she'd arrived in Prescot and fallen sick. She had no idea.

But all of that was simply too much, too soon, to say. She didn't have the strength, but she knew she would soon. She'd tell him then.

For now, she simply smiled and said, "I just knew."

Soon, as soon as she had the strength, she'd tell him she was sorry for asking him to leave her alone. The bet he'd made with Fenwicke—that had been a different Max. The Max who had only seen her from a distance and hadn't really known her.

She'd always thought her illness would repel any possible suitor. She'd thought no man would want her if he knew how sick she became.

Max was still here. He knew her now, he knew all of her; he'd slept beside her during the worst of it, and he was still here.

There was a certain masculine roughness inherent in Max's touch. And she loved that. She loved how he'd held her against him while she'd been sick. How she'd wake in the throes of feverish delirium and take comfort from his heavy, even breaths.

She heard him suck in a breath, and finally, she opened her eyes.

"You're not feverish," he said. His eyes were wide and shining.

She shook her head. "No. I'm getting better."

"Was it the Peruvian bark lotion?"

"The Peruvian bark lotion?"

"You told me to put it on you yesterday—last night—so I spread it all over your body."

She laughed softly. "You did? I don't remember."

"You were unconscious."

"Well, I don't know," she murmured, "it might have been that." Or maybe it was just Max. Maybe his tender care had frightened the malaria right out of her.

Before she knew it, he'd gathered her into his arms. "Then you shall have it every time you're sick, love. As much of it as you need."

She slipped her arms around him and laid her head on his shoulder. "Thank you."

"Are you really feeling better?" There was hope—and vulnerability—in the question.

"Yes," she said. "I know from experience when the fevers take a turn. This one...well, it's gone."

"Thank God." He bent to press a kiss on her forehead.

"Max?"

"Yes?"

"Was I very awful? I mean...when I was sick? I mean, I know sometimes I'm not completely lucid. And my sisters say I'll jabber and drool and toss and turn. And they say I've yelled at them and once I threw hot soup at Jessica."

"And I'd wager Jessica was there to take care of you the next time you fell ill, even after the soup-throwing incident."

"Well, yes."

"She loves you unconditionally."

There was a short silence, and then she hesitantly asked. "And you?"

He pulled back a little, using one hand to tilt her head up to look into his face. "I love you, too, Olivia. I thought I was going to lose you..." He shook his head, his frown darkening his eyes. "And I've never felt so lost. I need you. You've become a part of me I cannot bear to lose."

"I'm so sorry," she whispered.

His eyes widened. "Sorry? For what?"

"For telling you I didn't want to see you. For sending you away. It was stupid of me."

"I knew you needed time. But if you thought I was going to let you go that easily...Well, I wasn't."

She'd known that, too, deep inside. "I'm so sorry I fell ill and that you were forced to take care of me."

His arms tightened around her. "I *want* to take care of you."

She looked up at him, frowning. "Why?"

"Because I love you. And when you love someone you want to care for them. You want to make them happy."

"I wish I could care for you. I wish I could make *you* happy."

His lips quirked into a smile. "You have made me happy, Olivia. Because I think you just told me you love me, too."

She sighed, feeling happy, content, fulfilled, and so much better. "Oh, Max. I think you're right."

A few days later, Olivia had begun using her new supply of quinine that had come from London, they'd hired temporary servants to help with the house as well as a man to repair the broken-down door, and Olivia took her first steps outside since her arrival. Though she was still recovering, it felt wonderful to be outdoors.

"You know," she murmured, "when I lived with my mother and sisters in Antigua, they'd never let me see the light of day for a full month after one of the fevers, because Mother was convinced exposure to the outside air would make me relapse."

Max drew to a halt beside her, frowning. "Are you sure it won't?"

She laughed. "It won't." She leaned up on tiptoes and kissed his cheek, not caring if any of the servants were watching. After her illness, she and Max were beyond behaving discreetly. "I promise."

He squeezed her hand. "Good. But if it does, thank God you have your medicine now."

"Yes." She tilted her head at him and asked softly, "Is it selfish of me to revel in the fact that you seem to care so much for me?" she asked musingly.

"*Seem to* care? God, Olivia. I do care."

She smiled. "Then is it selfish of me to revel in the fact that you care so much for me?"

"Not at all," he said. "Everyone should have someone who cares for them. And everyone should revel in it."

She bit her lower lip, looked up at him from under her lashes, and asked, "Do you revel in the fact that I care for you?"

He stopped and turned to face her. Cupping her cheeks in both hands, he tilted her face up to him. "I do. I revel in it, and I thank God for it. Every minute of every day."

He bent down, and for the first time since she'd awakened from the fever, he kissed her, smooth and soul-piercingly deep, his tongue, soft and warm, seeking hers, dueling, and ultimately conquering. After long, sensuous moments, he pulled away, still holding her face, and pressed his forehead to hers.

"You're a minx," he whispered, breathing hard, the heat of his exhalations washing over her cheeks.

She smiled and traced the powerful muscles on his back with her hand. "I've missed you, Max."

"I've been right here, sweetheart."

"You know what I mean."

He pulled back and looked into her eyes. "I've missed you, too."

Despite the chill bite in the air, her body heated from the inside out.

He cocked his head in the direction of the house. "Shall we return to the warmth of the house?" His eyes glinted wickedly. "Of the bedroom?"

"What will the servants think?" she breathed.

He raised his brows. "Perhaps that we're madly in love?"

She laughed as he took her hand and tugged her toward the house.

When they arrived, the man-of-all-work Max had hired, Peebles, was waiting for them at the door. "Ah, Your Grace, you received mail today."

"Mail!" Olivia clasped her hands at her chest. It was the first bit of mail they'd received since they'd arrived in Lancashire. "Maybe there's news about Jessica and Beatrice."

They followed Peebles inside, and sure enough, sitting atop the small table in the entry hall, was a short pile of mail. Olivia retrieved the top letter. "This one is from a Samuel Childress. Do you know him?"

Max frowned and took the letter from her. Without

another word, he slid his finger under the seal to open it. As he read, Olivia glimpsed the name on the letter now at the top of the pile.

"Oh, it's a letter from my sisters!" She tore off her gloves, tossed them onto the table, and opened the letter, and then gasped at the first line:

Neither Jessica nor Lady Fenwicke has returned to Sussex. We all assumed they were still in Lancashire.

Slowly, she looked up at Max, and nearly took a step back when she saw the stark look on his face that surely mirrored hers.

"What is it?" she whispered.

"It's Fenwicke. He's left London."

"Did he go home to Sussex?"

Max glanced at Peebles, then reached for the remaining letters. "We'll read them in the parlor, Peebles, thank you. You may go."

"Yes, sir." Peebles swiveled and left, and Olivia followed Max into the parlor.

They both sat on the sofa before Max said, "After we escaped from Fenwicke in London, I hired a man to watch him. I didn't want him coming after you again, and if he started anything, I believed I'd know well in advance.

"However, it seems Fenwicke left London even before you and I did. He let it be widely known that he was bedridden, but he wasn't. He left Town secretly at night. I think he knew—or assumed—I was having him watched."

"So your man discovered all this?"

"Yes, a few days ago. He obtained the information from one of Fenwicke's servants. But it seems even he hadn't any idea of where Fenwicke intended to go."

"Oh, dear," Olivia breathed.

Max nodded, tightlipped. "If he finds Lady Fenwicke in Sussex—"

"He won't," Olivia said bleakly. "She and Olivia aren't there. Phoebe said they should have been here when I arrived."

"Which means..." Max said slowly.

"...Fenwicke has found them," Olivia finished, her chest growing tight. "Oh, Max. That horrible man has my sister!"

She jumped up from the sofa, turning on him. "Where would he have taken them?" She blinked hard. God... after what Fenwicke had attempted with her, what would he do to Jessica? And...oh God...what would he do to his runaway wife?

"We have to find him," she said. "He might...he might murder them."

Max stood and pulled her into his embrace. "He has a house near Manchester. It's his nearest property. I'd wager he took them there."

"But what if he didn't?"

"I'll find them, Olivia." His voice was firm. Confident.

"Oh, no. No, Max."

"No?"

"You wouldn't leave me here!"

"You're too weak—"

"I'm going with you. Do you think I can sit here, helpless and among strangers, while my sister is in trouble?"

"You'll be safer here, Olivia."

"I'll be safer with *you*."

He sighed, hesitated, and finally nodded. "You're right. I wouldn't feel comfortable letting you out of my sight. But when we arrive in Manchester, you'll remain in the hotel until I return with Jessica and Lady Fenwicke."

She nodded gravely. "Of course."

"Are you certain you're not too weak to travel?"

"I walked three miles today," she pointed out. "At least that much."

"And it took you most of the day."

"I'm getting better, Max. Truly. By the time we arrive in Manchester, I'll be good as new."

Holding her upper arms, he pulled her forward and pressed a hard kiss to her forehead. "God, I hope you're right."

By late that evening, they'd hired a comfortable traveling carriage with lanterns that would light the roads at night. Max had fashioned a bed for Olivia on the forward-facing squabs, and he sat on the rear-facing seat, watching her as the carriage rattled along and she snuggled into the warmth of the blankets. It seemed she could never be warm anymore without him lying beside her.

"This is wrong," she murmured.

"Wrong?" He raised a dark brow, but his features were muted in the dim lantern light coming in through the windows. "Why?"

"I'm cozy and buried under piles of soft blankets, but you look terribly uncomfortable."

He smiled and bent forward to rub a knuckle over her cheek. He seemed to like touching her like that, and she nuzzled into his touch. "I'm fine. Get some rest, all right?"

"I don't think I can." She was too worried about Jessica and Beatrice.

"Try."

"I'll try," she promised.

They traveled on in silence for a while. Max plumped up one of the extra pillows and leaned against the side of the carriage, but his eyes didn't close. Instead, she could feel him watching her.

"I wish you could lie next to me," she murmured.

"So do I, Olivia. So do I."

Chapter Twenty-three

They arrived in Manchester late the following day. Max had visited the area before, and he knew the layout of the city and the general location of Fenwicke's house. He found a hotel and took rooms for him and Olivia under an assumed name. If something happened to him, he didn't want to leave any clues for Fenwicke to find her here.

According to local knowledge, Fenwicke was not currently in residence, but Max didn't believe that for a second. He posted Peebles and another man at Olivia's door, the former with a pistol he was given free rein to use to protect the lady. Olivia's maid was in the room with her with explicit instructions to report anything suspicious immediately to one of the men.

He sent for a meal for them both, because he didn't want to head for Fenwicke's until dusk. When he was finished with all the preparation, he dismissed the servants and turned to her.

She looked up at him, her blue eyes wide but so trusting. So full of love. No woman had ever looked at him the way Olivia Donovan did. No woman had ever made such feelings surge through him with just a look.

"I'll return soon with your sister and Lady Fenwicke."

She nodded, then lowered her eyes. "I'm afraid for you, Max."

And for the first time, the realization that Fenwicke wanted to kill him, and that he would probably do his damn best to succeed in doing so, slammed Max square across the chest.

"Look at me, Olivia."

Slowly, she raised her eyes. "Fenwicke is so bad. He's truly insane. I fear he'll do whatever he can to wreak his revenge on you...on me, on Jessica, and on Beatrice."

At that moment Max understood that he must come back. He couldn't let Fenwicke win this time, because if he did, Fenwicke would come after Olivia next. He'd find Olivia, and once he did, he'd have his way with her.

Max wasn't going to allow that to happen.

"I'll come back to you. All right?"

Pressing her lips together, she nodded.

God, his hunger for her had never receded, but she'd been ill and recovering, and he'd tamped it down. But now it burst free, ravenous.

He pulled her tight into his arms, taking her lips in a feverish, hungry kiss. She tasted soft, like the purest lily. Sweet and delicate.

She fisted her hands into the back of his coat and tugged him closer, her response to his kiss as voracious as his own. He angled his face, cupped a hand behind her head, and kissed her deeper, gliding his tongue in a seductive warm stroke over hers.

When she whimpered into his mouth, his cock responded, growing steel-hard in an instant.

There was a knock on the door, and Max groaned out loud.

"It's our dinner," Olivia said. "I'll tell them to come back later." While Max waited, she opened the door and murmured to the person standing outside. Within a minute, she'd closed and bolted the door and was standing in front of him once more.

As he pulled her into his arms again, her hands moved to his front, and he realized that she was unbuttoning his coat. He reciprocated, working the buttons on the back of her gown and pushing it down, baring her pale shoulder to him.

He moved his lips over the curve of her shoulder, then thrust the dress lower. The chemise caught on her stays but her dress and petticoat fell to the floor, and he went to work on the ties of her stays, reveling in how tiny her waist was compared to the largeness of his hands.

She pushed at his shoulder. "Off," she commanded, and he saw that she'd unbuttoned both layers of coats. He shrugged them off, then pulled his shirt over his head, exposing his torso. While he'd done that, she'd loosened her stays and was lifting them away.

He kicked off his shoes, then unbuttoned his trousers and pushed them over his hips while he watched her shimmy out of her silky drawers.

"You're so damn perfect," he groaned. He swept her into his arms and carried her to the bed, dropping her with a little bounce that made her gasp. He crawled over her, and bent down to rake his teeth over her neck. She squirmed, wrapped her hands around his neck, and whispered, "Yes, Max. Yes."

He slid his fingers between her legs. She was already wet, already ready for him. His cock was pulsing. He couldn't wait another second.

He pushed inside of her. She was tight and warm, her body gripping him, caressing him, so sweet and hot. There was nothing better than the feel of his Olivia around him.

He'd never let this go. Never let *her* go. He was so damned in love with her. Fenwicke was going to rot, and Max was going to marry Olivia and spend his life with her.

Burying his face in her neck, he thrust again and again into the warm heat of his woman. She wrapped her arms and legs around him and her body squeezed around his cock, tightening like a vise until she seemed to press all around him, exquisite pressure that he couldn't control.

Suddenly, she cried out, rippling over him and around him, and the pressure built until every one of his muscles shook with it. Then, in a sharp explosion, the tension released, starting at the base of his spine and spreading through his ballocks and cock and into her.

Into the woman he loved.

He'd never come inside a woman before. And the significance of it, combined with the urgency of this moment, and the bursting sensation of his love for her—it all combined to create the most explosive orgasm of his life. Bright spots erupted in his vision, and he shook and undulated, yanking her against him and bringing her along. He came and came until it seemed like it would never end.

But eventually, the tremors of his body and the pulsing of his sex receded and finally stopped altogether. Distractedly, Max noticed that their bodies were covered with a sheen of sweat, and Olivia's usually pale cheeks were flushed such a pretty pink he had no choice but to bend down and press kisses to them, one by one.

She looked up at him, with those beautiful, long-lashed blue eyes. "I love you so much, Max."

"I love you, too."

Neither of them mentioned the fact that he'd come inside her for the first time. He knew they'd discuss it later. There wasn't time now. It was almost dusk. Time to find Fenwicke and the ladies.

He pressed a kiss to her lips and then with a sigh, rolled off her and rifled around for his scattered clothing, tugging it on quickly.

She pulled the blankets to her chin, watching him in silence. Finally, he sat on the edge of the bed and slipped on his shoes, then looked down at her one last time, committing her pretty oval face to memory.

"You look like a woman who's just been well loved."

"I have," she murmured.

"Good." He bent down and gave her a final, lingering kiss. "Good-bye, sweetheart."

Max would have preferred to go on horseback to Fenwicke's house, but he had two ladies he was hopefully going to be taking away from the house, so he took the traveling carriage instead. When the coachman pulled up to the front of the house, Max took a moment to survey the scene.

The place was older and smaller than Fenwicke's Palladian home in Sussex. It was a dark-timbered Tudor-style mansion, with small diamond-paned windows and a tall turret rising from one end.

Max climbed down from the carriage, feeling the weight of his pistol in his coat pocket. He hadn't had his pistol on hand the last time he'd met with Fenwicke. This time he was prepared. He instructed the coachman to be ready to drive as soon as he emerged from the house.

He walked up to the front door and knocked as if he were a regular visitor.

A tall, weasel-faced man answered. "Good evening."

Damn. This was the man who'd answered the door when he, Olivia, Stratford, and Jessica had been searching for Lady Fenwicke, only to discover that Fenwicke had arrived in Sussex that day. Max pulled his hat lower over his eyes and cast his gaze downward. He had remained in the background protecting Olivia that day, so he could only hope this man didn't recognize him.

"Mr. Smith," Max said gruffly. He handed over the card he'd swiped from someone at the hotel's dining room. "I'm here to see the Marquis of Fenwicke." He hesitated before continuing. "Fenwicke and I were old school friends. I heard he recently arrived, and I wished to welcome him to town."

They had known a youth by the name of John Smith at Eton, though Max doubted the man had made his home in Manchester.

"Yes, sir." The servant gestured Max inside the entry hall. "Please excuse me while I see if the marquis is at home."

"Of course."

When the servant stepped away, Max quickly hurried down the three separate corridors leading from the entry hall, looking in open doorways and listening for odd sounds. The first corridor led him to what were obviously the kitchens and dining room, along with the servants' quarters, which were eerily dark and motionless. He hurried back and went down the long corridor leading in the opposite direction. Nothing but a series of closed doors and utter quiet. The corridor was lined with ancient-looking life-sized portraits of men and women whose eyes seemed to follow Max as he hurried along.

Going back to the entry hall, he took the third corridor, which was very short and led to a large ballroom and a curving staircase. As he entered, he heard the sounds of the servant's shoes tapping on the stairs, so he retreated to the entry hall, managing to look like he'd been waiting indolently for the servant to return.

"I'm sorry, sir," the man said stiffly, "but the marquis is not at home."

"I'm so sorry to hear that," Max said with brittle politeness. "Have you any idea when he'll return?"

"No, I'm sorry, sir. In fact, I'm not certain he will return at all. We were given to believe he might have left to attend a pressing matter in London."

"Ah." Max gave an understanding nod. "That's very good, then. I was on my way to London myself. I hope I shall have the opportunity to meet him there."

"Yes, sir." The man opened the front door in obvious dismissal, and bowed as Max turned to leave.

Max walked outside, murmured, "Drive out of sight of the house and then stop," to his coachman, and mounted the step, closing the door behind him. He rapped on the ceiling and the carriage jolted into movement.

A few moments later, after turning a sharp curve and traveling a little farther, it stopped. Max climbed out and hesitated, looking at the sky. It wasn't quite dark, but it would be in a short time. "Keep the carriage here until I return," he said to the coachman, "but check the road between here and Fenwicke's house every half hour. I might require your help when I bring the ladies out."

The coachman, who was familiar with the bare bones of Max's plan, nodded. "Yes, sir."

He looked a bit nervous, so Max clapped his hand over the man's shoulder. "Everything will be all right. I just need to retrieve the ladies, and we'll be on our way."

"Yes, sir."

Max left him and returned to Fenwicke's house at a slow jog. He didn't go the way of the road this time but instead went into the woods backing the house, emerging behind the structure on the side he'd surmised housed the kitchens and the servants' quarters.

He slipped from tree to tree, keeping himself well hidden behind the trunks of old chestnuts, and studied the back door.

He hoped it would be unlocked. Along with a stable, there was a barn in the back of the house, probably where they kept the henhouse. If the servants often walked between the barn and the kitchen, it seemed reasonable to think that the door wouldn't be kept locked. Although, he hadn't seen any servants besides the dour-faced man. If Fenwicke had dismissed most of his servants while he kept two women imprisoned, it was more likely the door would be locked.

After a few moments searching the environs for any sign of human movement, Max strode to the door and tried the handle.

Locked. Damn it.

But Max hadn't heard the sound of a lock turning when the servant had closed the front door behind him. Perhaps that door was kept unlocked during the day.

Pressing his back against the outside wall, Max inched around the house, stopping to peer into each window as he passed. Heavy draperies at every window blocked his view of the inside of the house, but he heard no sounds and sensed no movement from within.

That worried him. If Fenwicke and the gaunt servant were inside this house, where were the women? If they were upstairs, he imagined he'd hear some sound filtering through the windows. But he heard nothing. Only an uncanny silence.

He reached the front stoop. Scanning his environment and seeing no one, he edged along the exterior wall. He listened for a long moment before turning to face the door and trying the handle.

Unlocked. The door swung open on silent, well-oiled hinges, and Max stepped into the darkened entry hall.

After Max left the hotel room, Olivia had lain in bed for a while before rising and dressing herself. Her dinner came, and she managed to choke down a few bites. After that, there was nothing, really, for her to do but worry. So she paced the small room, and she worried, and then she paced some more.

She went to the small, square window and pushed open the draperies. The sun was struggling to cast its final rays of sunlight on the land before it gave up and slipped completely away. It would be full dark within half an hour.

She snapped the curtains closed, turned, and leaned against the window.

Olivia could help Max. She *must* help him, somehow. She'd go mad trapped in this room all alone while he was out there in danger. First, she needed to see Fenwicke's house to determine how she could be of help. Then she'd find something to do, something to make herself useful.

"You'll forgive me for this, Max, I know you will," she muttered under her breath as she pulled on her cloak. If she'd asked him outright, Max would never have allowed her to follow him to Fenwicke's house. It wasn't because he didn't trust her or that he thought she would do something stupid. It was because he wanted to keep her safe. Well, the feeling was entirely mutual: She would do whatever she could to keep him safe, too.

Leaving her dinner to grow cold on the table, she lifted her skirts and swung open the door. Mr. Peebles was there, slouched against the wall beside her door, and he jumped up when she peered into the corridor. She raised a brow at him. "What are you doing, Mr. Peebles?"

"Er...His Grace requested I watch over you, miss."

"Very well, then. I'm going out. I suppose you'll insist upon coming with me."

"His Grace didn't say you was going out, though, miss."

"That's probably because he didn't know," she pointed out.

That only seemed to confuse the man. He gave a feeble nod.

She passed him and went downstairs, hearing the dull thud of his feet behind her, and approached the hotelier to ask for the use of a carriage. Within a quarter of an hour, they were in a hackney coach on their way to Lord Fenwicke's house—a landmark everyone in Manchester seemed to know the location of.

The driver stopped on the darkened road—she'd instructed him to let her out a good distance from the house. When he came around to help her out, she frowned at a flickering light in the road behind them as Mr. Peebles descended from the servant's seat to stand beside her. "What is that?"

"We passed a carriage on the side of the road a ways back, ma'am." the driver said.

It was likely Max's carriage. She nodded, then looked ahead. "How far is Lord Fenwicke's house from here?"

"About a half mile or so."

"And where is his closest neighbor?"

"That'd be the Turleys, miss. That house would be another quarter-mile down the road past Lord Fenwicke's."

She smiled and nodded. "Thank you. Stay here until I return, if you please."

He nodded and didn't ask her any uncomfortable questions. She'd requested that before they'd set out, and she'd paid him well for his discretion.

She glanced at Mr. Peebles, gave a curt nod, and then set off, picking her way carefully down the road in the semi-darkness. It wasn't too difficult to see, for it was a clear, crisp, late-winter evening. Stars lit the night sky, and the moon was up, casting a dim silvery light over the landscape.

They turned down a sharp curve in the road, and the house came into view. Light spilled from four small upstairs windows, but it appeared that there were no other lights on in the house.

"Max, are you in there?" she murmured.

"What's that, miss?" Mr. Peebles's too-loud voice seemed to reverberate through the night.

She jerked to a stop and turned to him, pressing her finger against her lips. "Shh. They can't know we're here, do you understand?"

The man's head bobbed up and down. "Oh. Yes, miss. Sorry, miss."

"It's all right."

Peebles wasn't a very bright man and he wasn't much bigger than Olivia herself, but she agreed with Max's assessment that he was generally a good man, and had quickly become a loyal servant to them both. She'd grown quite fond of him.

"All right," she murmured. "Here's what we're going to do. We're going to search the exterior of the house. Once we approach, you go to the left, and I'll go to the right. We'll meet around the back. Tell me whether you hear or see anything. Any movement, any voices. Anything, understand?"

Peebles nodded gravely. "Yes, miss."

"All right. Let's go."

They approached the house, and Peebles didn't make a sound. He'd even miraculously managed to mask the sound of his feet on the gravel road. Olivia's feet were making far more noise than his were.

When they were within a few feet of the silent front door, Olivia glanced up at Peebles and nodded. Peebles turned away and slowly began to make his way around the perimeter of the house. Her heart beating like a caged rabbit's, Olivia turned to the right.

She lifted her dress so the dew-dampened grass wouldn't soak her hem, and picked her way over the grounds, keeping her eyes and ears attuned to any sound or sight that might be out of place. After a moment, a muffled sound came from the house. Hesitating, she glanced up at the window above where she was standing. Golden lamplight filtered through the closed curtain and lit a small square of grass on the ground.

Was Max in there? What was happening?

He could manage it, whatever it was. She had to believe in that. Fenwicke was in there. If she went into the house, she'd distract Max from his goal, increase his danger. She had to trust that he could deal with Fenwicke without her.

Her goal was to assess the exterior of the house and ensure that Jessica and Beatrice weren't imprisoned outside.

She dragged her gaze away from the window and searched the surrounding area. The house rose to her left—this part of it was built with wood, but there was a stone turret jutting out from the corner just ahead. There were windows in the turret but no lights. Could Beatrice and Jessica be trapped inside?

Possibly. If they were, Max would find them. Yet, why would Fenwicke keep two ladies prisoner inside his house? Surely, when people heard he'd come to town, he'd have visitors. Then there were the servants.

Olivia knew Jessica well enough to predict with some measure of certainty how her sister would react in this situation. She'd be outraged, and she'd let her voice be heard. If Jessica were in the tower, she'd probably be screaming her lungs out. Even the Turleys, a quarter of a mile down the road, would hear.

Unless he'd done something to her. Drugged her. Killed her.

Olivia swallowed the lump in her throat. No, she wouldn't think that way. Her sister was alive, and she was going to find her, because chances were that Fenwicke wasn't foolish enough to keep her in the house.

She turned again toward the house, squinting at it in the night. It looked like an older house—built during

Elizabethan times, or maybe even earlier, considering the stone tower. Such houses often had secret corridors, priest holes, and the like. If there was such a place, she thought that might be the likeliest location for Fenwicke to have imprisoned his captives.

Olivia tiptoed around the tower, watching and listening for anything out of the ordinary in the still, cold night.

She turned down the side of the house. There was a door centered between the front and back corners, the exterior shape of a brick fireplace, and a dark, high window below the gable. She walked to the door and held her ear against it. Total silence.

Pressing her lips together, she moved to the back of the house. Her heart jerked and then pounded unsteadily when she saw a dark figure hovering a few yards away, but then she realized it was Peebles, waiting for her.

She walked slowly toward him, taking in her surroundings. The windows on the ground floor were dark, but there were two lit windows on the first floor above. Two dark silhouettes of outbuildings stood several yards' distance from the back of the house—probably a barn and a stable, or possibly a cottage for the groundskeeper or steward.

She reached Peebles and pressed her finger to her lips, then pointed to one of the enormous chestnut trees and began to walk toward it. She slipped behind it, out of sight of the house, and asked Peebles, "Did you see or hear anything?"

"No, miss. All was quiet as could be. I'd think no one was there but for the lights upstairs."

Her too, except for that brief bit of murmuring she'd heard. Where was Max?

She gestured toward the two buildings, both of them visible but partially obscured by trees.

"I'd like you to search the far building," she whispered. "If there's nobody inside, see if you can get in and search the interior as well. But only if you're certain there's no one inside, understand?"

"Yes, miss."

"If you see or hear anyone, don't let them see you. Come straight to me. I'll be searching the closer building."

"Yes, miss."

"Good." She gave him a tentative smile. "And thank you, Mr. Peebles."

He looked down, a bashful expression passing over his face. "'Tis nothing, miss."

She took a slow breath, calming her shaking nerves. "All right, let's go."

Mr. Peebles strode away, treading with his amazingly silent gait through the grass. She followed, veering from his path to approach the first outbuilding. It was silent and dark. No lights, no sounds. She circled it at first and decided that it must be a barn. From peering into the windows, she could see animal pens, but she couldn't discern the movements or sounds of any animals. The place appeared to be abandoned.

After completing her circle of the building, she deemed it safe enough to try the door. It opened easily and glided wide without a squeak. That was surprising. Someone had recently oiled the hinges. This was odd, since the barn smelled like lye soap and dust—like it hadn't been recently used. She turned to the left and began to explore the animal pens one by one. They were all clean and empty. A narrow set of stairs along the back wall led up to a hayloft. Olivia climbed them—the boards squeaked and complained as she ascended, but there was nothing in the loft but an old black traveling trunk tucked into the far corner. When she opened it, the lid gave a loud, complaining creak, but the inside was empty.

She tiptoed back to the stairs and began to descend. About halfway down, she heard a soft *thump*.

She froze. There it was again. *Thump*. And again, louder this time. *Thump!*

"Jessica?" she whispered. She stepped down from the last step and hurried toward the source of the noise—it seemed to come from the opposite side of the barn, beneath the hayloft.

Thump. Thump. Thump!

The sound grew louder as she walked into the very last stall—what looked like a large pigpen. The space was empty except for a dark woven rug covering the floor.

She heard a voice—what sounded like muffled shouting. She'd know that tone anywhere. It *was* Jessica. And her voice was coming from below the rug.

"Jessica!"

More thumping and shouting.

"I hear you!" she said in as loud a voice as she dared. "Wait a moment."

She pulled back the rug, struggling with its heavy weight. She could only see the door thanks to the moonlight shining through the bare window, casting a soft silvery glow over the floorboards. It was the barest outline of a door, invisible within the design of the planking, unless one was looking.

But how to pry it open? There was no handle.

She fell to her stomach and spoke to the crack in the

floor. "Jess—it's me, Olivia. I'm going to get you out of there...but how do I open the door?"

She heard a muffled sound, then one word: "Crowbar!"

A crowbar? Where on earth would she find a crowbar? The barn was completely empty.

Well, there had to be one somewhere. If it was here, she'd find it.

She closed her eyes in a long blink of relief. Her sister sounded as energetic and full of life as ever. "It's so good to hear your voice, Jess."

She heard a faint, "You, too, Liv."

"I'll be back," she promised. "I need to find a crowbar."

She scrambled to her feet. There was nothing in this barn besides the trunk, and that wouldn't be of any help. She went outside and hurried to the adjacent building, finding Peebles standing near a window with his head cocked as if he were listening intently.

"What is it?"

"I cannot tell if there's someone inside, miss. I hear something...but it might just be a horse, aye?"

She peeked into the window, but the moon was on the opposite side of the building and she couldn't see anything.

She released a breath through pursed lips. "How good are you with your fists, Peebles?"

His brown eyes widened. "Well, I daresay I've been in a fight or two, but—"

"Good enough," she said quickly. "Look, if there's someone in there, I'll talk to him, but if he threatens to go to his master, we're going to have to stop him."

Peebles nodded, his eyes wide.

"All right. Come with me."

She walked to the door, took a deep, fortifying breath, and pushed it open, hesitating at the threshold. A horse whinnied, and the floorboards creaked as another horse shifted its stance.

It was a smallish stable, with stalls for six or eight horses and space for a carriage, but certainly not enough room for apartments for the stable boys and groomsmen.

She glanced back at Peebles. "I think it's just horses."

Still wide-eyed, he nodded.

"We're looking for a crowbar. Will you help me see if there's one to be found in here?"

"Yes, miss."

She moved to the far end and started opening doors to survey the stalls. The first two stalls she opened were completely bare save for the bales of hay piled inside, but when she opened the third door, she gasped in relief.

She'd discovered a veritable treasure trove of tools and farming and gardening implements. At the very front of the row of tools lined up against the stable wall was a crowbar as tall as Olivia.

She hefted it and went out of the stable. "Mr. Peebles! I found it."

"Oh, miss, you shouldn't be carryin' that." He hurried up to her and took it, frowning.

"Thank you. Now follow me, and we'll help my sister escape."

"Your sister—?"

But she was already hurrying out of the stable and back to the barn. She rushed inside and into the room where she'd found the hidden door in the floor. She pointed at its faint outline. "See? There's the edge of a door, right there. Do you think you can open it?"

He slid the edge of the crowbar into the widest crack between the door and the adjacent floorboard slat and pried it up, grunting. "Prodigious heavy."

Olivia chewed on her lip and watched him as he continued to inch the door upward. The bottom seemed to be made of solid metal—that was why it was so heavy.

When it was halfway open, she saw blue eyes peering out from a very dirty face and matted blond hair. Jessica's blue eyes.

"Olivia!" her sister cried. "Thank God you came."

With a grunt, Peebles pushed the door one more time, and it fell open with a resounding *thump*.

Jessica scrambled up and out of the hole and threw herself into Olivia's arms.

Chapter Twenty-four

Max methodically searched every downstairs room of Fenwicke's house. He started with the kitchen and servants' wing and found it completely empty, though he was certain servants usually occupied the place. There were clothes strewn over chairs and soiled dishes in the scullery, which gave the impression that people had departed in a hurry.

The stiff formality of the rooms occupying the opposite wing, the wing bearing all the enormous portraits, made it obvious that those rooms were reserved for formal activities. Some of the rooms had been locked but the open ones were cold and stark. Max walked through a darkened drawing room, a study, and a library, all of which were sparsely furnished with dark, uncomfortable-looking furniture.

Max exited from the library and resolutely headed back toward the stairway. He had no doubt that he'd find Fenwicke and his weasel-faced manservant upstairs. Max was aware of the possibility that there might be others, though it stood to reason that Fenwicke wouldn't have thought anyone would be looking for him here. The world still believed him confined to his bed in London after a near-deadly sickness.

At the bottom of the stairs, Max drew his pistol, the weight more comfortable in his hand now that he'd spent a bit of time last autumn using similar weapons for hunting at Stratford House. Then, it was a tool for sport; now, it was a weapon that could save his life, and the lives of two innocent women.

He ascended the stairs slowly, wary of making noise and alerting anyone to his presence. He listened for any noise coming from the upstairs rooms and watched carefully for movement above him.

He reached the top of the staircase. Corridors led to the left and right, but Max focused on the right, where he could see light seeping out from beneath one of the doors.

He moved toward the door, trying to be as silent as possible on the wood slats of the floor. He reached the door and leaned close to it to hear if any noises were coming from inside.

After a minute, he heard a very faint, very low humming noise. He reached for the handle and tried to open the door, but it was locked from the inside.

Was it Fenwicke's bedchamber or the servant's? Max had no idea. He explored the rest of the corridor, finding four empty, unlocked bedchambers, and then tried the opposite corridor. At the very end was another locked door, but there was no light emanating from this one. He remembered the lights he'd seen from outside when he first entered the house. One of those lights would most certainly have corresponded to this room. Perhaps its occupant had gone to bed.

Which left the room with the light on. He'd take care of the occupant of that room first and try not to wake the occupant of this one.

He returned to the room with the light on and knocked softly on the door.

"What is it, Thompson?" Fenwicke's voice snapped out. "Have you finished packing? I want to be gone by dawn."

"Yes, sir." Max spoke on a cough, with his fist muffling his voice. So, Fenwicke planned to leave Manchester. It seemed Max's arrival as John Smith had alerted Fenwicke that something was amiss.

"What's that?"

There was a click as the lock tumbled, and then the handle turned and the door opened the merest crack, showing a sliver of Fenwicke's face.

Max kicked the door open. He put so much force into the blow that Fenwicke stumbled backward and the door slammed into the wall.

Damn. The noise would awaken the bloody manservant.

Fenwicke recovered quickly. He lunged away, but Max's eye had caught on something at the far corner of the room, and he couldn't tear his gaze from it.

"Good God," he whispered.

There was a naked figure slumped there. Her back, criss-crossed with welts and bloody lines, was facing Max, and her head lolled forward.

Was she dead or unconscious?

With a choke of outrage, Max rushed toward the woman, tearing the blanket from the top of the bed as he passed it.

Pillows went tumbling to the ground. When he reached her, he wrapped the blanket around her and slid his arm beneath her. She moaned softly but didn't wake as Max gently lifted her into his arms, trying not to disturb her many wounds. Lady Fenwicke slumped against him, a dead weight in his arms.

"Oh, what a hero," Fenwicke sneered from behind him. He heard the click of a cocking gun.

Max froze, realizing he'd stuffed his pistol into his coat pocket without even thinking about it when he'd rushed to help Lady Fenwicke.

"Turn around, Wakefield," Fenwicke said.

Clutching the unconscious Lady Fenwicke to his chest, Max slowly turned.

The man's face was stone cold. He held a small silver pistol he pointed at Max's chest.

"How dare you," he said, his lip curling, "break into my home and then touch my wife in such an unseemly fashion? That's a hanging offense, Wakefield."

"Kidnapping is a hanging offense," Max growled.

"Kidnapping one's own wife? I don't think so."

"You have kidnapped Miss Jessica," Max pushed out.

"Miss Jessica? I don't see anyone by that name here. I was having a lovely evening with my wife when a villainous duke entered uninvited. In a fit of rage, he rendered me unconscious and then he proceeded to brutalize my beloved wife. That's what the world will know.

"Now unhand my wife, Wakefield. I'd prefer not to be forced to shoot through her to get to you, but I will if I must."

"I'd advise you not to do that. Be a gentleman for once and let me lay her down first."

Fenwicke merely cocked an eyebrow. He kept the

gun trained on Max as he went to the bed and laid the poor woman on it. She whimpered again, and murmured something Max couldn't quite understand. He covered her as best he could with one of the blankets.

Straightening, he slowly turned to face Fenwicke. He felt the heavy weight of the gun in his pocket and wondered if Fenwicke had seen it when he'd first kicked in the door.

"My lord, is there—?" Weasel-face was at the door. He'd stopped in midsentence, his mouth hanging open, his gaze traveling from Lady Fenwicke lying prone on the bed, to Max, to Fenwicke and the gun.

"Thompson," Fenwicke grated out. "You will bear witness to this event. The Duke of Wakefield broke into my home and proceeded to beat my wife to a bloody pulp. I shot him, killed him, to save her."

The man's face went still, and his focus settled on Max like a shard of ice. Weasel-face was definitely loyal to his master.

"Yes, sir," he said.

"You damned bastard." Fenwicke sounded not only disgusted but anguished as he continued. "You thought you could get away with doing this? With breaking into my home, my sanctuary? With hurting my wife?"

For the first time, his eyes slid away from Max to go to Lady Fenwicke on the bed. Max's hand went to his pocket, but before he could reach the gun, Fenwicke's gaze snapped to him again, and he stepped forward, pointing the gun at Max's chest.

"No, Wakefield. I know what's in there. I'm not blind, and I'm not dumb. Now, very slowly, retrieve that pistol from your pocket and lay it on the floor. Any fast move and I'll shoot, do you understand me?"

Hell. The crazy marquis was going to shoot him either way, wasn't he? Max's gun was already cocked, ready to shoot. If he could pull it out slowly, then get a shot off before Fenwicke could...

Well, it was his only hope.

Slowly, Max raised his empty hand, then slipped it into his pocket, his fingers scrambling to grasp the gun in the proper position.

Now.

He whipped the pistol out of his pocket, aimed, and fired as he dove to the floor in an attempt to avoid the shot he knew would be coming from Fenwicke.

Two shots rang out, deafening in the confined space of the bedchamber. Pain exploded in Max's side as his body slammed to the floor. Dimly, he heard a thud as Fenwicke fell directly in front of him. He hadn't seen where he'd hit the man. He hoped it had been in the bloody head.

He raised his own head to see Fenwicke crawling toward him, dragging his leg and leaving a bloody trail behind him. The servant was shouting something Max couldn't understand. It sounded like a woman was screaming—perhaps Lady Fenwicke.

Through blurred eyes, Max saw Fenwicke's hands reaching for him. Using his elbow, he slid his body to the side so Fenwicke's hands just missed catching his neck and cracking his skull on the floor. Fenwicke made a snarling noise. "You shot my leg, you bastard!"

Fenwicke was coming for him again. Max slid on his back, curled his fist, and punched Fenwicke in the thigh, in the exact place where he'd shot the man. His side screamed with pain.

Fenwicke gave an agonized, rage-filled howl. There

was more shouting in the periphery of Max's awareness, but he kept his focus on the enemy.

Max surged upward onto his knees, shoving Fenwicke's shoulder as he rose. Fenwicke fell back onto the floor, curling in on himself as if to protect his injured leg.

Max clenched his teeth. His side burned like someone had taken a torch to it.

Fenwicke wasn't finished. He struggled up onto his elbow, then leveled a solid punch to Max's stomach. Max hunched forward, and then Fenwicke copied Max's first strike. He leveled a second punch at Max, this time in his bloody, injured side.

Max hissed through his teeth and struggled to keep himself upright. The pain was excruciating. It shot through his entire body, and he couldn't hold back the grunt as he thumped back onto the floor. His eyes had closed of their own volition—it hurt to even open them, but he did.

Fenwicke loomed over him, his mouth warped into a ghastly grimace.

Max's gun should be close by. It was a weapon he'd acquired from his uncle, who even in his dotage had kept a case filled with examples of the newest advances in weaponry.

This pistol felt like Max's other weapons, but in truth, it wasn't like any other weapon Max had ever shot before. This was a revolver.

He saw it at the periphery of his vision and reached for it. Fenwicke didn't pay him any heed, probably assuming the gun had spent its one and only shot.

Max's fingers caught the grip of the gun, and he raised the pistol up, cocking the hammer.

Fenwicke finally paid attention as the gun clicked. Over Max, his body jerked in recognition of the noise.

For the slightest second, Max hesitated. He'd spent his whole life trying to avoid being like his father. Trying to choose a path leading away from brutality and violence.

But this man had nearly killed his own wife. He'd kidnapped Jessica Donovan. And he'd attempted to rape Olivia.

He deserved to die.

Max buried the barrel into Fenwicke's ribs. And he pulled the trigger.

When the two gunshots broke the quiet of the night, Olivia's heart clenched. She jerked away from Jessica and looked between her sister and Peebles.

"Who came with you, Olivia? Are Jonathan and Sebastian in the house?" Jessica asked, her voice rising in panic.

"No," Olivia whispered, looking at her sister with dread rising her gorge. "It's Max."

She turned, lifted her skirts, and ran. She tried the closest door to the barn—the back door of the house, but it was locked. Her heart pounding with panic, she ran to the front door, barely noticing her sister and Peebles just behind her.

The door opened easily, and they hurried inside. "Upstairs," she directed. She was sure the gunshots had come from the upper story.

Glimpsing the bottom edge of the banister beyond an arched doorway, she ran to the stairs and took them two at a time. At the top, she saw an open door to the right and heard a scuffling noise.

That was Max. He was alive. He had to be.

She sprinted down the corridor and rushed inside just as yet another gunshot exploded in her ears. She reeled to a halt, her senses overwhelmed by all that she saw.

Beatrice was sitting up on the bed, looking pale and stark. Her dark hair was loose around her bare shoulders, and she clutched a blanket to her chest.

The man who'd opened the door to them when Fenwicke had been in residence in Sussex stood in front of Olivia, panic twisting his long face. He was shouting, but her ears were ringing from the gunshot, and she couldn't discern his words.

Just behind him, two men lay still on the floor. Deep red blood pooled around them. She recognized Fenwicke's dark, slicked-back hair. He was slumped over another man, hiding most of his body. But Olivia recognized the color of the coat. The shape of the hand lying limp on the floor.

"Max!" She lunged past the shouting servant and fell to her knees beside the two men.

Were they both dead? Neither of them moved.

"No!" she sobbed, shoving at Fenwicke's heavy form, trying to get him off Max. "No. No. No."

She heard voices behind her, shouting, but she didn't hear what was being said. With a great heave, she thrust Fenwicke's limp body off of Max.

There was blood everywhere. All over him.

"Oh, God, no," she whispered. She cupped his face in her hands, his warm cheeks roughened by a day's growth of beard. "Max...Max, can you hear me?"

His eyelids fluttered, and Olivia's heart leapt to her throat. She couldn't speak as he opened his eyes. He blinked a few times, clearing the cloudiness away until his clear green orbs focused on her.

"Olivia?" he whispered. His brows drew together in confusion.

"Are you hurt? Tell me where you're hurt."

"I'm all right. He just nicked me..."

"Oh, God, Max. You're covered in blood!"

"It's his. Mostly his." Both of them glanced to where Fenwicke lay, his body unmoving beside Max.

"Is he...dead?" she whispered.

"I think so." Max struggled to sit up, wincing.

"No," she murmured. "Lie down. You're hurt."

He sounded bone tired, but he sat up shakily. He frowned at her. "What...why are you here?"

"I needed to be here. To help."

His gaze drifted just beyond her shoulder, and she turned to see Jessica embracing a sobbing Lady Fenwicke. "You found your sister."

"Yes. She was under the barn in a priest hole."

He gripped her wrist, and despite his apparent exhaustion, his grip was hard. "Why did you come here? You could have been killed."

She shook her head. "No, I knew you'd need my help." She bit her lower lip. "But once I heard the gunshots, Max, I couldn't..."

"What should I do with 'im, Your Grace?" Peebles dragged the cowering manservant toward them, holding him by the scruff of the neck and pointing his pistol at him. "He tried to sneak away, but I caught 'im."

Max's eyes went icy when he looked at the man. He struggled to stand, and this time she helped him. He awkwardly rose to his feet, pressing his palm over his side, grimacing.

"Hold him," Max said coldly. "The ladies might confirm his presence when they were taken from Prescot, in which case he will be prosecuted for aiding and abetting a kidnapping."

Olivia glanced at Jessica and Beatrice, who clung to each other as they watched the proceedings. They both looked pale and scared, and Beatrice looked like she might faint at any moment, but Jessica held her firmly upright.

The man went white. "I didn't know anything about any kidnapping, sir!"

Max eyed him dispassionately. "I daresay that'll be for the courts to decide."

He turned away and slowly, painfully knelt down beside Fenwicke and took his pulse. Looking up at Olivia, he shook his head. A muscle twitched in his jaw. "I wish you didn't have to see this."

She bent down to help him back up, and she led him to one of the armchairs. He gratefully lowered himself into it.

"I'm glad I saw it." She knelt down before him. She laid her cheek on his lap, and he ran his fingers over her hair. "I should, perhaps, feel horrible about that, but I don't. I'm glad he's dead, Max. It's good for me to see it. It's good for me to know that I'll never have to be afraid of him again."

Chapter Twenty-five

Spring had arrived. The forest was unfurling its color—every shade of green imaginable covered the trees and shrubs in baby leaves. A thick layer of velvety grass draped the ground, and the sun peeked out from behind puffy clouds.

A season for regrowth, rebirth, and renewal. For all of them.

Olivia turned from the window to face her family. Jonathan and Serena were sitting together, reading, with Serena's head resting on Jonathan's lap as he idly played with her hair. Phoebe and Sebastian were arguing good-naturedly over which song Phoebe should learn to play on the pianoforte next.

Jessica was on the floor playing pat-a-cake with Margie. And Beatrice was beside her, laughing and playing along. Beatrice was living with them indefinitely, and she was welcome to stay for as long as she liked. Olivia hoped she would stay for a very long time indeed. She was such a kind girl and so innocent, even after all the horror she'd been through. And lately, they'd begun to witness her smiling and laughing again, and they'd all rejoiced in it.

And then there was Max. He had convalesced here at Stratford House from the gunshot wound in his side. He'd lost a good bit of blood and had been weak for a while, but the bullet had gone clean through him.

Olivia's gaze wandered to where he sat near the fireplace. Meeting her eyes, he lowered his newspaper and crooked a finger at her in a silent *come here*.

Smiling, she crossed the room until she stood beside him. He folded his newspaper and set it aside before rising. "Are you ready?"

"I am," she returned.

They linked arms and said their good-byes. Everyone glanced up and wished them a nice walk, then went back to their pleasant activities. As they left the drawing room, Olivia gave a happy sigh.

"What is it?" Max asked.

"I just love seeing my family so content. And I'm happy that Beatrice is finally emerging from her shell and beginning to enjoy life again."

"I am, too," Max said gravely.

"I'm happy you're here, too."

They went to the kitchen where the housekeeper handed them the bundle they'd requested. By the time they emerged onto the lawn, they were both smiling. They walked past the crumbling tennis court in comfortable silence.

"I think it's warm and dry enough for us to start playing again," Max said.

Olivia bounced on her toes. "Oh, yes! Let's play tomorrow if it doesn't rain."

"I'll look forward to it." Max grinned at her delight with the plan. "Just be easy with me, all right?"

She laughed. "I'll try."

They turned from the exposed lawn into the shade of the forest. Olivia allowed Max to take the lead, and she smiled to herself when she realized he was heading toward the spring.

When they arrived, Max bent and placed the bundle from the housekeeper on the flat rock where he'd been crouching the very first time she'd encountered him here. He unrolled the blanket and laid it on the ground beside the rock. Then he helped her to get comfortable on the blanket, and she leaned her back against a tree trunk, looking at the spring.

"Oh, look, Max," she breathed. "The geese are back."

Taking his seat beside her, the basket with their luncheon in it on his lap, he glanced at the pond. "So they are."

A proud mother goose swam by, followed by seven of the tiniest goslings.

"Oh," Olivia murmured, "they must be newly hatched. Aren't they precious?"

She felt Max's eyes on her rather than the geese, and she glanced at him to see him giving her a soft smile.

"Would you like to eat? Mrs. Timberfield packed some bread and cheese. And a bottle of wine."

"All right," she said.

Max laid the bowl of cubed pieces of bread and cheese between them, and he poured wine into the small glasses the housekeeper had provided for them. Olivia sipped at the wine and popped bits of bread and cheese in her mouth.

She leaned back against the tree trunk, listening to the

drone of the spring insects and feeling more contented than she ever had.

"Olivia?"

"Hm?"

"How do you see the future?" he asked her.

Gazing at the pond, she smiled. "I see it here. In England. With my family. All of us finally happy."

Suddenly, she felt unsure. She would have included Max in that idealistic picture, but did she dare? She couldn't make any assumptions as to what his plans were. All she knew was that he'd long since given up on withdrawing when they made love...and that she risked pregnancy every time they came together.

But the thought of bearing Max's child—even out of wedlock—didn't seem as appalling as it once had. If it turned out that she could bear children, she'd love to raise Max's son or daughter. Having his baby wouldn't change who she was. It wouldn't affect her family's love for her.

She slid a glance at him to see him gazing soberly at her. "What about me?" he asked softly. "Do you ever think of me when you think of the future?"

She moved the bowl away from between them and scooted closer to him, wrapping her arm around his chest and leaning up to kiss his jaw. She returned his question with one of her own. "Do you think of me, Max?"

He captured her chin in his palm and tilted her face up to meet his lips.

His kiss wasn't gentle. It was powerful, possessive, and it thrummed with an energy that seemed to resonate through his body and over her before diving into her heart.

The kiss deepened until it wasn't a kiss anymore. She

dimly realized that her breast was exposed, that his hand caressed it, the blunt tips of his fingers running over her nipple, sending bursts of pleasure through her, down to reside between her legs.

She squirmed to release some of the pressure building there, and she felt the length of him, solid as steel against her thigh. He tugged her down until he was over her, and she was flat on her back staring up into those intense green eyes.

He jerked his gaze away from her and moved down her body until his lips closed over her nipple, and she gasped at the sensation.

"Oh, Max. I want you."

"Do you?" he asked.

"Yes. Yes, please."

He looked up at her, his lips glistening from their kisses, his eyes intent, focused on her face. Serious.

"When?" he asked her.

"Now," she whispered. She wrapped her arms over his shoulders and drew him close.

He kissed her again, but pulled away within moments to look at her again. "Just now?"

"No," she whispered. "No. I want you now..."

He clutched her skirt and drew it up over her legs.

"And tomorrow..." she continued.

His fingers dragged over the sensitized skin of her calf.

"And forever," she admitted. She closed her eyes tight and waited. She'd just revealed her deepest desire to him. She had opened herself completely to him, giving him the power to laugh at her, to tell her that he hadn't changed his mind about marriage, or that she was too sickly to qualify to be the duchess who would always stand at his side.

A part of her hoped he'd enter her and they'd both ignore what she'd just said. That they could continue living in the present, so she wouldn't have to think and worry about the future.

"Open your eyes, Olivia." His voice rasped with desire. His questing fingers found the slit in her drawers, and she arched up as he stroked the sensitive flesh between her legs.

She couldn't deny him. She opened her eyes to find him staring at her intently, his gaze seeming to bore through her and straight into her soul.

"I love you," he murmured. His sex nudged her entrance. "I'm going to love you forever."

He pushed in, seating himself deep inside her. She gasped at the invasion, but at the same time, her body arched up and opened for him, as if welcoming him home.

He held himself there. Staring into her face, he said, "There is no other woman for me."

His words were fuel to her furnace, and as he moved, his body gliding, so large and velvety smooth deep within her, he stoked the flames, and she burned, outside and in. She came quickly and violently as fire whipped through her body, leaving her undulating under him, breathless and then crying out his name as the rapturous pleasure spread through her.

He followed shortly afterward, thrusting forcefully inside her, so deep and so hard that she could only hold him and take whatever he gave her. But there was only pleasure, powerful pleasure that only months ago she wouldn't have believed a human capable of.

And then he thrust deep, and his body went rigid then released with a shudder, and she felt him pulse inside her in that vulnerable moment of a man completely losing himself in a woman's arms. *Her* arms.

He slumped to the side of her, pulling her against him. There were clothes tangled everywhere, but she didn't care. She snuggled against him and sighed, utterly content.

She was the only woman for him. The only woman he loved.

A few moments later, he shifted, and she felt him adjusting her bodice back over her breasts and her skirts down to cover her ankles. He pulled up his own trousers and adjusted his shirt and stock.

"I fear we're hopelessly rumpled," she murmured, not caring in the least.

He grinned. "Well, I'd rather not face Stratford with pistols at dawn."

"Oh, it won't come to that," Olivia said. "My sister would never allow it."

He chuckled, then his face turned serious. "I brought you something."

"Did you?"

He turned and rifled through the basket that had contained the food. She watched him, curious, as he removed a tiny box.

"What is it?" she asked.

He opened the box and tilted it toward her so she could see the contents. A diamond ring lay on a bed of scarlet velvet. It was a single diamond, round cut, and larger than any Olivia had ever seen.

"It's a ring," she said unnecessarily.

"Yes. Do you like it?"

She reached out to touch the glittering stone. "It's the most beautiful thing I've ever seen."

"It was my mother's. I want you to have it, Olivia."

She blinked hard, looking from the ring to his eyes.

"And I want you to be mine. Legally."

"Legally," she repeated. She was suddenly incapable of intelligent speech.

"Yes. I want to marry you."

"Oh," she whispered. "Are...are you sure?"

He groaned. "How can you ask that? How can you question my certainty?"

He closed his eyes and shook his head. He laid the ring box down on the blanket and cupped her face in his hands so she looked at him as he spoke. "Listen to me. I need you, Olivia. You're the most beautiful person I've ever known, inside and out. You're brave, strong, intelligent, and wise. I love you. I want you, and I need you. I want to spend my life at your side. I want to have you in my bed every night, and I want to wake up every morning with you beside me."

She flinched. "Max, I don't know if I can bear children—"

"I never planned to marry, so I never planned on having children. My cousin will inherit the dukedom. My desire to marry you has nothing to do with potential heirs. I want to marry you because I love you more than anything in this world. I want to marry you because I can't imagine my life without you." He stared into her eyes, so solemn, so intent. "I want you to be my duchess, Olivia. Please...say you will."

Pressing her lips together, she nodded. "Yes, Max," she whispered, "I'll be yours. Always."

His breath released in a sigh, and he bent down and kissed her tenderly, his lips moving softly, gently against hers in a caress so sweet it was like a warm wash of honey over her body and through her soul.

Pulling away, he reached for the box with the ring in it. He removed the ring and slid it over her finger. He smiled down at it, then looked up at her. "We're..." He took another breath, and his smile widened to a grin. "We're engaged."

Biting her lower lip, she nodded. For the first time in her life, she truly believed that her infirmity didn't preclude her from being worthy of being a wife. Of being a *duchess*.

Max jumped up, pulling her up with him. Lifting her by the waist, he spun her around until she was giddy with laughter. "We're engaged!"

She threw her arms around him. "Yes, we are. And there's nothing in the world that would make me happier right now."

"Speaking of the world," he murmured into her ear, "I want to share the news with it."

"Hm, well, you're more than welcome to shout it to the treetops, though I'm not sure the geese and birds would really care."

"But your family will." He stepped back, suddenly looking nervous. Vulnerable. "What will they say? I know the earl and countess were expecting you to live with them—"

"They'll be elated for us."

"Are you sure?"

"Yes. Because they'll see how happy we are, and they'll know it's the right thing for us both."

His broad smile returned. "Shall we tell them right away?"

"Do you want to? They're probably all still in the drawing room. We could tell them all together."

"Good, then let's inform your family, and then let's inform the world. I'll put a notice in the papers as soon as I can."

She agreed, and they hurriedly gathered the leftover food and folded the blanket. As they left the geese, Olivia waved goodbye to the mother goose and her seven babies, who'd witnessed a very private moment between her and her betrothed.

She was going to be a duchess. But that was simply an accidental side-effect of what she was truly going to become, of what she truly wanted: to be Max's wife. His companion, for the rest of her life.

Olivia and Max hurried back toward Stratford House to inform her family ... and to inform the world.

After five years in the West Indies,

Serena Donovan is back in London.

But so is the one person she never

expected to see again . . .

Jonathan Dane—her very own

original sin.

❦

Please turn this page for a

preview of

Confessions of an

Improper Bride.

Chapter One

Portsmouth, England

Serena hadn't been on a ship for six years. She'd had no desire to go near a ship. But she'd spent the past several, miserable weeks on the *Islington,* watching over her younger sister Phoebe with hawk's eyes, ensuring she kept safely away from the deck's edge.

Phoebe liked her freedom, and she was on the verge of wringing Serena's neck out of frustration, but Serena didn't care. It was far better to have a sulking sister than to have the unthinkable happen again. These weeks at sea had brought back so many memories of Meg. Each day had served as a painful reminder of the hole left in Serena's life.

Serena stood at the rail, keeping her back to her fate— a fate she hadn't asked for and had never wanted.

She stared out toward the open sea. A lone ship was passing the round tower that marked the harbor entrance and making its way out to sea, its sails puffed full with wind. A part of Serena wished she were on that ship, headed away from England. Cedar Place was a safe haven, a refuge, a place where she could be herself. England was none of those things. Here, she'd be nothing but a fake. A poor replication of a priceless original.

Once she disembarked from the *Islington,* Serena would begin to spin a web of lies that would ensure her three living sisters' futures. A person who admired honesty above all else, she nevertheless intended to live a life of deceit.

How would she manage it? Especially in London, a place fraught with danger, with its society and parties and ladies with sharp eyes looking for an opportunity to spread any scathing bit of gossip. If she was caught, society would rip her to shreds.

Serena and Phoebe would be staying with their aunt Geraldine in St. James's Square. Aunt Geraldine was a viscountess, the widow of Lord Alcott, one of the most respected members of Parliament in his day. Serena knew from her last visit to London that her aunt was ruled by the expectations of society, and she bowed to its every whim.

When the sisters left in disgrace six years ago, Aunt Geraldine had loathed Serena and despised Meg by association. Even worse, she lived two houses down from the Earl of Stratford, Jonathan Dane's father. This time, Serena had begged her mother to arrange housing elsewhere, but they couldn't afford suitable lodgings in London. Aunt Geraldine was the only reasonable choice.

Serena squeezed her eyes shut. Jonathan Dane probably wouldn't be in London. Six years ago, his father had ambitions for him to take holy orders, and if that had happened, he'd be residing at his family seat in Sussex or at some other vicarage far away from Town. She fervently hoped Jonathan wasn't in London. If he was, he could only be a reminder of all the pain and heartache of the past, and of her willful deception of the present.

If he was in London, she would avoid him at all costs. Because, as much as she aspired to be more like Meg, she was still Serena. If she came face-to-face with Jonathan Dane, it was likely her claws would extend and tear him apart. If that happened, all would be lost.

She must remember that. There was more at stake here than just her reputation.

With shaking hands, Serena drew out the letter from the pocket of her pelisse. Careful to pin it tightly between her fingertips so the breeze wouldn't tear it from her grip, she read it for the hundredth time.

My dearest Meg,

I waited breathlessly for your last letter, and when it arrived, I tore it open right away. I cannot express the level of joy I experienced when I read your assurances of love. And my happiness only increased when I read that you will be returning to England, and that you have agreed, with your mother's blessing, to become my wife.

I'm equally delighted to hear that you and your sister, Phoebe, will come to London for the duration of the summer. It will give us an opportunity to plan our wedding, and to reacquaint ourselves in the flesh after so many lonely years of separation.

How I long to look on your sweet face again, my dearest. I shall come to Portsmouth the instant I hear of your arrival. I look much as I did the last time we met.

> *With my sincerest love,*
> *Wm Langley*

Carefully, Serena folded the letter and replaced it in her pocket. She returned her gaze to the horizon and the ship slowly slipping away through the waves, becoming smaller with every moment that passed.

She hated lying. She hated herself. She hated her mother. She hated England. She hated everything about this situation.

"This! This very moment is the most exciting moment of my whole, entire life!"

Serena turned to see nineteen-year-old Phoebe grinning at her, her face young and alive, and her expression bright with happiness.

More than anything, Meg would want to see Phoebe and their other sisters, Olivia and Jessica, well situated. All Serena wanted was their happiness. She couldn't stand it if anything horrible happened to them. She'd do anything to shield them from an experience like she'd had on her last visit to London.

She'd do this for her beautiful, innocent, lovely sisters. To ensure their future.

"It is very exciting," she said to Phoebe, her voice grave.

Phoebe didn't perceive the sadness leaching into Serena's voice. With a pang, Serena remembered she'd never been able to hide such things from Meg. Now, though she possessed what most people would consider a tightly knit family in her mother and sisters, no one really knew her.

Nobody would ever really know her. It was too late for that. She'd sealed her fate in stone in the summer of 1822. From that point forward, she'd been the only person in the world to know her true self. Even after six years, the loneliness that thought provoked was nearly unbearable.

Blinking hard, she turned to gaze back out to sea. Looking in the opposite direction, Phoebe clapped her hands together and stood on her toes, craning to see through the thick lines of rigging blocking her view. "Oh, do look! There is a boat approaching. Can it be the one meant to bring us ashore?"

Serena looked over her shoulder in the direction her sister was pointing. The long boat, filled with empty seats, with abundant room in the stern holding area for their luggage, bobbed toward them, its rowers driving the oars through the murky water in long, precise draws. "I believe so."

"We should make certain we've packed everything, shouldn't we?"

"Yes." Serena didn't move, though. Rooted to the spot, she stared at the horizon, where the dark blue of the ocean faded through haze into the crystalline blue of the sky. She was about to become someone she'd despise. She was about to do something unforgivable.

What would Meg do?

That question had guided Serena's life for the past several years. She had grown calmer, and she gave far more forethought to her actions than she had before her sister's death. Phoebe was the one who'd taken over the role of hellion in their family.

For Phoebe's sake, she'd do this. For Olivia's and Jessica's sakes. If she betrayed her mother now, her sisters would be the ones to suffer. Mother was no fool—she knew exactly what drove Serena. She knew that Serena would never willingly cause pain to her sisters, and she knew exactly how to use that truth to manipulate her eldest daughter.

"Well?" Flicking a tendril of blond hair out of her face, Phoebe stamped her foot lightly on a deck plank. "Are you coming or aren't you?"

"I'll come down in a moment, Phoebe. You go ahead and make sure Flannery has gathered all our things, all right?"

"Humph. Very well, then." With a swing of her jewel-blue skirts, Phoebe turned and disappeared.

Squeezing her eyes shut, Serena curled her fingers around the deck rail. She didn't want to do this. She despised lying. Despised even more that she would aspire to standards she couldn't attain. She could never succeed in living up to Meg's goodness.

What would Meg do?

Meg wouldn't risk their sisters' reputations. Phoebe, Olivia, and Jessica needed freedom from their mother, and from Antigua, once and for all.

Serena's sisters needed to marry, and marry well. They could never do so if Captain William Langley discovered the truth and revealed it to the world.

Jonathan Dane, the Sixth Earl of Stratford, stared broodingly at his ale. The delicious brew at the Blue Bell Inn had lured him to Whitechapel tonight, and the smooth amber liquid shimmered in his glass.

No, he fooled himself. It wasn't the ale that had drawn him here. He'd been a frequent customer at the Blue Bell

Inn for years, but he hadn't come for a while. And he knew damn well why he'd come tonight.

Meg Donovan.

She would arrive in England soon—within the next day or two. Jonathan had little previous connection to the lady. The problem was that on the outside she was identical to her twin sister. Serena…the woman whose death he was responsible for. The woman he'd loved…and betrayed.

Meg would be in London. He'd undoubtedly see her often, considering the fact that Langley had asked him to be the best man at their wedding. And each time he looked at her beautiful lips or gray eyes or blond curls, he'd be reminded of Serena…of kissing those lips, of gazing into the depths of those eyes, of sifting those curls between his fingers.

Suppressing a groan, Jonathan thrust away the sudden flood of memories. This happened on occasion—just when he thought he was free of her, she swept through his memories, blazing a trail through his dark, cloudy mind and leaving a bright, glittering stream of happiness in her wake. After all these years, the memories served nothing but to remind him of how worthless he had become.

"I've been searching for you all evening. Suppose I shouldn't have been surprised you decided to come here, of all places."

Jonathan blinked at William Langley, Post Captain in His Majesty's Navy, as if he were viewing a ghostly apparition. The man standing at the end of the table was so strictly composed and so straitlaced, most people didn't hesitate to call him priggish. Jonathan knew otherwise. Langley wasn't priggish, he just had a strong sense of a man's moral duty. He was a good man, but a human one, through and through. Still, he wasn't one to go chasing after Jonathan at such a late hour. Something was wrong.

"Why are you here?" Jonathan asked, his senses going into full alert. "What has happened?"

"It's . . . well, it's Miss Donovan." Langley slid onto the bench across from him, his face twisted in consternation.

Jonathan's gut churned. He'd tried to be happy for Langley. Really tried. But every time his friend mentioned his betrothed, he felt the sour burn of jealousy scraping over his throat.

Langley placed his hands on the table and leaned forward. "I received word that her ship arrived in Portsmouth today. And, well, I thought I'd come find you."

"Seems you succeeded in that, at least." In one long draught, Jonathan finished his ale.

"I remembered this was the tavern where you . . . well . . ." Langley's voice trailed off. "It was just a guess."

Jonathan rubbed his thumb over a bead of condensation on his glass. "A good one."

Langley nodded.

Jonathan finally looked up at him. "So why are you here, Langley?"

Casting his gaze to the table, the other man adjusted his cravat. "I was wondering . . . well, you were acquainted with Miss Donovan."

Jonathan pressed his lips together. Unable to speak, he gave a slow nod. "Yes. I was acquainted with her."

"Well . . . will you accompany me? To Portsmouth, I mean. I'm to escort her and her sister to London."

"Accompany you," Jonathan repeated, enunciating each word carefully. "To Portsmouth." He stared hard at Langley. Was the man sotted? No, Langley rarely drank.

But other than the deep gray circles beneath his eyes, he looked pale as death.

"Yes. Today. I've received word that her ship has arrived." Langley's Adam's apple moved as he swallowed. "I thought you might...you know...help. If it became... difficult between us. Awkward. If I say something—"

Jonathan raised his hand, stopping the man midsentence. "Let me see if I understand this correctly. You've sought me out *here,* at this hour, to ask me if I might travel with you to Portsmouth later today to meet your betrothed."

"Yes. That's right."

Jonathan stared at Langley incredulously. The man had been a captain in the Navy. Accustomed to barking out orders and having them obeyed without question. Accustomed to having the lives of hundreds of men under his control. Accustomed to leadership.

Yet he was deathly afraid of meeting his beloved after a six-year separation. Poor Langley.

Langley blew out a breath through his teeth. "What if I say something wrong? What if I...?"

Jonathan shook his head. "By all accounts, the lady is as besotted with you as you are with her. There's nothing you could possibly say that would offend her."

Langley gave him a baleful look.

As much as Jonathan could sympathize with the panic of a man about to face the shackles of marriage, there was no way in hell Jonathan would be going to Portsmouth. He knew he'd eventually come face-to-face with Serena Donovan's twin sister, but it wouldn't be today. He'd had months to prepare for the eventuality of seeing her, but he wasn't ready. Not yet.

He was a damn coward.

Well, he'd always known that, hadn't he? He'd been a coward six years ago. Nothing had changed.

"I can't go to Portsmouth today," he said in a kindly voice. "Sorry, old chap. I've a meeting with my solicitor, and it cannot be missed."

Langley's face fell. "Damn," he said under his breath.

Jonathan drew back a bit, unused to hearing Langley curse. "You'll do fine."

Langley grimaced. "I hope you're right."

"Of course I am right."

"But...you will come to the soiree?"

"Of course I'll be there." He didn't want to go to Langley's soiree, but he would. He'd promised Langley he would go. That would give him a full week to prepare for his reintroduction to Meg Donovan.

Serena and Phoebe ate in the common room at the inn, where they were fed a heavy breakfast that made Serena feel weighted down and greasy. Neither of them was used to such lavishness, but Mother had scraped her pennies so Serena, Phoebe, and their new maid, Flannery, could spend one night in this particular inn. Even this breakfast had been an extravagance, and Serena's purse was uncomfortably light after her payment for it.

But of course they couldn't give the appearance of genteel poverty. That simply wouldn't do.

Today Serena wore her new cherry-striped silk with puffed sleeves and a satin-net trim on the skirt and cuffs. She hadn't worn it on the ship, per Mother's orders. She'd wanted Serena to reunite with William Langley in a spotless, crisp new gown.

"Are you ready?" Phoebe patted her coiffure. Of the five sisters, Serena and Meg had resembled Papa, with golden-streaked blond hair and gray eyes. The three younger girls looked more like their mother, with the same snapping blue eyes and a reddish gleam in their blond hair.

"I'm ready." Serena sighed. As ready as she'd ever be.

"I'm stuffed like a pig," Phoebe announced.

Serena's brows snapped together. "You should be happy Mother's not here," she said under her breath. "She'd whip you for that. Especially if you spoke that way in the presence of her sister."

Phoebe elevated her nose primly. "Which is exactly why I shall not speak so in Aunt Geraldine's presence. I'm sure Mother would hear of it immediately and fly all the way from Antigua like a rampaging dragon to punish me. I'm not stupid, you know."

"Don't be impertinent," Serena chastised mildly.

Phoebe probably didn't remember, but Serena had been equally impertinent before she and Meg had gone to London six years ago. Everything had changed when she'd returned without her sister at her side. She'd withdrawn into herself.

Mother had been devastated by Meg's death, but she had been somewhat gratified to learn that the bulk of Serena's rebelliousness had drowned along with Meg. Unfortunately, Serena still had a scandal of enormous proportions hanging over her head, ruining any chance whatsoever of a respectable gentleman asking for her hand in marriage.

Her rebelliousness hadn't drowned, though. Serena had just forced it to plunge below the surface. It threatened to emerge every day, but she kept it firmly concealed.

Serena and Phoebe retired to a sitting room where they pretended to sew while they spoke in muted tones and awaited Captain Langley's arrival. Eventually, a gentle knock sounded on the door, and Serena froze, needle poised.

"Come in," Phoebe called.

The door opened a crack to reveal a maid. "There's a gentleman come, miss. Says his name is Captain Langley and he's arrived to escort you to London."

This was it. This first meeting would decide once and for all whether Serena had the nerve to go through with this charade. Her heart thumped through her body, as loud as a clanging church bell. She was surprised no one else seemed to hear it.

Phoebe set her embroidery aside and rose, brushing her skirts straight, and Serena realized she was expected to do the same. Moving her limbs was like moving solid iron. It took every bit of strength her body contained.

Can I lie to this man? Can I be what—and who—he wants me to be?

How could she? This was all her mother's doing. Serena hadn't even known what was happening. She should end the ruse right now, before the lie spread through London, before it was too late.

Serena stood, straightened her spine, and nodded to the maid. "Show him in, please."

It seemed like hours passed before Captain Langley appeared in the doorway. He was quite a handsome man, tall and lithe, with angular features and dark brown hair. He wore a stiff collar, a snow-white cravat, and a dark blue coat. His eyes were his most handsome feature, Serena thought. Meg had always spoken highly of his eyes. They were kind, expressive eyes, of a rich, deep brown.

"Captain Langley," she said in the smooth, cultured London accent she'd spent endless hours practicing under her mother's watchful eye. "It is so lovely to see you again."

"And you, Miss Donovan," the captain said. His voice was soft, but his bow was stiff. "I trust your voyage was comfortable?"

"Indeed it was. Please"—Serena gestured toward Phoebe—"allow me to introduce you to Miss Phoebe Donovan, my sister."

Phoebe bobbed a curtsy, and Langley gave another stiff bow. "Miss Phoebe."

When he turned back to her, hope and expectation brimming in his expression, tears surged up in Serena so powerfully and so quickly she almost couldn't contain them. She dipped her head so Langley wouldn't see the shine in her eyes.

How could she possibly meet his expectations?

When she was little, Papa used to say that he could always tell Serena from Meg because Serena had the silver gleam of a sprite in her eyes, the spark that promised mischief. He'd always teased her about it.

He hadn't been there to see the change in her after Meg died, but Serena had seen the difference in the looking glass. The sprightly gleam faded into cloudy shadow, and her eyes had changed from sparkling silver to flat gray.

Langley strode forward and gathered her hands in his own. His hands were large, firm, and comforting.

"Miss Donovan." His breath hitched, and he squeezed her fingers tightly and shook his head, seemingly at a loss for words. Then he murmured, "Meg. I never thought you would come after...I mean, I hoped—I prayed—that I would see you again, that you would respond with an acceptance to my offer of marriage... But to have you here... my love—it is a dream come true."

As his words sank in, it struck Serena for the first time that her mother's lies had deeply affected another person outside the core of their family. This man truly did love Meg. He'd loved her for years. Captain Langley would be devastated if he learned the truth of what had happened that day on the *Victory*.

She looked up and stared into those deep brown eyes brimming with emotion. Langley was a good man, a respectable man. He was the man Meg had loved, and now Serena had the power to destroy him.

She squeezed his fingers in return. "I missed you," she whispered.

The shock of losing his beautiful bride-to-be, Meg Donovan, to the icy waters of the Atlantic changed Captain William Langley's life forever. Little does he know, an even larger surprise awaits him . . .

Please turn this page for a preview of

Pleasures of a Tempted Lady.

Chapter One

William Langley gazed over the bow of his ship, the *Freedom,* at the rippling gray surface of the ocean. Though the seas had finally calmed, a slick of seawater coated everything, and half of his small crew were still snoring in their bunks, exhausted from keeping them all afloat through last night's storm.

He ran his fingers through the beads of water along the top rail of the deck. They were soaked through and it'd probably be a month before they dried out, but they were no worse for wear.

Now they could go back to the task at hand—seeking out smugglers along the Western Approaches. In the nearly windless morning, the *Freedom* crept along in an easterly direction. They were about halfway between Penzance and the Irish town of Cork, though it was likely the storm had blown them off course, and they wouldn't get an accurate reading on their position until the skies cleared. God only knew when that would be. In the interim, he'd keep them moving east toward England so they could patrol the waters closer to the coast.

"She did well, didn't she?"

Langley glanced over his shoulder to see his first mate, David Briggs, approaching from the starboard deck.

He smiled. "Indeed she did." His fingers curled over the deck rail as Briggs came to stand beside him. The *Freedom* was a newly built American schooner rigged with triangular sails in the Bermuda style, a sight rarely seen among the square-rigged brigs and cutters on this side of the Atlantic. But his schooner was fast and sleek—perfect for the job she had been assigned. And sturdy, as proven by her stalwart response to last night's storm.

She was, above all, his. Will owned what some might call an entire fleet of ships, but since before the first nail was hammered into place, the *Freedom* had been his. Three years ago, his carefully rendered plans had been sent to Massachusetts with detailed instructions on how she should be built. And now, with every step along her shiny planked deck, the satisfying twin prides of creation and ownership resonated through him.

The only area in which Will had relinquished control was in the naming of his ship. The name he'd wanted for her would be too obvious. It would raise too many smirking eyebrows in London society. Even his best friends in the world—the Earl of Stratford and his wife, Meg—would frown and question his sanity if he'd given the ship the name his heart and soul had demanded.

So instead of *Lady Meg,* he'd agreed to the moniker suggested by the American shipbuilder—likely as a joke, since they knew well that he was a consummate Englishman—*Freedom.* It seemed everything the Americans created had something to do with their notions of freedom or liberty or national pride. Yet, surprising himself, Will had found he wasn't opposed to the name. For him, this ship did represent freedom.

Being out here again, on the open sea, on this beauty of a vessel and surrounded by his hardy crew—all of it was freeing. The bonds that had twisted around his heart for the past two years, growing tighter and tighter, stifling him until he was sure he'd burst, were slowly unraveling.

Out here, he could breathe again.

He glanced over at Briggs, who was scrubbing a hand over his eyes. "Sleep well?"

"Like the dead."

"You should have slept longer."

Briggs raised a brow at him. "I could say the same to you, sir."

Langley chuckled. "Touché." Briggs was right. He'd achieved no more than two hours of sleep in the predawn hours. He could have slept longer, but he'd been anxious to survey the *Freedom* in the light of the day. He was glad he had. The anxiety and energy that had compelled him into action since the beginning of the storm was gone now, and he felt . . . not exactly happy, but peaceful. For the first time in a long while.

"No sightings this morning," Briggs said.

"No surprise there," Will answered.

Briggs nodded thoughtfully. "Aye, well, it's bloody foggy."

"And we're too far offshore." Will had a theory that the particular ship they were pursuing—a brig smuggling thousands of gallons of rum from the West Indies—remained close to the shore for several weeks at a time.

Instead of using one cove as a drop for its cargo, it used several—dropping a few barrels of rum here and another few there so as to throw the authorities off their scent. These smugglers were wily, and they had proved elusive to the coast guard as well as the revenue cutters for over two years now.

The *Freedom* was, in essence, a spy ship—with only four guns and a crew of twenty they probably wouldn't stand in a fight against a fully armed brig with a crew of a hundred. Their task, instead of capturing the pirates, was to log the brig's activities and hand over the information to the revenue officers, who would, in turn, seize the ship and its illegal cargo, and prosecute the smugglers.

Briggs sighed, and Will clapped a hand over his shoulder. "Patience," he said in a low voice.

Briggs was a few years younger than him and anxious to find the culprits, whereas Will tended to take things slowly, as if they had all the time in the world. The truth was probably somewhere in between. If they waited too long, the brig would be on its way back to the West Indies for its next load of cargo, and they would miss this window of opportunity.

Briggs turned to Will and nodded, the edges of his blue eyes crinkling against the glare. "Aye, captain. But we've been out here a fortnight already and haven't seen any hint of 'em." The wind had picked up, and it ruffled through the other man's tawny hair and sent wisps of fog swirling through the rigging behind him.

"We'll find them." Will squeezed Briggs's shoulder. Neither man said any more; instead both turned back to gaze out over the ocean. The sea was slowly gathering strength after its rest from the gale, and the schooner sliced through the small waves at a faster pace now. Will took a deep breath of the salt air. So much cleaner than the stale, rank air full of sewage and coal smoke in London.

"What's that?" Briggs asked.

Will glanced at the man to see him squinting out over the open ocean.

"What's what?"

Briggs pointed straight ahead. "That."

Will scanned the sea. Could he have been wrong all this time? Could they encounter the smugglers' ship way out here? Even as he thought it, he realized how unlikely it was. More likely they'd come across another legal English or Irish vessel.

Seeing nothing, he methodically scanned the blurred, foggy horizon once again, and then he saw it: the figure of a boat solidifying like a specter from the fog.

Will frowned. This vessel was far too small to be this far out at sea on its own.

After half a minute in which they both stared at the emerging shape, Briggs murmured, "Holy hell. Is it a jolly boat?"

"With a broken mast," Will said, nodding. "I don't see anyone in it. Can you?"

Briggs leaned forward, squinting hard. He shook his head, but then frowned. "Maybe. Lying on the center bench?"

The mast looked like it had snapped off to about a third of its height, and half the sail appeared to be draped off the side of the little boat, floating in the water. No one was attempting to row.

The boat was adrift. And the *Freedom* was headed straight for it.

Will could see at least one figure now—or at least a mound of pinkish fabric piled on one of the benches. Beside the bench, he saw the movement. Just the smallest shudder, like the twitch of a frightened puppy crouched beneath one of the bench seats.

He spun around and shouted out an order to Ellis, the man at the helm. They'd been sailing close-hauled, and he told Ellis to turn into the wind on his command. If they timed it properly, rather than barreling right over the little boat and tearing it to splinters, they could pass it on the port side without getting its floating sail tangled in their keel or rudder.

"Aye, captain!" Ellis answered.

Will heard a shout. He turned to take stock of the other seamen on deck. There were six additional men, four of them clustered near Ellis and pointing at the figure of the boat emerging from the fog. The other two had been at work swabbing the deck, but were now looking at the emerging vessel in fascination.

"Fetch the hook," someone shouted, and a pair of seamen hurried down the port deck where the telescoping hook was lashed.

Everyone else was still asleep, but Will could easily make do with the nine of them. The *Freedom* was sixty feet of sleek power, and one of the most impressive of her attributes was that her sails were controlled by a series of winches, making a large crew unnecessary. In fact, Ellis and three others could easily control the ship while Briggs, Will, and the other seamen secured the little vessel.

"We'll draw alongside it on our port side," Will murmured to Briggs. Even after such a short time aboard the new ship, Will had impeccable timing when it came to the *Freedom*. Briggs and the crew often laughed that the ship was such a part of him he could command it to do anything he wanted with a mere thought. The truth was, Will knew the *Freedom* intrinsically. He could predict with great accuracy how it would react to any manipulation of its sails and rudder—certainly a result of knowing everything about the ship since its earliest conceptualization.

"Aye, sir," Briggs said. "I'll prepare to secure it portside."

"Very good." Will turned back toward the jolly boat as Briggs hurried toward midship. He could see the figure on the bench more clearly now, and he swallowed hard.

It was definitely a woman. The pink was her dress, a messy, frothy, lacy concoction spattered with the muck that was part of the inner workings of any sailing vessel. She lay prone and motionless on the bench. Beside her, the brownish lump wasn't entirely clear. A dog, Will thought, probably dead afraid, with its head tucked under its body.

He waited another two minutes. The wind had begun to gust, and Will adjusted his plan to compensate. He waited, on edge, judging the wind and the closing distance between the two vessels. Finally he shouted, "Haul up!"

Ellis responded instantly to his order, turning the wheel so the *Freedom* sailed directly into the wind. The sails began to flap wildly, but Will heard the whir of the winches, and soon the sheets were pulled taut.

The *Freedom* lost speed quickly as the jolly boat approached, and they drifted to a halt just as a seaman reached out with the grappling hook to snag the gunwale of the small vessel.

Will ran to the port side while Briggs lashed the boat to the *Freedom*'s cleats and one of the seamen secured a ladder. He had already descended the ladder when Will arrived at the scene.

"There's a lady here, sir!" The seaman, Davis, who was really just a boy, looked up at Will wide-eyed, as if uncertain what to do.

"Can you carry her, lad?" Will called down. The poor woman hadn't budged, and her matted hair and torn clothing covered her features. He hoped she could breathe through that thick tangle of blonde hair. He hoped she was alive.

Davis looked rather horrified at the prospect of carrying her, but with a gulp that rolled his prominent Adam's apple, he nodded. Widening his stance for balance in the bouncing jolly boat, he leaned over and gingerly tucked his arms under the figure of the unmoving woman and hefted her up.

Will saw movement from the corner of his eyes, and he glanced over at the lump he'd thought was a dog.

Two brown eyes stared at him from under a mass of shaggy brown hair. It was looking up from its position curled into a ball on the floor of the jolly boat, but it was no dog. It was a child, and he was creeping backward, as if he were considering escape.

Seeing that his first mate had looked up from his task and had noticed the child as well, Will nodded at Briggs. "Go down and grab him," he murmured. "Best hurry, too—the boy looks like he's about to leap overboard."

Briggs leapt over the side of the *Freedom,* his movements graceful. The man had a way about him on a ship—no matter where he was from the bilge to the top of the mast, he was inherently graceful and self-composed, even in twenty-foot seas.

Briggs's fast motion evidently frightened the boy, because he hurried backward, and when Briggs stepped over the bench toward him, he scrambled up the gunwale and leapt overboard. Briggs was lightning quick, though. He whipped out his hand, grabbed the urchin by the scruff of the neck, and hauled him back into the boat.

Without making any noise, the boy kicked and flailed, his hands gripping the strong arms around him and trying to yank them away.

"Feisty one, aren't you?" Will heard Briggs murmur above the slap of the waves against the jolly boat's hull. "But don't worry, lad. We're here to help you, not hurt you."

That seemed to calm the boy enough for Briggs to get a firmer grip on him, and Will turned back to Davis, who was struggling with getting the lady up the ladder. Another seaman, MacInerny, had climbed halfway down to help, and they'd managed to heft her halfway up.

Will bent over and reached down for her, managing to grasp her beneath the armpits, and with the two seamen's help, he managed to pull her the rest of the way up. It wasn't that she was heavy—she was actually a slip of a thing. But the movement of the ocean combined with her dead weight and frothy torn clothing combined to make it a cumbersome process.

Cradling her head, Will gently laid her on the deck.

"She's breathing," Davis gasped as he scrambled up the ladder. "She lives!"

Will heaved out a sigh of relief.

Holding the little boy—who looked to be about five

or six years old, though Will was certainly no authority on children—Briggs stepped onto the deck. The four men hovered over the woman. Crouched near her feet, Davis cleared his throat and tugged her dress down over the torn and dirty stockings covering her legs.

With his heart suddenly pounding hard, Will raised his hand to push away the blonde mass of hair obscuring her features. Her hair was dense with wetness and salt, but he cleared it away from her face, his callused fingertips scraping over the soft curve of her cheek.

"Oh God," Will choked, his hand frozen over her hair. "Oh my God."

"What is it, sir?" Briggs asked.

Will blinked away the water threatening to stream from his eyes.

Was he overtired? Had the intensity of the storm and lack of proper sleep caused him to have strange, perverse dreams?

No. God no, he was awake. There was too much color—the dewy flesh of her skin, the light brown of the freckles of her nose, the pink and white of her dress. Beyond the rancid smell of bilge water—originating from the boy, he thought—he could smell her, too. She'd always smelled like fresh sugar, like the sugar cane from the plantation in Antigua where she'd been raised.

Was she a ghost?

Half fearing she'd evaporate like fog beneath his fingers, he clasped both sides of her face and turned it upward, so she would have been staring at him were her eyes open.

"You're real," he whispered. Leaning down, he held his cheek over her mouth and nose and felt the soft puff of her breath.

Davis was right—she *was* alive.

How could this be? She'd been lost at sea eight years ago—on the other side of the Atlantic. Had she been adrift all this time, like some sleeping beauty, waiting for him—her prince—to find her and kiss her awake?

Did he dare hope that this wasn't some cruel joke of fate?

"Meg," he breathed. The dewy feel of her skin beneath his fingertips swept through him like the stroke of a rose petal. "Meg? Wake up," he murmured. "Wake up, love."

The urge overcame him, and forgetting the men staring at him, at them, he bent forward and pressed his lips to hers.

THE DISH

Where authors give you the inside scoop!

♥ ♥ ♥ ♥ ♥ ♥ ♥ ♥ ♥ ♥ ♥ ♥ ♥ ♥

From the desk of Jennifer Haymore

Dear Reader,

When Olivia Donovan, the heroine of SECRETS OF AN ACCIDENTAL DUCHESS (on sale now), entered my office for the first time, she stared at the place (and me) wide-eyed, as if she'd never seen an office—or a romance writer—before.

Bemused, I offered her a chair and asked her why she'd come. I was surprised when she got straight to the point; honestly, from the way she looked, I'd expected her to be far more reluctant.

"I want you to write my story."

I leaned forward. "Well, just about everyone who comes through my door wants me to write their story. To get me to do it, however, requires...more."

She carried a reticule looped around her wrist, and at this point she began to riffle around in it. "How much more?" she asked. "I haven't got much, but whatever I have—"

"Oh, no. I didn't mean 'more' in the sense of payment."

She frowned. "Well then, it what sense *did* you mean?"

"Well, I write about love...the development of relationships, the ups and downs, the ultimate happily ever after."

She gave a wistful sigh. "That's exactly what I want.

But"—she clutched her reticule so hard, her knuckles went white—"I fear I shall never have it."

I raised my eyebrows at her. "Why not? You're a lovely young woman. Obviously well bred, and from the looks of that silk and those pearls you're wearing, you're not lacking in the dowry department."

She gave me a wry smile. "I believe there's more to it than that."

"Look, I'm pretty familiar with your time period, Miss Donovan. In the late Regency period in England, looks, breeding, and financial status were everything."

She shook her head. "It's partially him...well, the man I'm thinking about, the one I'm hoping..." She hesitated, then the words rushed out: "Well, he's going to be a *duke* someday."

I blew that off. "In one of my books, a duke married a *housemaid*." (And this lady was no housemaid, that was for sure!) "Honestly, I can't see why any future duke wouldn't want to pursue a lady like you. You'd make a lovely duchess."

She licked her lips, hesitated, then whispered, "There's where you're wrong. I fear I'd make a terrible duchess. You see, I'm...ill."

I looked at her up and down, then down and up. She was a little thin, and pale, but ladies of this era kept themselves pale on purpose, after all. Otherwise, she looked healthy to me.

She stared at me for a moment, blinking back tears, then stood up abruptly. "I think I should go. This is hopeless."

She wasn't lying. She really believed she'd never have a happy ending of her own. Poor woman.

"No, please stay, Miss Donovan. Please tell me your

story. I promise, if there's anyone who can give you a happy ending, I can."

"Really?" she whispered.

I raised three fingers. "Scout's honor."

She frowned, clearly having no idea what I was talking about, but she was too polite and gently bred to question me. Slowly, she lowered herself back into her seat, still clutching that little green silk reticule.

I flipped up my laptop and opened a new document. "Tell me everything, Miss Donovan. From the beginning."

I truly hope you enjoy reading Olivia Donovan's story! Please come visit me at my website, www.jenniferhaymore .com, where you can share your thoughts about my books, sign up for some fun freebies and contests, and read more about the characters from SECRETS OF AN ACCI-DENTAL DUCHESS.

Sincerely,

♥ ♥ ♥ ♥ ♥ ♥ ♥ ♥ ♥ ♥ ♥ ♥ ♥ ♥ ♥ ♥

From the desk of Kristen Callihan

Dear Reader,

I fell in love with classic movies at an early age. While other kids were watching MTV, I was sighing over Cary Grant or laughing at the antics of William Powell and Myrna Loy.

There was a fairytale aspect about these films—from the impeccable clothes and elegant manners to the gorgeous décor—that took me out of my own world and into a place of dreams. Much like a good romance novel, if you think about it.

Watching old Fred Astaire movies had me dreaming of living in New York City in an apartment done up in elegant shades of white. *It Happened One Night* had me yearning for a road caper with a handsome stranger. I coveted Marilyn Monroe's pink satin dress in *Gentlemen Prefer Blondes*...all right, her diamonds too! But hands down, my favorite aspect of classic movies was the dialogue.

Back in the 1930s and 40s, the tight rein of censorship turned scriptwriters into masters of innuendo. Dialogue back then wasn't merely conversation; it was banter, the double entendre, a back-and-forth duel of words and wit. It was foreplay.

Therefore, it wasn't any surprise to me that when I started writing my own stories, dialogue would play a key part in my characters' relationships. Before the touches, there are the words.

In my novel FIRELIGHT, the verbal foreplay between my hero, Lord Benjamin Archer, and my heroine, Miranda Ellis, is particularly important. Archer hides his appearance behind masks, determined not to let Miranda see what lies beneath. In turn, Miranda hides her true nature behind the mask of her beauty. With so much hidden, they must rely on verbal communication to slip past their physical walls.

And so we have a dance of words. Words that say one thing but mean another. Words that test and tease. Words that make the sexual tension between Archer and Miranda burn hotter and hotter, until it can do nothing less than combust.

Hope you enjoy the heat,

♥ ♥ ♥ ♥ ♥ ♥ ♥ ♥ ♥ ♥ ♥ ♥ ♥

From the desk of Hope Ramsay

Dear Reader,

Among the things I love best about small, rural towns are the events they hold. Some of these events commemorate national holidays, others celebrate civic pride. And still others, like festivals and county fairs, seem to be mostly about having a real good time.

You can find small-town events everywhere. Even in the suburban landscape around Washington, DC, small towns maintain their sense of identity through their festivals, fairs, and special days. Alexandria, Virginia, where I currently live, throws an annual birthday party for its hometown hero, George Washington. Imagine parading through the streets in the February cold and snow. Seems strange, but it's a big annual event. It's fun. And my kids have fond memories of marching in that parade as members of their scout troops.

So it should come as no surprise that, when creating the world of Last Chance, I made sure to give it a festival complete with a parade, a barbecue, dancing, games of chance, and carnival rides. What better place to turn the matchmaking church ladies of Last Chance loose? The fact that they set up a kissing booth to raise money for a good cause should come as no surprise to anyone. Of course, I couldn't let the women have all the fun, so I also gave the local men a demolition derby where they could wreck cars to their hearts' content.

It was a lot of fun to send a member of the British aristocracy off to attend Last Chance's Watermelon Festival. Since my hero comes from a small village in the UK where they light bonfires on Samhain, Lord Woolham surprises the locals by taking to my county fair like a duck to water.

His Lordship enjoys his visit to Last Chance so much that he decides to stay. I hope you enjoy your visit too.

Hope Ramsay

♥ ♥ ♥ ♥ ♥ ♥ ♥ ♥ ♥ ♥ ♥ ♥ ♥ ♥ ♥

From the desk of Cynthia Garner

Dear Reader,

I have been a fan of the paranormal since I was a kid. My teenaged years were spent watching re-runs of Christopher Lee and Peter Cushing in those wonderful Hammer horror films. When Frank Langella played Dracula and later on Gerard Butler...whoa! Tall, dark, and sexy won the day, except...those Draculas were evil. While I don't mind an evil vampire every now and again (they keep us on our toes, right?), I highly prefer them to be one of the good guys. Or at least a reforming bad guy who's struggling against his inner big bad.

When I first came up with the concept of an interdimensional rift being the origin of Earth's creatures of lore, excitement at the wonder and unlimited potential of such a world made me giddy. And it takes a lot to make me giddy. But a lonely, hot-bodied vampire named Tobias was my first indication that my gleefulness wasn't going to end anytime soon.

Add a feisty heroine who's part demon, part human, and full-on furious with this yummy vamp, and you have all sorts of fun as each of them fights their feelings for the other, determined to keep their relationship on a professional level while they investigate a string of murders.

Yeah. Like that ever works—in fiction, at least. We want our characters to be heroic, but flawed. And you can't get much more flawed than when you fall in love and completely complicate your life.

My website has some extras from KISS OF THE VAMPIRE: a deleted scene, a map showing where the bodies were found as well as an X-marks-the-spot where the final battle took place, a page of Nix's investigative notes, and a brief interview with Tobias Caine.

Look for Dante and Tori's story in my upcoming *Secret of the Wolf.*

Thanks for coming along for the ride!

Happy Reading!

Cynthia Garner

cynthiagarnerbooks@gmail.com

Lawrence Balingit

As a child, JENNIFER HAYMORE traveled the South Pacific with her family on their homebuilt sailboat. The months spent on the sometimes-quiet, sometimes-raging seas sparked her love of adventure and grand romance. Since then, she's earned degrees in computer science and education and held various jobs from bookselling to teaching inner-city children to acting, but she's never stopped writing.

You can find Jennifer in Southern California trying to talk her husband into yet another trip to England, helping her three children with homework while brainstorming a new five-minute dinner menu, or crouched in a corner of the local bookstore writing her next novel.

You can learn more at:
JenniferHaymore.com
Twitter, @jenniferhaymore
Facebook, http://facebook.com/jenniferhaymore

ISBN 978-0-446-57315-3

57315

UPC

0 70993 00799 7

SECRET SEDUCTION

With her pale hair and slim figure, Olivia Donovan looks as fragile as fine china, and has been treated as such by her sisters ever since a childhood bout with malaria. But beneath her delicate facade, Olivia guards a bold, independent spirit and the kind of passionate desires proper young ladies must never confess . . .

It was a reckless wager, and one Max couldn't resist: Seduce the allur~~ing~~ ~~for~~feit part of his fortune. Yet the wild, s~~~~ined he'd fall in love with t~~~~ould he have guessed that a dangerously unpredictable rival would set out to destroy them both. Now, Max must beat a madman at his own twisted game—or forever lose the only woman to have ever won his heart.

"AN AUTHOR
TO WATCH!"
—NICOLE JORDAN,
New York Times
bestselling author

Available in
August 2012

www.HachetteBookGroup.com
Also available as an ebook
Art Direction by Claire Brown
Cover illustration by
Gregg Gulbronson
Handlettering by Ron Zinn
Cover © 2012
Hachette Book Group, Inc.
Printed in the U.S.A.

$7.99 US / $8.99 CAN.

ISBN 978-0-446-57315-3

50799

EAN

9 780446 573153